T0131422

True Romance

11 Stories of Love and Laughter

Other books in this collection:

When Love Goes Bad
Falling In Love...Again
Forbidden Love
Losing It For Love
When Love Sizzles
Love In Strange Places
Bedroom Roulette
Women Undone
Mothers In Love
Battlefield of Love
Nine Romantic Stories To Remember

Second Acts Series– by Julia Dumont
Sleeping with Dogs and Other Lovers
Starstruck Romance and Other Hollywood Tails
Hearts Unleashed

Infinity Diaries – by Devin Morgan
Aris Returns, A Vampire Love Story
Aris Rising, The Court Of Vampires

Age of Eve: Return of the Nephilim – by D.M. Pratt

TRUE ROMANCE

11 STORIES OF LOVE AND LAUGHTER

The timeless love stories from
True Romance and True Love live on.

A BROADLIT BOOK

BroadLit

May 2014

Published by

BroadLit ®
14011 Ventura Blvd.
Suite 206 E
Sherman Oaks, CA 91423

ISBN 978-0-9890200-8-4
Produced in the United States of America.

Visit us online at www.TruLOVEstories.com

This collection is dedicated to all of you who are looking for true love or have already found it.

TABLE OF CONTENTS

MY HUSBAND'S SURPRISE

Thursday I took the day off from work and discovered that my husband was cheating on me.

It was a rough day that started with my twelve-year-old daughter wailing that she didn't have any clean clothes for school. At the same time, her brother, thirteen, complained that there wasn't one clean shirt hanging in his closet.

"Who was supposed to do the wash this week?" I asked.

"Jen," Don said.

"Don," Jen said at the same time.

As they pointed accusing fingers at each other, my husband called up the stairs to complain that there wasn't any coffee. "I told you yesterday morning that there wasn't any left. I thought you were going to pick some up, Vickie," Abe accused.

Maybe there comes a time in every working wife and mother's life when she finds that her house has gotten away from her. As I raced around trying to find Jen and Don some clothes, at the same time assuring Abe that instant coffee wouldn't kill him, I knew I needed time to deal with things.

Maybe it was the pile of unwashed clothes downstairs that convinced me; maybe it was the fact that my kitchen floor hadn't had a good scrubbing in months. Abe had been "meaning to get to it," but he'd been working late this month, so there went the floor. Let's face it, I told myself, if I want something done right, I have to do it myself.

I called the accounting firm where I worked and talked to my supervisor. She said, "Sure, take the day off. You have sick days coming. Besides, the office can survive without you. But your family might die without clean socks."

My supervisor was about my age, newly divorced, and somewhat bitter about family life. So I paid no attention to her little dig and pitched right in to do the housework. Soon, the washing machine and dryer were whirring under heavy loads; the bathroom had been scrubbed, washed down, and polished; the house had been vacuumed to within an inch of its life; and the kitchen floor didn't stick to my feet anymore. Before tackling the refrigerator, which was next on my list, I decided to fold the first batch of wash and put it away.

It was while I was stacking Abe's socks in his drawer that I found the box. It was a long, flat, white box embossed with the name of one of the most exclusive boutiques in our city.

Surprised, I flipped open the lid. Then I lifted out the slinkiest, sexiest, skimpiest nightgown I'd ever seen.

The nightgown looked very expensive. I'd never owned a gown like this in my life, and I was shaking my head over Abe's foolishness when I happened to glance at the tag on the back. It read size eight—eight, for heaven's sakes—when I can barely squeeze into a twelve. What was Abe thinking? I wondered.

And then my heart took a nosedive onto the now-clean bedroom floor because it hit me that this nightgown—this gorgeous, frothy, expensive little bit of nothing—was not for me!

It was for another woman. Abe and another woman? As I thought this, I caught sight of my face in Abe's bureau mirror. I wasn't wearing makeup—unless you could count the smudge of dirt on my cheek. My hair had gotten frazzled during the morning's housework and stuck out all around my round face. I didn't even look at the rest of me, mercifully covered by an old flannel shirt and jeans that were too tight. I wasn't a candidate for even a second chance in a beauty contest.

And then I got a mental image of the woman for whom Abe had bought this sexy gown. She'd have gorgeous hair, gorgeous nails, a face and body to match, and a low, sexy voice. As the picture formed, I groaned. "Oh, boy," I muttered. "Marcie Evans."

Marcie Evans was a secretary, newly hired by the big boss of the company where my husband had been a salesman for years. Marcie had all the qualities I'd thought of, and then some, and Abe thought she was a total knockout. How did I know that? Well, when I admired Marcie's looks at the company picnic a couple of months ago, he'd looked slightly guilty, the way husbands look when they've been thinking less than pure thoughts. "Oh, Marcie?" Abe had said. "I guess she's not bad looking."

Marcie and Abe—Marcie and Abe together. My mind made horrible pictures, and my stomach twisted so sharply that I nearly threw up. I wanted to tear the nightgown into a hundred pieces, toss the thing in the trash, and then burn the trash. But then, Abe would know I'd found it. Maybe he'd say nothing—but then again, maybe he would talk and that would force a showdown. So, okay, let's have a showdown, I thought, but then another idea came: Suppose Abe told me that he wanted to leave me for Marcie?

I felt worse as I envisioned life without Abe. Life without Abe sitting in the corner chair reading his paper; without Abe and the kids concentrating hard over a game; without Abe's warm body in bed next to me at night. Darn it, Abe hadn't just been a part of my life for fifteen years, he was my life. No matter what he'd done, I couldn't stand the thought of losing him.

I put the nightgown back in its box and replaced the box in Abe's sock drawer. Then, I went downstairs and, standing in my now-spotless kitchen, I felt my anger flare. Abe and I had two great kids, a home that we'd bought recently after saving for years, a college fund to which we contributed a hefty chunk of our paychecks every month, and a shared dream of traveling the world one day. We'd come a long way since we were starry-eyed kids in love, and we'd grown together. No way was Marcie Evans going to cash in on all this—no way! The problem was, how could I compete with her? How could I even begin to try?

I tossed the problem around all day. By the time evening came around, I was almost a wreck. Miraculously, Abe didn't have to work late, and watching him out of the corner of my eye, I saw that he appeared to be nervous, too. When the phone rang during dinner, he actually jumped. I noticed that jump, heard the odd note in his voice when he said he'd get it, and saw his disappointment when the caller turned out to be one of Jen's friends. Later, after dinner, we watched a made-for-TV movie about a middle-aged man who was cheating on his wife.

"What do you think about a man like that?" I asked. Abe looked uncomfortable. "I think a man who cheats on his wife is really low," I went on. "Here, she's given him the best years of her life and when he's tired of her, it's good-bye."

"You don't know the man's side of it," Abe protested. He didn't meet my eye as he added, "There're always two sides to a story, Vickie."

I couldn't help it, the next words blurted out of me: "So it's okay for a man to two-time his wife?"

He shrugged. "All I'm saying is that there may be times when a man needs more than he's getting at home," he said.

I'd had doubts before this, even with that sexy nightgown upstairs in Abe's sock drawer. Now, as I saw my husband's eyes follow the beautiful, glamorous actress on the TV screen, I knew there was another woman. I wanted to come right out and ask him if it really was Marcie, but I kept my mouth shut.

That night, when Abe had fallen asleep—he was exhausted from work, he said—I lay awake thinking. The images of Marcie and Abe, of Marcie in that nightgown, flashed in and out of my brain. I didn't know which way to turn until I suddenly thought of my supervisor, Brenda. Since her divorce, stylish, pretty Brenda had been up to her ears in men. She'd know what to do.

Of course, I couldn't level with Brenda. I didn't know her that well, and besides, I couldn't bear to talk about what I suspected about my husband. Instead, the next day I asked her how she managed to look so gorgeous all the time.

Brenda looked pleased. "I diet and I exercise," she told me. "Aerobics down at the health club. You know the place, don't you? You pass it on the way to work."

She was wearing an emerald-green suit with a long, slim skirt that flared at the base, and she looked stunning. I took a long breath and plunged. "I've been thinking of trying aerobics myself," I told her. "Maybe I could go with you."

She looked surprised, but said, "Sure, anytime."

"How about tomorrow after work?"

Brenda cautioned me that aerobics would be hard. She also instructed me to bring a leotard and a towel with me to work the next day. I had a leotard at home, but when I tried it on, I nearly chickened out right then and there. Then, while I was standing in front of the bedroom mirror trying to suck in my stomach, the phone rang.

It was Abe. "Look, honey, I won't be home for dinner," he told me. "An important client came into town today, and I'm meeting him after work. We may get involved in a lot of shoptalk—you know how it is."

"Sure," I said, adding mentally that I suspected just how involved he would get. And while I was picturing Abe and Marcie holding hands in a romantic restaurant, I watched my blimpy self in the mirror and resolved that no matter what, I was going to slim down.

The next day found me ready to go to the health club. Brenda had to wait for me because, at the last minute, our boss had dumped some work on me and instructed me to get it done before I left.

"Tell him you don't have the time to do it today," Brenda prodded me. "Nobody else here would put up with this, Vickie."

I knew she was right, but I wasn't good at confrontations with the boss, so I worked fast while Brenda waited.

Then we went to the club where I filled out a form and was weighed and measured. So far, so good. But when I followed Brenda to a room where an aerobics exercise was about to begin, she looked doubtful.

"You're sure you want to do this?" she asked me. "It's pretty hard work for someone who's just starting."

Brenda wasn't kidding. After a while, I could hardly think anymore. The aerobics instructor was a slim, trim, twentyish kid who jumped around like a jumping bean, while her class grimly followed. I was so exhausted, I thought I'd die. I was grateful when, after the exercise session ended, Brenda suggested we get some coffee.

"You know, Vickie," she told me, "you were the last person I'd expected to want to start exercising. You always looked so—uh, comfortable, before."

What she meant was that I was comfortable like the proverbial old shoe that everyone took for granted. It was true. At home, my family expected me to pick up after them, and at work, it went double. My boss wasn't the only one to dump extra work on my desk—a lot of the other accountants figured that good old Vickie would do jobs that they didn't want to do or couldn't get to. Good, old, hardworking, wishy-washy Vickie, who was slightly overweight and was losing her husband to a glamorous young woman.

I told Brenda that I was trying to shape up, and as she nodded, I noticed how beautifully her hair was cut and styled. I commented on it, and she was pleased and told me where she'd had it done. "It's expensive, but a good cut's worth it—it helps attract m-e-n." She spelled out the word and added that men noticed a woman's hair, her figure, her walk. Then she laughed. "I guess you wouldn't have to worry about that, though, with a sexy guy right at home, Vickie."

I swallowed my coffee the wrong way. Right then, I didn't need any reminders about Abe's sexiness. I told Brenda I had to drag my weary body home, where I found Don looking into the fridge.

"Hi, Ma," he greeted me. "What's for dinner?"

Abe had called to say he'd be late again, and the kids turned their noses up at the chicken and salad I served. "Mom's on a diet again," Jen remarked. Her tone of voice implied that she was sure my diet wouldn't last. She was right—the last few times I'd tried to slim down, I'd given up too easily, but now I had a real incentive.

After dinner, the kids usually scattered to do their homework, but today I held them back. I was aching too much to stand up, let alone wash the dishes. I was even too tired to listen to their protests. I told them what to do, crawled upstairs to take a hot shower, and then I flopped down on our bed to rest. I'd meant to stay up and wait for Abe, but I was so weary that I went straight to sleep and didn't even hear him come in.

For the next week, I was constantly tired. I hurt, I ached, and I agonized over each move. Many times, I nearly gave up, but I kept thinking about what Brenda had said about men noticing a woman's looks. I thought constantly about that sexy nightgown that was still in Abe's sock drawer. A couple of times, I'd checked to see whether he had moved it, but it was still there. It got to be a kind of symbol for me. I reasoned that since he hadn't actually given it to Marcie yet, it meant there was still time for me to get him back. It was a crazy way to reason, I guess, but it kept me going.

Another thing that kept me going was a change around the house. As the pounds melted off, I started to delegate more jobs to the kids. They'd halfheartedly done chores before, but now with me coming in late every day from my exercise class, I had to rely on them to do certain things. If Jen and Don didn't set the table and put a casserole in the oven or make a salad, dinner that night would be late. The kids griped a little, but they soon settled into their new routine. They threw wash in and folded it on a regular basis, ran the vacuum, and mopped down the kitchen floor—maybe because they were secretly proud of their mother for sticking to her guns this time. At this point, my life would have been really in decent shape if it weren't for Abe.

He still worked late several times a week. Usually, I was too exhausted from the aerobics to stay awake till he got home, so there were days when we hardly spoke to each other. That seemed to suit Abe fine. I was sure he was continuing to see Marcie because he still jumped when the phone rang. And there were other signs—the new ties he wore to work, the eager look in his dark eyes. Brenda had told me the signs that told her that her husband was having an affair before their divorce, and Abe's behavior followed all those guidelines.

One evening toward the end of my second week of exercising, there was a phone call from her. Jen took the call and said, "Dad, it's for you—some lady."

Abe nearly broke his neck getting to the phone, snatched up the receiver, then shot a guilty look at me before starting to speak, about business in too-loud tones.

When he hung up, I asked casually who it was.

"Just something about work," he told me. "Nothing important."

I looked long and hard at this guy who I'd been married to for fifteen years and whom I still loved so much that it hurt. He was still so handsome that when he smiled at me, my bones turned to jelly. We'd shared good times, hard times, the birth of two kids. We'd been friends, sweethearts, lovers. Yet, for the past couple of weeks, we'd been living a lie. Suddenly, I couldn't stand things the way they were.

"Abe," I said, "we need to talk." He just looked at me. I took a deep breath. "The other day I found—"

But I never got to complete my sentence because just then, Jen wandered in with a question about laundering her new, expensive sweater. She looked so young and pretty and innocent that my heart twisted. I'd been ready to ask Abe about that sexy nightgown, despite the consequences. But now I was reminded that if our marriage broke up, the kids would be caught in the fallout. With an aching heart, I answered Jen's questions.

Abe smiled after her as she left the room. "She's a great kid," he said, and there was real love in his voice. "They're both great kids.

Look at the way they help around the house these days."

That night, I peeked into Abe's sock drawer again and saw the box still hidden there. Maybe, I thought, with Abe's love for his family and the new me, there's still hope. . . .

I continued to work out. I continued to diet. Within a few weeks, I noticed a difference: not just because my clothes felt looser and my body felt tighter, but because I was changing, too. It was as if my character was firming up along with my body. At home, it was now taken for granted that the kids helped out, and at work I put my foot down. My day now had to be stretched to include my aerobic workouts and I no longer was a pushover for doing the other accountants' unwanted jobs. And when the boss tossed a report on my desk around quitting time one afternoon, I quietly but firmly informed him I couldn't get to it before I left.

"I have an appointment right after work," I told him. "I'll be glad to work on this first thing tomorrow morning, though." He blinked at me and looked surprised, but rather meekly agreed.

The appointment I had was with Brenda's hairdresser. She was expensive, but when I came through our door that evening, the look on my kids' faces was worth it. "Wow, Mom, you look great," Jen exclaimed, and Don rolled his eyes.

"Hey, Ma, way to go," he said. Then he grinned. "Wait till Dad sees you."

But when Abe came home that evening, he hardly looked at me. "You had your hair done," he commented, and his words were as indifferent as the kiss that landed somewhere in the air near my cheek. He was as jumpy as a cat on hot coals, and whenever the phone rang, he ran to get it. There was no doubt that he was waiting for a phone call, and I had no doubt from whom that call would be.

It came after dinner. The kids were washing and wiping the dishes to the sound of their CDs, and the kitchen was so noisy I hardly heard the phone ring. But ring it did—once, before Abe snapped it up. He was in the bedroom, and I was near the phone in the hall.

Quick as a flash, I lifted the receiver to my ear.

"You're sure," I heard Abe say eagerly. "You're sure, Marcie?"

Marcie. If ever there'd been any possibility for doubt, there was none now. I hated her. I hated her low, husky voice that purred into the phone.

My husband didn't say anything for a moment. Then he drew a deep, shaky breath. "Then we're on our way," he whispered.

I replaced the receiver in its cradle and leaned up against the wall. I was drained of any hope. My drastic makeover hadn't worked. Whatever it was that had held Abe back till now, he wasn't going to hold back any longer. They were "on their way" and it was over between us.

Walking as though in a dream, I went to the kitchen. There I sent the surprised kids off to do their homework and started wiping dishes myself. I was still at it when Abe poked his head into the kitchen and said he had to go out for a while. I just nodded, unable to speak. He was going to her, of course. "If I'm late, don't wait up for me," Abe added.

The door closed behind Abe as I wiped the last dish and put it away. Then I went upstairs to our bedroom, shut the door, and looked at myself in the mirror. "Now, what?" I asked.

There were no easy answers, but I had to admit that the woman who looked back at me from the polished glass wasn't the same one who had found that sexy nightgown weeks ago. This woman was slimmer and well-groomed. And looking beyond the surface appearance, I'd gained poise and confidence. At work this afternoon I'd proved this to be true—but now, I was up against the big one. This time, no matter what happened, I had to get Abe to tell me the truth because I couldn't live with the lies any longer.

I had no idea what would happen when I confronted Abe. Maybe he'd deny everything. Maybe he'd want to leave me. That thought nearly killed me, but when the sharp pain subsided, I knew something I hadn't known a few weeks ago—that, if necessary, I could go on without him. I could still be a good mother to the kids. I could still be a good, productive person. I could survive.

I drew in a long, shaky breath and saw my mirror-image blur behind sudden tears. Resolutely, I wiped them away. Then I brushed back my new, stylish hair and went out into the living room to wait for Abe.

He was late. The kids had gone to bed by the time his key turned in the lock. He looked surprised to see me sitting up and waiting for him, but before he could speak, I said, "We need to talk, Abe."

"Talk about what?"

"About us." Once I'd gotten that out, the words came more easily. "I started in on this a while ago, but we got interrupted." He was looking at me warily as I added, "I know about it—I know it all, Abe."

"You know?" Abe blinked. "Who told you?" Then he exploded. "It had to be Al Collins from the office who told you, right? He could never keep a secret." He paused and then added, "So you know about Hawaii."

He was going to take Marcie to Hawaii. That was the last straw. Hawaii was one of those places we'd both dreamed of traveling to together, and now he was going with her. "Abe," I cried, "you couldn't."

"Sure, I could. We're going to Hawaii on your birthday."

I stared at him, and he started to grin all over his face. "I thought you knew everything, but I guess you don't. The company had this big contest, see. The sales reps who sold over a certain amount last quarter were going to get to go to Hawaii with a guest—free. Hey, listen, what with the kids' college fund and the house mortgage and all, I figured this might be the only way we could go."

I couldn't take it in. I heard what he was saying, all right, but the words weren't registering. Abe was taking me to Hawaii? "But what about Marcie?"

His grin never slipped. "Marcie was great. She knew how much I wanted to take you to Hawaii, so she helped me by keeping me posted about how I stood in the sales race. You know, being the big boss's secretary has its advantages. She even called me at home a couple of times to give me tips on some really big clients."

He came over and took my hands. I clung to his hands like a lifeline. I wanted to cry. I wanted to laugh. This had been Abe's secret, and all the time I'd thought . . . .

"Abe," I told him, "I love you."

He put my arms around him and kissed me, and we held each other tightly for a long time. Our next kiss was different. It was the kind of kiss that even after fifteen years sent the blood skipping through my veins.

It sure had been, but there was one last question left unanswered. I pushed away from Abe and looked up into his face. "While I was cleaning your sock drawer," I began, "I found a box."

He looked disappointed. "You found it!" he accused. "I meant it as a surprise! I got it so you could wear it in Hawaii." He let go of me and went upstairs to get the white box. Then he handed it to me. "Since you found it anyway, you can model it tonight."

I started to ask him what had possessed him to buy a size eight. Then I saw the look in his eyes and understood: that Abe saw me not as I was, but through the eyes of love. To him, I'd always be a size eight. To him, I was perfect. And truly, wasn't it that way for me, too? After all, I never noticed Abe's slightly receding hairline or the few pounds he'd put on since we were married. I never noticed the lines around his eyes, except to think they made him more handsome. To me, Abe was every bit as sexy as he was the day we fell in love.

My voice sounded husky as I told him again that I loved him. "But, Abe, about this nightgown . . ."

I never got a chance to finish my sentence. I never got to wear the nightgown, either. I'll say this much for it, though—it looked fine draped over the chair by our bed! THE END

HOW AN UGLY DUCKLING WON MY HEART

The day my roommate, Amy, and I discovered that our hip measurements had increased, we knew we had to do something.

"I figured I would have to pay for that soft office job sooner or later." Amy moaned. "I just didn't think it would be this soon." We both worked as secretaries at a baked-goods distributing center, and did a lot of sitting.

"We have those perfectly good bikes we brought from home," I pointed out. "And there's a fantastic park across the street with a path running all the way around. I bet it's four miles around. So what are we waiting for?"

That very evening after work, we started our course of exercise. "Why haven't we done this before?" I asked as we skimmed past trees and shrubbery and beds of bright summer flowers. I felt like a thinner person already.

How lucky I am, I thought, breathing in the grass-scented air, to have a good friend like Amy beside me to share these special times. We came from the same little town, we'd been best friends in school, and had decided to come to the city together and get jobs. We hadn't expected to find positions with the same firm, but we lucked out in that area. Life is good to us, but it would be better for me if only I could have a nice boyfriend like Amy's Barry, I thought as we pumped happily along.

Approaching the shimmering little lake in the center of the park, I noticed a jogger who had stopped to examine his shoe. "Wow! Check out Mr. Good Looking," I said, ogling the gorgeous guy with the terrific body.

"I know him," Amy said. "That's Ed Kosner. I met him at Barry's company's Fourth of July picnic." Barry worked for U.S. Crafts, the big employer in this area, and Amy often attended their special affairs. "Hi, Ed," she called as we pedaled past the handsome young man.

"Hi," he said, with the blank look that implied lack of recognition. Amy was great in every way—except looks. She wasn't ugly, but she had one of those ordinary faces that people forgot. Of the two of us, I was always called the pretty one; still, Amy was the one who had landed herself a guy since coming to the city. We'd met Barry at a singles' dance. I was taken aback when he went for Amy instead of me. In high school, the boys had always picked me. I was happy for her, though. She deserved a good man like Barry.

"Ed's unmarried, has a good job, and from what I heard, he has no steady girlfriend," Amy said. "I can understand why," she added wryly.

I certainly couldn't. With his face and physique, the girls should have been flocking. "Let's sit on this bench and pretend to be resting when he comes running by. I want another look," I said.

"It's okay with me to sit for a while," Amy said with a puff as she flopped off her bike. "But don't start anything with Ed," she went on as we collapsed on the bench. "He's stuck on himself and you don't want to get involved with that kind of guy."

Poor Amy, I thought. She's just hurt because he doesn't remember her and didn't pay any attention to her at the picnic. Congratulating myself for wearing my new shorts, I twined one leg over the other in what I considered an eye-pleasing arrangement.

In due time, Ed came pounding by and paid no attention to either one of us, or to my stunning legs. We'll just see about that! I told myself. If he jogs here regularly, I'll find some way to increase my visibility!

We were about to go when another jogger trotted down the path.

This one was as plain looking a man as Amy was a woman. When he spotted us, he did a double take, and then dropped to the grass beside us.

"You ladies have the right idea with those bikes. With a pair of good wheels you can get up enough momentum to rest your legs now and then, and not only when you're taking time out."

"Yeah, it's the only way to go," Amy answered. I merely nodded and turned toward the lake. A pair of swans glided by on the far side. How graceful, how totally beautiful they were, surely one of God's greatest creations.

"Did you know the male swan is very protective?" the jogger said. "When the female is laying eggs or the new brood is hatched, you'd better stay away. He'll attack. Those feathery wings contain some mighty hard bones. They can break your leg and they've been known to actually kill."

I pretended not to be listening, but Amy said, "Really? I'm glad to know that. I'll make sure to stay away from them." She could never bear to be rude, and she cast this perfect stranger her sweetest smile.

"The male is called a cob and the female is a pen," the jogger persisted. Evidently, he felt we needed educating.

"What is this, a class in zoology?" I muttered.

"He certainly is well-informed," Amy whispered. Then she grabbed my arm. "Look, they're leaving the water." The snowy white pair waddled up onto the bank, revealing long reedy legs that seemed inadequate support for their bodies, which now seemed very bulky. The graceful look had vanished, leaving them as awkward in appearance as a couple of ostriches.

"Well, I'll be going on," the jogger said, evidently giving up on us. He smiled, causing his mouth to spread from one big ear to the other, and his little squinty eyes to squeeze shut.

"I hope I'll run into you again," he added. "My name is Cass Ellis, by the way." He sprang to his feet.

"Perhaps we'll meet again. Good-bye, Mr. Ellis," Amy said,

minding her manners as usual.

We continued the new routine every evening and, though it happened slowly, the unwanted inches on our hips began to decrease. There were always joggers and other cyclists on the path. We usually saw both Ed and Cass—Handsome and Homely. Cass always smiled and spoke, but Ed ignored us, though we always stopped to rest at the lake. There we would be, staring at him as he sprinted by. I liked a man who kept his mind on what he was doing, and Ed Kosner certainly had that characteristic.

The trouble was, he was always going in the same direction we were, so that we might pass each other, but we'd never meet face-to-face. Several times I suggested to Amy that we reverse our route, but she said that by doing so we would have the sun in our eyes. I figured I could wear my sunglasses, but I didn't want to push it. Amy was so sure that Ed wasn't worth bothering about. She had spoken to Barry about him, and told me his co-workers didn't like him.

They're just jealous, I thought.

I was secretly pleased when Amy told me Barry wanted her to meet him several evenings a week to play tennis. Without her breathing down my neck, I would find some way to turn Ed's eyes from staring straight ahead of him.

First, I got out my sunglasses and tried the reverse direction. Even with the sun protection, the glare was so blinding I didn't recognize Ed if or when I met him.

I dreamed up another tactic. There were two ways around the lake—one branching off from, and then rejoining, the other. The route we'd been following was the long way, with curves and slopes. The other cut straight across the narrow end of the water, where the swans hung out. It was mostly used by mothers with little tots, the elderly, folks who liked to feed the swans, and joggers and bicycling cheaters.

I'll take the shortcut, I thought, and sit in wait at the far end for my victim. I would be concealed by a bush at the point where the two paths came together again, but I would be able to peer through the foliage and see him coming. Then I would scoot out on my bike and just barely avoid running into him. Or perhaps, I would let myself actually graze him a little bit. That would wake him up. I would fall all over myself apologizing and he would laugh and tell me no harm was done. Then he would invite me to have coffee with him at the little café at the park exit.

The next time Amy went off to play tennis, I headed for the shortcut. As I turned onto the little path, I saw a sign reading: BEWARE. SWANS BROODING. MALE BELLIGERENT.

Well, the male would scarcely attack a bicycle, I thought as I sailed past the warning sign.

One of the swans—evidently the prospective father, as the female would have been on her eggs—was standing on the bank about halfway to my bush. As I drew near, he glared at me through mean little eyes, then lowered his head and lumbered purposefully toward me, letting out hissing sounds. So the stupid bird thought he could fight a pair of wheels! I could pedal way faster than he could get around.

That's what I thought. But those scrawny underpinnings were more muscular and fit than they seemed. He kept gaining on me and, before I knew it, he was batting at my rear wheel with one large wing.

"Hey, bug off!" I screamed.

He kept alongside me, swatting and hissing, and then he caught his wing in the spokes. The bike toppled and I tumbled down, and then flung myself onto the nearby lawn. He couldn't get at me. As much as he thrashed around, he couldn't free himself.

Something had to be done about him. I couldn't leave the poor bird there with my bicycle.

Nobody was in sight. No mothers with little kids, no kindly senior citizens, no nature lovers with their bread crumbs.

Of course not! They had read the sign, too, but, unlike me, they had taken the warning seriously!

On the other path, though, which I could see slanting down toward the one I was on, was a man in runner's shorts. Ed. "Help!" I called. "Hey, mister!"

Ed charged through the shrubbery that separated the two paths, and stood shaking his head at what he saw. "What gives?" he asked as the swan thumped and heaved helplessly about. "What are you doing on this trail anyway? Didn't you see the sign? Can't you read?"

"I agree I was stupid," I said a bit crossly. "What we have to do is free this creature."

Big eyes turned to study me. "What do you mean 'we'? You got yourself in this mess. You get yourself out." He turned and jogged on.

"You're gross. Don't you care about the swan?" I screamed after him. "You use the park. Shouldn't you help preserve its wildlife?"

He just laughed over his shoulder and kept banging one foot in front of the other until he disappeared into a clump of pines.

Meanwhile, the swan flapped and flailed madly about, hissing and making scary throaty sounds. Could he have a heart attack? I wondered. What if he dropped dead on me? I had to find a telephone and call someone. But who? Police? Fire department? By the time I could get hold of a responsible person, the poor bird might have expired. What was I going to do? I had to help that swan. Maybe I could dial 911 if I could get to a phone in time. I just had to!

I had to try. I started to run off, when a pair of feet appeared through the brush and skidded to a stop beside me, along with the body that went with them. They belonged to Cass. "Hey, now!" he said, scratching his head. "Look, you hold him tightly by the neck like this, and I'll work on his wing."

"I can't hold him. He'll bite!" I screeched. What was wrong with this man?

"Not if you do it like this," he assured me.

"All right," I quavered. "Nice swan, pretty swan," I said in what I hoped were soothing tones as I put my two fists around his lengthy throat. I was trying to be as gentle as I could be. I was so afraid of hurting this beautiful swan.

"I'm continually fascinated by the family instincts of some animals," Cass said as he carefully manipulated a quill. "Can you believe this cob's small brain telling him he must guard his wife while she creates his kids?" Cass seemed genuinely amazed at this.

"It is amazing," I agreed. "Nice cob, pretty cob," I crooned.

Cass loosened a section of wing, and then another, until he succeeded in untangling the whole thing. Instead of appearing grateful for his release, the swan shook a wing at us as if it were a fist, then with a final angry glare, stalked back to his mate.

"Cass, I can't thank you enough," I said. "I don't know what would have happened if you hadn't come along when you did."

"I always wanted to rescue a maiden in distress. Now I intend to carry you off to that little café at the east exit. Here, hop on your bike"—he held the bike upright for me—"and I'll lead you along. Just come with me. We both need something to relax us. You did a great job. I was really impressed."

By the time we got our coffee, we were chatting and laughing like old friends. Cass was fun, and knowledgeable in numerous areas. The café, he told me, had an interesting history. Nearly as old as the city itself, it had been a meeting place for writers and artists, and our state song had been written at one of the tables. It was fascinating to be with him. I had never been around anyone who knew so much. Not only had he saved the swan, no one else could have done that— he knew so much about so many different things!

"Cass," I said, "you have a very good-looking mind." In fact, I wondered why I had ever considered him outwardly homely. I liked the laugh lines around his eyes and mouth, the easy tilt of his nose, his powerful shoulders. I found myself longing to be held close to that broad chest. I don't know what took me so long to appreciate such an amazing guy!

Two nights later, after we had dinner together, I got my wish. It was every bit as wonderful as I had imagined. Later, after he had escorted me to my door and we shared one last kiss, I thought about how surface deep beauty really is. The most handsome person, namely Ed, was ugly inside. That lovely, graceful bird, the swan, had its ungainly aspect. Then, take Amy. The expression "Beauty is as beauty does" certainly fit her.

I'm trying to be more like her. I certainly want to keep Cass as a friend, and I'm hoping that someday soon, we'll be more than that. THE END

ENGAGED TO THE WRONG MAN

My fiancé, Tyler, and I needed to find an apartment before our wedding, but none of the ones we'd seen fit the bill.

"Tyler Barrington, it is absolutely impossible to find an apartment in our price range that has covered parking and twenty-four-hour security patrols!" It was satisfying to say the words into the phone, even though Tyler had already hung up. I finished the last bite of my sandwich and stirred a packet of sugar into my lukewarm coffee as I picked up the newspaper again. Our wedding was only three months away, and we still hadn't found an apartment to live in. Oh, there were plenty of rentals advertised—but Tyler was very particular. Every day at lunch, I would call to tell him about the perfect, affordable, centrally located apartment I had discovered, and inevitably he would find something wrong. Or else his mother would point out some fatal flaw as soon as he told her about it. I was beginning to think we would spend our honeymoon sitting in a real estate office studying brochures and leases.

I sighed and went back to examining the classified ads. I was so absorbed in the real-estate listings that I didn't even hear Craig, my boss, come in.

"Ahem," he said. He got my attention, all right. Startled, I spilled coffee down the front of my blouse and all over an ad for an apartment complex that had a sauna and swimming pool and covered parking. I hated to admit it, but I was a natural-born klutz—one of those people doomed to go through life spilling coffee, tripping over cracks in the sidewalk, and bumping into people with shopping carts in the supermarket.

"Sorry, Josie, I didn't mean to make you jump like that," he said. Craig eased his body onto the corner of my desk and gave me a boyish grin. "Listen, Kevin is due at the clinic for physical therapy at four, but we've got a problem with one of the computers and I can't get away. Can you pick him up at school and take him over there?"

Craig's wife, Pam, had been killed in a car accident a year ago, and since then, my secretarial duties had gradually expanded to include Cub Scouts, swimming lessons, trips to the dentist, and even an occasional conference with Kevin's fifth-grade teacher. I didn't mind, though. Kevin was a sweet, sensitive kid—exactly the kind of son I hoped Tyler and I would have someday. Kevin had been thrown out the car when his mom was hit head-on by a drunk driver, and had suffered severe injuries to his legs. Since then, he had undergone four operations. At first, doctors predicted he would spend the rest of his life in a wheelchair, but Kevin had surprised everyone with his courage and determination. His left leg was still encased in a cumbersome brace from ankle to thigh, but he was walking more confidently every week.

"Sure, Craig," I said. "I'll be glad to. Shall I drop him at your apartment afterward?"

Craig nodded. "Thanks, Josie. You're an angel. One of these days Kevin will trade in that leg brace for a football uniform, and I'll double your salary and make you a vice president."

"Forget that!" I laughed. "Just find me an apartment within ten minutes of here with luxury features, new carpeting, and covered parking—and a rent that Tyler and I can afford."

It wasn't until after Craig left that I remembered that Tyler had arranged for us to look at a condo over in Woodridge after work. I made a mental note to call his office and tell him to pick me up at the hospital.

Later that day, as Kevin and I were headed for the clinic, our taxi got caught in traffic. Luckily, the appointments were running behind schedule at the clinic. Once we got there, I discovered that the air-conditioning in the waiting room was broken. I read an article on fishing in mountain streams, which I hoped would make me feel cool. But it only made me feel bored, so I gave up. I patted the perspiration off my forehead with a tissue, and walked down the hall to the snack bar to get some ice cream.

I returned just as Kevin reappeared, looking exhausted and drained, which was typical after a therapy session. I started to say something sympathetic, but suddenly his eyes turned toward the door and his face lit up.

"Uncle Pete!" he exclaimed. The pain disappeared from his expression, and it was replaced by excitement. I turned to see a tall, good-looking stranger. Although he was quite a bit younger than Craig, the family resemblance made it obvious they were brothers.

"Hi, I'm Pete Barnes, and you must be Josie Sanders." The man's smile was easy and confident as he greeted me. "I had to come to the city on business, and Craig said I just might catch this young fellow here before he left." His eyes dropped to the front of my blouse and I felt my face turn pink under his stare.

"Uh—very artistic," he said, cocking his head to one side and squinting critically. "I'd never have thought to put the green and mocha side by side like that—it's a bit flamboyant perhaps, but a nice touch, especially with those little flecks of chocolate."

I looked down in dismay at a generous dollop of mint-fudge ice cream that had dripped from my cone to join the coffee stain on the front of my white blouse.

"Oh, no," I groaned. "I'll never be able to get this clean again!"

Pete and Kevin laughed. "There's still some clean places over by the pocket," Kevin noted. "You should spill some cherry soda there."

Pete shook his head. "No, it calls for something more dramatic. I think pizza would be just the thing. Do you think I could persuade you to join Kevin and me for a giant-size pepperoni special with extra cheese?"

Before I could answer, Tyler's voice interrupted us. "Josie, what's going on? My secretary gave me a message to meet you here." Tyler scowled as he planted himself firmly between Pete and me.

I glanced at my watch guiltily. "It can't be five o'clock already!" I exclaimed.

"It's almost five-twenty," Tyler said crossly. "And I've been searching all over—do you have any idea how big this hospital is?" He looked at my blouse. "My God, Josie, don't you have anything decent to wear? Surely you don't plan to go looking at apartments with food spilled all over your clothes." He turned and glared at Pete and Kevin, as if they were somehow responsible for the stains.

Pete extended his hand and introduced himself, ignoring Tyler's rudeness. "I was planning to take my nephew out for pizza," he offered. "Perhaps you and Josie would like to join us."

"No thanks," Tyler responded curtly. "Come on, Josie, we're late."

"I'm sorry," I apologized over my shoulder as Tyler hurried me down the hall. "Tyler promised his parents we'd have dinner with them tonight."

Traffic was heavy on the downtown parkway and by the time we got to the Woodridge exit it was nearly six o'clock. That didn't improve Tyler's mood, either.

"I don't know why you had to be so rude," I chided him. "Pete was just trying to be friendly. And you wouldn't even look at Kevin when I introduced him to you."

"Well, Craig Barnes has no business expecting you to baby-sit for a kid like that. That's not what you went to business school for."

I bristled. "What do you mean by 'a kid like that?'" I demanded. "Kevin Barnes is just like any other ten-year-old kid, except he's going to walk a little slower for a while."

Tyler sighed patiently and shook his head. "Josie Sanders, when are you going to learn to toughen up and stop letting people impose on you?" He pulled into the parking lot next to a sign that read, NO

PARKING-TENANTS ONLY. "Come on, honey, smile. It's too nice a day to fight." He leaned over and gave me a quick kiss. I smiled obediently and followed him into the manager's office.

The apartment didn't have a dishwasher and the nearest laundry facilities were two miles away in a shopping center. But Tyler insisted on taking a complete tour anyway. It was after eight by the time we got to the country club where we were to meet Tyler's parents. I was ravenous.

"Sorry we're late," Tyler apologized. "Josie volunteered to play baby-sitter to the boss's kid and it put us behind schedule."

I started to protest, but Mrs. Barrington gave me a withering look. "Undoubtedly your kindness was appreciated by your employer, dear," she said coldly. "But your social obligations to Tyler should have come first."

Tyler's parents had never tried to conceal their disapproval of me. They had made it abundantly clear that a lowly secretary—especially one who tended to spill soup and use the wrong fork for the shrimp cocktail—would not fit in with their high-society friends.

"Now, now, Camilla. I'm sure Josie didn't intend to be inconsiderate," Mr. Barrington said placatingly. He smiled at Tyler and me. "And it really wasn't any problem; we just went ahead and ate without you."

He motioned the waitress to clear the table, and I noted wistfully that there was half a potato left on Mrs. Barrington's plate. My stomach was begging me to grab for it. "We'll have to hurry," Mr. Barrington went on, standing up. "I managed to get four tickets for the ballet and we don't want to miss the first act."

I realized with dismay that we were not going to be allowed to eat at all. Tyler was smiling agreeably; his stomach apparently didn't care for the last little scraps of Mr. Barrington's steak that the waitress was carrying away. I managed to snatch a handful of bread sticks as we got up to leave. Mrs. Barrington glared at me, but I pretended not to notice.

The next morning I was busy filing invoices when Pete Barnes strolled into the office, carrying one yellow rose. I stood up as he handed it to me, bumped my shin on the open file drawer, and uttered a very unladylike exclamation as I dropped the file folder full of papers.

Pete raised an eyebrow in mock disapproval. "Really," he said, "a simple thank you would have been adequate."

"Oh, no, I didn't mean . . ." I stammered. My face turned bright red as it always did when I got flustered. Then, seeing the twinkle in his eyes, I gave up and laughed with him. "Now you know the real me," I told him. "I try to hide it, but the awful truth is that I'm an incurable klutz, and I swear whenever I run into things."

"That's not so awful," he said cheerfully. "I find klutziness kind of appealing. It brings out my protective instincts. By the way, it's too bad you couldn't join us last night. Kevin and I really pigged out on pizza. Did you have fun on your date?"

Wryly, I described my efforts to absorb culture in spite of starvation. I put the rose in a glass of water on my desk and Pete helped me gather up the papers I had dropped.

"Listen, how about letting me buy you a cup of coffee and a doughnut at the snack bar downstairs?" he suggested. "It's the least I can do for a woman who almost collapsed from hunger last night."

"Well . . ." I glanced at my watch.

"Come on," Pete insisted, taking my arm. "I need a cup of coffee, even if you don't. Craig and I have to go to a very boring meeting with some computer people."

When I got back to the office, fortified by two cups of coffee and a jelly doughnut, the phone was ringing and it was Tyler. "Where have you been?" he demanded. "I've been calling for half an hour."

"Uh . . ." I tried to think of a plausible explanation.

"Listen, Josie, I just called to tell you I have to break our date tonight. Mother phoned and told me she and Dad are going to a party over at the Thornfields' and she promised them she'd bring me along."

I bit my tongue and mentally counted to ten so I wouldn't say anything I'd regret later. The Thornfields were a very prominent family. And they had a twenty-year-old unmarried daughter who conveniently just happened to be home from college for the summer. And wouldn't you know, she just happened to be the girl Tyler had dated all through high school! It was bad enough that Camilla Barrington did not consider me a suitable match for Tyler, but this maneuver was so obvious it was almost insulting!

"Come on, Josie. It's only a dinner. Besides, Mr. Thornfield is on the board of directors at the bank. I can't very well refuse, can I?"

"No, apparently not," I said frostily.

Tyler completely missed the sarcasm in my voice. "Good girl," he said in the tone someone might use when talking to a clever dog that has just fetched a stick.

"Oh, Mother said to remind you about the garden party a week from Saturday. Alexis and Phillip will be arriving the night before, so we'll all have dinner at the club."

I gritted my teeth. Alexis was Tyler's older sister. She was nearly as snobbish as Mrs. Barrington. Her husband, Philip, was rich and self-centered. The garden party was in honor of Alexis's birthday. I wasn't looking forward to it.

"Josie, are you listening?"

"Oh—I'm sorry, Tyler, what was that again?"

"Mother said for you to get a new dress. I told her you were planning to wear that blue one you wore to the club and she said you really ought to wear something more formal."

"Tyler, for heaven's sake, I haven't even finished paying for the blue dress yet! I can't just run out and buy a new outfit every time she has a party."

There was a silence followed by Tyler's exasperated sigh. "Look Tyler, I have to go now," I lied. "Someone is calling on the other line." Without giving him a chance to argue, I hung up.

Craig Barnes came in as I was glaring at the phone. "Uh, oh," he said. "Don't tell me—you just found another perfect apartment and Tyler rejected it because the drapes were one inch too long." Craig didn't like Tyler very much, and he never bothered to hide his opinion. "Hey, I know just the thing to brighten you up," he said when I explained my bad mood. "I promised Kevin I'd take him and Pete to a football game tonight. Kevin is crazy about football, you know. How about joining us?"

I declined. Football definitely wasn't my idea of fun. And, from what I had observed, Kevin wasn't interested in the sport, either. On several occasions I'd tried to tell Craig that, but he couldn't seem to accept the idea of his son not being an athlete.

"Aw, come on, Josie, don't look at me that way," he protested, reading my mind. "Football is good for boys. If you had it your way, Kevin would grow up to be a sissy. Just you wait until next fall. He'll be playing in the peewee league, and I bet he'll turn out to be a running back, too, just like I was."

Craig had a faraway look in his eyes and I knew he was picturing Kevin scoring the winning touchdown while everyone cheered. Totally unrealistic, of course. The doctors had said that if the therapy was successful, Kevin would eventually walk with only a slight limp. But football was out of the question. Forever. I sighed, because there was no way to convince Craig of that.

Craig handed me a stack of reports to process and the air-conditioning men arrived to work on the thermostat, so I pushed my problems out of my mind and settled in for a long afternoon at the computer. Then I went home, washed my hair, and hoped that Tyler was having a rotten time at the dinner party.

I didn't see Pete again until Wednesday. He'd picked Kevin up after school and had taken him shopping. When they came in, Kevin had a package tucked under his arm and an ear-to-ear grin.

"Josie, look what Uncle Pete bought me!" Proudly, he opened the bag to show me a camera and a book on photography. "He's going to teach me how to develop my own pictures, too. Tonight we're going to . . ."

"Hey, son, did you forget? I thought we were going to try tossing the football around a little after dinner." Craig had come out of his office and was looking at the camera equipment disapprovingly.

Kevin's face fell. "But Uncle Pete has to go back home tomorrow," he said. "Besides, my leg still hurts from the last time we played. Why do we have to play so soon?"

Craig's frown deepened. "Listen, son, the first thing a good athlete has to learn is discipline. And that means pushing yourself physically and not whining. Otherwise you'll never make first-string."

I saw Pete's jaw muscles tighten up. "Go on out and wait for us by the elevator, Kevin," he said curtly. "Your dad and I will be along in a minute." As soon as the office door shut he turned to Craig. "Don't you realize the harm you might be doing to that boy?" he demanded angrily. "Didn't you listen to the doctors when they told you that—"

"Doctors," Craig said harshly. "What do they know? If we'd listened to them, Kevin would probably still be in a wheelchair!" He pounded his fist on the desk. "My son has guts, Pete. You mark my words. Next year at this time I want him out on that football field with the other boys."

"And he can be," Pete insisted. "As a sports photographer, but not as a player. If you weren't so stubborn you'd admit that."

"No way!" Craig retorted. He strode out of the office and slammed the door.

"Sorry, Josie." Pete apologized. "But for a smart man, that brother of mine sure can be stupid sometimes." He shook his head in frustration as he left.

Tyler called an hour later to tell me he'd pick me up after work to go see an apartment he'd heard about. The previous tenant had just been transferred to the West Coast and it hadn't even been advertised in the paper yet. For once, he actually sounded excited, and the more he described it, the more I found his enthusiasm contagious.

As we drove in through the gates, my spirits sank. I could tell right away that it was out of our price range.

"Let's just leave, honey," I suggested to Tyler as the manager came out to greet us. "There's no way we can afford this." But Tyler ignored me and as we walked through the apartment, he drooled over the gas fireplace and ceiling fan and built-in microwave. Then we toured the laundry room and swimming pool, which had a sauna and clubhouse, complete with an outdoor barbecue pit. As we walked back toward the office, Tyler paused beside the sun deck.

"How do you like it, honey?" he asked.

I shrugged. "It would be okay, I guess, if we were rich."

Tyler grinned. "I signed the lease this morning. We can start moving our things in the week before the wedding." I stood there with my mouth open.

"It was all Mother's idea," Tyler went on. "She and Dad are going to take care of the rent for the first year. Mother says she just can't bear to think of us stuck in some tacky, run-down place miles from everywhere."

I forced myself to smile, but inside I felt numb. I didn't want Tyler's parents to pay our rent. I especially didn't want Camilla Barrington to pick out our living-room furniture, which was exactly what Tyler was telling me she'd already done.

"She found it at Savon's." That obviously impressed him—Savon's was a top-of-the-line furniture store. "A sofa and two matching chairs, and a teak coffee table. They'll be delivered next week." He chuckled. "I haven't seen Mother this excited in months. She and Amanda were out shopping all day yesterday."

"Amanda?" I asked, getting more annoyed.

"Yes, Amanda Thornfield. She's majoring in interior design at college, you know. She's very talented."

Oh, that's just dandy, I told myself. Not only was my mother-in-law choosing my apartment, but she had enlisted Tyler's old girlfriend to decide how to furnish it. Amanda had probably picked out our sheets and towels and decided where to put the bed, too. I knew already that I was going to hate the sofa.

"Josie? Is something wrong?" Tyler tilted my chin up and peered at me anxiously. "You don't even look surprised."

I laughed, a fragile laugh that was dangerously close to tears. "Oh, Tyler, nothing your mother does surprises me anymore."

"Yes," he agreed cheerfully. "She surely is a generous person."

When Tyler drove me home he wanted to come in for a while, but I pleaded a headache.

"Headaches are caused by stress," he whispered, nibbling at my ear. "I bet I know how to make you relax."

I pushed him away. "Look Tyler, I'm not in the mood, okay?"

"Well, you don't have to act so huffy about it," he snapped. "After all, we are going to be married in a few weeks." He walked me to my door and left without even saying good night.

Whenever I got depressed, it made me even klutzier than usual. When Craig got depressed, he drank coffee by the gallon and swore a lot. By Friday afternoon, I was tripping over chairs and spilling file folders down behind the desk. Craig had dark circles under his eyes, and the new secretary from the purchasing department refused to come in our office because Craig had already screamed at her twice on Thursday for no reason at all.

Kevin arrived just before five. Craig had left for the conference room carrying a coffee-stained budget draft and swearing a blue streak.

"Where's Dad?" Kevin asked. "He's supposed to take me to the shopping center." I noticed he was carrying the camera case.

"He had to go to a meeting," I told him. "He ought to be back in a few minutes. Have you taken any pictures yet?"

Kevin looked down at the box and bit his lip. "No," he said softly. "I've decided to take it back to the store. I'm going to exchange it for a football helmet."

"Oh, Kevin, honey, are you sure that's what you really want? I can talk to your dad if you want and try to—"

"No!" There was a long silence. When Kevin spoke again his voice was very quiet, almost a whisper. "Josie," he said, "when you're a kid you have to do things even if you don't want to."

Craig returned just then and they left. But Kevin's words kept running round and round in my brain as I got dressed that night to go to dinner with the Barringtons. I put on my gray wool dress and brightened it up with a shiny red belt and a necklace. It didn't matter, though—no matter what I wore, Camilla Barrington was sure to find fault with it. I'd probably spill food all over it anyway. *Hey, Kevin, I* thought to myself, *even when you're not a kid, you still have to do things even if you don't want to.*

At least Tyler and I weren't late this time. We met the Barringtons in the lobby and Alexis and Phillip walked in right behind us.

"Josie, darling!" Alexis gave me a big phony smile and reached out to hug me. She aimed a kiss at my cheek, but I had just turned to greet Phillip and it landed on my nose instead. Well, it was her own fault. They all knew perfectly well how uncoordinated I became when I was nervous. Phillip elected to shake hands instead.

From there, the evening went steadily downhill. I dropped my napkin on the floor immediately, and as soon as the waiter handed me a menu I managed to dip the corner in the butter dish. It was Tyler who spilled his whole glass of red wine on my lap, though. That wasn't my fault at all. I was just sitting there, listening politely as Camilla described the cute little mirror she had bought us for our entrance hall. Tyler was very apologetic, and Alexis, of course, shrieked in dismay so that everyone in the dining room turned to stare. Camilla glared at me.

I was depressed for the rest of the night. Maybe Camilla figured I had passed on my clumsiness to Tyler like it was some sort of repulsive social disease.

Our evening broke up early. Alexis and Phillip said they were too tired to go anywhere and Camilla suggested that I ought to hurry home to soak my dress if I wanted that stain to come out. Tyler kissed me good night in the car.

"I'm sorry about the wine, honey," he said for about the hundredth time. That pretty well killed any feelings of passion he was arousing in me.

"It's okay," I assured him. He walked me to the door.

"Remember, Alexis's birthday party is at three tomorrow. Don't be late. Both of my parents have this thing about being punctual."

I waved good-bye and went inside. Amanda Thornfield was going to be at the party. It was a good bet that she wouldn't be late! I put my dress to soak and wrapped Alexis's birthday present. The paper tore and I started all over again. It took me four tries before the ribbon looked presentable. I set it on the kitchen counter where I couldn't possibly forget it. I taped a reminder on the bathroom mirror just in case.

The next morning, I skipped breakfast and did a double exercise session, determined to look willowy thin and graceful. I planned to skip lunch, too, but relented. Willowy thin was nice, but not if it made my stomach growl. I compromised with skim milk, yogurt, and a hard-boiled egg. Tyler phoned at one to make sure I hadn't forgotten to wrap the present. "And, Josie," he added, "to me you're beautiful no matter what you wear—even that blue dress Mother doesn't like."

After he hung up, I mulled that over and tried to decide if it was a compliment. Then I lay down on the sofa for a few minutes to rest my eyes. An hour later the phone shrilled, jolting me out of a sound sleep. Glancing at my watch, I was horrified to discover it was after two o'clock and I was hopelessly behind schedule.

"Hello?" I answered.

"Josie?" I recognized Pete's voice. "Hey, I came down for the weekend to rescue my nephew from the deranged football fanatic," he informed me cheerfully. "I'm going to talk some sense into that thickheaded brother of mine even if it takes all night. How about helping me?"

"I don't think it will work," I told him, holding the phone under my chin while I grabbed a towel and wriggled out of my jeans and sweatshirt. "Besides, I happen to have a date."

"Break the date, then."

"Pete," I said. "I'm engaged to be married, remember?"

"Josie, if you want some good advice, break the engagement, too." Pete's light, bantering manner suddenly became serious. "I only met the guy once, but I knew right away he wasn't the man for you. Craig agrees, by the way. He says Tyler is weak-willed, selfish, and spoiled. And his mother is a domineering old barracuda."

"Craig had no right to say that!" I protested.

"Well, actually, he didn't say it in those exact words." Pete chuckled. "I laundered his language a little. But seriously, Josie, give it some thought. And make sure you don't let people change you into something you never wanted to be."

"Thanks, Pete. And good luck with the football fanatic." I hung up and hastily showered and applied my makeup and dabbed on the perfume that Tyler had given me for my birthday. I scrabbled desperately through my dresser drawer, looking for my earrings. I found them just as the taxi pulled up and honked.

The taxi driver refused to hurry. "What's the point?" he shrugged. "With that construction work on the parkway, the traffic is backed up all the way." I groaned and as we crept along, I stared at my watch and pictured Tyler pacing back and forth impatiently, while Camilla fretted and fussed. Maybe I'd tell him the taxi had had a flat tire. Or that we'd been in an accident.

When we pulled up in front of the Barringtons' home, the driver whistled softly. "Pretty classy place," he said admiringly. "I haven't seen so many expensive cars since the mayor's funeral."

"Here." I shoved some money at him and rushed up the steps to the front door. Mr. Barrington had even hired a valet service to park cars and take the guests through the back gate to the patio. A band was playing there, and next to the pool stood a buffet table covered with fancy appetizers. There was a bar, too, and Tyler was standing there with a drink in his hand and a very annoyed expression on his face. When he saw me he set the drink down so hard that it splashed onto the tablecloth. I decided to forget the flat-tire story and go with the truth.

"I'm sorry, Tyler. I forgot about the detour on the parkway and it took longer than I expected."

Then Alexis and the rest of the family walked up to greet me and I knew what Tyler's next question would be about: the present. "I left the present in the taxi," I said miserably.

Alexis laughed her shrill, phony laugh and said it didn't really matter, and Tyler apologized to everyone for my thoughtlessness.

Tyler's father smiled tolerantly. "Now, now," he said to Camilla. "Try not to let it spoil the party for you. I'm sure Josie will learn to organize herself better once she and Tyler are married." He patted my arm. "Isn't that right, dear?" he asked.

Just then one of the waiters walked by and my elbow must have bumped his arm. Camilla Barrington gasped as a whole tray of cocktail shrimp and little chicken sandwiches clattered onto the brick patio, leaving a trail of hot sauce down the back of my dress.

It was an omen. No doubt about it, fate was sending me a message I couldn't ignore. And that's what I told Pete on the phone an hour later.

"Did you break your engagement?" he inquired.

"Yes, did you teach Craig a lesson?"

Pete laughed. "No, we settled peacefully."

"Good," I told him. "Because I just happened to stop at the bookstore on my way home and I got Kevin a book on action photography. Is it okay if I stop over for a while?"

Well, I wound up going over there, and Pete and I have been dating each other ever since. It's spring now and football season is long past. Craig is doing a lot better about accepting Kevin's physical limitations. The other day, he came into the office at lunchtime with a newspaper in his hand and he actually skipped right over the sports page without pausing.

"Look at this!" He grinned, tossing the paper on my desk and pointing to the picture on the society page. It announced the engagement of Tyler Barrington to Amanda Thornfield. She was a lovely girl with long hair and a flawless smile and a big glob of spicy mustard running down her picture.

"Hey, your sandwich is dripping," Craig observed. I giggled and made a mental note to show Pete the picture when he came by to pick me up for our date. Somehow it seemed like a very fitting way to close that chapter in my life. THE END

THE SECOND HONEYMOON

A humid August wind whipped around our tiny compact car as we sped along the gray highway toward northern Wisconsin. I looked over at Sam, separated from me by the bucket seat, and saw the lines of strain and worry about bills and the mortgage starting to appear on his otherwise smooth skin. It was a weekend to get away from it all, a time for a second honeymoon. Well, almost a second honeymoon. Between our first wedding trip to the national park and this one, five years had gone by, and we had two very active little boys along with us this time.

We hadn't planned it that way. A family camping trip had been the last thing we wanted. But the planning had begun at the last minute, sort of, when Sam came home one hot, sizzling July night. He looked so absolutely worn out that I'd said, "What I wouldn't give to be back at our lake on a day like this!"

"Our" lake wasn't ours at all, of course. It belonged to the people of the state of Wisconsin. But to us, it was a special place. Sam and I had spent our honeymoon there. We'd never forgotten it—and we'd never been back, though we'd been promising ourselves that trip for five years.

"It's not impossible," Sam said, wiping his face with a wet towel.

"What's not impossible?" A squirt of lemon hit me in the eye. "Oh darn! I wish I could think of something cooler than tuna fish salad."

Sam went on, dreaming out loud. "At our lake, it's cool enough at night to broil steaks over a fire. We'd even need blankets at night."

I stood there like an idiot, wiping my eye. Then, I continued pouring iced tea for us and cold milk for the kids, fetching paper towels, and shutting Kiki, our ever-hungry poodle, out on the back porch so we could eat in peace, without having him beg and yap for handouts. I love dogs, all of them, but sometimes, when the kids and the dog and this miserable heat all ganged up on me at once, I simply didn't want to deal with them.

Anyway, Sam finally translated what he meant. "It's not impossible to go back to our lake, honey. Our fifth wedding anniversary's coming up, and I've my vacation time."

Now, my Sam's a man in a million! How many husbands remember any wedding anniversary, let alone what number it is?

Well, we did our best to keep our plans a secret. First off, what to do with the boys? We needed strategy. We had to do something to make our kids want to spend two weeks with Grandma, Aunt Carol, and Cousin Phil on their big dairy farm.

Lucky for us, the kids didn't need much convincing. The next evening, we drove out to the farm. And guess what? Of all the years of not leaving the farm, this was the time Sam's folks had chosen to go on a tour of French Canada! Only Harry, the hired man, was there, along with two extra men to run things.

So that eliminated one place where we could leave the boys. They'd have loved to stay on the farm, too. Bobby didn't want to leave. He was downright insulted that Cousin Phil had hired men to feed the herd. He said he could've helped Harry—and he wasn't even in school yet! Both our boys are independent little things.

We went down a long list of relatives—it was hopeless. Everybody was either away, sick, or had some other excuse. I was miffed for a while, thinking nobody loved our kids or us. But, really, to park two little noisy boys in somebody's quiet house in the middle of a heat wave was a lot to expect.

After that, we started on friends and neighbors. Again, we batted exactly zero. All our friends and neighbors had their own whimpering, fretting, itchy kids to drag through the endless heat.

Nicole, our next-door neighbor and good friend, sighed. "Frankly, I'd like to ask you to take my three little demons with you. Did you know they all have poison ivy—and my husband and I haven't had a full night's sleep in a week!"

Boy, when you say the words "population explosion," I know what you mean! Around where we live, everybody seemed to have too many kids. At least it seemed that way during the summertime.

But we did have three offers of help—when it came to Kiki! Yes, it was easy to board our dog, but nobody would take the kids!

So we finally came to a great decision: we'd take our children on our second honeymoon. "Well, it's legal anyhow," I kidded Sam. "Think of the people who trot around with their kids without bothering to get married!"

At that point, Sam was all for staying home and forgetting the whole thing. But I had the bug; I simply had to have another early-morning swim in the cool water of "our" lake. I had to wake up under canvas, and see the tracing of leaves overhead. I insisted that I must breathe fresh air again.

Mostly, I appealed to Sam's sentimental streak. "Darling, I just ache to go back to that wonderful place where all our happiness began!"

He couldn't resist that. So, on August eighth, we set out like a band of nomads in our overstuffed car. We had a trunkful of toys, so we had to stow all our clothes in the backseat, along with the boys. Behind our car, we dragged a rented trailer, loaded with camping equipment. You'd have thought we were going on a ten-year safari.

On the way out of town, we left Kiki with some friends who had volunteered to take him in. Ordinarily, he'd have howled to see us go, but these friends had a lovely lady poodle, you see.

Then, off we went.

Four-year-old Bobby, the mischievous one, started bouncing as soon as we hit the road. He pulled his little body halfway out of his car seat, and over into the front seat to whisper in my ear, "Hey,

Mommy, I have to go to the bathroom."

"We're almost there," I said irritably to my oldest child. I was eager to get there and to start reliving those memories as soon as possible. "Can you wait?" I asked as I put him back in the seat.

"Sure," he answered heartily and grabbed his brother's coloring book.

Three-year-old Tommy howled loudly, right into Sam's ear. His round cheeks were all red and puffy, and his eyes spilled out tears of childish misery. He held up the snapped stick of red crayon to me and sobbed, "Bobby broke my crayon, Mommy." Those watery eyes begged me to rectify the situation.

I couldn't restore the broken crayon, but I did say, "Bobby, be more careful in the car," and added one of those stares that showed him I meant business.

"It's not my fault!" Bobby shouted his defense. "It was an accident!"

Tommy knew he wasn't getting his revenge. He knew he had a broken crayon and nothing was being done about it. The tears started oozing out again as he scrunched up his small face and let out a real scream.

With Tommy making tearful accusations about the broken crayon and Bobby holding his own with all the logic of a four-year-old, we arrived at the camping grounds. Sam pulled the car to a sudden halt by the entrance and practically leaped out to talk with the ranger. I knew the feeling. He had that desperate need to talk to an adult to keep his sanity.

After Sam slammed the car door ferociously, I had a spirit-sagging vision of how the trip was going to turn out. With two children, I couldn't recapture the romance of being the new bride, Angela Carter. In fact, this vacation wasn't going to be that much different from being at home. I couldn't control the boys, and as I gazed at the pine forest, I realized glumly that we'd have to baby-sit every second. Otherwise, they would run all over the park.

I trotted them both off to the bathroom and washed Tommy's face. Miraculously, with one look at the postcard-perfect lake, the boys forgot all about their argument. They raced back to the car and pleaded with Sam to take them fishing.

"Later, boys," Sam subdued them swiftly. "First, we have to set up the tent. Get in."

Why does it always take a man's deep voice to command little children? I asked myself as I saw the two kids hop into the car.

Walking up to him slowly, I hugged Sam. "Darling, did you get the same campsite?" I asked.

Sam's astonished eyes told me he'd never even thought about getting the same place. He started apologizing at the same time I began reassuring him that it was all right.

Bobby fidgeted impatiently in the backseat. Breaking into our jumbled apologies, he started clamoring to go. "Come on, come on," he chided me in a good imitation of the way I spoke to him sometimes when he dawdled.

"Never mind, Sam." I dismissed my own wishes to keep peace with the kids.

"Maybe I should change sites for you," he mumbled, hesitating indecisively for a moment.

I could see Bobby was looking around for something to do, and trouble was imminent. "Well, come on! Let's get going," I teased him in the same tone of voice Bobby had just used on me.

That was the last time I had a chance to talk with Sam about anything personal all afternoon. He set up the tent while the boys "helped" him, and I unpacked the utensils and made lunch. After lunch, they went off to fish, and I stayed behind to do the dishes.

This trip wasn't anything like the last time. Five years before, Sam and I had barely waited until he had set up the tent and put down the sleeping bags. We'd made love eagerly in our small tent in the daylight, without a thought about the people camping nearby. Later, we'd looked out at the children in the park and made plans for a family of our own. I never realized how different it would be to travel with children!

"Mommy, I almost caught a fish this big!" Bobby announced, coming up behind me and gesturing some outrageous size.

"The kids got tired of fishing," Sam explained. "Too much of waiting around for them."

The sun played on the streaks in his hair, and I felt like encircling his waist with my arms and pressing myself against him. But the kids wanted to go swimming, and, instead, I dutifully dug the bathing suits out of the car. In the small tent, I helped the kids out of their undershirts. Then, Bobby took off for the lake.

"Wait a minute!" I cried, but he was gone.

"I'll watch him," Sam volunteered, and he sprinted through the trees in Bobby's direction.

I finished dressing Tommy and walked him slowly and tediously down to the lake where Sam was. Maybe I'd been foolish to have two children so close together, but I wouldn't really want to be without either one of them. I couldn't regret energetic Bobby, my firstborn, for all the trouble he caused, and not Tommy, my baby, whose little body wriggled against mine as I coaxed him into the water.

We spent the afternoon trying to teach Bobby how to swim, and Tommy played near the shore. The splashing and thrashing in the water and the shrill screams of delight from the children never stopped for a moment. I wanted to lie on the shore with Sam and watch his firm, muscular body, clothed only in his swim trunks, as he moved about in the sunshine. The thought of the nearness of his body drove me to try to make the kids play in the sand, but my plans never worked out. One or the other of them was never ready to come out of the water for any length of time.

The activity of the children stole our privacy that afternoon. I tried to share my intimate thoughts with Sam, but the children's sharp demands for attention kept interrupting my reminiscences before Sam could answer me, and it seemed like he didn't remember any of the memories I cherished. We had almost grown to be strangers, instead of better lovers, with the years of marriage and the addition of children.

At last, blankets of gray shadow muted the early colors of fall, and Sam took the boys to the playground, while I cooked dinner. It was just like fixing supper at home, except that I wasn't bothered by requests for cookies from those two upturned faces that reminded me of newly hatched, hungry sparrows.

The rest of the evening, we all sat around the campfire and toasted marshmallows. After watching the fire and popping enough amorphous white blobs into the children's open mouths, I felt we had gone through all the motions of a camping trip in the real Boy Scout tradition. So I hustled them off to bed. They nestled down for the night quickly and were almost asleep when I zipped them in.

"When are you and Daddy coming to bed?" Bobby asked sleepily, propping himself up on his elbow.

"Later on. Just go to sleep now," I told him as I gently pushed him back down again. He started to drift off to sleep, thank goodness.

Sam was watching the embers die out when I slipped down next to him on the picnic bench. The woods were cool and quiet in the dark. Overhead, the branches rustled in the wind, and from far away, we could hear the faint noise of other campers.

This was more like our honeymoon—the cool nights alone together when there was nothing else to do but make love. I didn't try to make conversation, because I knew the talk would get around to the children, or their swimming lessons, or work. That would ruin everything. I was here for a second honeymoon, so I decided to start having one.

I looked into Sam's tired eyes for a moment and smiled at him. He held me in a tight embrace, and I kissed him in all the ways I could think of to show him I loved him. For a while, there were no children, no other campers, no one else—just Sam and me in a dark wilderness, with the wind rustling the branches of trees. He slid me off the picnic table onto the ground. I didn't know where I landed. I didn't care. I just knew my passion for Sam.

"Mommy!" a young voice shrieked in fear. "Mommy, Mommy, Mommy!"

It took me a second to remember where I was, and then I rushed into the tent. "Bobby, what's wrong?" I cried, kneeling next to him.

"I had a bad dream," he snuffled as he climbed into my arms. "I dreamed there was a big bear outside, sniffing around."

"There aren't any bears in this park, silly," I comforted him. I was a little embarrassed and sheepish that we'd frightened him with our lovemaking. "Go back to sleep now."

"No!" he stated resolutely. "I'm scared! Will you sleep next to me, Mommy?"

Sam was standing in the entrance, and I turned to him for help.

"I better move your sleeping bag next to him," he told me. "I don't think Bobby will get back to sleep any other way."

I wanted to bawl like a baby at my disappointment. Sam didn't understand how much this trip meant to me and what I intended it to do for us. I had arranged it for his relaxation and to rekindle the spark of love. Our romance was dying slowly like the embers of the fire outside our tent. Nothing was working out as I had planned on this trip. Nothing! Sam was too busy with the kids to think of romance. We were practically becoming slaves to our own children by fulfilling their every demand.

With a grudge against my own child, I climbed into the sleeping bag. I could see Sam outside, throwing sand on the embers, and I felt as though he were putting out our love just as deliberately.

The next morning, the children were up at seven, and I had to get up right away to watch them. Here, there weren't any cartoons they'd settle down for. I made breakfast, and the smell of it aroused Sam.

I got out a quick "Good morning darling, hope you had a good rest last night" before I had to warn Tommy for the eighth time not to go near the fire.

"I slept pretty well," Sam said. He yawned, stretching his arms over his head. "We better take the tent down after breakfast. We have to start back by noon."

The kids were having such a great time playing that they didn't want to leave. "All right," Sam compromised with his uncanny knack for appeasing children. "One short hike and then off we go. Agreed?"

But the boys didn't want to hike. "Swim again!" Tommy offered, his face brightening.

"No," Sam answered craftily, "we've already done that. Let's explore!"

"I'm going to look for buried treasure," Bobby announced, picking up on the idea.

The three of us followed Sam, with Tommy begging Sam to carry him. I lagged behind, dragging my feet over the gravel path and kicking bitterly at the larger stones. I didn't have the spirit to keep up with them. Sam walked way ahead of me with the kids. A fine second honeymoon this was!

The last time we'd walked down that path, Sam had started to run after me in the woods. I had fled down the path and dared him to catch me. I had been giggling too much, and I hadn't watched where I was going, when all of a sudden I'd caught my foot in an old, gnarled tree root on the ground. I had fallen heavily and knocked the breath out of myself. Sam was beside me in a second, and when I'd recovered my breath sufficiently to realize I'd also sprained my ankle, he laughed that he'd caught me at last and had carried me back to the tent where we made love again. Well, that was all in the past.

I looked up from my reverie and saw Sam walking back towards me. Bobby and Tommy were farther off. I pasted on a smile that did not animate the rest of my face, but it was an attempt at a happy greeting. I was coming closer to him when suddenly, I wrenched my ankle and started plunging downward. In a moment, Sam's strong arms reached out to break my fall.

"You did it again!" Sam laughed at me and pointed to the old tree root I'd stumbled over once again. "I knew you would!"

He'd remembered where the dangerous old tree root lay, but I had forgotten. He had his special memories, too! They were different from mine, but they meant the same to him as mine did to me, I realized.

"I guess I'm all right now." I smiled. He didn't carry me, but he walked with me every step of the way.

Going back home, the kids weren't any less noisy, but I didn't mind them so much. They couldn't steal our intimacy anymore. Our closeness lay in our love for each other, not just in our bed. THE END

MAMA'S FAVORITE SHIRT

Four little pairs of eyes watched as I traded envelopes in the church collection plate. I hoped that they were too young to understand what I was doing. Quickly, I tucked my husband's original envelope in my coat pocket. I worried that inquisitive Justin would ask, "Mommy, why is Daddy's offering in your pocket?"

I tried to remain calm as I scanned the congregation to see if anyone had noticed. Martin, my husband, had already left the sanctuary to set up the coffee urn in the social hall. We had a short social following the church service each week. Martin had been glad to volunteer for the job of starting the coffee. The minister's sermons always bored him, sometimes even upset him. Besides, Martin could hardly make it through a solid hour without a drink. He was an alcoholic. Martin didn't think he was, but I knew, and the children knew, too.

I realized that no one had seen me make the swap, except for the kids, that is. We always sat in the last row so that Martin could leave easily. People were careful not to look around rudely during the offering. Still, I felt myself begin to blush. I felt prickly hot all over. I just knew that everyone could read the guilt on my face.

The deacons carried the offering baskets to the front, and the congregation broke into song. I knew that the envelope with Martin's name on it only contained five dollars instead of the usual forty-dollar tithe. The forty dollars was in my coat pocket.

Martin had been brought up to give a tenth of everything he made to the church. He made four-hundred dollars a week, which meant forty went into the collection plate. When he got a bonus at

Christmas, he put a tenth in a special Christmas offering. Even when his company insurance paid for the birth of our children, he gave one tenth of the payment to the church.

For seven years, I had watched a tenth of Martin's earnings go to the church. Even when he had made only eighty-five dollars a week working as a salesclerk, eight-fifty always went into the collection plate. It had been hard to make ends meet then on such a small income. Now, it was just as hard on four hundred a week. After the ten percent came out, there was still a lot left. That would be plenty of money if it weren't for Martin's drinking.

Martin was a manager at a microwave plant. It wasn't an executive position or anything. He still wore work clothes like the other men under him. I wasn't sure how well we could live on what Martin made, but I knew we didn't live as well as the families of the men under him.

We lived in a little two-bedroom frame house. Most of the men in the neighborhood worked for Martin—like my best friend Patty's husband. He made two-hundred-and-fifty dollars a week working on the assembly line. They lived in a house exactly like ours. The whole development had only three kinds of houses: houses without a garage, garage on the left, and garage on the right. But Patty's house was freshly painted, and she and Larry, her husband, had planted little bushes and trees. We just had the one scrawny tree that the contractor had planted in each yard. Inside, Patty had secondhand furniture the same as we did, but she had bought cute little decorator pieces which really spruced the place up.

Patty and Larry had three kids. They always had good shoes, jeans, and shirts to wear. Patty managed the family money. She always paid the mortgage, utilities, and other bills. Then she carefully picked up the groceries, shopping all the sales and using coupons. She had a real neat list of priorities, including clothing, gifts, and everything. At the end of the month, Patty and Larry split any leftover money equally for their spending money the next month. It really seemed to work out great.

I never saw any money at all. Martin managed it all—if you could call it managing. He cashed his entire check every week and went straight to Wavelength's, his favorite bar. He only paid the bills when the creditors made him nervous. Since he picked up the strangest collection of groceries, it was hard to give the kids nutritious food. I often wished that they were eligible for the free-lunch program at school. And I had to beg for money to buy clothes for them. I felt like a terrible mother. My children were so poorly cared for. I gave them lots of love, but I knew they needed more.

Suddenly, the church was united in song. The sermon was over, and I hadn't heard a single word of the morning's message. I joined in the singing.

"Good morning, Mrs. Conner," the lady in the pew ahead of me said, just as she did every Sunday morning. Everyone began to greet family and friends around them.

"How are you today?" I responded, not really expecting an answer. I tried to help pick up the purses and Sunday school artwork, using just my free hand. Then I hurried my little ones to the bathroom. It would be a good place for me to slip the offering envelope into my pocketbook.

Ellie and Dina took forever in the bathroom, and for a change, I was glad. It gave me a chance to collect myself. I had to make myself stop thinking about what I had done. If I didn't, I'd never get through the day. I could think tomorrow when Martin was at work and Mark and Justin were at school.

After awhile, we were ready to move into the social hall. The boys and Ellie quickly scattered out to visit with their friends. Dina clung tightly to my hand as Mrs. Montgomery cornered me to talk.

Martin spotted me and moved from across the room toward me. I was accustomed to the sensation that everyone was staring at me. It was certainly obvious to me that Martin always caught a drink before the rest of us arrived for our coffee. I was sure that everyone else could tell as well. Martin always reeked of alcohol.

But this morning, I worried that they could see my guilt as well as Martin's. Surely they would understand that I needed the money. Martin so often bought a round of drinks for as many men as were now sipping coffee here. I only knew about that because Mark's Sunday-school teacher had nervously approached me about it. He had been in the bar one night when Martin, who was already quite drunk, had bought a round for everyone in the place—which was more than twenty men! That was more than two years ago, and I still shuddered to think of what I could have bought the children with the money.

"There you are," Martin said as he came up.

"We were just discussing the morning sermon," I responded.

"What was it about?" Martin questioned.

"Now, Martin," I stumbled nervously, "you can't expect someone to repeat the whole sermon for you every week." I hoped he wouldn't ask me again.

I wondered how many of my church friends suspected that I drove Martin to drink. Looking at me and at the children so unkempt, they might well wonder which came first—Martin's drinking or my sloppiness. Perhaps they saw Martin as a good provider and me as an undeserving wife and mother. Many probably wondered why I wasn't able to cook better meals for my kids. They couldn't be expected to know that the kids were dirty today, not because I didn't want to bathe them, but because we were out of soap. You can only do so much with water. When Mark's Sunday-school teacher had come to visit me, he had spoken of wifely duties. He had made me feel that Martin was drinking because I was doing something wrong.

For all of the seven years of our marriage, I had bent over backward to be the perfect wife and mother. I didn't know how to cook when we got married, but I learned quickly. I had Mom to thank for that. She told me, "Keep it simple. Men don't like fancy foods anyway." How right she was. I learned to fry. That seemed to be the key to Martin's heart. I cooked hamburger, fried chicken, French fries, hash browns, fried eggs, and grilled-cheese sandwiches.

Once, when we had company, I made a spinach soufflé. Martin put me down in front of everyone. "I can't imagine what got into her," he said. "She never cooked garbage like this before."

I held the tears inside and mumbled an apology. "I'm so sorry. It looked real good in the magazine. I just thought you might like it."

Martin had laughed. "That's the problem with women today. They should never have taught them to read." The other two men had laughed, and that encouraged Martin. He wasn't about to miss a chance for a few laughs. "Honey," he had continued, "I think where you really went wrong was when you decided to think." The men laughed all the harder. Their wives sat glaring at me as if I had somehow broken a rule and brought on all of the discomfort. Then Martin ordered me to the kitchen to make something people could eat.

I had put the soufflé on the table for the kids, and they had eaten ravenously. I got out some burger patties and fried them while I sliced up some leftover potatoes for hashed browns. There was already a salad on the table. When I had carried the newly cooked food out, Martin had said, "Now that's more like my little woman." Turning to the men, he added, "You just gotta give women a little direction now and then."

That was the last time I took a chance on a recipe. My women's magazine showed delicious dish after dish with guarantees that they were man-pleasers. I knew they wouldn't please my man, so I never tried them.

Suddenly, Martin was snapping his fingers in front of my face. "Hey, it's time to head home. What's wrong with you, anyway? Cat got your tongue?"

"Oh, I'm sorry," I stammered.

On the way out, with our children between us, Martin got mad at me. "I was really embarrassed. How dare you daydream when the preacher's wife was talking to you!"

"I'm sorry. I didn't mean to," I said meekly.

On the way home, I decided I had better keep busy all day, or I would really come unglued and confess to Martin what I had done. So when we got home, I fried up some ham steaks and heated frozen French fries. We ate pretty well when Martin ate with us. The kids kept asking me questions which I never seemed to hear. Finally, I suggested the kids help me with some kitchen work, and they all disappeared.

The children never helped me with the housework. Martin said they shouldn't have to. He said he never had any chores when he was growing up. I can remember his exact words.

"My mother managed the housework all by herself. We kids never had to help her, and she did a better job than you do, too. If you weren't any good as a housewife, you shouldn't have gotten married. You should have been an old-maid secretary or something."

Well, after that day, I worked on cleaning any spare moment I had. At first, I used all of the convenience products advertised in the magazines. I soon realized they were too expensive when Martin, who did the shopping, came home yelling, "If you think I'm going to spend my money on all that junk on your shopping list, you're crazy. My mother used vinegar and elbow grease, just like you're going to have to do." Vinegar worked pretty well, even though the kids complained about the smell.

I said as little as possible during dinner. When Martin came to the table, I saw he was already working on a drink. The kids looked nervously at me. I couldn't bring myself to speak. Finally, Dina said, "Mom, shouldn't we say grace?"

"Of course, honey," I squeaked out, my voice cracking.

"God is great. God is good. Let us thank Him for our food," Dina said.

"You might thank me, too," Martin added. "I made the money to buy it."

Dina chimed in, "And thank Mommy, too, for cooking it."

Martin was annoyed. "It's her job to make dinner."

We completed dinner in silence. Martin lay down on the couch to take a nap. The kids went outside so as not to wake him up and unleash his anger.

Martin woke up shortly after I finished cleaning up the dishes. He took a quick drink from the bottle in the kitchen, kissed me on the cheek, and left for an afternoon with the guys. I was in bed when he stumbled in late that night.

Martin was running the shower when I woke up the next morning. Before long, he emerged, looking refreshed and ready to go. He put his uniform on, as well as his company jacket. He bent over the bed, kissed me, and remarked, "Don't you imagine it's time you got me some breakfast?"

I made pancakes. They were the easiest breakfast food for me to make. They were Martin's favorite, so I had made them many times in seven years. "Don't be putting fancy stuff in them," he had said. "You put the fancy stuff on top after they're cooked." He ate enough to feed all four of his children, but what was left over wouldn't half feed them. And there was nothing in the cupboards to make more batter with. Soon he was gone.

One down. Four to go, I thought to myself.

Martin was an unusual alcoholic. His drinking didn't seem to affect his working. No matter how drunk he got at night, come morning, he was ready to go. All the men who worked for him really seemed to like him, even admire him. I couldn't figure out how he made it through the day without drinking. I started to think that maybe he did drink because of me.

Soon the kids clamored into the kitchen. Sadly, I looked at the ragged clothes they were wearing. I thought of the forty dollars hidden in my underwear in the dresser. I was thankful for the money Mom had sent for my birthday. It had given me something to substitute in the envelope that I had traded for Martin's real envelope. I wished I could afford to go down to that new discount department store and buy each of my children a new pair of jeans, but I knew I had to save the money for Mark's glasses. I wondered—worried, really—about how much they were going to cost. That sick feeling came back to my stomach. It was the same feeling deep in the pit of my stomach that I had felt when Mark had brought the note home from his teacher. "Dear Mr. and Mrs. Connor," she wrote. "Recent eye testing at school has indicated that Mark should have further testing at an optometrist's office. If you have any questions, please contact the school nurse." At the time, there was a huge stack of overdue bills on the dresser in our bedroom.

"Mommy, are there more pancakes?" Dina asked.

"No, honey. That's it."

"Well, I'm still hungry," Mark said nastily. I almost resented his attitude, considering what I was doing to get his glasses. Then I caught myself. After all, the poor little boy was just hungry.

"Let me see what I can find," I said as cheerfully as possible. I looked through the refrigerator and found some leftover potatoes. I dished them out.

"Yuck," Justin moaned. But they knew it was the best I could do, so they filled their tummies.

"Have a good day at school, you guys," I said as I zipped Justin and Mark into their coats.

"We'll try," Justin offered.

"School gives me headaches," Mark added.

I kissed him on the cheek. I told myself that I had to get the glasses soon. The optometrist had warned against waiting too long. I was so relieved when the optometrist had allowed me to carry the bill myself. I didn't dare add it to Martin's collection. I watched the boys kick rocks down the sidewalk and then disappear from sight.

When I turned around, the girls were already involved in a game with my pots and pans. I collapsed at the table, and I considered what might be left for me to eat. I remembered some stale rolls. I toasted them, and they tasted pretty good. I didn't really need much when it came down to it.

Martin had always been the one with such big dreams. He had promised me a big house, lots of children, and plenty of money. All I had wanted was a comfortable little home and a couple of children. Please don't get me wrong—I loved all four of my children. Martin had been so pleased that his first and second babies were boys. I had been glad when the third baby was a girl. Before Ellie's birth, I had suggested not having another child after Ellie was born. An increasing number of my friends had had their tubes tied when they felt their families were complete. Martin was furious. He wanted lots of children. So before Dina was born, I signed to have the operation following delivery. It still scared me to think what Martin would do if he found out.

As it was, the kids were just a year apart—Mark was six, Justin was five, Ellie was four, and Dina was three. This year, when Dina turned three, I looked into enrolling them in a day-care center so that I could work. Martin and I had ended up in the biggest argument ever. I told Martin that we needed the money for the children. He promised to do better by the children, but life hadn't gotten any better.

I had searched the newspapers from cover to cover, looking for work to do at home. It was hard to tell what work was legitimate. I couldn't take in any work that Martin could learn about. Finally, I resorted to entering contests. All I could do was hope. I just hoped that if I won something that I could keep the money to spend as I needed.

Finally, in desperation, I had pleaded with Martin to let me handle the money. I waited until a Sunday after church, because it was the time when Martin was the least drunk.

"Martin, I don't know how to say this," I had begun, "but we are really in financial trouble."

"I'll take care of that. Don't you worry about it," was all he said.

"I can't help but worry," I went on. "There's never enough food, and the kids need clothes. I know we have all kinds of bills that aren't paid."

"I have all kinds of bills. They are no concern of yours!" he shouted. "And I'll get groceries and clothes." Martin had stormed out without eating dinner.

He was home before dinner was even ready. He carried a bag of groceries which he just about threw at me. Then he left again. I was glad to see the sack had bread and peanut butter, but the other items weren't at all what we needed. There was soda, potato chips, candy, and some expensive, exotic fruit. Well, at least the fruit was nutritious.

The next day was Monday, and when Martin came home from work, he had dresses for the girls and fancy shirts for the boys. In a way, I was glad for them, because the kids would look nice at church. The clothes were only a little bit big, but would work just fine. I wondered if these purchases meant less beer or more unpaid bills. I feared the latter. Many times, I wondered about what would happen when the creditors closed in on us.

My last resort was to try to convince Martin to get help, either for his drinking or for our money problems. I had tried to guess how he would react and then tried to figure out what to say, but it had turned out all wrong.

"Martin, remember when we were going out together?" I began tentatively.

"Yeah, those were the days."

"Remember all the dreams we had?" I went on.

"Kind of. We talked a lot then," he said.

"Well, it seems to me that we mostly got what we wanted. You have a good job, we've got a nice house, and we have four great kids."

"I guess it's not too bad."

It's now or never, I thought. Out loud, I said, "I was just thinking. If we could maybe get rid of some of our overdue bills—well, maybe everything would be better."

Martin looked at me angrily. "I'm not going to get into this discussion again. I mean it! Just drop it!"

"Martin," I had yelled, "you have to stop drinking. You just have to! It's wrecking everything. I can't take it anymore!" I had yelled so loud, I felt like my head would explode. I burst into tears. Martin started to come to me, but he turned and walked out the door. That was only a couple of weeks ago.

I knew as I sat at the table that my only recourse was to continue to take Martin's church offering. That way, I would be able to slowly get Mark his glasses and all of the children clothes and shoes. They really needed shoes. I could buy extra groceries for the school lunches. I would save five dollars each week to put in the exchange envelope. That would leave thirty-five a week. It would really help.

As the week drew on and Sunday approached, I worried about the kids catching me. I decided I had to let the boys in on what I was doing. I worked on a speech. "Mark, Justin, you are both big boys now." What can I say to make them understand? I wondered. "I need you guys to help me out. Mom is doing something that you might not understand. I'm going to be switching church envelopes. We can't afford to give so much to the church. We need more clothes and food."

But then, I knew I would hear the inevitable question: "Does Daddy know?"

I realized I could not mix the kids up in this. I would just have to make sure that the boys didn't catch me: I started making the switch at home before we even left for church. It worked real well. I never got caught.

I was careful to only buy things that Martin wouldn't notice. I bought secondhand clothes, so that they wouldn't stand out. It also made the money go further. I only bought food for lunches. Martin never talked to the kids, so he never heard about what they had eaten. I felt so good sending the boys to school with a sandwich, a piece of fruit, and a thermos of milk. Life was so much nicer.

In the afternoons, I often thought about what I was doing. I wasn't sure if I was stealing. I wondered if God would punish me for not giving more to the church, but I had made my choice.

Life went on this way for several months. Martin didn't change. He continued to drink, to stagger in late, and to bring us a few crazy groceries. I thought he had caught on to what I was doing, but I decided I was wrong. It seemed easier and easier to make the trade. There was always forty dollars in the envelope.

I guess we were in the calm before the storm. Once, after work on a Wednesday, Martin didn't come home from the bar until early Thursday morning. He crawled into bed and slept past noon. I tried to get him up to go to work, but couldn't.

When he finally roused himself, he dragged himself to the kitchen table. He looked as vulnerable as a small child. I had never seen him like that before.

I busied myself getting him a cup of coffee. My hands were trembling as I set the coffee in front of him. Martin had never missed a day, or even an hour, of work.

Martin tried to speak several times before he said, "I have a choice to make."

I was speechless. I just sat there waiting for him to get a hold of himself.

He just looked at me, bewildered. Finally he spoke. "Randy, that's my boss, caught me drinking at work."

"Oh, no," I said.

"Well, I guess it's no surprise to me," Martin said. "It's a miracle I didn't get caught sooner. Seems he suspected me for a long time."

"He fired you?" I was afraid to hear his answer.

"No, not straight out. I can stay on if I start going to AA–Alcoholics Anonymous. The plant has a policy to help alcoholics, but I'm not an alcoholic. I'm really not."

I wasn't sure what to say. I didn't want to upset him further. "My idea is you could just go along," I said. "I mean, you could pretend so you could keep your job."

"Yeah, I thought about that," Martin replied. "There's more, too. The creditors have called and talked to Randy. Can you believe that? Well, Randy wants me to turn all our debts and then my paychecks over to some kind of financial advisor. I'd lose control of everything!"

"Oh, honey," I whispered, taking his hands in mine. I felt sorry for him—even though I had to admit it would be the best thing that could happen to him.

Martin lay around the house all day. He was so sick from the drinking binge the night before that he didn't even take a drink all morning. Just before quitting time, he called Randy and made an appointment to see a financial advisor. Then he pulled himself together with a shower and put on his best clothes. He even left me with a tender kiss.

Martin came home resigned to his "fate." He ate a little dinner, and helped me get the kids to bed. He even read them a story. Dina snuggled up to him and said, "Daddy, I like you like this."

Martin went to work in the morning, which made things seem more normal. I felt compelled to get the house in order.

I didn't want to have any distractions when Martin came home. I whipped up a tuna salad and put some peaches in the refrigerator to chill. I wanted to be able to set dinner on the table without taking time away from Martin.

I was surprised when Martin came through the door with another man—another alcoholic from the plant. He was going to take Martin to the AA meeting. He had dinner with us, and then the two of them left. I held hope in my heart.

Martin was very quiet when he came home. As I rolled over to go to sleep, he said, "I was just going through all the motions. Then I got up in front of everyone. I feel stupid saying it, but I fell apart. All of a sudden, I knew—I knew I was an alcoholic."

I cuddled up next to him. I couldn't think of anything to say. I wanted to help him, but I didn't know what to do.

The next day, Martin's boss called me and gave me an answer. He told me about Al-Anon, a group for families and friends of alcoholics. There was a meeting downtown that night, he told me, and he even offered to drive me there. I accepted his offer, glad that there was some way I could help my family. I called a neighbor to watch the kids.

Martin continued to attend his AA meetings, and I went regularly to the Al-Anon sessions. Together, we met with the financial advisor, and she helped us straighten out our financial mess. She made Martin realize that I could be trusted with money, and I took over the grocery shopping. The advisor also saw that all our large bills were paid off, and set up a payment schedule for us to follow each month.

Eventually, Martin and I also began attending a marriage encounter group sponsored by our church. We each learned some painful truths about ourselves, and I was able to admit to Martin that I had had my tubes tied. I also told him about the way I switched offering envelopes. He was upset at first, but he later said he knew I had no other choice.

Someday soon, with God's help, I know our family will get back on the right track. We've got people who care about us looking out for us. More importantly, Martin and I are now looking out for each other. THE END

I FOUND MY MAN IN THE CLASSIFIED ADS

When a fifty-two-year-old widow decides she wants to marry, I told myself, *she's just like the man marooned on a desert island who decides he wants to get home for Christmas. But there remains one big question: how?* I sat brooding over my morning coffee, my television set chattering away unheeded. I'd gotten into the lonesome habit of keeping it on all day, just for the companionable sound of the voices. *Admit it, Doris*, I thought to myself, *you're in a tough situation.*

I was tired of living alone. I was sick of the women I played bridge with once a week. I hated going to the movies by myself. And worst of all, I—Doris Stillman, the best cook in the world—had taken to eating TV dinners because I couldn't stand the idea of cooking just for myself.

My son, Bobbie, had been bugging me again to move in with his family. I'd been telling him for the two years since Carl, my husband, died, that I didn't want to be a burden. But that was only half the truth. My son has five children—little dears, all of them, but noisy. And my daughter-in-law is a willing, but, let's face it, lousy cook. I could see my days stretching out ahead—as baby-sitter and head chef in my son's house.

"Mom," Bobbie would say, "we want you with us. We want you safe and comfortable in your declining years."

Each time he made that remark, I aged six months. The picture he had of me—as a little old lady with gray hair and a sewing basket, a sort of period piece to go with his wife's Early American decor—just left me cold. Not that I didn't love him for his sweet sentimentality that turned me into a sweet old woman, but I just couldn't play the part. I didn't feel a bit old. It had never ceased to surprise me when I looked into the mirror and saw the telltale gray at the roots of my hairdresser's latest artistic triumph!

But how can you hope to explain to a loving son that you still feel sweet sixteen? I just never bothered to try. Bobbie would have been shocked at the thoughts running through my head. I was a little shocked myself. When Carl died, I thought my life had ended. In my grief, I was half sorry to discover it hadn't. I kept hearing Carl's voice shouting the words he'd used on so many umpires at baseball games: "Look alive, you dope! The game's not over yet!"

The game surely wasn't over for me, not yet. I was determined to get back in there somehow. But I didn't know where to begin. To distract myself, to put off thinking about it, I picked up the morning paper. I always read it from one end to the other each day, and so I waded in. There was a crisis in the Middle East. The soldiers were popping bombs on some distant point of the map. Bloomingdale's was having a sale. I could get anything I wanted at Bloomingdale's—except a man!

Then I folded the paper to the classified section. It occurred to me that maybe the way to head back into a life of my own was to find a job. But I told myself that was a pipe dream for a woman of my age, whose only experience consisted of thirty years of being a wife!

The first ad I saw caught my eye. The item read: "Male widower, wants woman one day a week to clean small apartment and cook dinner." I read it over three times, and then I telephoned.

When a woman's voice answered, I almost laughed at my sharp sense of disappointment, for surely this meant the job was taken. But then the voice at the other end of the line informed me that she was the man's daughter. She was spending the day in her father's apartment in order to interview applicants for the position. I said I'd be right over.

Luckily, the apartment house was close by, and easy to get to by subway. Within half an hour, I was dressed and on my way, excited by the spirit of adventure, but a little scared at the thought of what my son would say if he knew.

I found the place without any trouble. It was only a couple of blocks away from a bustling neighborhood shopping district. But the building itself was quiet and sedate. I found the sixth-floor apartment, took a deep breath, and pushed the bell.

The young woman who answered struck me as a bit snooty. She was dressed in navy blue, and her purse and designer scarf lay on a chair in the little entrance way. "My father is at his business," she said, and her tones implied no less than Wall Street. "Uh, do you have references, Miss—"

I had to think quickly. I didn't want to give my real name. I guess I was thinking of my son and his inevitable disapproval. "My name is Dotty," I lied. "No, I don't have references. You see, I've never worked before. But I've spent my life keeping house, and I'm a very good cook."

"Well," she said, "I keep trying to get my father to move in with us. We have plenty of room." Her tone implied a mansion of some kind. "But he has his own busy life, full of interests." She seemed to suggest financial interests. "And he likes his independence."

Good, I thought. Already I had discovered two things I had in common with Mister Widower—a desire for independence, and children who had their harmless pretensions. I was heartened by the small apartment, too.

"You see," she went on, "every Tuesday night, Dad has his old cronies over for cards." As she said it, I spied the poker chips inside the glass cabinet. "I thought it would be nice if—if he had someone to straighten the place up for him and prepare a late supper for the four of them. He finally agreed. Of course—Dad is a bit messy."

Messy, all right! Though the place had been hurriedly straightened, I spied a tie hanging over a bedpost in the next room. If I'd listened to his daughter, I wouldn't have cared much for Mister Widower.

But I took everything she said with a grain of salt. I liked a man who wasn't too neat—a man like my Carl.

"Of course, I don't expect you to stay late," she said. "Dad doesn't get home till after seven. So you could just come in at noon, clean up the place, and then prepare a meal that he can heat up later. You could be finished and gone by five-thirty or six."

"You mean—I've got the job?"

She sniffed, glancing at her watch. "Well, nobody else has called, and I have to get to the nail salon. Yes, the job's yours if you want it."

Did I! But, in the language of my grandson, I "played it cool." We settled on a salary, and then she picked up her purse and scarf. "Well, uh—Dotty, you can just start right in, since today is Tuesday." She handed me the key to the apartment. "Dad will leave the key under the door mat," she said as she was leaving. "And when you go, you can just put it back there. And he'll leave your money on the hall table. Do you have any questions?"

I only had about a dozen, but I was determined to answer them for myself. And I did. In the next few hours, I cleaned the place from top to bottom. But the cleaning was only incidental. I was looking for clues to Mister Widower's personality. His daughter had given me a bleak picture, but I soon began to replace that with a far more interesting one of my own.

Dusting his bureau, I inspected his masculine-looking hairbrushes. A bald man wouldn't need those brushes. I peered closer. No signs of falling hair. Good!

Next, I tidied up his medicine chest, knowing some widowers turn into hypochondriacs. But I found only aspirin, nose drops, vitamins, hair gel, and his shaving things. The hair gel confirmed the heartening clue of the brushes. And the ad on the pack of razor blades read: "For the man with the tough beard." Excellent. Mister Widower was the real virile type.

Then a thought struck me and I searched further. Sure enough— no denture cleaner! He used ordinary toothpaste. He had his teeth.

When the mail came that afternoon, I discovered his name—something his daughter had failed to tell me. It was Mr. P. McDougal. I liked the sound of it. And the mail itself was interesting. There was a statement from a savings bank, a copy of a gourmet magazine—he liked good food, and that gave me a real advantage—and a dentist bill, which confirmed the clue of the toothpaste.

P. McDougal. What did the "P" stand for? Patrick? Peter? Paul? Then I realized that something about that gourmet magazine had begun to bother me. I wondered in dismay if he might be fat. Well, there was one way to find out. I hurried to his closet and inspected his suits. They were tailored to fit a man of above medium height, lean, and broad across the shoulders. I breathed a sigh of relief.

Humming happily, I investigated his laundry hamper and found seven shirts bundled, ready to be sent out to be cleaned. Seven shirts. A fresh shirt each day. He was orderly! Then I had an idea. I'd seen a do-it-yourself laundry just down the block, so I decided to launder the shirts myself, for I'd noticed he was particular. They had been only lightly starched, and that meant he was a persuasive man—as anyone knows who's dealt with laundries!

A check in the refrigerator showed only a small supply of beer. Good! Carl had been a beer man himself. The bare refrigerator meant I'd have to do some grocery shopping if I was going to cook a dazzling meal. So I took my purse and spent more than my week's wages on groceries while the shirts were running in the washing machines. Then, bustling back to my new job, I realized I was happy as a lark—doing a man's laundry, getting ready to cook for him. His daughter said I should be finished and gone by six, and that meant I wouldn't meet him—not that day anyway. But, I told myself, there are more ways than one to cook a goose.

I imagined Mr. P. McDougal getting home that night. First, he would see how clean and tidy the apartment looked. Then, he would discover the carefully laundered shirts. And last of all, his gourmet plate, and he would taste my delicious meal. He would see what a competent housekeeper I was. That ought to put ideas in his head about the other six days of the week. I ironed the shirts beautifully and hung them on his closet door where he'd be sure to find them. Then, for the next hour and a half, I worked happily in the kitchen. When the meal was on the stove, I set the table for four, pleased to find in the buffet the linen and china that had probably belonged to the late Mrs. McDougal. The dining-room table looked lovely. Then, just to show my approval of a poker-playing man, I set up the card table in the bay window alcove, found two decks of cards, and put out his poker chips.

Leaving soft candles burning, I took one last look around and, satisfied, pulled the door closed behind me. It was six o'clock. By then, I had a complete picture of P. McDougal in my head: a distinguished-looking gray-haired man, above medium height, who carried himself straight and wore his clothes like a banker in a Wall Street ad.

By then, I was so curious to see him that I headed for the neighborhood Italian restaurant on the corner just across the street, planning to wait around in hopes of catching a glimpse of him. And to my surprise, I felt hungry for the first time in weeks. *No TV dinner for me tonight!* I thought happily.

The restaurant was cozy, with red-checkered tablecloths and little individual lamps on top of each table. It fit my mood exactly. I took a seat at a table for two near the front window, and immediately began craning my neck to see out—though he wasn't due home for an hour.

"And what will the lady have?" a voice with a smile asked me.

Feeling as if I'd been caught red-handed, I looked up at the waiter standing in front of me. I could tell something about me amused him.

"A cocktail before dinner? Or perhaps you're waiting for someone?"

"No," I said, flustered. "I'm—alone. I don't usually have a cocktail."

His smile deepened. "Then perhaps a little wine with your

dinner," he said, as if that settled the matter. "I can recommend the veal parmigiana."

"Well, all right," I said. "But—no wine."

He took painstaking care in noting down my entree, my vegetables, and the way I preferred my spaghetti. When I finished my meal, he beamed, asking, "And will you have your coffee now, or later?"

"Later," I said, even though I knew that coffee with dinner usually kept me awake.

"And for dessert?"

Why didn't this man go away? I wanted to study the sixth-floor corner window of the building opposite me. But I turned back to the menu.

The waiter said, bending over my shoulder to point, "The parfait is excellent—and for a lady who doesn't have to watch her figure. . . ."

Surprised, I handed him the menu. For an average-looking guy, the man had a surprising amount of savoir-faire. "All right," I said. "The parfait."

He smiled and walked away. I immediately turned back to the window. But a moment later he was back, brushing my shoulder as he placed a wine glass on the table. He held a small bottle of wine for my inspection. "Compliments of the management," he said.

"But—"

"It's our best Chianti. It enhances the veal. I highly recommend it. And the management realizes you are a new patron. We hope you'll come back—often."

Speechless, I watched him open the bottle and pour out a drop of the red wine into my glass. Then he stood waiting. If I hadn't been a TV fan, I wouldn't have known what to do next. But I picked the glass up, daintily, and sniffed. Then I nodded wisely. He was as pleased as I was at my display of sophistication. He poured the glass full.

If I had hopes to continue to watch the apartment house across the street, I had another thought coming. That waiter didn't leave me alone for a minute. After all those years, I'd finally run across an attentive waiter—just when I needed him the least! Even while he wasn't serving me, he stood near the door, leaning against the wall with his arms folded and watching me with that hint of a smile on his lips. Any other time, I might have been flattered—he wasn't a bad-looking man—but under the circumstances, I was only annoyed. When I left at five after seven, the lights were still as I had left them in the apartment across the way. He might have come in, or he might not have. I had no way of knowing with the distraction of that waiter.

Unknown to me, he had followed me to the door. "Can I call a cab for you?" he asked.

"No—no thanks," I answered, flustered because again, he must have seen me eyeing those windows.

"Then you must live in the neighborhood," he said.

"No. No, I don't," I said, walking briskly away toward the subway. "Good night!"

"Have a nice evening," he called after me.

Well, really, I thought, *the man was actually flirting with me!* Then a small voice replied: *Isn't that just the idea? Isn't that just what you wanted, Doris?*

I smiled to myself. *Yes,* I answered. *That's exactly what I want. But I've set my sights on a different man.*

And I had. The different man, as it turned out, wasn't indifferent to my subtle scheme of seduction. The next Tuesday, I found the key under the mat, let myself in, and discovered a note beside the money he'd left on the table. "You're a marvel," it read. "What a meal! And the shirts are just right. I'm leaving grocery money. If you need more, let me know. And, by the way, what's your name?" It was signed "P. McDougal." I read it twice. I hadn't expected things to move along so fast.

That day I carried my investigations further. He seemed to wear only black shoes, and he kept them highly polished, and on shoe trees. The shoes had no arch supports and they weren't deformed or out of shape by corns or bunions. From the size of them, he was a man with a firm foundation.

But, I asked myself, *what does he do with his spare time, except play poker?* There were no golf clubs, and not many books. I found part of the answer that day as I vacuumed the bedroom. The television set, which faced his bed, was turned to the channel that, the night before, had showed a pro football game from the West Coast. I knew because I'd watched the whole thing myself—just like when Carl was alive.

And then I found out how my man put himself to sleep at night. Under the bed was a thick book of double-crossword puzzles. A new book! One I hadn't known was out. I'd been a double-crossword fiend for years. I picked it up, found the page his pencil marked, and frowned down to see what had stumped him. I found it: a three-word phrase of nine letters meaning "exactly." That was easy. I carefully lettered in the words "on the nose."

But the double-crossword answers were like peanuts to me. I could never stop with one. The rest of the afternoon, I kept puzzling over the next item that had stumped Mr. P. McDougal, trying to think what on earth it could be—an eight-letter word for "narrow-necked bottle in wicker jacket with handles."

While I did the laundry, shopped, and cooked, I thought of the puzzles. We'd make a fine team, for he knew answers that would have exasperated me, like: "openings in the bow of a ship that cables pass through." He'd neatly printed in "hawseholes," where I would have bitten my pencil in two.

Already I felt at home in his apartment, with the big wing chair for reading, the ample desk, the very old oriental-looking rug. I liked his late wife's taste. As I watered his plants, I realized they were pampered and tended. They looked as if someone frequently dusted their leaves, and the soil was black and rich. That meant he was lonely—for plants are living things and sometimes take the place of family and pets for people who live alone. Didn't I know? Since Carl's death, my African violets had thrived on my lavish attention.

I stayed a minute later that night. Just before I closed the door, the answer to the puzzle clue came to me and I hurried back to the book to write in "demijohn." I left in triumph and by six-thirty I was comfortably seated at my table in the Italian restaurant across the street. My waiter came almost immediately, as if he'd watched for me. "It's Tuesday night again," he said and smiled. "Why only on Tuesdays?"

He didn't miss a thing. I felt like a woman of mystery as I arched my brows. "It's my night for romance," I said.

He smiled. "You know, I'll soon be imagining a kind of nostalgic rendezvous about a man who never comes. Like in some old movie."

"Starring Irene Dunne," I said, smiling. "I remember. In one of them, it turned out that the man was dead—very sad."

"Not sad at all," he said. "Remember, she met another man there, at the rendezvous point. It was love at first sight."

"I don't remember that at all," I said.

He chuckled. "Maybe I made it up," he said. "I like happy endings. You know, it's a joy to talk to you—someone of my own generation. The restaurant has gotten popular with the pizza crowd. But they come later—and I manage to get off before then."

Again he deliberated over my meal. "I guess I might as well leave it up to you what to order," I said. "Surprise me."

"Nothing would please me more," he said with a look that made me blush.

When he was gone, I peered out between the window plants. No light yet in the sixth-floor apartment. Then my waiter returned with a cocktail. "It's very light," he said, "and it's on the house."

"The house will go broke at this rate," I said.

"Well, it'll be for a good cause," he answered.

"Just what is the cause?" I asked, smiling.

He thought for a moment, and then said, "Romance, I guess. The management is very much in favor of nights set aside for that. Romance and mystery. Where do you come from? And where do you disappear to when you leave here?"

"That's my secret," I said.

He gave a little shrug. "But you can't keep it forever."

The next week, I had several surprises. Again, there was a note from P. McDougal. "Dotty, you're a whiz! What's a ten-letter word meaning 'sportive?' Not too much water on the plants, please. No late supper tonight. Frank's got the gout. Charlie has a cold. And Tommy's found a lady-love." He signed it: "P. M."

Well, I liked him. He sounded lively. Since I didn't have to cook, I spent most of the afternoon polishing the late Mrs. McDougal's silver that had become tarnished from disuse. It was a lovely pattern, very much like my own. How well they would go together! As I polished, I daydreamed about a table set for a holiday feast—for our children and grandchildren. Then I had to laugh at my imaginings.

Before I left, I composed a note that included a recommended diet for Frank's gout, a home remedy for Charlie's cold, and congratulations to Tommy. Then I added a P.S. "the ten-letter word for sportive is frolicsome." Already, I had begun to feel like a part of his life.

But my confidence was short-lived. When I walked out into the crowded street, I again felt lonely and sad, not much a part of anything. I'd worked for him for a month, and we still hadn't met. The late shoppers surged around me—men just off the subway, women who'd run out to buy something they'd left off their shopping lists. Only I seemed to be alone and purposeless. But then I headed toward the restaurant across the street. My spirits lifted as soon as I went through the door, though I still felt a little tired. I sank down at my familiar table and put my fingers to my eyes for a minute.

"Feeling tired and letdown? What you need is some of our lasagna."

I looked up. There he was, smiling and warm, like an old friend. "That sounds like a prescription," I said.

"New dress?" he asked. "That color goes fine with your eyes. You don't often see eyes that blue."

"Flattery," I said, "will get you everywhere." My discouraged feeling faded fast. Outside, I might have felt lost and alone in the crowd. But here I felt at home, cozy, even pampered. I tried to think of something to say to my redheaded man, but just then the bartender called him.

"Sonny, here it is."

Two thoughts fought for the upper hand then: *Could I possibly be like a flighty teenager who imagines she's falling in love with two men at once?* It certainly seemed that way. The second thought was: *His name is Sonny.*

He returned a minute later, bringing a tall glass to me. "I asked the bartender to make this. Try it. I think you'll really like it."

I sipped, feeling very daring. But I hardly tasted the drink. I was too busy looking at Sonny. I tested the sound of it. "Sonny," I said aloud.

"That's what my friends call me," he said. "Want to be friends?"

"It feels as if we are already," I admitted.

He smiled. "What about you? What's your name?"

"Doris," I said.

"Doris, let me guess what you're like."

"Guess away," I said. "What are you—a character expert?"

"A regular Houdini," he said. "First of all, you're a new widow."

"How did you know?"

"That one's easy," he said. "You're no old maid. You're too easy for a man to talk to. Old maids are skittish. And they tend to be either too skinny or way too fat. But you—you're just right. Oh, no doubt about it—there's been a man in your life."

"That's the male ego talking," I said, laughing. "Maybe I'm a happy divorcée."

"That's out," he said, shaking his head. "No man in his right mind would ever let you go."

The drink was going to my head. Or could it be the soft lights? I felt a little dizzy, light-headed. "Go on," I said.

"For another thing," he said softly, "you're lonely."

I smiled. "And here I thought I was putting on a good act." But he'd grown serious.

"One lonely person always recognizes another. My wife died six years ago."

Another waiter brought out a huge tray, and Sonny slipped into the seat opposite me. I was afraid he would get fired on the spot. But I liked it. I liked the independence it showed, and I wanted his company—wanted it very much. "So—you're having dinner with me," I said.

"I'd like to have dinner with you every night," he answered with a twinkle in his eye. "If there's anything I hate, it's eating alone."

"That, I can understand," I said.

We talked for two hours, Sonny and I. I forgot to look out my window, forgot to study that sixth-floor apartment. I learned that he had three children, all grown and married. He was a grandfather, and he was a baseball fan.

And I told him a little about myself, about Bobbie and my grandchildren, about Carl and our years together. When I left that night, I was filled with a warm glow, but I told myself it was mostly just the wine. I felt torn, as I remembered P. McDougal and all we had in common. "But," I told myself, "a bird in the hand is worth two in the bush."

It wasn't that easy, though. I felt silly to admit it to myself, but I still couldn't put Mr. P. M. out of my mind, no matter how much I scolded myself for foolishness.

During that next week, I puzzled about what I should do. I finally decided I had to meet P. McDougal. I told myself I'd probably detest him on sight. I'd find him vain, self-centered, and unattractive. Then I'd be glad to allow my feelings for Sonny free rein. On the other hand, I half expected it to be love at first sight, and the idea saddened me because I would have to give Sonny up. Such a short

time before, my life had been dull and routine. Now here I was, filled
with turmoil, with hope, with plans.

I spent that morning in the beauty parlor and got the works—
shampoo and set, manicure, facial—which I didn't need. *It's now or
never,* I told myself.

But when I got to the apartment, I discovered that P. McDougal
had taken the situation out of my hands. In dismay, I read his note.

"Dear Dotty, I don't know how to thank you for what you've
done for me. The shirts, the excellent food, the way the apartment
looks—these things have convinced me of something I hardly realized
before. I have been a lonely man since my wife died. But I won't
be much longer. I suspect I would fall in love with you if I weren't
in love already. But, unfortunately, I won't need your services after
today, for tonight I pop the question. And you deserve all the credit
for convincing me to want to marry again. P. McDougal"

Overcome by self-pity, I sank down in the big wing chair. Well,
it was over. My dream had backfired. And it served me right for
acting like a fool over a perfect stranger. Those words rang in my
head—perfect stranger. That was exactly what he'd become in my
mind—perfect. And now he would always remain a stranger.

I dragged myself through the afternoon, even washing the
windows and scrubbing the floors. I would leave my love nest in
order for the new woman, his wife.

As I pulled the door closed for the last time and replaced the key
under the mat, I reminded myself that "there's no fool like an old
fool." It was past six, and I remembered that Sonny would be waiting
for me. I tried to be glad, but instead I felt only confusion.

Outside, the street was still crowded. And as always, I didn't feel
like a part of that crowd. Instead, I felt as I had before I'd found my
job—lonely and left out of life. But the restaurant looked inviting,
and I squared my shoulders as I headed across the street toward it. I
tried to focus my mind on the memory of Sonny's smile, but I half
feared by then that he'd only been playing with me. That would be

just my luck!

I was still a woman divided when I entered the restaurant that night. And I felt such a letdown when a strange waiter met me at the door. "I'll show you to your table, Miss," he said, leading me toward the back.

I could have cried. *Where was Sonny?* A small voice whispered inside my head: *You've waited too long, Doris. You've discouraged him.*

"But—I always sit up front. Here," I said. My usual table was vacant.

But the waiter seemed not to hear. He walked on, toward the back, where the dining room became L-shaped. When I rounded the corner after him, I saw a table set for two, with candles lit and a white cloth replacing the red and white checkered one. How I envied the woman who would take her place there, opposite her man.

The waiter stopped beside the table, smiling a little. He drew back a chair and waited for me to take it. "But this isn't my table," I said. "It must be reserved for someone else."

"It's reserved for you," he said. Then the kitchen door opened and out walked Sonny. My heart did a childish somersault. He did not wear an apron. He was dressed up in a suit, shirt, and tie, and he moved purposefully toward me, smiling like the cat that captured the canary. He took the chair the waiter held and seated me, wordlessly.

"What does this mean?" I asked as he sat down opposite me. The waiter withdrew, returning a moment later with a chilled bucket of champagne and two long-stemmed glasses.

Sonny took the bottle and popped the cap. "My," he said, "you're sure dressed up tonight, Doris. How did you know we'd be celebrating?"

I felt a little guilty then, for I was dolled up for a different man. But I made myself ask in a small voice, "What are we celebrating?"

"Several things," he said. "For one, Paul Neuman's birthday."

"Nonsense," I said. "It is not."

"Oh, yes it is," he said. "Doris, meet Paul Neuman Schafer—the bartender!" He raised his glass, and I turned to look at the laughing man behind the bar.

"Oh, be serious," I said. "What are we celebrating?"

"It's our anniversary," he said. "We've known each other exactly five weeks tonight."

I laughed. "All right," I said. "Let's celebrate. I just lost my job today."

"What kind of job?" he asked.

"Oh, I had a job working once a week for a gentleman in this neighborhood. Mr. P. McDougal."

He looked stunned. "You worked for P. McDougal?"

I nodded. "But he fired me today."

"Well," he said, "you don't know when you're well-off."

"You—know him?"

"I've known him for years," he said. "Intimately, in fact. He's quite a fellow—handsome, witty, exciting."

My curiosity had gotten the best of me by then. "Does he come here often?"

"Almost every day."

"If he's all you say he is then why am I so lucky to lose my job?"

"Well," he said, "he has a lot of very serious faults, too."

"Do you—have you met the—the woman he's going to marry?" I asked, green with jealousy.

"Indeed I have," he said.

"What—what's she like?"

"Oh," he said shrugging, "she's middle-aged, snooty, hard to get acquainted with."

"Doesn't sound pleasant." I sniffed.

He smiled. "Shall we drink to them, Doris?"

How could I refuse? Half-heartedly, I raised my glass to my lips as Sonny said, "To P. McDougal and his lady." I was thinking, ironically, that this was carrying things too far.

"You—you were sweet to do this," I said. "I needed to be cheered up." But I sat there feeling forlorn somehow.

"I wanted to get to know you," Sonny said. "But I guess there's only one way for a man and woman really to get to know each other."

"What way is that?" I asked.

"By getting married," he said.

I gasped, almost choking on champagne.

"Oh, I know this is sudden," he said. "But we're old enough to dispense with a time-consuming courtship, Doris. I promise to court you gallantly—on our honeymoon."

"Honeymoon! You certainly are sure of yourself!"

"Yes," he said and sighed. "It's one of the faults I was talking about. Doris, I guess it's time to confess. What—what is a four-letter word for phony?"

"Fake," I breathed, staring at him, unable to sort out my suspicions.

"That's the word I'm looking for," he said. "Doris, my friends call me Sonny, but my dear old Irish mother named me Patrick."

"Patrick—"

"McDougal," he said.

"You!"

"Me!"

"But—oh! I can't believe it. How long have you known?"

"Known I had to have you? Since the first night you walked through that door."

"No. How long have you known who I am? That I was—me?"

He grinned. "Not till you told me, tonight. Now I see I should have known all along. The fact that you came on Tuesdays, the way you kept looking out that window—at my apartment—admit it!"

"How conceited!"

He chuckled. "And I thought you were looking at the sky, taking an inordinate interest in the weather, when all the time—"

"Ah," I said, "so it's you who are—handsome, witty, exciting!"

His grin broadened. "But with faults. I'm not the tidiest man alive. I often have holes in my socks. And I'm a bear before I have my morning coffee."

"And me! So, I'm middle-aged and snooty!"

"And beautiful, charming, attractive in every way. I forgot to add that."

We sat eyeing each other—P. "Sonny" McDougal and me. Then, at the same moment, we burst out laughing. "You are a scoundrel," I said.

He hung his head. "I have to admit, I am."

Still laughing, I reached across the table and covered his hand with mine. "I don't mind if a man is a bit of a scoundrel," I said.

The waiter brought the food then. When he withdrew, I said, "You're sure you won't get in trouble with your boss for this?"

"But you see—I am the boss," he said. "One of them, anyway. Paul Neuman, the chef, and I—we three are partners. We opened this place years ago."

"You're full of surprises," I said.

"Marry me and you'll find out," he said, smiling.

"How do I know you'd make a good husband?" I teased.

"I had thirty years of experience," he said. I saw a fleeting shadow cross his smile.

"I know all you must be remembering," I murmured.

He met my eye. "You have your memories, too, Doris," he said. "I loved my wife very much. When she died, I thought the world had ended. Now I know it hasn't. And I owe it to you—all those good dinners, ironing my shirts, keeping my place neat—it's one of those funny twists of fate. I want to live again."

"So do I," I said simply.

He reached for my hand. "Then—let's start over, together."

"My son will have a fit." I laughed.

"So will my daughter. She always wants to manage my life for me."

"That's my son, too. He wants to manage mine."

"We'll just have to be—disobedient." He laughed. "Say yes, Doris."

But I'd become self-conscious. The bartender was watching, with a smile of approval. The waiter stood nearby, grinning, too. And at the kitchen door the chef looked out. When I met his eye, he winked. "We have an audience," I said.

"Then let's get out of here," he murmured.

"But—the dessert!"

"I know what I want for dessert," he said. "I want to walk with you, holding hands. Then I want to take you home in a taxi, where I'll try to steal a kiss."

"You're very persuasive."

"You don't know the half of it," he said, rising.

He took my arm. Paul Neuman Schafer winked as we passed the bar. Outside, the street was noisy, full of people. The lights had come on. I took his arm, feeling suddenly a part of life again, and no longer left out and lonely,

He squeezed my arm against his side and drew my hand into his. And together we made our way into the hustling crowd, back into life again. THE END

I LEARNED TO TRUST
MY HEART

"Billy, where are you going?" I called sharply from the kitchen. I had just heard the front door of the apartment creak open, and, even without looking, I knew it was my eleven-year-old son, Billy, leaving. Tricia, my five-year-old, was playing in her room, just down the hall from me. "I thought I told you to stay in your room until you finished those math problems!"

I heard the front door creak shut again, and in a few minutes, Billy appeared in the kitchen doorway looking sheepish, his head drooping and his eyes fixed on the floor around my feet. He was dressed in his baseball uniform, and he held a glove, old and tattered, in his hand.

"Well, did you finish them?" I asked impatiently.

"Yes, ma'am," he mumbled. My heart softened for an instant, and went out to this little boy of mine. These days, Billy seemed to be growing by leaps and bounds, and in no time he would be grown and gone from me for good. Already he was getting big; he reminded me more than ever of his father, my husband Ronnie. Those twinkling eyes, that easy smile, his charming, irresistible manner—yes, just like his father. Too much like his father.

"And what about your paper route?" I asked sternly.

"I can get that done after practice," he answered, lifting his head up, his eyes hopeful, his voice wheedling. "I've got my route down to forty-five minutes flat now."

"Mr. Larson called just last night to complain that his paper was late and all tangled up in his bushes, Billy. Do you call that doing a good job?"

"Aw, he's just an old grump," he said. "Everybody else on the route likes me." Billy sounded cocky, sure of himself—just like Ronnie used to be. *Just an old grump. How many times had Ronnie said words like that just after he'd been fired from yet another job?* Suddenly, this memory made me furious.

"That paper route is your responsibility!" I lashed out at Billy, my voice shrill and loud. He shrank away from me and clutched his glove to his chest, as if for protection. But I couldn't seem to stop myself. "Somebody has to teach you to do a job right. You get out there on your bike and start right now—no practice for you today!"

"But, Mom!" Billy cried. His face was scrunched up in misery and disappointment. "I promised Coach Wilson I'd be there today. He said he'd help me with my pitching. He said that if I practiced hard enough, I could pitch in the big game next month—the big game in the tournament." He looked up at me with such a forlorn, pleading expression that I almost gave in. After all, he was just a kid. . . .

But as I gazed down at him, I was again reminded of Ronnie.

"No," I said flatly, finally. "Baseball is just a game. The paper route is a job, and job always come first." I hardened my face towards him.

"But this is really important!" he cried. When he saw I wasn't going to give in, he threw his glove to the floor and glared up at me with blazing eyes. "You won't listen! You don't care . . . you hate me!" he shouted. "And if you won't let me go, I hate you, too!" He shot me one last furious look, and then stomped back to his room. I heard the door slam loudly—his last comment to me.

I sagged at the sink, suddenly exhausted. It seemed like there was an awful lot of door slamming going on around here lately. I could still hear Billy's words echoing in my head, "You hate me . . . hate me. . . ."

"Oh, Billy," I whispered. "I don't hate you. Don't you see that I'm only doing what's best for you—that I love you very much?" I knew he couldn't hear me, but somehow the words helped lift the heavy, leaden feeling I had inside.

I'm just so tired, I thought. Working all day at that tedious job as a file clerk, then rushing to the grocery store, getting to the daycare center at five, hurrying home to check on Billy, fixing dinner, doing the dishes, starting the laundry—it was all too overwhelming. Being both mother and father, breadwinner, and homemaker—all at the same time, and all by myself. I couldn't take much more. My paycheck barely covered our expenses, and I was near the breaking point. I was blowing up constantly, like I did today.

Oh, Billy, I thought again. *If only you weren't so much like Ronnie; I can't, just can't, let you grow up to be like him!*

Ronnie . . . how could I now so bitterly resent the man I had fallen in love with at first sight, the man I had married two days after my high school graduation? He had been my knight in shining armor then, the "older man" all my girlfriends giggled about and envied me for.

Actually, he was only nineteen to my sixteen when I first met him, that summer before my senior year in high school. He was the only guy I knew then who was really out on his own, with a real job, a car, and even his own apartment. He had dropped out of school and left home a few years before, and was now working for a construction company. The first time I saw him, all golden-tanned and strong, was on the roof of a house being built next door. I had come out in a bikini to sunbathe in our backyard when I heard the long, appreciative whistle. I looked up, right into his mischievous eyes, and my heart was his in an instant.

Before long, I was baking oatmeal cookies and mixing lemonade to take over to him on his breaks. We would sit together in the shade of a big willow by the back fence and talk, laughing when his boss yelled at him to get back to work—Ronnie did take a lot of breaks. But I didn't care then. His irresistible charm had hooked me, and I was head over heels in love, grateful that Ronnie even gave me the time of day.

By the time school started, we were seeing each other regularly. At first, it was only out to the drive-in, or maybe to get a hamburger after classes, but soon Ronnie had talked me into going over to his apartment. I would fix us some dinner, and then we'd relax with a few beers. After that, the late, dark hours were ours alone. I even spent the entire night a few times, either sneaking out of my house after midnight or telling Mom and Dad I was sleeping over at a friend's.

And all my girlfriends were more than willing to cover for me. Eager to graduate and get out on their own themselves, they were awed with Ronnie and our "grownup" arrangement. I was on cloud nine. Ronnie told me he loved me and I believed him; things couldn't be better.

Then, in April, I found out I was pregnant. I was immediately overjoyed. Nothing could make me happier than to have Ronnie's child, and I was ready to settle down and be his wife. I rushed right over to his apartment after school and blurted out the news. Ronnie was silent for a long moment. "That's . . . that's just great, babe," he said finally, looking at my radiant face. But I saw the shadow pass over his face, and noticed the way he edged backwards, as if trapped. I saw, all right, but I was so happy myself, I just ignored it–then.

We were married after graduation, and I moved into his apartment the same day. We didn't have money for a honeymoon, but I didn't care. Now his apartment was mine, too. I set to work, joyfully turning it into a home for us both.

And at first it was a happy, cozy home. Ronnie worked on several construction jobs, made good money, and when he came home at night, I was waiting with a hot dinner and open arms. We had a lot of fun those first few months–Ronnie was always one for a good time–and even when he got laid off, he found other jobs right away. He was one of the best carpenters in town, and almost everybody liked him. He liked his work, too, and after Billy was born, I was just as happy and busy myself. We were both thrilled with our new son; Ronnie spent hours playing with him when he got home each night.

But when Billy was only a few years old, our luck began running out. Ronnie started getting fired, job after job, for arguing with his bosses. He did expert work, but the trouble was that he just couldn't take orders. He wanted to do everything his own way.

"I just love being outside all day, and working with my hands," he'd say to me earnestly as we cuddled in bed late at night. "I could do a really fine job, too, if people just left me alone. But I'll be darned if I'll do things the way everybody tells me to. First, it was my folks telling me to go to school when I knew I wanted to be a carpenter, and now it's them—those big, hot shot bosses. They're all just a bunch of know-it-all grumps."

At first I listened sympathetically; I admired the pride of craftsmanship he showed. But as time went by, he was home more and more, without work and complaining about everything. I had to budget tightly to make the small salary he occasionally brought home stretch far enough even to feed us, and I was beginning to change my mind about his so-called high ideals.

"But, Ronnie," I said one night after he had launched into another tirade about his latest boss, "you have to learn to get along with people—that's just part of life. You have responsibilities now, and you've got to think of Billy and me." *And maybe one more*, I thought. I hadn't told him yet that I was pretty sure I was pregnant again.

"Yeah, responsibilities," he mumbled, turning away. He stared at the wall a moment, then suddenly grabbed his coat and started out the door. "I'll see you later," he said over his shoulder. "I'm going out to play baseball with the guys and have a few beers afterwards."

I was left there, alone with Billy, and fighting one of the pounding headaches I had been getting so often lately. Ronnie was doing this more and more, spending all his time playing baseball or football with his buddies, and then staying up to all hours drinking. I couldn't take much more.

What had happened to my "knight in shining armor," the "older man," who I thought would take care of me? It seemed that when the going got rough and life became more of a chore than a fun game, Ronnie couldn't handle it. I lay down on the couch, thinking what a burden it would be to tell Ronnie about my new pregnancy. It seemed so long ago when I had been so happy to tell him about Billy. Then, uneasily, I also remembered the trapped look he'd had when I told him.

By the time Tricia was born, Ronnie couldn't get a job in construction work anywhere in town. He had gained a reputation for being a hothead, and nobody would hire him. He tried working as a salesman, a mechanic, even a short stint as a trucker, but nothing would satisfy him. He drifted from job to job—and also began drifting further away from us. He grew moody and brooding. Where was the carefree, confident Ronnie I had fallen in love with? Either he would be gone all day, or sit for hours in his easy chair and stare at the wall.

By this time, I was frantic. We had no money for food, or even new shoes for the children. I began to nag and yell at Ronnie constantly, until I was a total wreck and Ronnie so withdrawn that we could barely look at each other.

One night, when he came home at midnight and I started in on him, he finally exploded.

"Leave me alone!" he shouted. "You're just like everybody else—let me do what I want!" We stared angrily at each other for a moment,, and then suddenly, he sagged, deflated. He looked up at me with haunted eyes. "I need to find . . . to find something . . ."

"What, Ronnie?" I said pleadingly. "What are you looking for? You've got us."

"I know," he said, shaking his head. "But don't you see that that's not enough. I need to find out who I am, by myself. I never really had the chance to." He looked at me pleadingly now, but I couldn't understand. I was tired of trying; I needed some security myself.

"Ronnie," I said in a low voice, "you'll always be looking and never find what you want—unless you look right here, at what you have." I gave him a chance to respond, but he just looked at me blankly. At that moment, I knew I was on my own.

That night Ronnie slept on the couch, and when I got up in the morning, he was gone. We waited for weeks, but he never came back. When I finally went to a lawyer and the courts found him, I didn't even care anymore. In the past few years, all my love for Ronnie had drained right out of me. I was exhausted and bitter. By the time we finally got a divorce, and I was awarded child custody, I had turned numb. I didn't care where Ronnie went or if he ever "found himself." I had two children to take care of—what was I to do?

Those next few years were the roughest I ever had to face. I really learned what being "grown up" meant. Somehow, after months of searching, I was able to land my file clerk job, rent a cheap apartment, and find adequate day care for my daughter, Tricia. But we were barely scraping by now, and I was starting to wonder if anything was worth the nervous, angry woman I had become.

Like today, yelling at my own little son so fiercely, making him think that I hated him. . . .

I gazed out the kitchen window at the bird feeder balanced on the ledge. Billy had made it for me for Mother's Day last year, and I had to admit it was a beautiful piece of woodwork. He had definitely inherited his father's talent and love for working with his hands. But bird feeders weren't going to feed us, and certainly were not going to do Billy much good in the future; I had learned that much from his father. That's why I insisted that he do well in school, especially in subjects like math and science, so he could get a good job someday and learn early how to listen, take orders, and do a job right.

I sighed and swished the last dish dry. My feet ached from standing all day at work, and I still had three loads of laundry to get through. I heard the apartment door wrench open and slam, and I knew Billy was gone on his route. I winced at the sound, but steeled myself. Someone just had to teach him.

Wearily, I walked out into the living room. There, scattered all over the couch, were Billy's books and papers, untouched since he had thrown them there after school. So he hadn't done his math problems! Instantly angry again, I stomped over and grabbed the books. He was going to get this homework done before he went to bed tonight or no more baseball all year!

As I started toward his room, a thin envelope fluttered out of a book to the floor, and I saw my name written across the back of it. Puzzled, I slit it open. It was a notice from Mr. Wilson, Billy's math teacher: Billy was failing the class.

My anger drained away as quickly as it had welled up. Why hadn't Billy told me? Had I really given him a chance? Was he that scared of me?

I scanned the letter again. Mr. Wilson wanted to see me tomorrow for a parent-teacher conference. I remembered that Billy had told me his coach was Mr. Wilson, too. I wondered what kind of a man would encourage Billy to play baseball when he knew Billy was failing one of his most important classes. Didn't anyone believe in discipline and hard work anymore?

The next day, I worked through lunch so I could leave early from work to see Mr. Wilson. I was a little apprehensive as I walked down the narrow corridors of the school, but I was determined to get to the bottom of Billy's troubles.

I found Room 401, the room marked by Mr. Wilson on the note, and pushed open the door. It was empty, except for the straight rows of short desks and a young, tall man wiping the blackboard in front of the classroom.

"Excuse me," I said, clearing my throat. "Could you please tell me where I can find Mr. Wilson?"

"That's me," the man answered, turning toward me with a boyish grin and warm brown eyes. "But please, call me Roy." He took a step forward and stretched out a large, capable-looking hand.

I was caught off guard for a moment. Was this handsome, young man really Coach Wilson? I had expected an older man, with a crew-cut and strict, rough features. But this man—Roy—was not only handsome, but he looked at me with such friendly, attentive eyes that I had to shift my gaze.

"I'm Billy's mother, Sarah James," I murmured, handing him the note. "I'm here to discuss Billy's math grade."

"Oh!" he said as his eyes lit up. "I'm glad you could come, Mrs. James."

"Well, I suppose if I'm calling you Roy, you might as well call me Sarah," I said, blushing. For some reason, this unexpected man made me feel giddy.

But this isn't right, I thought; I was here to talk over a very serious matter. I straightened my skirt a bit, thrust out my chin, and cleared my throat again. "Now what's this about Billy flunking?" I asked in what I hoped was a stern voice.

"Well, Mrs. James. . . Sarah . . . Billy's a very bright boy and he tries extremely hard, but he seems to have a block when it comes to math."

"A block?" I said, confused. How could Billy be bright, like Roy said, and still be failing?

"Yes, a mental block," Roy said gently. "You see, the reason Billy can't grasp the basic concepts is because he tries too hard. He forces his mind and wrestles with the ideas so much that he actually blocks them. What he needs to do is relax and let them come naturally." Roy paused a moment to glance at me.

I must have still looked puzzled, because he went on. "That's why I try to encourage him in baseball. He enjoys it so much that all the pressures or problems that bother him in class are gone. I hope to help him transfer some of that enjoyment to math class."

At the mention of baseball, I stiffened. "Baseball is not going to get Billy anywhere," I said a little sharply. "I see no reason why he should spend as much time as he does at it. Block or no block, Billy would be better off doing his math homework."

Roy gave me a funny look, and suddenly switched from his teaching voice to a more personal one. "Say, what is all the emphasis on math anyway?" he asked, peering at me closely. "It's an important subject all right, but some people do better in other areas. He's a great ballplayer and, Mr. Bardin, the shop teacher, has shown me some of the woodwork Billy did in his class. I think Billy shows much more promise in those directions."

"It seems you've taken quite an interest in my son," I snapped. I didn't need to be told that Billy was headed in his father's footsteps.

Roy turned a little red. "Billy just reminds me of someone I once was . . . very close to," he mumbled.

"Well, Billy is my son, and I'll thank you to stick to your teaching while I handle his future," I said, suddenly very angry. "Good night, Mr. Wilson!" With that, I marched out of the room, leaving him staring after me.

All the way home, I argued back and forth with myself about my angry parting with Roy. *After all, it really wasn't any of his business,* I kept telling myself. *He had no right to meddle in Billy's life—or mine.* But deep down, I couldn't forget the genuine concern in those brown eyes or that friendly smile. And although I finally decided the best thing to do would be to forget him, I knew it might be some time before I could shake his face from my memory.

It didn't help matters much when Roy showed up at our front door a few days later. I was clearing the remnants of our dinner off the kitchen table when Billy bounced in excitedly to tell me who was here. Thrown off balance for a second, I glanced around the messy kitchen and down at my rumpled clothes. I still hadn't changed from work, or had a chance to straighten up the apartment. Hurriedly, I ran a comb through my hair, took off my apron, and tried to pull myself together as I walked out into the living room to greet him.

"Hi," Roy said, a little embarrassed. He looked defensive, as if preparing himself for another angry outburst, and I couldn't blame him. But I also detected a determined set to his chin and an insistent gleam in his eye.

"I came to get you all for baseball practice tonight," he said, giving me an especially emphatic nod. "I thought it was time everybody saw what our practices were like." He confronted me challengingly.

"But I have dishes and cleaning and . . ." I said, flustered. Why did this man make my insides feel so fluttery when he looked at me like that?

"Now, what's more important," Roy said with a wink at Billy, "dirty dishes or the team's star pitcher?"

Billy nearly melted on the spot with that remark. I could tell he just adored Roy. And for some reason, that got my anger up again. I would go—just to put a stop to this nonsense once and for all.

"All right," I said coolly. "Just let me get Tricia." Roy looked triumphant, and yet also disappointed at my chilly tone. I saw his face fall a bit.

He and Billy walked ahead of Tricia and me on the way to the park, deep in conversation about the "Big Game," as they called it, scheduled in a few weeks. I began to relax a bit. As much as I hated to admit it, it was really nice seeing Billy up there with a man—I had always felt unsure about my role as both mother and father since Ronnie left.

With all the enthusiastic parents at the practice, it wasn't long before I, too, was swept up in their excitement and cheering. I even surprised myself by hoping for a victory in the upcoming tournament and finding out how much fun I was having.

I also discovered that Roy was right about Billy. Usually so sullen or cocky at home, Billy was a totally different boy on the ball field. He listened carefully to all of Roy's instructions, and cheerfully did whatever was best for the team, retreating without a squabble when his turn was over and joking with all the boys and girls at breaks. I had to admit, he was a good pitcher, too—I could tell he put every ounce of effort into throwing the ball just right, just the way Roy told him to.

As I watched my big boy out there, with pride swelling up in my throat, I began to change my mind about my objections to baseball.

Maybe there was something to what Roy had said. I relaxed even more, and as my worry ebbed a little, I realized this was the first time in months I had dared to let go like this. I was so afraid to let down my defenses these days; I guess I had been using my worry and anger to protect myself from getting hurt again.

By the time practice was over, I was in such high spirits I gave Billy a big hug and Roy a grateful smile.

"You were right," I said, blushing a bit as I looked at Roy. "It was really wonderful to see my son in action."

I was glad to see Roy's brown eyes light up again. "In that case," he said, returning the smile, "why spoil the evening by going home now? How about some burgers and ice cream over at my place?" Tricia and Billy cheered and jumped up and down at the prospect, and so I laughed and gave in. But my heart did its own flips at his suggestion.

Roy lived only a few blocks from the park, in a small cozy house with a big backyard and lots of trees. He even had a tiny shop in his garage where he did woodworking projects to give away as gifts. His craftsmanship was beautiful, every bit as good as Ronnie's, if not better. I could now understand Roy's sympathy and encouragement towards Billy's talent.

Roy was gallant and fun as he showed us around and barbequed the burgers. Before long, it was evident he had bewitched both my children with his charm. *But it was a different kind of charm than Ronnie's,* I thought as I watched him wrestle with Billy and swing Tricia until she giggled with delight. Roy's charm came from pure, simple caring.

"How do you ever find time for all this?" I asked him as we relaxed in lawn chairs with coffee after dinner. "Teaching, coaching, woodwork, the house. I barely have the energy to read the newspaper when I'm done with work and chores around the apartment," I laughed wryly.

"Oh, it's all just fun for me," he said eagerly. "I love doing everything I do—I get so much out of helping the kids, working with people . . ." His voice trailed off, and he gazed after the children for a long moment. "It can get awfully lonely here by myself if I don't keep busy."

Something in his face made me reach out and touch his hand. "Have you ever been married?" I asked gently.

"Yes, once," he said in a low voice. "I had a son, too, who would have been Billy's age right now if . . ." For a moment, the air between us was filled with a painful silence. "I lost them both, my wife and son, in a car accident six years ago," he finally said. "I learned how precious life was then, and I vowed, never to waste it."

I could think of no words to console him, to erase the jagged pain I saw etched across his face. I squeezed his hand gently and sat, without a word, as a lump formed in my throat. And here I thought I had problems! I found I was admiring this man more and more.

"Well, you certainly have a gift for life, Roy," I said at last. "You've discovered something about my own son I never saw before. I haven't seen him so happy in years. I think I'd like him to continue with practice and pitch in the tournament."

Billy, who had come up beside me, heard that last remark and let out a whoop. "Oh, boy, oh, boy!" he shouted.

"But," I said, turning to Billy firmly, "only on one condition. You have to promise to spend as much time on your paper route and math homework as you do in practice."

"Oh, I will," he said earnestly. "Coach will help me, too, won't you?" He turned to Roy with hopeful eyes.

"You bet I will!" Roy answered with a grin. I was relieved to see that his sad memories had faded, at least for the time being, and that he was his cheerful self again.

"And the last thing we have to do is put you in training," Roy said to Billy, with a severe expression but laughing eyes. "That means early to bed, for one thing—starting tonight."

"Aw, Coach!" Billy said with a groan. "We were just having a good time."

"A star pitcher needs lots of sleep," Roy said with a chuckle. "And math class comes early in the morning." He winked at me.

It was time to go, I knew, but I found myself very reluctant to leave the peaceful backyard—and Roy's company. As he walked us to the corner and the children skipped ahead, Roy took my arm.

"And when will I see the star pitcher's mother again?" he asked in a low voice.

"Oh, I'll hang around at the next practice," I said, looking up into his face. "And next time, I'll provide the dinner." I was glad for the darkness so he couldn't see how nervous I felt, and so the children didn't see when he leaned down and gave me a soft, tender kiss.

I said good-bye, and nearly floated on the way home. *What a lovely night it had turned out to be,* I thought when I walked into our apartment. I didn't even mind the dirty dishes. I spun through the rooms and whisked things clean, with renewed energy.

The next couple of weeks were hectic, however, and quickly sapped my brief burst of energy. Our manager at work was replaced by a new one, and the whole office was turned upside down. The new boss changed everything around to suit his ideas. He wanted all the filing done his way—and just after I had gotten the old system down pat, too. The hours at work were long and frustrating with his criticizing eyes peering over my shoulder at every turn. I came home at night exhausted and cranky from the strain.

Nothing very soothing was waiting for me there, either. There were dishes, laundry, Tricia cranky herself from hours at the day-care center, and Billy out on his paper route or at baseball practice. After dinner, I'd help him with his homework, going over problem after problem in his math book, or I'd play with Tricia to make up for all the extra attention I was giving to Billy. I knew I was spreading myself too thin, but certain things just had to get done. Usually, it was way after midnight before I could sink gratefully into bed.

But at least one very nice item was added to my busy schedule in those weeks, someone who made up for everything else: Roy.

Sometimes I would watch the kids practice. I enjoyed being outdoors and I liked being with Roy. But when I didn't go, he'd come over after baseball practice, bringing Billy home and then staying for dinner. He was always cheerful and willing to help clear the table, tutor Billy, and admire Tricia' s toys. After we tucked the kids into bed, Roy would stay for coffee and sit up with me in the living room—just us, together, alone.

The more time I spent with Roy, the more my admiration and love grew for him. He was never too tired to listen to and encourage me, and I began to really enjoy sharing my daily struggles and joys with him. Bit by bit, I was letting my defenses down again, letting Roy in. I was letting someone get close to me again, finally. I realized I was falling as deeply in love with Roy as I had with Ronnie many years before. And although I also knew that it was different this time, I was still scared. I vowed over and over that I would never let myself be hurt like I did before, with Ronnie—but I just kept on loving Roy. I couldn't help myself. I was too happy.

And then, just when I thought everything was going so perfectly, it happened again: my luck started running out. Rumors began to fly at work that the new boss was installing a new, more efficient system, which would eliminate half the work—and half the jobs. Since I was one of the most recently hired, I would be among the first to go if the rumors were true. What would I do then?

And Billy, who had been so conscientious at first, began to neglect his paper route and homework as the baseball tournament approached. It was only a week away now. I came home from work every night to another complaint from Mr. Larson about his newspapers, and more than once I caught Billy practicing his pitching stance in his bedroom when I had told him to finish his homework. I could understand his excitement, and yet I was still worried. I knew from bitter experience that games should never come before responsibilities. I started reacting sharply to Billy again.

But the worst blow of all was Roy. Just when I needed him the most, he seemed to suddenly have no time for me.

His excuses began on the one night we had planned as a special date for just the two of us, alone. After the kids were already in bed, he was to come over for a late dinner and, hopefully, a quiet, romantic evening. I had spent my lunch hours all week and too much money shopping for just the right candles and wine and special ingredients for the gourmet dinner I was preparing him. But when the big night came, and I looked with satisfaction at the glittering, candlelit table, I knew it was all worth it. It had been a tough week, and I needed this time alone with Roy. I was just slipping into the gorgeous new outfit I had bought for the occasion when he called.

"Sarah," he said abruptly when I answered the phone, "I'm afraid I won't be able to make it tonight. I've got a million last-minute things to arrange for the tournament, and a mound of papers to grade that came in today—final grades are due next week."

"But we've planned this evening for weeks!" I wailed. "I have the kids all tucked in, the good china out. . . ." Miserably, I looked down at my new outfit. I had paid a fortune for it, and now Roy wouldn't even be able to see it. Suddenly, I was reminded of all the nights I had sat alone, dinner spoiled, waiting up for Ronnie. "You could come if you tried," I snapped. "Obviously you don't really want to come—you don't really care." My voice was rising shrilly, but I couldn't control it. "You're just making excuses, I can tell; I've heard every one in the book."

Roy was quiet on the other end. "I'm sorry, Sarah," he said finally. "I thought you would understand."

"Oh, I understand all right," I laughed bitterly. "I understand more than you think!" With that, I slammed down the phone and burst into tears. I glanced around the room, all set up for our special date, and grew angrier by the minute.

"Just like Ronnie," I fumed to myself. "All wrapped up in himself and his projects, thinking everything else but me is more important, letting me down just when I finally let myself need him." I strode furiously over to the table and blew out the candles. *Well, I'm not about to let myself get hurt like that again. This time, nobody is running out on me! I can get along perfectly well by myself, just like I did before I ever met Roy. I'll just forget him.*

But at the thought of good, gentle Roy, and my love for him, my anger quickly faded. I went over to lie down on the couch, lost in a confusing mixture of thoughts. Was the same thing happening with Roy that had happened with Ronnie? Or was Roy really busy, with good reason, tonight? I didn't know what to think. I was hurt, puzzled, angry, remorseful, all at the same time. I decided to wait and see if Roy called back, and if he did, I would apologize.

But I waited in vain for his call, and finally, fell asleep right there on the couch. The next morning I woke up, cramped and miserable, still dressed in my outfit. I barely had time to think as I scrambled to get ready for work. The way things were going at the office, I couldn't afford to be late.

All day, I alternated between resentment and despair. I felt so badly for having shouted at Roy. But then, hadn't he ruined an evening we had planned for weeks? Couldn't he even commit himself to one, simple evening? And why hadn't he called back? As much as I tried to be fair, I couldn't shake the haunting memories of Ronnie and what he had done to me.

By evening, I felt terribly lonely, but I had made up my mind to forget Roy for good. The only one I could count on was myself, I decided. From now on, I wouldn't allow anyone to get close to me. It hurt too much to be let down.

All that next week, I refused to even talk to Roy, and walked around in a daze. It seemed that my whole life was shaky, ready to cave in any moment. In a few days, it collapsed completely.

It happened the day before the "Big Game." I left for work, smiling a little over Billy's obvious excitement, in spite of myself. I was even humming a tune when I walked into work, and feeling better than I had all week. But when I checked my box, I found a note saying that the new manager wanted to talk to me. Instantly, my good mood vanished and was replaced by fear. I approached his office, wondering what I had done wrong.

He told me the news I was terrified to hear: I was laid off. I had two weeks to work, and then the new system would be installed. He said that two weeks was enough time to find a new job, but I knew better. I had struggled for months just to land this one—jobs were scarce these days.

The rest of the day passed, like a nightmare. I forgot about everything else in an all-consuming terror. I was cut adrift again, just like when Ronnie had left me. What was I to do now?

When I got home, the apartment felt empty. I gave Tricia a cookie and then glanced out the window. There, in the middle of a mud puddle in the street, was Billy's math book. He must have dropped it there on his way home from school. The rest of his school things were scattered on the couch. The phone rang, and suddenly, my heart leaped up. Maybe it was Roy! I could tell him what had happened today; he would help me and tell me what to do.

But it was just another complaint from Mr. Larson. It seemed he hadn't gotten his paper yet tonight, and he'd "had it up to here."

Well, so have I! I thought to myself as I slammed down the phone. I was silly to think it might be Roy calling—I knew I would have to depend on myself as usual.

Just then, Billy strolled through the front door, whistling and tossing his glove up in the air.

"Where have you been?" I confronted him harshly.

Billy looked at me, first surprised, then wary at my indignant tone. "At baseball practice," he answered. "The Big Game is tomorrow."

"I know very well what tomorrow is," I snapped at him. "But what about today? What about your paper route? I just got another call from that Mr. Larson. And as for your schoolwork—well, I can see just how much you care about that!" I pointed fiercely out the window.

Billy's face was blank as he glanced out the window, but quickly filled with guilt when he saw the mud puddle and upturned math book. He edged toward his room.

"I know now that I've been too soft on you," I shouted, suddenly exploding. "But that's going to change right this instant, do you hear? From now on, you're going to work, and work hard. That means no more baseball—ever! And I forbid you to play in that game tomorrow. You'll have to learn what responsibility means, even if you learn the hard way!"

By now I was nearly shrieking in my rage. Tricia had come around the corner to stare at me with wide-open eyes, and Billy's face was covered with fear and anger.

"Leave me alone!" he cried as he ran past me to his room. "Why won't you ever let me do what I want?!" He slammed the door resoundingly, and I was left with his echoing cry. "Let me do what I want." It sounded uncomfortably familiar.

But I was still too furious to think. I stomped into the kitchen and began slamming pots and pans around until my anger could subside. It took quite a while, but within an hour I had prepared dinner and cooled off a bit. I called Billy first. No answer. I went and knocked on his door, and then opened it. The window was wide open; Billy was gone.

I immediately felt a piercing stab of panic and regret. *What had I done? Where was my little boy?* And then I remembered where I had heard the last words that Billy had shouted at me: They were also the words Ronnie had said, the night before he left. And he had never come back.

"I have to get a hold of myself," I whispered to the empty room. "Billy will be back. He'll be back when he gets hungry enough."

Firmly, I made myself leave the room. I would do a few chores and wait. *Young boys run away all the time,* I told myself. I bustled about, giving Tricia her dinner, doing the dishes, cleaning out the bathroom, putting Tricia to bed—but still, no Billy. By that time, it was dark and a thunderstorm was building up in the sky. I paced back and forth, checking the window every two seconds and trying to control my welling panic. I was just about to call the police when the doorbell rang. I jumped up and raced to answer it.

There, dripping on the welcome mat, was a very tired, very sheepish-looking Billy, clutching the hand of a handsome man—Roy.

I was so happy to see them both. I just breathed a long sigh of relief, then hugged and scolded Billy at the same time as I whooped him off to a bath and then to bed. I would listen to explanations later.

When I came back into the living room, Roy was still there, sitting motionlessly on the couch. "I found Billy on my back porch when I got home," he said, standing up as I entered the room. "It took some time before I understood what was going on, but I finally got the story. We had a long talk, and I finally persuaded him to come home."

"Thank you," I said stiffly. "But I don't need your help." I was shocked at the way I sounded; I really was glad to see Roy. But I felt defensive and hopeful and bitter all the same time. I was afraid . . . afraid of letting go again.

"Hey, what's the matter with you?" he asked in a soft, puzzled voice. "I thought we had something special going, and then suddenly you won't even talk to me, and now you're mad when I bring home your own son. What did I do?"

"What did you do?" I said, my voice rising in pitch. "You stole my little boy away, turned him against me! You made him believe he could get by without working and left me to pick up the pieces, alone, without a job. . . ." Suddenly, I was sobbing uncontrollably.

Roy reached out to pull me close, and against his sturdy chest, I poured out everything: my lost job, my precarious marriage with Ronnie, my fear, terror, and helplessness all these weeks and months and years. When I finished, Roy held me quietly for a few minutes.

"Now I understand," he finally said gently, still cradling me in his arms. "I never really knew how to handle your anger before, but now I see where it's all coming from." He paused for a moment and looked deeply into my eyes. "Oh, Sarah, don't you see what you've been doing? You've been living in the past, so terrified of what happened before that you expect it to happen again, now, with Billy and with me. And, by expecting it, you are actually making it occur."

I stared at him, stunned. What was he talking about?

"Take Billy," he said, still in a soft, gentle voice. "By demanding so much out of him, by trying to keep him from turning out like Ronnie, you're driving him in the same way Ronnie was driven all his life. You're not giving Billy a chance to find himself now before it's too late. And if you don't, he'll end up just like Ronnie, in spite of your intentions."

"But Billy's route . . . he gets complaints. . . ."

"Billy's just a boy. So he got excited and made a few mistakes, like we all do. And I know Mr. Larson," Roy chuckled. "He just likes to complain."

Roy looked at my uncertain face and went on earnestly. "But you've seen Billy at baseball practice—you've seen how seriously he takes it. Do you know why he came over tonight? He told me he just couldn't let down the team. He felt responsible to pitch in the Big Game. And look at this." Roy reached into his pocket and pulled out a sheet of paper. On it was Billy's final math grade: He had passed!

"This took a lot of hard work," Roy said. "Billy told me he was so excited to tell you the news he must have dropped his book on the way into the apartment."

My heart sank, and I sat weakly on the couch. If only I had given him a chance . . . and I had nearly lost him.

All at once, I looked up at Roy, as a thought hit me. "And you?" I said, my voice trembling. "Oh, Roy, I'm so sorry . . . all my anger."

"Well, I must admit I was confused," Roy said, taking my hand. "I picked up the phone a million times to call you, but I thought you were through with me; I decided to wait for your call." This time he tried to avoid my gaze. "You see, after my wife died, it took a long time for my emotions to heal. I'm still afraid of being hurt."

So he was afraid, too! I gripped his hand. And here I had been treating him like Ronnie. He was about as far away from Ronnie as you could get.

"And I'm so sorry about spoiling your evening last week," Roy said. "It's just that I was really busy—I feel a huge responsibility to my work and to the team. I was going to invite you out for the next night to help make up for it all, but you hung up."

I winced at the reminder, but Roy smiled, "You've got some temper!" He laughed. "But if you'd held out and gone with me the next night, I would have given you this."

Roy pulled a gift-wrapped box out of a sack I hadn't noticed him bring in. "I've been working on this a long time," he said. Inside was the most beautiful, handcrafted wooden music box I had ever seen. As I looked up at him with wondering eyes, he said, right before he kissed me, "It's meant as an engagement present—that is, if you agree."

Well, I certainly didn't disagree, and it was the best decision I ever made in my life. I thought about everything Roy said, and I finally was able to see what I was doing and why. Oh, it took some time, but my anger is nearly gone now, and I'm learning to let Billy go and enjoy life. He's a wonderful boy and a wonderful carpenter—the shop teacher told me last week that Billy was his best student in over ten years of teaching. And now that I understand that Billy can take orders and be responsible, I'm not so worried about his future. What matters most is that he's happy.

And with a father like Roy to guide him along . . . well, I'm pretty happy, too. Roy doesn't take his responsibilities lightly, and I know he will be around for a long, long time. I can tell just that by looking at the beautiful music box on the dresser in our bedroom. Every time I hear its lilting melody, I'm thankful that I found Roy—and myself—in time. Life truly is a precious gift. THE END

MY IN-LAWS THREW
ME OUT

That night we got married, I had only known Bill for two weeks. But I think I loved him from the first moment I saw him. It was funny I should feel that way. He wasn't handsome or what you'd call charming. No, it wasn't like that at all. Only his red hair set him apart from any of the other Marines coming into town from the nearby base. That, and his height. There was just something about him that wrung my heart, and a feeling like that is stronger than any thrill or excitement can ever be.

He was so shy, too, as if he weren't used to talking much to girls, even one who was just waiting on him in a store. "I—I'd like to look at a nightgown. Something real pretty with lace," he said.

It was silly, but I couldn't help but feel that sudden pang of jealousy as I took down the box of the sheerest ones in the shop. "What size?" I asked, trying to make my voice sound cool and crisp.

At first he only looked dumfounded. Then his hands outlined a space that would have made two of me. The smallest it could have been was a forty-two, and I felt a glow of triumph as I put the lid back on and pulled down another box. As I took out the large, tailored gown and held it up for him to see, I saw the light leave his eyes. "But I wanted to get my mother the prettiest nightgown in the place," he said.

Oh, so it was for his mother. Hearing the tenderness in his voice as he spoke about her made me realize how much I liked him. I had never known my parents, but it wasn't my father I missed in all those foster homes where I had lived. It was always a mother I dreamed about during the lonely hours. A soft-looking, loving mother who would have cuddled me in her arms.

"There are other things I'm sure she would like," I said. "A bag or a scarf or—or I might even be able to order a nightgown in a larger size. If I can, do you want me to telephone you?"

His eyes lit up again. "That would be cool," he said. "Only it's not so easy getting calls at the base, unless you happen to be in the barracks all the time. Maybe it'd be better if I drop by in a few days."

But I didn't have to wait to see him again. He was waiting outside the store when I got through work. "I got a better idea," he said. "I thought maybe you and I could have dinner together. That is, if you don't have another date."

It was something I had never felt before, that crowding feeling inside of me, as if the excitement and happiness were almost too much, coming together like that. "I don't have another date," I said, and I sounded the way I felt, as if it were poetry I was saying, not just those simple words. It embarrassed me, having my heart go flying into my voice like that.

Then he grinned, and suddenly, I wasn't ill at ease any more. "I feel like celebrating," he said. "I just got word this morning that my college application was accepted. Mom will be so excited when she hears I'm really on the way to being an engineer. Of course, I could never have done it without this G.I. thing." His grin came a little sheepishly. "I'm not talking about myself too much, am I? It's just that this means so much to me I have to tell somebody about it."

"You can tell me," I said. "I like to listen."

That was the way it all started, sitting there in the restaurant, listening to his voice quickening in excitement, and knowing more and more with every passing minute that no one had ever meant so much to me before. Outside of his plans, it was his mother he talked about most, not what a boy on his first date with a girl usually does. But that only endeared him to me the more, with the feeling of all I had missed settling like an ache in my throat. Just hearing him talk about his family—his mother and father and Pete and Jack, and his younger brothers—it was almost as if I was seeing them in front of my eyes.

"I guess always being so poor made us stick together more than a lot of families do," he went on. "Dad had a bad accident at work when I was only a kid, and was only able to do odd jobs after that. It was grim sometimes, never knowing if we could manage the next month's rent.

"But Mom helped us when the going got rough, talking about the time our ship would come in and we'd have the house and backyard she was always dreaming about. She had one of those oversized piggy banks, and when I worked after school, she'd make a big deal of putting the money in the bank for our house. So you can see how it makes me feel, being actually on the way to earn the kind of money that will get Mom her house and all the other things she's been wanting."

The lump in my throat grew so big I could hardly breathe. "She's lucky having a son like you," I said. "But you're even luckier having a mother." And then somehow, I couldn't stop talking, though I had never been able to tell anyone how I really felt before. About being alone, I mean, and not having any family. It was so easy to talk to Bill. Just as easy as it was listening to him.

Afterward, I was sorry I had told him so much, because I was afraid it was only pity that made him keep on seeing me. Even after I found out I couldn't get the nightgown he wanted in a larger size and helped him pick out a bag for his mother instead, he kept on seeing me. And though he would always give me that quick, shy kiss when he left me at the door of my rooming house, I was sure it was just a part of his being sorry for me. That was the way I had felt about him at first. But it wasn't like that any more. Now, it was as if the whole world ended every time we said good-bye, and only started coming alive again the next time I saw him.

Sometimes it seemed as if I could hardly stand it unless I knew he felt that way about me, too. Unless he said something to at least give me a little hope that someday he might. But he didn't. Not until that night we were really saying good-bye.

It was raining so hard that night; one of those hard September downfalls that didn't let up for a moment. We had had dinner and gone to the movies, and then it was time for him to catch the last bus that would get him to his train in time. We didn't have long to wait, but even in those few minutes, we were drenched. But it didn't make any difference. I didn't notice the rain—all I felt was the pang of knowing we were saying good-bye and this time I would never see him again.

I was trying so hard to laugh and be happy so that he wouldn't have only that dismal, bedraggled picture of me to remember. But when the light filtered through the rain at the bend of the road and I knew the bus was actually coming, I couldn't hold my tears back any longer. It was shameful, I know, having so little pride. But there are things that mean so much more than pride, and love is one of them.

He must have seen the light the same instant I did, for suddenly, his arms were wrapped around me and his face was pressing against mine. "Don't cry, Maggy," he whispered. "I'll be seeing you again. Honest, I promise."

And when he kissed me, it wasn't the way he had all those times before. His mouth pressed down on mine so hard it was almost as much of a pain as a joy, and the way I loved him was different from before, so wild and sweet that life wasn't even worth living unless his arms would always be holding me and his mouth always waiting for mine.

The bus stopped and he almost pushed me away from him, though he still held onto my hand. "Maggy, there's something I've wanted to tell you," he said, and his voice sounded as if it had an ache in it, just like the one in my throat. "I love you. I didn't feel I could tell you, because I didn't think it was right asking you to do all the waiting it would mean. That is, if you love me, too—"

"Oh, yes," I said. "Oh, Bill, I think I loved you the first minute I saw you."

He kissed me again, and then got on the bus. "I'll write you," he called down from the steps. "The minute I get home I'll—"

The rest of his words were lost in the roar of the engine as the bus started up, and I started running beside it, hoping he would say it again. There was so little to remember, and I didn't want to miss a word of anything he had said.

Then suddenly, he threw his bag off the bus, and I saw that he was about to jump. I started to scream a warning, but he was already on the ground and running toward me before I could even squeeze his name past the fear in my throat.

"I had to come back," he said. "I can't leave you until everything's right between us." He picked up his bag with one hand and held my arm with the other. "We'll go find some place where we can talk."

But even the diner was closed when we got back to the main street, and there wasn't anywhere that we could escape the rain. "I should have kept right on going," Bill said as we started walking toward the rooming house where I lived. "Here I am, trying to give you pneumonia—and for what? Just so we'll have to go through saying good-bye all over again. You know what? I wish I hadn't met you until four years from now. It's going to be tough, Maggy, so far away from each other and having to wait all that time."

Maybe if I had stopped to think I wouldn't have been so shameless, putting my longing into words. "I couldn't take it, Bill," I said. "I just couldn't, that's all. And I don't see why getting your degree has anything to do with it. There are plenty of wives working to help their husbands get an education, and I've always been able to get a job anywhere I've ever been. Oh, Bill, why can't we get married now? Right away."

"That's what I mean." His voice sounded almost mad. "I should have stayed on that bus instead of putting both of us through the wringer like this. Look, Maggy, it isn't only you and me. It's my family, too. I've got to help them. You can see how I can't run out on them."

"I wouldn't like it if you did," I said. We were almost at the house, and I began fumbling in my bag for my key. "We can both help, Bill. You'd be surprised at how economical I am, and—"

"That's out," Bill said. "Completely out. I couldn't marry any girl expecting her to help me with my obligations. It just wouldn't be fair." He took the key out of my hand and led me firmly to the door. "Look, Maggy, we can't keep on standing here in the rain. We can talk it over in our letters and—"

He was opening the door, and I felt even worse than I felt when I had seen the bus coming. "What good will letters be?" I demanded. "Oh, Bill, let's get it settled now one way or another. We can go up to my room and talk. It's so late everybody will be asleep."

"You sure it'll be all right?" he asked. And then, as I nodded, he put his bag down inside the door. "I don't want to go like this, either, Maggy, with everything up in the air. But I don't want to leave you without holding you again, even for a few minutes, only—"

"It'll be all right," I whispered. "Nobody will know." But I felt ashamed as we tiptoed up the steps. It seemed so cheap and furtive, taking all the shine off the way we felt about each other.

Only I didn't think of that when we were in my room and Bill took me in his arms. Everything was so right then, with him holding me close, not even kissing me, and just pressing his cheek against mine. It was as if he was feeling all the things I was feeling, too. As though he was showing me there wasn't anything wrong about our being there alone. We didn't even talk. We just held each other. And then, in just that second it took the door to open, all the sweetness was gone.

I knew Mrs. Simpson, my landlady, was strict, but I didn't think anyone could have so little understanding. "We were just saying good-bye," I stammered. "It's raining so hard, and there wasn't any place we could talk, and—"

She was small and thin, and her voice came almost in a whimper that was even worse than screaming would have been. "I knew I shouldn't have taken you in," she whined. "A girl coming from nowhere with no references or nothing. And here, just like I thought, you turn out to be nothing but a common tramp."

Her voice rose as Bill started to protest, and her pale eyes narrowed as she looked at him. "And I'll take no back talk from you, either. I'll have you know I run a decent rooming house, and I want you to leave this minute or I'll call the police.

"And as for you," she said, turning back to me. "I want you out of here in the morning. And what's more, I'll see to it that you don't have a chance to contaminate some other decent woman's house. Anybody else would send you packing this very minute. But I was always too softhearted for my own good. I couldn't even chase a stray cat out on a rainy night like this."

Bill was so furious his face was white. "Don't worry—she won't be staying!" he exploded. "So if you'll just get out of here, we'll start packing."

Her laugh sounded even dirtier than the way I felt. "Oh, no, you're not getting away with anything like that," she said. "I wasn't born yesterday. I'll stay right here until I see the last of you safely out of my house."

I was trembling so hard I dropped the first shirt I tried to take out of the closet. And so it was Bill who took them all out and pulled them off their hangers and packed them. I felt so dirty after all those things she said I wanted to take a bath and try to scald all that filth away. But even more, I wanted to get away from her just as fast as I could, and so I didn't even go into the bathroom to change into dry clothes. Still, even if I had, it wouldn't have done much good, for the rain was coming down as hard as ever when we left the house.

Bill didn't say anything as we started walking down the road to the center of town. I was sure everything was spoiled between us until suddenly he put down our bags and took my hand. "I've changed my mind, Maggy," he said. "About not getting married right away, I mean. After what just happened, I couldn't go and leave you alone. I'd be worried sick about you all the time. So if you still want to get married, Maggy, I want it, too."

I didn't even try to fight my tears after that. "Oh, Bill," I said. "If you only knew how much I want it. But not if it's just because you feel sorry for me. That's one thing I couldn't take, Bill. If you're asking me to marry you just because you feel sorry for me—"

"Sure I feel sorry for you." He was grinning again. "Who wouldn't feel sorry for any girl having to take what you took tonight? But I love you much more than I feel sorry for you. And there's something else I was thinking when I was packing back there. I was thinking you'd have to live with my folks so we could make ends meet. And maybe that's too much to ask you, living with your in-laws like that."

"Too much?" I said. "Oh, Bill, if you only knew how happy I'd be. Why, it would be like having a family of my own at last." And I wasn't saying it to make him feel better. I meant every word of it. Then, I felt a prickle of apprehension. "But what about them? How will they feel having some strange girl coming right into their house like that?"

"That's one thing you won't have to worry about," Bill said. "Mom's always missed having a daughter of her own, and Dad always goes along with anything Mom likes."

He let go of me, and signaled an oncoming car hopefully. It seemed to go past us unheedingly, but when Bill picked up the bags again, it stopped a few yards down the road. We ran toward it.

The driver gave us a long, hard look. "Where you bound for?" he asked. And when Bill told him the nearest railroad station, he nodded. "I'll be passing within a couple of blocks of it. You look okay to me, but you'd better sit here in front. I'm not taking any chances with hitchhikers in the backseat." But he wasn't as gruff as he sounded. He even went out of his way to leave us right at the door of the terminal.

There wasn't anyone else in the waiting room, and after we had gone into the restrooms and changed into dry clothes, Bill bundled his jacket into a pillow and made me lie down on one of the benches. "Try and get a little sleep," he said. "You could use some."

I tried, but I couldn't sleep, and Bill must have been as wide-awake as I was. When I finally sat up, he came over to me and put his arms around me. We didn't talk, we just sat there, holding each other until the first sign of light began coming in through the dusty windows.

"Look," he said. "The sun's coming out. You'll have a nice day for your wedding after all, Mrs. Cooper. And I've been thinking, honey—what's the sense of waiting till we get home? Mom would want to make a ball out of it, having all her friends and the neighbors in, and I'd rather have it this way, just you and me. I figured it all out when you were asleep. One of my buddies got married here with hardly any waiting at all. That's one good thing about wearing a uniform. People are always willing to help you out, and they got their blood tests overnight. It'll be all right, Maggy. We'll find a motel for you to stay, and I can go back to the base for the night."

It was just like Bill had said—everybody was nice about helping a Marine and his girl. The sun was out clear and strong the next day. Before noon, we were being married in a big old-fashioned church, and in another hour, we were on the train. The corsage Bill had given me was beginning to droop, and our wedding breakfast was ham sandwiches and cups of coffee, but I didn't care. I didn't need the good omen of the sunshine to know that there couldn't be a happier bride anywhere.

There was a diner on the train after we made connections in Washington, but neither of us could eat dinner. Bill was too excited, he told me, and now that we would be getting to Jersey City in another hour or so, I was beginning to get nervous. I wished Bill had called his folks about our marriage instead of wanting to surprise them.

But I didn't realize what a really big mistake it had been, until

I saw his mother's face as she opened the door for us. She looked exactly like anyone's idea of an old-fashioned mother. She looked so soft and comfortable, with the sort of face that seemed made for smiling. Only the smile left quickly and her mouth tightened as she stared at me, and I knew I had done everything wrong. I should have waited downstairs and let Bill go up alone to prepare her. Any mother should have been allowed those first moments alone with her son after not seeing him for so long.

But Bill didn't sense what was going on. He was still grinning as she tried to break away from the hug he was giving her. "Hey, Mom," he said. "Is this any way to welcome your son and your new daughter-in-law?"

"Daughter-in-law?" she cried. "What do you mean—daughter-in-law? As if I haven't had troubles enough without you walking out on me for some girl I haven't even laid eyes on before! Here, your father's been laid up almost all summer, and I was thinking everything was going to be all right with you getting out of service so I'd have more than just your allotment to manage with. And now that you're out, you got to spring this on me!"

Nothing Bill had ever told me had prepared me for a scene like that. It was the first time I realized that he didn't see his mother with his mind and his eyes, but only with his heart. Not that I couldn't understand some of the things she was feeling, but she was turning out so differently from the picture of her that Bill had given me. I had never thought her tongue could have such a cutting edge. And Bill didn't seem to realize it at all. He was still grinning as though she was a child having a temper tantrum.

"Now, Mom," he said. "You know you don't mean a word of what you're saying. As if I'd walk out on you, or as if Maggy would, either! You'll love her, Mom, once you get to know her. You always wanted a daughter, and now that I've given you one, the least you can do is kiss her."

She began to cry then, and that made it easier for me to go over to her. But I didn't want to force her to kiss me. So I held out my hand instead, and after a moment, she took it gingerly and then dropped it as though it had burned her fingers.

"Come on back into the kitchen," she said. "There's no need standing out here with all the neighbors to hear my own son turning me down."

Bill didn't say anything, and there just wasn't any answer I could come up with. We went through the parlor and the three small bedrooms into the kitchen. Bill's father and brothers were playing cards at the big table in the middle of the room. The boys gave us an embarrassed nod, got up hurriedly, and left the room. Mr. Cooper looked after them as if he didn't know whether he should call them back or not. Then he coughed self-consciously. "Well, I see you're home, son," he said. "We've been looking for you since yesterday morning."

"He had better things to do than think of his family." Mrs. Cooper began sniffing again. "He was busy getting himself married to this girl here."

This time Bill couldn't hold back his hurt feelings at what she was saying. "Her name is Maggy, Mom," he said. But even as he reproved her, the gentleness was still there in his voice. "I guess I played it all wrong, springing it on you like this without any warning. But then everything happened so suddenly and—"

Bill's mother looked at me then, not him. "A man suddenly marries a girl, what kind of a marriage is that? What kind of a life, either?"

"Take it easy, Mom!" All the gentleness was gone from Bill's voice, and his eyes blazed. "Don't go saying things you'll be sorry for afterwards. And get this straight—I married Maggy because I love her. Nothing else figured in it. Nothing, do you hear?"

"Now, now, son," his father said. "There's no need to talk to your mother like that. She's upset, and why shouldn't she be? She wore herself out, making a big dinner for you yesterday, and you never show up. Then when you do, you bring a wife with you. It's hard for a mother, losing her son to any girl, especially one she's never even seen before."

"It's like I always said," Mrs. Cooper brushed her hand against her eyes. "It's why I used to pray my heart out for a girl, knowing what a comfort she would be in my old age. A daughter marries and you gain a son. But a son marries and you lose him. That's as true as the Gospel. It happens all the time."

Bill was able to laugh then. "If that's all that's worrying you, Mom, forget it," he said. "You couldn't lose me even if you tried. And as for Maggy—you should have heard her telling me that it would be like having a family of her own, being with all of you. Come on, Mom, be yourself and make us a cup of coffee. Even a stranger's never been in the house this long without you rustling up something for him to eat."

"It's already made," she said. "I've been keeping it hot, waiting for you. And there's the chocolate cake I made yesterday. I just let the boys have a piece of it."

She cleared the table and put a cloth on it. I could see how close they all were, and for a minute, the sickness inside of me went away. Bill took the cups and plates down from the cupboard, and his father took the coffee off the stove and began pouring it into the cups. The boys came back, and as we sat around the table, there was such a good feeling of family unity and contentment, in spite of the redness around Mrs. Cooper's eyes.

"Well, it's like old times, almost," Mr. Cooper said, clearing his throat. "That's what Mr. Kendrick said last week when I saw him at a Union meeting and told him you were coming back, Bill. He said your old job was there, waiting whenever you want it."

"That's another surprise," Bill said. "I won't be going back. I was just going to tell you. I'm going to college to study engineering, just like we used to talk about when I was a kid. Remember, Mom? I'll be getting help through the G.I. bill, and I figure I can always pick up a few bucks at night—"

"Aren't you forgetting something?" his mother broke in. "You don't just have us to think about any more, not that you seem to have been doing much of it lately. You got a wife. Or haven't you thought about that, either?"

I found my voice at last. "I'm going to keep on working," I said. "Not just to help out, but because I like having a job. I wouldn't know what to do with myself without one."

"And there's the money I've been sending home for you to put in the bank," Bill said. "We can always use that if we have to."

Mrs. Cooper's face whitened. "You mean you're even going to take the house money away from me?" she demanded. "Some of it's gone already, what with doctor bills for your father and all. But there's still enough for a down payment, with you being in line for a G.I. loan now. But I can see how it wouldn't be important to you any more, a house for your folks. You got only yourself to think about now. You and your wife."

"You're going to get your house, Mom," Bill said. "That's the first thing I thought of when I knew I could go to college. I can make enough to buy one, once I have a degree. Getting a house is more than the money you have to put down. Those monthly payments come high, and with my old pay it would be pretty tough. It'll be only four years more, Mom."

"All my life, all I've been dreaming about is a house of my own, with a backyard for the boys to play in and keep them off the street." Her hand went to her heart as she stared at him. "And now you talk about four more years as though they were nothing. I might be in my grave by then. Do you know that or don't you care, now that you have a wife? I guess all that counts now is a house for her, not me."

"Mom, please don't go on talking as if I don't even belong to the family any more," Bill begged. "We're even going to keep on living with you—that is, if you want us to. Everything will be so much easier that way, all of us together even when we get the house. A family, just like we've always been."

"Maybe," Mrs. Cooper said. "We'll have to see about that. How things work out, I mean. And it makes me feel better knowing I haven't lost you altogether. But it would be so much better in a house, Bill. I—"

"Look, Mom, we'll talk about it tomorrow," Bill broke in. "Maggy and I'll come over in time for lunch." Bill and I got up to leave.

His mother looked at him unbelievingly. "You mean you're not going to be staying here, after all you said about not leaving us?"

"It'll just be for a few days, Mom," Bill said. "Maggy and I need a little time to be alone, and—well, sort of get acquainted." He looked so boyish and embarrassed that I wanted to hug him. "After all, I hadn't even laid eyes on her until about two weeks ago."

He shouldn't have said it. I knew that even before I saw Mrs. Cooper stare at me in that intent, speculating way. She didn't say anything, but as the door closed behind us, I heard her break into a hysteria of sobbing.

"Oh, Bill," I said. "All I wanted was to make you happy. And all I've done is to make trouble for you."

"Don't talk like that." He put down the bags and took me in his arms, his hand brushing my hair awkwardly. "Don't ever say things like that, Maggy. You're everything I want. Everything! Always remember that. And Mom will be all right. Every once in a while, she goes into a frenzy like this, but she always comes out of it smiling. You wait and see, Maggy. Everything is going to be all right."

But it was hard for me to believe that, still hearing that muffled sobbing behind the closed door. It seemed to follow me all the way to our hotel, into the room where I clung to Bill so desperately, as if I were saying good-bye to him instead of just beginning my married life. Then, in a little while, all the tension was dissolved in the deeper feeling of our love and our need for each other. *It's only Bill and I who count*, I thought then. It was only Bill and I who could hurt each other. No one else, not even his mother, could threaten the wonder and content we were finding in each other's arms. . . .

Even though some of the little nagging fears came back the next afternoon as we climbed those stairs again, things didn't seem as impossible as they had the night before. Bill's mother looked calm as she opened the door for us, and when she led the way back to the kitchen, the table was set as if she was expecting other company, not just us. I felt as if it was her way of telling us everything was all right again, and I was so grateful to her. Not only for that, but also for not bringing up any of the unpleasantness that had spoiled Bill's homecoming.

The cold cuts and potato salad she set in front of us were so good there wasn't any reason she should apologize for them. But although we each took a second helping to reassure her, she still kept talking about the hot lunch she should have fixed for us.

"It's not that I didn't want to take the trouble," she said. "Only it took me so much longer at the doctor's than I thought it would. I knew I shouldn't have taken the time to go. But your father made me, just because I had one of my spells during the night."

Bill looked scared to death as he put his knife and fork down on his plate. "You're not sick, are you, Mom?" he asked.

"You don't have to look so worried," she said. "It's just that my heart kind of acts up every now and then when I'm upset or worried about something. And there's all those stairs to climb every time I have to go out to the store or something. There seems to be more of them for every year that goes by. But then none of us gets any younger."

"You should take it easier," Bill said. "There's no need for you having to go up and down them so often. The kids can run your errands for you."

"When they're at school most of the day?" The edges began coming back into her voice again. "Besides, what do they know about picking out vegetables and meat? Getting things nice and fresh is the least I can do for my family. But I was saying to your father, I'd give anything if we could find a place on the street floor without any stairs to have to worry about. Only try to find a place these days! Houses are all there are. But I guess there's no use talking about that any more, is there?"

"Gosh, Mom, I don't know," Bill said. "I just don't see how we could pull it off. But it's not that I don't want to. You know that, don't you, Mom?"

She bit her lips and her hand went up to her eyes again. "Of course I do, son," she said. "But don't you start worrying about me. You've got yourself to think of, you and your wife. And I guess that's just the way of nature once a man gets married. His mother has to make way for his wife."

I didn't want to cry then, not with his mother's tears already making Bill so miserable. But I couldn't hold mine back, not entirely, as I turned to her. "It's not going to be like that, Mrs. Cooper," I protested. "As if I ever could take your place with Bill. That's one of the things that made me love him right from the start, the way he felt about you."

But I guess I shouldn't have tried to reassure her, for she pushed away my hand and rushed out of the room. And as Bill got up so quickly and went after her, there was only sudden resentment instead of pity in my heart.

I don't like her, I thought. *I don't like her at all!*

But the shame came even as I thought it. It was true what Bill's father had said the night before. It can't be an easy thing for a mother to turn her son over to another woman. *I'm not going to let myself be a jealous wife,* I told myself sternly. *Bill has enough to worry about without that.* But I couldn't fill the emptiness inside of me that came as I realized how different everything was from the way I had thought it was going to be. And I wasn't surprised when Bill told me that night that he had decided not to go to college after all.

I knew how much getting his engineering degree had meant to him, but I didn't try to argue with him. His decision had come too hard for him, without me reminding him of all that he was giving up. I couldn't add my own disappointment to his burden. All I could do was try to understand as he began making his new plans for the future.

"The only way to look at it is like this," he said. "We're young enough so we can afford to wait. In another two years, Pete will be through high school and can help out. Even if he has to go into the Army, there'll still be his allotment. And I'll only be twenty-five then, and in the meantime I'll be getting all that practical experience in the shop. I thought of taking night courses, but I decided I'd be losing more than I gained, that way it goes on for years. Figuring it out, it would be more sensible to work nights and make overtime pay."

I had to protest then. "But you can't work nights too, Bill," I said. "That's too much to take on. You've got to think of yourself."

"It won't be all the time," he said. "Maybe just one or two nights a week. All the time-and-a-half in the world wouldn't be enough to pay me to stay away from you every night in the week. And, Maggy, I'll see to it that we have good times together, just you and me. It's not all going to be just work and saving." He took me in his arms, and it was the way it had been the night before, with my love for him easing the sting of my disappointment.

Maybe that night seemed especially sweet because it was the last time Bill and I were alone like that with nobody else to matter. The next day, we moved in with the family, and I tried not to let Bill see how much I had come to dread the thought of living with his mother. Later on, I felt foolish for worrying, because it was almost the way I had pictured it—as if I was really being taken into the family. Mrs. Cooper even hugged me, as well as Bill, when he told her about his decision.

She cried again. But it was different this time. Her tears came with smiles, like an excited child overwhelmed by an unexpected surprise. For the first time, I could really understand the feeling Bill had for her even when she was in a temper, feeling the warm glow in my own heart that came from having a part in giving her so much happiness.

"I know just the place I want," she said, when she had calmed down enough to talk. "It's a new development I went out to see last week. All ranch houses and no stairs, with attics that can be fixed up when we can afford it. Now, Maggy, don't start taking your hat off. The minute I get dressed we're going to go out there so you can see for yourself."

We had almost as much fun as she did, just sharing her excitement. Even the people on the bus felt it, and kept smiling at her as if her happiness made them feel happy, too. The trip took almost an hour, and I could see by the anxious way Bill kept looking at his watch that he thought it would be a long time to spend going to work. But his face brightened as we got off the bus.

It was almost like the countryside, with all the houses standing in the middle of their own big stretches of lawn. It was Saturday, and Bill kept glancing at the men working in their gardens, squeezing my hand in excitement. One of the houses had a "For Sale" sign in front, but when Bill stopped to look at it, his mother tugged impatiently at his sleeve.

"These are just all the old places," she said.

I had wanted to go into the gray-shingled house, too, and when we turned a corner and saw the development a few blocks away, I felt a pang of disappointment. The houses were all pretty and new, but they were so crowded together they almost touched each other, and the fenced-in space in the back looked like only an excuse for a yard. But inside the model house, everything was new and fresh, and I could understand Mrs. Cooper's delight as she kept passing her hand over the gleaming stove.

I could understand her disappointment, too, when Bill didn't confirm with the agent. "Look, Mom, we'll have to figure it out a bit first," he said as we walked away. "They're asking for plenty, and you have to think of all the extras that go in a new house. Why don't we look at the other place first?"

There was a man raking leaves in front of the first house we wanted to look at, and he seemed more upset than pleased when we asked if we could go in to see the house. "Things are in something of a mess," he said. "My wife is away, and I'm not much good at keeping things straight."

That first time I saw the man, Fred Lewis, I thought he must have been in his forties, though I found out later that he was only thirty-two. His build had something to do with it, because even though he wasn't overweight, he was stocky. But most of all, it was the deep lines around his eyes and mouth that made him look older. His eyes had a faraway look in them that made it seem as though they were focused on something we couldn't see at all.

We went in through the back door, and though the dishes were all washed and stacked in the drainer, it had the uncared-for look a room gets when there isn't a woman around. It was the same in the rest of the house. The plants in the sunny bay window had that same neglected look, and some of them were already withered.

But the charm of the place was there anyway. The comfortable chairs were so pretty in their new slipcovers, and the dark wood of the tables still gleamed under the film of dust. The shelves built around a window overlooking the garden were filled with books, with china ornaments grouped between them. As I went over to look at a painting of a silly-looking calico cat playing with a kitten, Fred pushed it farther back on the shelf.

"This doesn't go with the rest of the things," he said. "It's something my wife has had since childhood. I just thought I'd tell you since you seemed interested in it."

"You mean the house is for sale furnished?" Bill said, and the way he looked around with new interest showed that he had felt its charm, too. He asked the price, and even with the furniture included, it was far less than the other house had been.

His mother had gone into the kitchen again, but she came out as Bill was asking about taxes. She must have seen how interested he was, too, because she plucked anxiously at his sleeve.

"We'd better get going," she said. "I completely forgot we're having stew for dinner, and I have to get it started."

"How about putting a deposit down?" Bill said, and my heart sank as his mother pursed her lips. I would have felt at home if we were moving in that very minute, but even before she spoke, I knew it was going to be the other house we were going to live in.

"Bad enough a secondhand house with secondhand furniture, too," she said. "It's not that there's anything wrong with them," she went on quickly, as if to make up for the criticism. "It's just that I like my own things, instead of having something another woman has picked out."

"I can see how you feel," Fred said. "Peg—my wife—has always felt like that, too. Everything we have, she always had such fun deciding on it. That picture over the mantel—it took her weeks to make up her mind between it and a flower print."

"It's lovely," I said. "Everything is so lovely, I don't see how she can bear parting with any of them."

Bill's mother nodded. "Maybe I've done you a favor," she said, "and you don't know it yet. Maybe when your wife comes back—"

"She won't be back," he said. His voice sounded so cold it stunned me. But then I saw his eyes, and in just that instant his guard was down and the anguish was there. "She's incurably ill—in the hospital."

There wasn't anything to say after that. But as we walked toward the bus stop, Bill took my hand and held on to it hard. "The poor devil," he said. "You hear something like that, and you wonder if you have any right to your own luck."

"I know, Bill," I said. "It made me frightened, too."

"Still it happens to all of us," Mrs. Cooper added. "And at least he can comfort himself that he didn't deny her what every woman wants most, a house of her own. Son, I was just thinking, with all that crowd looking and all, don't you think we should go back and put down that deposit on the ranch house? I got it right here with me, and there isn't any other house that would suit me so well. I'd never get over it if we waited so long that all the houses were gone. And you heard what the agent said. You'll still get the money back if you decide against it."

"You really want it bad, don't you, Mom?" Bill said. "It's just that one house and no other will do—"

"It's not only what I want," she said. "That other house—there's stairs there, too. And no bathroom downstairs, so I'd be running up and down just the same as I do now. And the doctor says I shouldn't have to be climbing stairs all the time."

"Well, I guess that settles it," Bill said. "And I suppose all those new houses cost about the same. Are you sure it's really the one you want, Mom?" And as she nodded, with that little-girl look of excitement in her eyes again, I knew there wasn't going to be any more discussion about it. It had all been decided for Bill before he even came home from the service.

Bill and I didn't talk about our own disappointment in not buying the other house, but I knew he felt it as deeply as I did. Even after we moved into the new house, he'd look at the gray-shingled one longingly as we passed it. Then one Saturday afternoon, we saw a big black hearse in front of the driveway and a sad little group of people getting out. We hurried past, because we knew what had happened, even before we saw the mourning band around Fred's sleeve.

Again, Bill took my hand in that quiet, almost frightened, way. But we didn't talk about that, either. Ever since we had both started working, we had so little time to be together that we couldn't bear to let anything intrude on those brief hours together. We were like ostriches hiding our heads in the sand, trying to hide our worries from each other.

It wasn't only the mortgage we had to think of. There was the secondhand car Bill had to buy on time, and a week wouldn't go by that we didn't have to meet some installment payment for all the things Mrs. Cooper felt she needed for the new house. Some of them were bought without even consulting us beforehand, and the rest were wrung out of Bill with her tears. But living with her had become easier. She didn't seem to resent me so much now that she was having her own way with everything. But I couldn't find it in my heart to forgive her for what she was doing to Bill.

I knew it was the bills that kept him awake at night, just as they were responsible for all the weight he was losing. It frightened me even more than the way he had begun to perspire nights, his pillow so soaking wet in the morning it would still be damp the next night. That's why, when he told me he was taking on even more night work than he had been doing, I couldn't keep still any longer.

"You can't, Bill," I protested. "You're doing far too much already. And for what? We didn't need that new furniture for the living room, or the television set or the deep freezer or most of those other things your mother has been getting. And so what if we can't pay and they cart them all away? It would be better than you worrying and working yourself sick like this. Can't you see that, Bill? Don't you realize how unfair it is to me?"

He didn't understand what I really meant—that it was his health I was talking about, nothing else. He was sitting on the edge of the bed taking his shoes off, and for a minute he didn't answer me. He just sat there, staring down at his feet. Then, he looked up and I felt even more frightened than I had before, seeing the hopelessness in his eyes.

"I know, Maggy," he said. "Don't think it doesn't upset me, too, you using every penny you make paying for all the things I should be able to give you and my family. Oh, Maggy, if you only knew what it does to me seeing you still wearing the clothes you had when we got married. Never getting anything new for yourself. Never—"

But I wouldn't let him go on. I ran over to him, hugging his arm as I sat beside him. "That doesn't matter!" I cried. "As if I want anything else but what I have. You and being with you and you loving me. That's what I meant, Bill. That you have to take care of yourself for me, because you're all I've got and I wouldn't want to go on living if anything happened to you."

He didn't take me in his arms as he had in the beginning, holding me, loving me. It was as if his fatigue had wiped out the hungry thing our love had been. He held his cheek against mine and his hand kept smoothing back my hair, but it was more like the caress a man would give his sister than his wife. We had been married less than a year and it was already gone, that quickening longing that had once been like a fever in his blood.

"I did everything wrong, Maggy," he whispered. "I shouldn't have told you how I felt until I was really able to take care of you. We should have waited. . . ."

If I had thought about it, I would have kept back the bitterness I was feeling. But the words exploded out of my own hopelessness. "If we had waited, we wouldn't ever have been married. Your mother would have taken care of that."

He pulled himself away from me. "So that's how you really feel, Maggy," he said. "Just like Mom's been telling me, you don't like her. I thought she was just imagining things, but now I see she was right all along. But I guess it'd be too much to ask, having it different. Mom says all wives are jealous of their mothers-in-law."

The bitterness inside me really began pouring out then. "Mom says!" I cried. "Everything is what Mom says! Can't you think for yourself, Bill? Can't you see with your own eyes what she's doing to you? Smothering you so you can't even call your heart your own, much less the good sense you were born with. If you would just try to think for yourself for once, just once, you'd see how selfish and possessive she is. She doesn't love you, not the way I think love should be. She just owns you."

His face was white then. Only his brown eyes looked alive. "Shut up!" he shouted. "Don't you dare say things like that about my mother!"

Then, just as quickly, the fury was gone and his eyes looked as dead as the rest of his face. "Now that I know how you really feel, how can we go on, Maggy?" he said. "It was bad enough before, having to use your money to help keep things going. How can I do it now, knowing how you hate her? Maggy, I'm not mad any more. You've got to believe that. I'm just thinking, like you said I should. Maybe we should call it quits before we lose everything we've had, not just a part of it. If we go on like this, we'd get to the point where we'd hate each other. And I couldn't take that, Maggy. Hard as it would be, I'd rather lose you than hate you."

No other fear had been like this, so that there was nothing left inside me but that suffocating terror. "You don't mean that, Bill," I gasped. "Tell me you don't mean it." I flung my arms around him as though I was holding him to me with sheer force. And then as his arms went around me in that same urgent way, I felt his heart pounding against mine and I knew he was frightened, too.

I don't know how long we sat there on the bed, clinging to each other, our bodies seeking the reassurance that neither of us could find the words to give. Then, it was as if the violence of our fear had shocked us out of the worried numbness that had stifled us before. As if in having felt that terror of losing each other, we had found the vital forces of our love again. It was so long since Bill had held me in that eager, wanting way. It was so long since we had slept the whole night through locked in each other's arms.

The next morning, I woke feeling I could face anything with Bill so close to me again. He had to leave for work so much earlier than I did that usually, I was still asleep when he left. But that morning, his kiss woke me, and he held me with the same passion he had the night before.

"Whatever happens, we'll never fly at each other the way we did last night, will we, Maggy?" he said. "No matter how worried we get, we'll never take it out on each other again, will we?" And then, as I promised, his arms tightened around me. "Things will be easier now. There'll be something extra coming in. You just wait and see, Maggy."

It really seemed, at first, as if he was right. In the next weeks, we were even able to put a little money in the savings account we opened so proudly in the local bank. But as it turned out, I was the one who had been right. The extra work had been too much for Bill to take on. One night when he came home and almost threw himself down on the bed beside me, his body felt as if it was burning up with fever, and the next moment he was shaking with a chill. By the time the doctor got there, he was delirious.

The doctor said it was pneumonia, the kind the miracle drugs can't help. He refused to give us any false hope, as he called it, and his bluntness left me in a despair so deep I felt I would never be able to fight my way out of it. But after the first shock was over, Bill's mother seemed to have gained a strength I had never seen in her before.

"There's no need getting a nurse," she insisted as I started for the phone to call the agency the doctor had suggested. "What stranger could do for him like his own mother?" And as she began carrying out the doctor's orders, I felt ashamed of my own weakness, seeing her calm competence. She even found time to comfort me, putting her hand awkwardly on my shoulder.

"He's not going to die," she told me. "I won't let him. Now you stop worrying yourself and go to the store. There's nothing you can do here, and work will help take your mind off what's happened."

She was right in a way, for going through the motions at work did help a little. Only as the days dragged on and Bill still lay there in that drugged stupor, his glazed eyes not recognizing any of us, it got harder and harder to leave him. But I had to go. The money I was making was more important than ever now. It was the only thing I could do for Bill, with his mother taking care of all his other needs.

But the worst day of all was that Friday when the doctor said we could expect the crisis. I was so tense that morning that I was sick in the bathroom twice before I had to leave. My heart felt as if it was being torn into pieces as I stood in the door of our room just looking at him, not saying anything because he couldn't hear me even if I did. Even my heart wasn't talking to him, but just to God. I kept praying all day long. All the time I was going in on the bus, all the time I was selling hats, all the way home again on the bus, I was praying—and wondering, as I prayed, if it wasn't already too late for even God to hear.

I ran the whole way home from the bus. As I got near the house, my heart gave an awful lurch as I saw the boys weren't in the back playing handball, as they had kept on doing even while Bill was so sick. I couldn't even pray any more then. And when I reached the house, I couldn't move. I was so afraid I couldn't force myself to open the door.

Then I heard someone laughing, and I tore the door open so fast I almost fell. Bill's father and the boys grinned as I came into the kitchen, and Jack made an okay sign with his fingers. But I couldn't really believe the danger was over until I saw Bill propped up against the pillows, drinking the broth his mother was feeding him. I was so overcome with relief I couldn't even hold it against his mother that she hadn't called to tell me the crisis was past.

Bill pushed the spoon away when he saw me and held his arms out. That was the last thing I remember until I found myself lying on the floor, with Bill's mother bending over me, and Bill saying my name over and over again.

"I'm all right, Bill," I said. I tried to laugh, but I started to cry instead. "It's just the good news was too much to believe. It was the shock, I guess. That's all."

"Shock nothing!" His mother laughed. "I've been seeing signs for a couple of weeks, only I wasn't sure until this morning when you were sick. And now fainting like this, I don't need any doctor to tell me what's happening. You're going to have a baby, that's all that's the matter with you."

I wasn't so dazed that I didn't realize what it would mean. "Oh, no," I protested. "I can't be. Not yet." And I could see Bill was feeling the same way I was, not daring to be happy, only worried about all the extra expense it would mean.

But his mother didn't seem worried. "What do you mean, not yet?" she demanded. "And here you've been married almost a year. If you were a born mother like me, you'd be singing for joy instead of looking as if the roof had fallen in on you. The happiest times of my life were when I was holding a baby in my arms, and now soon I'll be having another one to hold and love. A grandchild all my own."

I was too worried then to realize Bill's mother was taking possession of my baby, even before it was born. Then afterward, when she seemed to accept me as one of the family at last, I was too grateful to her to look beyond her kindness. She fussed over me continuously, seeing to it that I had all the food the doctor had prescribed. I wasn't allowed to do anything around the house when I came home from work, and she insisted I stay in bed late weekend mornings, bringing my breakfast in on a tray.

It could have been such a happy time if I weren't so concerned about Bill. He was driving himself so hard, though the doctor had told him he had to take it easy. And even during the summer he didn't lose the hacking cough that had persisted after his illness.

Then, for a little time I couldn't even worry about Bill any more. It began that night I first felt the fluttering movement in me, and suddenly the baby became a living thing to me and not just that worrying responsibility it had been before. I lay there, caught in the miracle of this new love, so different from the love I felt for Bill. And as the fluttering came again, with it came the tenderness for that small unborn child that made it so wholly mine I couldn't share my joy even with Bill, not then in the very beginning.

The tenderness grew and grew until it matured into the rapture that came as I held my daughter for the first time. She wasn't beautiful, not then. Her little face was scrawny and red and wrinkled, but her eyes were blue and her hair was red and had a wave in it like Bill's, and her tiny hands and feet were so beautiful in their perfection that I cried like a fool as I held them to my lips.

Then Bill came in, and it was my first feeling of being a part of my own family, the three of us there together. Bill's eyes were wet, too, as he stared down at her, taking her tiny hand in his.

"Look at her fingernails," he said in an awed whisper. Then he laughed as if to cover up his sentimentality. "What do you know—she's been to the beauty parlor already, getting herself a manicure and wave!" But he was too shaken to hold that lightness long. "Wait till Mom sees her. She's carrying on like a crazy woman in the reception room. You'd think no baby's ever been born before. Maggy, what do you think about naming the baby Clara, after Mom? It would make her so happy."

He must have forgotten that long ago, just after we knew the baby was coming, I had told him Joan was my favorite name and if it turned out to be a girl, that was what I wanted to call her. But as he looked at me so pleadingly, I knew it wasn't that. It was his mother taking over again, crowding even into this special thing we were feeling for our little daughter, staking her claim to her before we had a chance to know she was ours.

But I couldn't deny that pleading in his eyes. I couldn't hold on to the resentment either. "All right, Bill, if that's what you want," I said.

"It's not what I want. Not especially," he said. "It's just that Mom was telling me how she had always planned to name her first girl, if she ever had one, after herself. It was her mother's name, too, and she told me how sad it made her to know that after she was gone there wouldn't be another Clara in the family. But if you've set your heart on calling her Joan—"

With his voice faltering and his eyes looking so miserable, I couldn't hold out against him. Maybe I was getting like the rest of the family, giving in to anything Mom wanted because it was so much easier living with her when she was happy.

That was why I tried not to resent it too much when Bill's mother took complete charge of little Clara when I came home from the hospital. She was the one who had all the fun of bathing her and dressing her, of wheeling her up and down the street and even putting her to bed at night. In the beginning I tried to assert myself, but it always meant either tears or angry, shouted words, making everybody unhappy because of her moods. The baby had become her life, crowding even Bill and his brothers out of her affections.

And she was spoiling her so dreadfully, giving in to her slightest whim, that in just a few months, Clara turned from a smiling angel into a little brat who cried constantly unless she was in her grandmother's arms. I made an even bigger effort to assert myself then, but it wasn't any use. I even tried to coax her, despising myself as I did so, telling her she was wearing herself out by doing so much for the baby. But that didn't help, either.

It was hard enough having to argue with her, but Mr. Cooper always chimed in with her when he was home. "Just leave it to Ma, Maggy," he said. "She always had a special way with babies. A born mother, if there ever was one."

I couldn't understand the way he was always taking her side in anything that ever came up, because she had never lavished her affections on him. Almost from the beginning, I had known he was just another outsider, the way I was. He might as well not have been there at all.

She smiled at him as she stuck the pacifier into the sugar bowl and then popped it into the baby's mouth. "Pa knows, all right, no one better than him, all the sacrifices I made for my children," she said. "And I know it upsets you with all I got to do for the baby, but it's my life doing it. I was always a homebody type, never worked outside my own home a day in my life. So it's different with me than a business girl like you. I never can understand what girls like you find in working outside the home. Sometimes I wonder if you wouldn't be happier if you went back to the store, for goodness knows you just seem so lost hanging around the house all day."

A little chill went through me at her words. I had lived with her long enough to know the suggestion for what it was—the beginning of a campaign to get me out of the house so that Clara would be completely hers. I had thought about going back to work myself, because I knew it would help relieve Bill's burden if I was bringing some money into the house again. But I always shrank from it, unable to face the thought of having to be away from my baby.

"I'd rather be with Clara," I said. "Certainly nothing means more to me than being with my baby. And just because I've worked since I was married doesn't mean I wouldn't rather have been home. It wasn't fun I was working for. It was because we needed money." And then as she bridled, I tried to appease her. "Besides, taking care of the baby is too much for you. You'll just make yourself sick."

Her laugh came at that. "Me? Sick? I've never had a doctor in my life. Even when I was having my babies, a midwife was good enough for me." And then, as I stared at her, her mouth fell and her face reddened. "Except for that time about my heart," she went on, so glibly that I wondered why I had never realized before that along with everything else, she was a liar, too. "I completely forgot about that, because I haven't had any trouble with it since I haven't had any stairs to bother me." *What a lie!*

It had been bad enough before, with Bill wearing himself out with all the responsibility of the house. For then, at least, there had seemed a reason for it, and no matter how much I had resented her extravagances, I had thought the house itself was necessary for her health. But now, all the resentment I had managed to repress before swept into my consciousness.

"How could you lie like that?" I cried. "And for what? A house? How could you put it before Bill's future? Before his health even?"

She got up from her chair so fast I thought she was going to drop the baby. I ran over to take her, but she slapped my hand away.

"Don't you dare talk to me like that!" she screamed. "You do it again, and I'll really open Bill's eyes to the kind of girl he married. You and your sweet talks when he's around, talking like butter wouldn't melt in your mouth, and when he's away, you show what you really are. But what could that poor boy be expected to know of a girl he only knew two weeks before you got him to marry you? But I'll open his eyes when I tell him what you said. And Pa here is a witness to it."

"And how do you think Bill will feel, knowing how you lied to him about your heart?" I said, and I couldn't lower my voice, even when little Clara began to cry.

"Now, now," Mr. Cooper said. "There's no reason for you flying off the handle like that. Ma didn't lie. It don't take a doctor to tell Ma her heart gave her trouble climbing stairs. Besides, you should be grateful to her, taking your baby off your hands like this, giving up her life to it like she gave it up to her sons."

"Grateful!" Mrs. Cooper sniffed. "There's many a young girl would get down on her knees to a mother-in-law who works her fingers to the bone making life easy for her. But she's not one of them. What other wife doesn't have to fret about her baby, or lift a finger around the house, or cook her husband's meals for him? But then I guess it's true what they say. The more you do for some people, the less they appreciate it. And I guess there isn't a house been built yet that's big enough for two women."

There was open warfare between us after that. Even though it was waged in silence, with neither one of us putting it into words again, it was there like a poison gas seeping through the house. I hadn't told Bill about the argument because I didn't want to pass on the bitterness of my own knowledge to him. He was caught in a trap that was hopeless enough as it was, without the realization that it was his mother's lies that had snared him into it. But I didn't have to tell him something was wrong. I could see he sensed it more and more as the days went on.

When he finally questioned me, I tried to convince him nothing was really wrong. "There's always bound to be a little friction with two women around each other all the time," I said. And then as he just nodded, his shoulders sagging even more than usual, I suddenly found the courage to make the decision I knew would be the only solution to the situation.

"I've been thinking I should go back to work, Bill," I said. "There isn't anything for me to do here, not even for the baby. So there's no reason I shouldn't be helping out in the only way I can."

"It'll be a help. No doubt about it," Bill said. "Only this time I'm going to set a limit to it. Your helping that way, I mean. I got all the credit books out the other night when I came home from work. The rest of you were sleeping, and so there wasn't anything to distract me. It comes out like this. All those loans were for two and a half years, and that means they'll all be paid by next June at the latest. Pete will be graduating then, and there'll be his help to count on, too. I could hardly believe it, seeing daylight again."

His drawn face looked boyishly handsome again, grinning like that. I felt as if a weight had lifted from my own shoulders, too, looking at the debt-free days ahead. Of course, there were still the mortgage payments to be met, but Pete would be helping with them. I felt as I did the day we decided to get married, with the sun coming out and everything so full of hope.

"Maybe you can even go to college," I said. "Maybe—"

His grin widened. "Hey, don't go so fast, Maggy," he said. "Give me a chance to draw a free breath first. But that will be coming, too. And someday, who knows, maybe we can get a little place of our own."

It wasn't even so bad leaving the baby as I thought it would be, now that there was such a real incentive for my going back to work. All the way to the bus that first day, I kept planning for the future, making up my mind that once the monthly payments were finished, I'd bank my salary for the time Bill and the baby and I could be on our own. Even if we only had one room, it would be like heaven.

I was so full of my dreaming I didn't notice there was no one else waiting at the bus stop but me. The bus seemed a little late in coming, but I didn't think much of that either until a car pulled up beside me.

"Didn't you hear about the strike on the radio?" a man's voice called out. And as I looked over, I saw it was Fred Lewis. He looked younger than he had the first time I'd seen him. The deep lines were gone from his face, and though it was late fall, he was still tanned. But that wasn't surprising, because there was hardly a time during the weekends when I happened to pass his house that I didn't see him working in the garden.

"I'm going to Newark," he said. "I'll be glad to drop you off any place you're going."

"That's where I'm going, too," I said. "And it would mean so much getting there, my first day back at my job."

"I'm doubly glad I caught up with you then," he said. After I slid into the passenger seat of his car, he told me, "I'm glad to have company for a change. I get tired of talking to myself. Your name is really Margaret, isn't it? I remember your husband calling you Maggy that day you stopped to see the house. It made an impression on me because that was my wife's name, too, though everybody called her Peg. I thought—well it was sort of a comfort thinking another Margaret might be living in her house, and you seemed to love it, too."

"Oh, I did," I said. "So did Bill. But it was really because of his mother we were buying a house—"

I floundered, not knowing what to say. But I didn't have to be embarrassed with Fred. He was one of those people who always seem to sense others' discomfort and have a way of putting them at ease again.

"I know," he smiled. "And I'm very grateful to her. That day you stopped in, I had hit rockbottom, both mentally and financially. Our savings were gone, and I'd decided the only thing to do was to sell the house. Particularly because it was a reminder of everything I was losing.

"But as I discovered, you can't trust your emotions at a time like that. After it was over, I was glad I'd borrowed instead of giving up the house. It turned out to be the only thing that helped at all, living there with all those memories of her to help me cope. So you can see why I'm grateful to your mother-in-law and to all those other people who preferred the new houses in the development."

"In that case, I'm glad we didn't get it," I said. "Even though I practically turn green with envy every time I pass your garden. Those chrysanthemums you had last month—I never saw more beautiful ones."

It was so easy getting to know Fred. He made me feel that I was doing him a favor when he suggested driving me back home after work.

He talked about Peg when he parked outside the house that evening. "I like talking to you," he said. "You don't get embarrassed when I talk about Peg. Most people do, even our friends. It gives me such a lonely feeling, not being able to mention her name."

He insisted on taking me to the door. "Peg always had someone for dinner Saturday nights," he said. "That's one of the things I've been missing. I was thinking it would be nice if you and Bill came over next Saturday, if you haven't other plans. I don't pretend to be the cook she was, but I've been told I have a way with a steak and French fries."

"That would be fun," I said. Then, I stiffened as the door of the house suddenly opened and Bill's mother stood there.

"Your dinner's getting cold," she said. "I thought I'd better tell you, unless you'd rather sit out there gabbing with your friend."

I couldn't have felt any more embarrassed than Fred looked, because it wasn't only what she said, but it was the way she stared at us as though we had been caught doing something shameful. I knew what she was thinking and how her mind worked once she got one of her impossible ideas. Suddenly, the prospect of going over to Fred's wasn't fun any more, knowing what she would make of it. She would spoil it not only for me but for Bill too, planting doubts in his mind that he would never have thought of by himself.

The door slammed behind her, and I tried to keep my voice steady as I turned to Fred. "We haven't any plans," I said. "But Bill has to work overtime so often. Let's leave it this way. I'll call you if we can make it."

"That'll be fine," he said. "I'll understand if I don't hear."

Neither of us could meet the other's eyes as we said good-bye, and I had to brace myself as I went into the house. As soon as I was inside, I knew the storm had already broken, because Pete and Jack were bolting down their dinner so they could make a quick escape.

I didn't have to wait for the coming tirade. "It's that widower, isn't it?" she demanded. "They're all alike, them and their sorrow! A decent wife gives the best years of her life to a man and what happens? He can't wait to bury her before he's after someone to take her place. Only most of them don't go so far as to chase another man's wife. But then I guess men can tell if a woman's easy. It's second nature to that kind of man to know a two-timer when he sees one."

It was all so illogical and unfair, and I couldn't defend myself without making her insinuations seem at least partly true. "He offered to take me home because of the strike," I said. "I wouldn't have been able to get to work this morning if he hadn't happened to come along while I was waiting for the bus."

She could twist anything to her own purpose. "So you didn't see enough of him this morning, you had to be with him tonight, too. And you sure took your time getting here. Almost an hour late! And even after that, you couldn't bear to leave him. Sitting in the car with him like that for all the neighbors to see."

I didn't want to fight with her. "It was the traffic," I said. "Everybody with cars drove to work this morning because of the strike."

"You don't have to explain," she said. "I'm not stupid. Naturally if they drove to work, they had to drive home, too. But what's that got to do with you? You didn't have a car to worry about. But then I suppose he was being so charming you wouldn't pass up the chance of being with him again, would you?"

"I had to get home," I said, and then my resentment of her unfairness made my own fury rise to meet hers. "I couldn't win anyway, even if I'd stayed in town and waited for Bill to get through his night shift so I could drive home with him. With the way your mind works, you'd have had me picking up someone on the street."

She laughed triumphantly. "I've got news for you! You wouldn't have had to wait for Bill. You could have come home on the bus, just as always. The strike was over at a quarter to six. It was on the radio. That's one thing you didn't think of, Miss Smarty Pants, isn't it? That I'd know it was over. Maybe you'll know better than to try to pull the wool over my eyes another time."

It wouldn't have done any good to tell her we were already on our way home by then. That even if we had known, there wasn't anything wrong in driving home together as we had. I was so sickened I couldn't eat any dinner, and though I knew it was only adding to her fury, I pushed my plate away and left the table. The baby was asleep in her crib when I went into the bedroom, but for once I woke her up and cradled her my arms, feeling some of the tension leaving as she cooed happily in my arms.

I didn't tell Bill what had happened, except that Fred had taken me to work and back again. I didn't even mention the invitation to dinner. Even though I knew that Bill would have liked to break the dreary routine of our days as much as I would, I knew that if we went, it would have only meant more unpleasantness.

I began living in the future, as if the present didn't even exist. I realize now how wrong it was, throwing away any part of life like that. Because no matter how bad things are, they're real, and there's always something that's good mixed in with the bad that you can hold on to. Like having Bill come home to me nights, and waiting up to have coffee with him. And enjoying the baby when she was so little and helpless. I had my husband and my daughter. But I was wishing them away, too, along with the bad. I was so impatient for those six months to hurry them off the calendar. It was only after they were gone that I realized how good they had been. Even the bad didn't seem so terrible when everything that came later was so much worse.

It happened so suddenly. That night, I heard Bill groaning and woke up to see his whole pillow covered with blood. His eyes looked so frightened, but he tried to smile. "Don't look so scared, Maggy," he said. "It's happened before, twice. And I always was all right afterward. It's nothing to worry about."

"And you didn't even see a doctor?" I demanded. "Oh, Bill—"

"He'd only have made me give up the night job," Bill said. "And how could I when—" He stopped, and there was only his frantic eyes pleading with me as the blood started oozing out of his mouth again.

I called the doctor, and he came right away. After he'd examined Bill, he beckoned me into the kitchen. Bill's mother had awakened, and as usual, she was so strong and confident in a crisis that some of my fear had gone. Only it all came back when I talked to the doctor.

"Of course there'll be tests," he said. "But I don't need them to be sure that the boy has advanced T.B. Now, please, Mrs. Cooper, don't look at me as if I'm signing his death certificate. So much can be done nowadays. And he's a veteran, isn't he? That means the best care in the best hospitals. But what's going to help him most is your hope and courage."

I kept thinking of that, the hope and courage, in those days before Bill was finally admitted to the hospital. I'd stand outside his door, forcing my mouth up into a smile, and I'd laugh when all I wanted to do was cry. I even lied to Bill, telling him the store had advanced the money for the last payments on what we owed, though they had turned me down flat when I asked them.

But I had locked my emotions in too hard. That was why I broke down that day after he had left for the hospital. I couldn't even wait until I could go into my own room and lock the door. I just sat there in the kitchen pounding my fists against the table until they bled.

"Now, now, there's no need carrying on like that," Mrs. Cooper said. "You've got to pull yourself together."

She wasn't being hard then, just matter-of-fact. And maybe she felt that sympathy wouldn't help me. But I know it would have helped, for when she left the room and her husband came over to me and awkwardly patting my head, I immediately felt better. "You just go on crying all you want," he said. "Get it all out of your system, Maggy." And it did help. As he sat there beside me, the wild resentment began going, and it was easier to take the sorrow without having to swallow the bitterness, too.

My only worry was for Bill then. I couldn't even think about all those debts at first. If the hospital had been near enough so I could see him, it would have been easier. But it was way up in New York, near the Canadian border. It cost so much to get there that Bill might as well have been in Europe.

But before another month had gone by, I had to think about the bills. Pete would be graduating in another month, and he had taken a job in the supermarket on afternoons and Saturdays, but the money he made didn't stretch very far. Every night when I came home, Mrs. Cooper had a new tale of woe about the collectors who had come around. And one Saturday morning, there was a notice from the bank that if they didn't receive two payments immediately, our mortgage would be in arrears. I was so worried I hurried right over to the village.

If I had stopped to think, I would have known the bank was closed on Saturdays. I felt as if I had come to the end of my endurance as I stood there, staring at the locked door. I had to fight to hold the tears back as I started toward home again.

It was one of those beautiful days in early May. I could smell the lilacs as I passed all the gardens. But I could only smell them. I couldn't see them through my tears. Then suddenly, I felt someone taking my arm, and as I turned, I saw it was Fred.

"You—you're crying, Maggy," he said. "What's the matter? Anything I can do?"

I couldn't answer. His kindness released the wild crying inside of me that I had managed to hold back before. His arm tightened on mine as he turned me around and led me back to his house. We went in through the gate and sat down on some lawn chairs that were in the front yard.

"Now then, tell me what's wrong," he said. And the way he said it, so interested and yet so forceful, too, I couldn't have held my worry back even if I had wanted to. And I didn't. It was like finding someone—a friend, a brother, a father—who I could lean on.

"I know what it's like," he said finally. "There's nothing as important as money when you really need it. And yet it doesn't mean a thing when you don't. That's the way it's been with me lately. I thought it couldn't buy a thing I really wanted until now, when it can give you a little peace of mind. Please let me help you, Maggy. It would mean a lot to me."

Even if I hadn't been so tired, I don't think I could have held out against his insistence on helping me. He was firm as he insisted I tell him everything I owed, and he was so businesslike as he jotted all the items down on the back of an envelope.

"Two thousand should just about cover it," he said then. "But I think we should make it three for emergencies. I'll go in the house and make out a check. And no back talk now. We'll figure out a way you can pay it back when Pete gets a job."

My heart was so filled with relief and gratitude, I couldn't wait to get back to the house to tell the others so their tension would be lifted too.

I thought maybe I had been foolish for telling them where I got the money from when I saw Mrs. Cooper looking at me in that speculative way. But she didn't say anything and she began bustling around, almost cheerful again, as she started fixing lunch.

It was the turning point, with everything beginning to look hopeful again. In another few months when Pete had a full-time job at the market, I was able to start paying Fred back, little by little. One wonderful weekend, I was even able to see Bill again. And best of all, he was beginning to get better. The doctor told me he thought Bill might be able to leave the hospital in another six months, provided he worked only a few hours a day when he came back home.

My heart was bursting with happiness that whole weekend. I was able to make plans again, tangible plans. When I talked to the hospital supervisor, he said there were always jobs available at the hospital, and though I wouldn't make as much as I did in the store, it would be enough to live on. Bill and I would be together, and I would have my baby again.

I was so happy I had to call Bill's mother right from the station and tell her when I got into New York on Sunday night. Then, when I was walking home from the bus, I saw the light in Fred's living room and suddenly, I felt I had to tell him the good news, too. I was so full of my happiness that I had to talk about it to anyone who would listen.

Fred was so interested, just as I knew he would be. "Come in," he said, after I had blurted out the part about Bill being so much better. "This calls for a drink to celebrate."

I had intended to hurry on home to give the family all the details, but I couldn't stop talking about it with Fred once I had begun. I talked so much I felt I had to apologize when I was finally leaving. But Fred just laughed.

"Apologize? For what?" He grinned. "If you knew what it meant to me, seeing a woman in the house again. You've made me feel alive again, made me realize that someday I might even be able to care for some other woman enough to share my life with her. I wasn't cut out to be a bachelor, Maggy. . . ."

It was later than I thought, and our house was dark when I got there. But as I was fumbling for my key, the door was thrown open and Mrs. Cooper stood there.

"I'm sorry," I said. "I stopped at Fred's to tell him about Bill and—"

"That's a laugh," she said. "You're so happy about your husband, you've got to fly into another man's arms to tell him about it. You had liquor, too. I smell it on you."

"One drink," I said. And suddenly, I couldn't stand arguing with Bill's mother when we should both have been so happy. "Please," I said. "Don't spoil it. Would I have told you about Fred if I had anything to hide?"

"You told me about the money he gave you, too," she said. "That's when I knew you didn't have any real decency, bragging about a man giving you money."

There wasn't any use talking any more. She was still muttering when I went into my room, and the next morning, she made a point of not talking to me as I had breakfast. But that evening, she was all smiles again when I came home. "Guess what?" she demanded. "The baby said her first word today. She said Mama." She picked the baby out of her high chair and hugged her. "Say it again, baby. Say Mama."

It was such a thrilling, wonderful feeling, hearing the word that linked her with me so intimately.

"Say it again, baby," I whispered. But when she did, all the warm, happy feeling was gone. Because as she said it, she threw her arms around her grandmother, and I knew who the "mama" had been for.

"See!" Mrs. Cooper laughed. "She knows who loves her, who her real mother is. And you scheming to take her away from me," she added indignantly. "Not only her, but my son, too. Well, we'll see about that."

I didn't realize it was really a threat. But even though I didn't understand the fullness of her cruelty, I was frightened enough to tell Fred about it the next time I saw him.

Every once in a while, he came home on the same bus I did, and it always made the trip seem shorter and less monotonous when I could talk to him. But that evening, he wasn't as comforting as usual.

"It doesn't sound good to me," he said. "Maggy, I hate to say this, but I feel we shouldn't have anything to do with each other anymore."

My heart sank even deeper than before. Not to see Fred or talk to him, when he was the only one I could confide in? "I wouldn't be able to take it," I said. "I feel alone enough as things are."

"I feel the same way," he agreed. Then his face brightened. "Maybe we could see each other in town for lunch once in a while. But I'll make sure I don't even ride home on the bus with you again."

Everything seemed the same as usual when I came home one night, after the third lunch with Fred. Mrs. Cooper was at the stove, and she didn't turn around. But that happened so often, and I didn't think anything of it, especially when her husband gave me his usual greeting.

It was only when I went into the bedroom and saw my suitcase standing on the floor that I felt the first premonition. I ran to the closet and opened the door, and all my clothes were gone. Then I saw that all the rest of my personal things were gone, too, and that even the baby's crib had been moved out of the room.

I ran back into the kitchen. "Why did you pack up all my things?" I demanded.

"I just thought I'd save you the trouble," she said, looking triumphant. "I rented your room today."

She went on talking, but I didn't hear what she was saying. "Where am I supposed to sleep?" I exploded, and I could see by her husband's startled glance that he hadn't known anything about it, either.

"I'm sure I don't know," she said. "And I don't care, either. Just as long as it isn't in this house. You think you're so smart, but I know all about you, sneaking around and seeing that man in the city. I was on to you all right. And when I hired a detective, he just found out what I already knew."

"There wasn't anything wrong," I said. "Even you should know that. But you're doing me a favor, if you only knew it. Now I can take the baby and go to Bill, without having to wait any longer. It was only because I thought you needed the money that I didn't do it long ago."

"I never wanted your charity," she sneered. "And now I don't need to take it any more. But you're not taking the baby. And you're not going to Bill. Not when I tell him all I know. You think he's the kind who will stand for such disgraceful happenings? Not my Bill, he won't."

"You can't upset Bill with your lies!" I cried. "Don't you see what it will do to him? He might have a relapse. Don't you realize that?"

"It's up to you to decide if I tell him or not." She looked at me shrewdly. "You just leave quietly, and I won't breathe a word of it. And the baby stays here, until Bill is out of the hospital and can see to it himself that you lead a decent life. If you try to take her now, I'll go up to Bill tomorrow. So you take your choice, and if anything happens to Bill, it'll be on your conscience. Not mine."

She turned on her husband as he started to say something. "You stay out of this, do you hear?" she shrieked. "I know what's best for my own grandchild."

There wasn't any choice after that. I couldn't risk upsetting Bill, now that he was really on his way to recovery. *And besides,* I told myself, *it would only be a few more months before he'd be out of the hospital and I'd be with him again, him and the baby.* But even knowing my mother-in-law inside and out, I could still wonder at her cruelty when she wouldn't even let me kiss the baby good-bye.

I found a room that night in the nearby town. It would have been easier and cheaper staying in Newark, but I couldn't bring myself to live so far from my baby. But though I'd swallow my pride and go past the house on weekends, I never saw little Clara. My mother-in-law attended to that.

Fred had called me just once since it happened, but I didn't see him any more. He realized how impossible it would be when I told him what had happened.

The only way I got any news of little Clara was when I would go into the market on Saturdays to see Pete. He had started going around with the pretty girl who lived next door. "We're thinking of getting married," he told me. "Maybe in another month or so, when I get my raise."

"I'm glad, Pete," I said. "And don't let anyone stop you."

"I know what you mean," he said. "My eyes have been opened since Mom's been acting up with me about Ruth. Only I can't help worrying about how she'll get along."

"She'll get along all right," I said. "She can rent out your room, too."

"I've been thinking the same way myself," Pete said. "That things will work out. And there's something I've been wanting to tell you. I don't believe all those things she said about you. Not any more. And I don't think Bill does, either."

"Bill?" I said, and then, as Pete told me that Mrs. Cooper had gone up to the hospital the weekend before, I knew I had to see Bill, too.

The only train I could make didn't get me there until Sunday morning. I thought I would have to wait until visiting hours, but the nurse let me go straight up to the ward. Bill looked so white, not nearly as well as he had the other time I had seen him. But he smiled when he saw me, and I forgot all those instructions I'd had about not kissing him as I ran over to him.

He just held me at first. "I knew Mom was exaggerating," he said. "I knew I hadn't lost you."

"As if you ever could," I whispered.

"Sure, I know my girl," he said, and as his arm went around me, I felt how much stronger it had become, and that took away some of the worry I felt because of the way he looked. "I told her a couple of lunches didn't mean anything. Even the money—"

"It was for the bills," I said. "They had to be paid. And I've been paying it back every week. Oh, Bill, Fred has helped me so much. Not only that way, but being so understanding. It meant so much to have someone I could talk things over with."

"I know," he said. "I know how tough things must have been for you. Mom gets crazy ideas at times. We all know that. But I hope you won't hold it against her. It'll be hard to go back living together if you do."

I couldn't believe he had really said it. But when he looked at me, his smile so uncertain and his eyes pleading, I felt as if something died inside of me.

"But we're not going back," I said, my voice sounding firmer than I felt. "You know the doctor wants you to stay here another year."

"I know," he said. "But I'm okay now. All the bugs have been knocked out of me. And I've got to take care of Mom now that Pete's getting married. Someone's got to take care of things."

The furious tears stung against my eyes. "She can take in roomers," I said. "She's got one now, in our room. She can even give them their meals if the room rent isn't enough. You've done enough, Bill. We both have. It's time we started thinking of ourselves."

Two red spots of color flamed against his white cheeks. His smile was gone and his mouth was a grim, tight line. "How can you be so hard, Maggy?" he said. "That's one thing I never would have thought of you, being so hard. You know Mom isn't well. She even suggested taking in boarders herself. Only she says her heart has been acting up again, having to take care of just one roomer."

"There's nothing wrong with her heart, Bill," I said. "She lied about that to get the house. She said—"

"She warned me that's what you'd say," Bill said. "She told me about the time you called her a liar. I thought she was exaggerating, but now I see she wasn't. Maggy, I still love you, but we can't go on after this. The way you hate Mom, it would be only hell for all of us trying to get together again. And I can't let her down, Maggy. If she died because I wasn't willing to do my duty to her, I wouldn't ever feel right with myself again."

"She won't die," I said. "She'll outlive all of you, except maybe Pete. He's the only one who has any backbone out of all of you."

"Please, Maggy, I can't take it," he said. "Just leave me alone for a little while." And as I left, I still didn't realize I was losing him, that I had lost him already. I didn't really know until I went back to the hospital that afternoon and the nurse told me Bill had said it would be better if he didn't see me again.

That was the way I thought it all ended, in the hospital room that day. I had lost both of them, Bill and my baby, too. I still loved Bill enough not to fight for my baby as Fred had suggested I do. I couldn't do anything that would add to Bill's burden.

I was seeing Fred again. After all, it didn't make any difference now if anyone misunderstood our relationship. I still loved Bill, but it was Fred who was helping me get through the toughest period I had ever had to face. I loved Bill, and yet after a while, I was able to love Fred, too.

Not in the same way. I could never feel that wild, crazy emotion for anyone else. But it was good, too, in its own way, that devotion to Fred that grew steadily stronger.

Then one night, when I was meeting him for dinner in a restaurant down the street from the house I had moved into in Newark, I saw that Fred wasn't alone. But it was only when I reached the table that I saw it was Pete who was with him. I didn't even think of Fred then. That wild beating in my heart was for Bill. All of it was for Bill.

Pete didn't have to tell me that something was wrong. My heart told me that. "Ruth made me come," he said. "She said it was only fair to tell you Bill is sick again."

I sat down, but I still had to hold on to the table to keep from falling. "He hasn't hemorrhaged again, has he?" I demanded. And then, as he nodded, I heard my voice rising and I couldn't keep it down, even though people were turning to stare at me. "Then why don't you do something about it? Why don't you take him back to the hospital? Why did you tell me? I should think you'd know by now there's nothing I can do."

"He loves you," Pete said. "He loves you so much, he'd rather die than live without you. That's why he won't go back to the hospital."

It was just instinct turning to Fred, the way I had been depending on him all year. "What should I do, Fred?" I asked.

"Go to him," Fred said. "That's what you've been wanting to do all this time." His hand went over mine then, giving it a hard squeeze. "Let's go now," he said then, smiling. "I don't think any of us is hungry."

It was only after we were in the car that I began to wonder if maybe Pete was wrong about Bill loving me. But I knew it was true, hard as it was to believe it, once I started thinking about it. And I felt as if things were going to be all right the minute Bill's father opened the door and I realized his smile was more than just a welcome. It was a relief so deep that his eyes were wet as he put his arms around me.

But it wasn't really true for me even then. It was only true when I went into the room that used to be ours and saw Bill's face. It was as if a million stars were shining in his eyes. And me—well, I was feeling the same way he looked. It was a minute before I even realized that the little girl peeking so shyly from behind the door was my own baby.

I called to her, but she was still so shy with me that it was Bill's arms she ran into. But that didn't make any difference, with me holding on to both of them and savoring it over and over in my heart. It was a while before I could even talk to Bill about the most pressing thing of all.

"You will go back to the hospital, won't you?" I said then. "It will be different this time. Clara and I will be with you."

Then suddenly, I wasn't confident any more. I was afraid again, sick with the old dread as Mrs. Cooper stood glaring in the doorway.

"He's not going to the hospital," she said, and her voice was so strong it made me feel even weaker inside. "He's going to stay right here where his mom can nurse him. That's what he wants. He's kept saying it all along. He wants to be with me."

Bill looked so weak it was impossible to think his voice could sound so firm. "I didn't say I wanted you to nurse me, Mom. I said I didn't want to go to the hospital. There's a difference. Because without Maggy, what was the sense of being patched up again? But now—I want to live now, Mom. That's why I'm going back."

She went pale. "You mean your own mother isn't enough to make you want to get better?" Her voice rose and her face turned red. "After everything I've given up for you, I don't mean anything to you any more. Is that how you feel? You're like Pete! You don't love me any more! Me, your own mother!"

Bill dug his elbow into the pillow, struggling to sit up. "Stop putting words in my mouth, Mom," he said. "I didn't say that. I don't even feel like that. Only I don't know if it's love I feel any more or just plain habit. But what I do know is that you'll never mess up my life again. I'm promising that not only to Maggy, but to myself. We won't let you run us or our child, either."

His mother stared at him unbelievingly, and for once, she couldn't find the words that had always come so easily before. And as her husband started to speak, she turned to him gratefully. I felt almost sorry for her then, with him saying none of the things she expected, just as Bill hadn't, either.

"You heard what the boy said," he said. "Leave it that way. I know how he feels. I let you get the upper hand, and I've been a licked man all these years. Guess I was always afraid of you and I guess I still am, but I want to say this. Never in your life did you love anyone except just yourself."

She found words then. "You know what you are, John Cooper?" she screamed. "A snake, that's all. A snake in the grass!" Her hand went out and she slapped him. Then she ran out of the room.

There was a red spot on Mr. Cooper's cheek where she had slapped him, but he didn't seem to feel it. He stood taller than I had ever seen him stand before. "There's something else, son," he said. "Something that even now I wouldn't have the heart to tell you in front of her. Things were never so bad like she made out. All these years I've been getting compensation for that accident. Not so much, but enough so we didn't have to starve. We really don't need your help, Bill. You just give Maggy and the baby any extras you can hand out. You don't owe your mother a nickel. Remember that. Any debt you ever owed her you've paid back with blood. . . ."

That was over a year ago. Bill is almost well again now. I see him every day in the hospital, all times of the day, because I'm working there. And on Sundays, I bring little Clara to the lawn just below Bill's ward so she can wave hello to him. Bill says it's hard being so near her and not being able to hold her, but in a little while he will be able to do that, too. For he'll be out in just about the time it will take me to finish painting the apartment I've rented for us. I'm so happy I don't know why I should be crying as I write it down. Maybe it's because happiness as deep as this needs a few tears, too, just to be able to bear it. THE END

THREE FATHERS FOR MY THREE BABIES

My eighteenth birthday didn't turn out to be the happy occasion I'd dreamed it would be. Not only did I have no one to celebrate with, I couldn't even tell anyone the truth about it.

At the restaurant where I worked, they knew it was my birthday all right. Mr. Harrison had given me the day off, and Vivian, the woman I worked with, had presented me with a pretty card with yellow roses on it. But they thought I was turning twenty! Claude's Diner was licensed to sell beer and wine. I'd known they wouldn't hire a minor, so I had lied and told Mr. Harrison I was nineteen when I'd applied for the job.

Eighteen had seemed like a magic age—the beginning of freedom from foster homes and the endless chain of social workers who had governed my existence since I'd been a child.

My parents had died in a car accident when I was five years old, and my memories of them had dimmed long ago. I remembered more about my Aunt Cora, Uncle Charlie, and my cousins Darlene, Wally, and the twins than I did about my parents.

I have no recollection of being told of my parents' death, nor do I remember the funeral. Perhaps Aunt Cora thought I was too young to attend and didn't take me.

I do remember the day the strange lady came to Aunt Cora's and took me away. Aunt Cora didn't have room for me, the lady told me when we were in the car. She was taking me to live with another family where I would have a bedroom of my very own and a "brother." She spoke with lively enthusiasm about what she called my new life, promised me happiness, and told me how nice my new foster parents would be.

But all I could think about was that Aunt Cora, who had always treated me like one of her own and who I'd thought loved me, didn't want me anymore and was sending me away. Having my own bedroom didn't sound inviting at all. Sharing Darlene's big double bed had always been much nicer than sleeping in my own room at home. But no one had even asked me.

With five-year-old logic, I figured there must be something wrong with me, some reason why my aunt and uncle didn't want me around. Not having room for me wasn't a good enough reason to me. There had to be something else to explain why they didn't love me, some fault I had that I couldn't see.

There were no visits from my aunt and cousins in my new home, not even a phone call—further confirmation that I was somehow unworthy of them. I didn't know what this shameful thing was, but I felt that it lurked somewhere inside of me and that I had to hide it. After a while, I became afraid to express myself and turned sullen and withdrawn.

Less than a year later, I was taken from my first foster home and placed in another one. The social worker, a different one this time, told me that maybe I would be happier at the new place. But I wasn't. To me, the move was another rejection, this time by foster parents.

I retreated even further into myself and soon I was moved again, then again, and yet again. No one wanted me for long. Looking back, I realize that I must have been a very unlovable child. The burden of my untouchable resentment and silence must have been hard for these foster families to cope with at the time.

By the time I was nine years old, I was being taken regularly to counselors, psychologists, and psychiatrists, and my resentment deepened into bitterness. I hated these poking, prying know-it-alls who fought to destroy my privacy, to invade the thoughts and feelings that were the only things I could truly call my own.

I didn't like going to school, where I could only look on in envy at the self-confidence of the other girls and the closeness between them. I made few friends, feeling it was useless to involve myself in friendships that would only have to be abandoned when I was moved again. There was the shame, too, of being homeless and without family and roots that helped kill my desire to be sociable.

When I entered high school, the attention of several boys came as a surprise to me, and I began to take a new look at myself. The mirror told me that I was no longer the skinny, awkward child I'd thought I would always be. I had filled out. I couldn't be called voluptuous by any means, but I had curves—neat, pleasing-to-the-eye curves. And I had nice eyes, and when I smiled, I might even be called pretty.

My discovery gave me new confidence and I began to make more of an effort to be friendly with my classmates. Soon, I found that the friendships I had always denied myself had only been waiting my acceptance, and I made friends easily.

Over the next few years, my confidence continued to grow. I could hardly wait until I was eighteen and on my own. Surely there was a place in life just for me—a place where my every action wouldn't be subjected to the approval and rules of social workers and foster parents.

I stayed in the same foster home for the first two years of high school. It was the longest time I had lived anywhere since my parents died. Mr. and Mrs. Bailey were very nice people. But having had no children of their own, they seemed to me to be out of touch, and I never became close to them. I was allowed to date, but only on special occasions—a school dance or homecoming game. And I always had to be home directly after the event. With life holding so much promise now, it wasn't enough. I longed to explore this exciting new world on my own.

The summer I was seventeen, I got a part-time job at an ice-cream parlor, Queenie's, a block away from the high school. I loved working. For the first time, I knew the pride of self-reliance. I no longer had to accept the allowance Mrs. Bailey gave me every Saturday. Through the years, weekly allowances hadn't been a part of every foster home. At some places they had been given reluctantly, never without the unpleasant reminder that money was hard to come by and shouldn't be spent frivolously. Consequently, whenever allowances were given, I felt a certain amount of guilt for taking them. Now I had money of my own. Money I'd earned myself. It was a good, satisfying feeling.

As September neared, I became depressed. My eighteenth birthday would come in February—midway through the school year— and if I wanted to receive my diploma, I would have to stick around for four months longer. The thought of so many months of the same old school routine, of constant submission to the unbending supervision I'd always been under, seemed unfair. I wasn't sure I'd be able to stand it after my birthday had passed and I knew I was free.

I didn't want to go back to school at all, and as I thought about the puppet-like existence I'd led all my life made me angry. It was time I voiced my own opinions and made some decisions on my own. A high-school diploma had been the social service department's goal, not mine. I had just been going along with them while I waited patiently for my release. I decided that the last six months of my wardship would be better spent gaining practical experience in preparation for my independence.

I phoned my social worker two weeks before summer vacation ended and told her of my wishes to find a full-time job rather than return to school. She wouldn't allow it. I used all my carefully thought out arguments and still she would not give in.

"By the time February comes, you'll see the wisdom in finishing out the year," she stated firmly.

I hung up almost in tears. The old resentment simmered, and this time it boiled over. I let the anger come. All my life I'd been moved here and there at the whim of others, being told what to do and what not to do. Well, I wouldn't submit this time! I didn't need them anyway. I was older and fully capable of taking care of myself.

I had nearly several hundred dollars already saved. Two more weeks of work would bring in almost three hundred dollars more. That would surely be enough to rent a room for a month, with some left over for food until another paycheck came in. I began applying for jobs in the nearest big city, which was a fair distance from the town I lived in with the Baileys. I'd be unlikely to run into anyone I knew there.

As the Labor Day weekend neared, I was beginning to lose hope of finding employment. Claude's Diner was my final stop on the Saturday of the long weekend. They had no ad in the paper, but there was a "Waitress Wanted" sign in the window. I was glad I'd spotted it. One of the waitresses had walked out earlier in the day and Mr. Harrison hired me on the spot. I was to begin the following Tuesday.

I left Claude's feeling elated. I had found a job, and if I could find a place to stay right away, I could be moved and settled and ready to begin my new life. It was nearly two o'clock in the afternoon and my final shift at Queenie's began at six. The newspaper I'd bought earlier that day was still tucked under my arm, so I looked around for a place where I could open it up and search the ads again. The bus stop halfway down the block had a bench in front of it. I headed for it and sat down, spreading the paper on the bench beside me.

I thumbed past the classifieds, where I'd circled the jobs that had sounded promising, and stopped when I came to the rental section. I looked for places that would be close, within walking distance if possible. There were several in the area, and the closest one was a room only two blocks away. The rent was a little more than I had expected and would seriously deplete my bank account, but there would soon be more coming in. I would manage. Hopefully, the room hadn't been rented yet.

It hadn't. The room was in the basement of an older, family-style home. It was large, with a double bed and a dresser placed on one side and a small fridge, a sink, and cupboards on the other. A two-burner hot plate sat on the counter. The bathroom was located in the far corner of the basement. Linen and a few dishes would be supplied if I needed them, the middle-aged landlady told me. She had introduced herself as Mrs. Ivers, and she seemed nice enough.

"It's a quiet place," she said. "There's only my husband and me and our grown daughter living upstairs."

My decision to take the room had already been made. I gave Mrs. Ivers the money for the first month's rent and told her I would move in the next day.

On the bus ride home, I thought about what I'd done. Handing over the money had made it final. There was no turning back. But I had no regrets. There was no one I was really hurting by running away. I would leave a note for Mr. and Mrs. Bailey, telling them that I had a job and a place of my own so they wouldn't panic over my disappearance. The information would be passed on to the social worker, I knew.

I got home, changed into my uniform, and made it to Queenie's with ten minutes to spare. My shift ended at ten o'clock, and I went straight home to my room, where I began to sort through my belongings. I didn't have much: my clothes, a jewelry box, a small portable CD player, and, thankfully, my own set of luggage.

When everything had been arranged for quick transfer into the suitcases, I undressed and climbed into bed. I lay awake for a long time, anticipating the days ahead and my new independence. Finally, I slept.

The next morning, I was awakened by Mrs. Bailey, asking if I was going to church with her and Mr. Bailey. The invitation was extended every Sunday, but I was never forced to go or made to feel guilty if I chose not to attend. Sometimes I went, more often I didn't. Today I had other plans and told her I wouldn't be going.

I got up, showered, dressed, and made my bed. That done, it would still be half an hour before Mr. and Mrs. Bailey left for church. In the top drawer of the bureau, I found the notepaper I'd received three Christmases ago from my previous foster parents, and

I sprawled across the bed to write my letter to the Baileys.

It was nearly done when I heard the closing of the front door and, soon after, the sound of the car starting up. A few minutes later, the car pulled away and I folded the completed letter, slid it into an envelope, and stood it against the mirror where it would easily be seen.

I quickly packed and when I was almost finished, I stopped long enough to phone for a taxi. I had to be out before the Baileys returned, which I estimated would be in little more than half an hour. I was waiting in the front hall when the taxi came. I told the driver to take me to the bus station. My plan was to wait there fifteen minutes, then take a different taxi to my new home. I hated to spend the cab fare, but I figured it would be worth it to cover my tracks. The stopover, I thought, was necessary in case the police were sent after me. It was almost inevitable that I would be spotted getting into the taxi by at least one of the neighbors, and if the driver was asked where he'd taken me, he could only direct them as far as the bus station. It would be hard to guess where I'd gone from there.

The two fares put another dent in my finances, but there was still my final paycheck from Queenie's, which would be issued on Wednesday of the following week. After all the trouble I'd already gone to, this added precaution would be worth it.

The only hitch was collecting my last paycheck from Queenie's. It might be risky, I realized, as I inserted the key Mrs. Ivers had given me into the lock on the back door of my new home. Would the social worker be waiting for me there? Would I be sent to yet another foster home? The Baileys wouldn't want me back after I'd run away. There would be another strange family to get used to—new rules and demands. The efforts of the past weeks would all be wasted. I would be right back where I started.

Maybe, I decided, it would be safer to wait until Friday to pick up the check. The social worker wouldn't hang around for days waiting for me to come in.

I shrugged, telling myself I'd worry about that later. Right now I wanted to get settled, then find a store that was open on Sundays and buy some groceries with my remaining money.

The work at Claude's was completely different from what I'd been doing at the ice-cream parlor, but Mr. Harrison was patient and I learned fast. Plus there were tips, something I hadn't expected. They certainly helped, and I'd had no trouble getting my paycheck from Queenie's, either. Julie, the manager, didn't even seem surprised to see me. Apparently she didn't know that I'd run away. She asked how school was going and told me to drop in once in a while and say hi.

But I hadn't been back since. Although a month had passed, I was still on edge, expecting a social worker or the police to appear at any time and claim me as a runaway. More than ever now, I didn't want to be discovered. My new life was satisfying. I felt whole and important. And there was Doug. I was sure that any day now, he was going to ask me out. . . .

I really had that on my mind one Friday as I wiped the front counter for the third time. It had been slow for the past hour, but the crew from the construction site down the street would be coming in any minute now for coffee. Doug would be one of them. Serving them was the highlight of my day. They always joked and teased me and made me laugh.

Doug had the most beautiful smile I had ever seen, and warm eyes that I'd often turned around to see studying me with unconcealed interest. I'd never had a man look at me that way before, and it sent shivers down my spine and made my stomach do flip-flops. The boys I had known in high school hadn't had that effect on me, that's for sure. I wondered if this was what it was like to fall in love.

Finally, the door swung open and six dust-covered men in work clothes walked in, hammers and measuring tapes swinging from their belts. They sat down at the counter and I asked, "Coffee for everybody?"

"Coffee, guys?" the foreman asked, leaning forward on the

counter and looking down for responses.

Coffee it was for all of them, and slices of cherry pie, too. After I'd set down the last of the steaming cups of coffee and plates of pie, I turned to the coffee machine to change the filter and make a new pot.

"So where's that big, tough boyfriend of yours, Cindy?" Gabe, the foreman, kidded me.

"I told you, I don't have a big, tough boyfriend," I said. "I don't even have a little fragile one."

They all roared at this.

"Then why are you blushing?" Gabe asked.

And if I hadn't been before, I certainly was now. I turned away, still laughing but embarrassed. I blushed so easily and hated it when I did.

Just then, two more customers came in and sat down in one of the booths in my section. I took menus to them, then went to the cooler to get the beer they wanted. After I'd served them beer and taken them their food, I returned to the counter and refilled the men's coffee cups. They were all busy with shop talk, but Doug's eyes never left my face as I filled his cup. Still, he said nothing, just smiling slightly when I met his gaze.

More customers came in then and I had no time to wonder about his thoughts. When a lull came again, the men were gone. I was disappointed. Doug wouldn't be in again until Monday.

"Don't worry, Cindy. He'll be back." Vivian, the buxom, dark-haired waitress who worked with me on the day shift, had come up beside me. Her words surprised me. I hadn't told her about my crush on Doug. I was afraid she'd think I was acting immature. Vivian was in her early thirties, married, and had a ten-year-old son, differences that to me equaled a whole generation gap and all the misunderstandings that usually went with it.

"He's just as interested in you as you are in him," she continued, smiling and eyeing me mischievously. "I just hope for your sake he's not married. Do me a favor, Cindy. Put your dreams on hold until you find out, huh?"

I smiled back at her, suddenly glad she knew how I felt. It lowered the barrier I'd put up between us, making me feel more at ease. "I will," I assured her, also hoping that Doug wasn't married.

Both Vivian and I worked Monday to Friday and alternate Saturdays. It was my turn to work the following day. The shift was a short one—from noon until four-thirty in the afternoon. Near three o'clock, I looked up and was surprised to see Doug coming through the door. He was alone and I almost looked away again before I realized who it was. I'd never seen him in anything but dirty work clothes. He was dressed now in clean jeans, a red plaid shirt, and a denim jacket.

He smiled and sat down at the counter. "Just coffee, Cindy," he said.

I poured the coffee. He'd come by to see me, I just knew it, and my excitement was hard to contain. My hands were shaking as I set the coffee down in front of him. When my hand was free of the cup and saucer, he suddenly reached for it and held it gently.

"I was thinking," he said. "If you really don't have a boyfriend, there would be no one to object if I was to ask you to go out with me, would there?" He said it teasingly, but there was no mistaking his seriousness.

"I guess not," I said, trying not to sound as eager as I felt. "Unless it might be your wife or girlfriend."

Doug laughed and said, "No wife and no girlfriend. Can I pick you up when you get off? We can have something to eat, go to a movie afterward, if you like."

"I'll have to go home and change first," I told him. "I get off at four-thirty. You can pick me up at my place at six. Is that all right?"

"Sure is," he said, taking a pen from his shirt pocket. "What's your address?"

I told him and he wrote it down on a napkin.

There were a few more customers that had come in and I had to go and wait on them. Doug left soon afterward, saying, "See you at six."

When my shift was over, I almost ran all the way home. After I'd showered, I couldn't think of what I should wear. Finally, I decided on my nicest jeans and a white sweater with tiny pink flowers all over it. I knew it wouldn't be a fancy evening. Doug wasn't a fancy sort of guy, which suited me just fine. I preferred casual people and casual places. I brushed my hair and put on fresh makeup, and my reflection in the mirror over the dresser told me I looked just fine.

The one small window in my room faced the front of the house. It was high and I had to stand on the bed to watch for Doug. I didn't want him coming right in and seeing how I lived. I would meet him at the door.

He was right on time, and I was both nervous and excited as I ran up the basement stairs. This was the first date I'd ever had that wouldn't be monitored by an adult.

Doug's eyes swept over me with approval when I opened the door and stepped out to meet him. He took my hand as we walked to the car.

"Anywhere special you'd like to go?" he asked. His smile and manner were easygoing and confident. I felt my nervousness beginning to disappear.

"I'll leave it up to you," I said.

"Do you like seafood?" he asked.

"I love it," I told him.

"Then we'll go to the Pier and have supper. We can decide what else to do from there."

The Pier was a cozy, dimly lit restaurant. I loved the rough wood decor that was meant to look like the galley of an old ship. We ordered lobster tails and baked potatoes and talked the whole time, trying to learn as much about each other as we possibly could.

Doug was twenty-three years old and had moved to the city three years before. He had initially come to escape reminders of a broken engagement. It seems that after a two-year relationship, Annette, his high school sweetheart, had suddenly decided that he wasn't good enough for her. She had broken their engagement and married a young lawyer two months later.

I told Doug about my childhood, but not that I'd run away from my last foster home. I was afraid if he knew I was only seventeen, he might be reluctant to ask me for another date. Even that early in the evening, I was hoping that before the night was through, he would.

By the time we left the restaurant, I was floating on a cloud. Doug liked me. I knew he did. We'd decided to go to see one of the new horror movies playing, something we discovered we both enjoyed. Doug went to the snack bar for popcorn and sodas. We walked inside the darkened theater and he said, "I usually go to the stock-car races on Sundays. Would you like to come?"

Would I? You bet I would! Of course, I told Doug yes. Then we sat down to watch the movie.

Doug took me straight home after the movie ended and walked me to the door. His kiss was light, almost platonic, and he held me for only a minute. But I wasn't disappointed. I would be seeing him again the very next day.

"I'm glad I finally got up the nerve to ask you out, Cindy," he said. "See you tomorrow." He turned and headed back down the walk, waving as he got into his car. When I went in the house, I was bursting with happiness.

That was the beginning of a closeness I had never shared with anyone before. Within a few weeks, I knew without a doubt that I was deeply in love, and I was sure that Doug felt the same way. I told him the truth about my age, wanting our love to have a foundation of honesty and trust to grow on. Doug sympathized with my lonely childhood and seemed to understand my need to run away and become independent. The night I confessed, he held me close, stroking my cheek and kissing me.

I was amazed by my newfound happiness. The love I'd been denied as a child was being awarded to me now tenfold by Doug. He just had to be the most caring, compassionate man in the whole world, I thought. Life was finally going my way.

Doug shared an apartment with his friend Perry, who worked as a bartender at one of the local hotels. Sometimes Doug and I double-dated with Perry and his girlfriend, Justine. She was a barmaid at the same hotel and several years older than me. We got along, but never struck up a friendship of our own. To me, Justine seemed very mature and worldly, and I felt young and gawky in comparison.

We didn't double up very often. She and Perry liked to go to bars and nightclubs, and I wasn't old enough to get in. Doug and I went to dinner, to movies, and often we spent the evening in the apartment just watching television and stuffing ourselves with pizza or Chinese food we had delivered.

It was Christmas Eve when Doug and I made love for the first time. There had been invitations to Christmas dinner from both Mrs. Ivers and Gabe, Doug's boss. We thanked them both, but planned our own day. We wanted it to be a special occasion—just the two of us.

Perry was spending the holidays with his brother's family, so we would have the apartment to ourselves. We'd set up and decorated a small tree. A turkey in the last stages of thawing sat in cold water in the kitchen sink. The gifts I'd bought for Doug were under the tree with the rest of the presents, three that were addressed to me from Doug and a few others we had received from the people we worked with. A bottle of sparkling cider was in the refrigerator chilling, and we only had to make cranberry sauce and stuffing so they would be ready for the next day.

When that was done and the dishes were all washed and put away, we settled down on the couch to watch a Christmas special on television. Doug had opened up the cider and poured us each a glass. When the first commercial came on, he put his arms around me and kissed me tenderly.

"Happy, Cindy?" he asked when we finally drew apart.

"Very," I told him. "This is the best Christmas I've ever had."

It was, too. All my other Christmases had been spent in houses where I'd felt more like a guest than a part of the family. With Doug, I felt loved and wanted.

Suddenly I knew I wouldn't be going back to my cold basement room that night. I wanted to stay with Doug, make love, and wake up with him in the morning. Up until now, the thought of total intimacy had frightened me. Where I'd succeeded in overcoming almost all my fear of personal relationships, sex was the one area that I'd remained afraid of.

But this night was somehow different, and with my decision came the feeling that making love with Doug was right—and long overdue. I had fought against my ever-increasing desire for a long time, and Doug had been so patient with me. He'd never gotten angry or tried to talk me into it.

When I looked into Doug's eyes now, he pulled me closer and covered my mouth again with his. Abandonment felt sweet. With my reserve gone, the kiss swept me away. There could be no stopping then, even if I'd changed my mind, which I didn't. Doug went slowly, almost too slowly. Admitting my need to myself had created an urgency in me that consumed me completely. We made love right there on the couch, even though his bedroom was only a few steps away.

Afterward, I lay in Doug's arms feeling peaceful and magically complete. "I love you, Cindy," he whispered. "I swore I'd never fall in love again, but I can't help it." He smiled and tapped me on the nose. "Now don't go leaving me, you hear?"

"Loud and clear," I murmured, snuggling against him. "I couldn't leave you even if I wanted to. I love you, too, you know."

In time, I vowed, I would prove to Doug that I wasn't like his old girlfriend, Annette. And when he was free of all his doubts, Doug would ask me to marry him. I was sure of that. Christmas Day was like a miniature honeymoon for us. We didn't do anything special, just lazed around the apartment, made love, and went for a long walk, holding hands and laughing over silly things.

The next day, I had to go back to work and so did Doug. Perry returned that night and we no longer had the apartment to ourselves. But during the next month, we found other places to share our love. A few times, I snuck Doug down into my room, where we whispered so Mrs. Ivers wouldn't hear us. Once we took a drive to the country and stayed in a motel for the weekend.

Toward the end of January, a change came over Doug that seemed to have no cause or explanation. He was often lost in thought and hardly paid any attention to what I was saying. I began to wonder if he was changing his mind about loving me. After a week of this strange detachment, I questioned him timidly.

"Of course I still love you," he said, sounding concerned, and for a moment I thought the old Doug had returned. But he immediately drew away again. "It's a problem I have to figure out by myself."

I tried to get him to confide in me, but he wouldn't, and with the hurt his refusal caused me came a slight twinge of anger. What was the matter with him, anyway? Didn't he know how much I loved him? Love was meant to encompass both the good and the bad. I wanted desperately to share his problem, but he just wasn't letting me in.

A few days later, I walked the two blocks home under a torrent of rain. I was soaked to the skin by the time I got there and surprised to see Perry's car sitting in front of the house. He called me over.

"Doug flew east this morning," he said. "Some family problem or something. He asked me to give you this." Through the car window, he held out a white envelope that obviously contained a letter.

I stared at Perry in disbelief for several seconds before I found my voice. "Did he say when he'd be back?" I asked, reaching for the envelope. I felt like crying. First the odd withdrawal, and now Doug had left town without even phoning me at work to say good-bye.

"He said in a week or two," Perry replied. "But maybe the letter will be more specific." He started the car. "You'd better go in now, Cindy," he said, laughing. "You look like a drowned rat."

His remark reminded me of how bedraggled I must look. "You're right," I said, attempting a smile. "Thanks for bringing this to me. I appreciate it."

I headed for the house and Perry drove away. Inside, I hung my soggy coat over the doorknob and tore open the envelope, hoping it contained an explanation for Doug's hasty departure. But it was only a short scribbled note. "Dear Cindy," it said. "Had to go home for a while. Will be back before your birthday. Love, Doug."

Was someone in his family ill? But that didn't make sense. An illness wouldn't require secrecy, would it? Well, my birthday was on the twenty-fifth, only two weeks away. Doug would be back, and hopefully the problem would be resolved and he would explain everything. I would just have to wait.

But my birthday came and went and still Doug wasn't back. Neither Perry nor I had heard from him. I had phoned Perry several times and learned that Doug had taken only one suitcase and had left on the spur of the moment, not even leaving the address of where he'd be staying. That wasn't at all like the Doug I'd thought I knew so well. What had changed him so drastically in such a short time?

And now I had a new fear. I'd missed my period and was worried that I might be pregnant. Why I hadn't seen a doctor and gotten started on the Pill right after Doug and I had become sexually involved, I didn't know. I'd been taught about birth control in school. There was no excuse for my neglect or Doug's.

Several more weeks passed and still there was no word from Doug. I'd been phoning Perry nearly every day, and I knew I was beginning to get on his nerves. By this time I was positive I was pregnant. My period still hadn't come. At night, I'd lie awake for hours, wondering if there had been an accident and Doug was in some hospital so badly hurt he couldn't even tell anyone to notify me.

I couldn't eat much either, even though I'd been lucky so far and hadn't had any morning sickness. I'd begun to lose weight, and Mr. Harrison was beginning to lose patience with me at work. I was making a lot of mistakes—mixing up orders and adding bills up wrong. If only Doug would get back, I thought constantly. We could get married and then everything would be all right. He loved me and wouldn't let me down. I was sure of it.

Though Vivian was sympathetic, I didn't tell her about my pregnancy. I was ashamed and didn't want her to know how dumb I was.

Perry's girlfriend, Justine, came in on a Monday afternoon. I hadn't seen her since the last time the four of us had gone to the arcade together the Sunday before Doug had left. She told me she wanted to talk to me when I got off. "Can I pick you up?" she asked. "We can go for a drive."

"Sure," I told her, glad for the opportunity to avoid returning to my lonely room.

"Okay," she said. "I'll be outside. See you then."

I wondered what she wanted to talk about. It had to be about Doug. Had she and Perry heard from him? Luckily, we got busy soon after she had gone and I didn't have time to wonder whether the news would be good or bad.

Justine was parked right in front when my shift was over. She smiled at me after I'd got in and closed the car door. "You look beat," she said. "Hard day?"

"Not really," I replied. "I haven't been sleeping much lately."

"Let's take a drive through the park," she suggested. "Maybe some fresh air will do you good. How's the job going? Still like it there? I used to work in a restaurant, but I like bar work better. Tips are better, too."

She babbled on, making small talk as she drove. It was another wet, depressing day, and I thought of how well it matched my mood. Then Justine slowed, pulled into a parking area, and shut off the car.

She settled herself sideways on the seat and looked at me.

"Have you heard anything at all from Doug?" she asked.

"No," I replied. "Have you or Perry?"

She sighed and studied me for a while. I knew then that she'd heard something and my heart started racing. I waited for her to continue, growing more anxious with each passing second. Finally she spoke.

"I hate to be the one to tell you this, Cindy, but someone has to." Justine paused again. "Doug is gone for good. Two days ago, he phoned Perry and asked him to pack the rest of his belongings and ship them to his hometown. He said he was going to write to you and explain everything. Seems Annette and her husband didn't hit it off too well. They got a divorce and she and Doug are going to try married life together."

It took a few minutes for her words to really sink in. Doug wasn't coming back at all? He was going to marry the girl who had once jilted him? I had believed so totally in Doug's love, had been so sure that he would return as soon as he was able to. The thought that he was ditching me hadn't even entered my mind.

The hurt and outrage I felt then could only be expressed in ragged, gulping sobs. Justine patted my arm and tried to console me, but I found little comfort in her words.

"I've been putting off letting you know," she admitted. "Doug knew how much you loved him and that you'd take it hard. It hurts, I know, and it will for a while. But before you know it, there'll be someone else and you'll forget all about him."

She let me cry. It was a long time before I regained some control. "What am I going to do, Justine?" I sobbed. "I'm pregnant."

She looked surprised. "Does Doug know?" she asked.

"No," I said. The word came out harsh and angry. Pride had reared up in sudden, grim determination. "I don't want him to know now." I was crying again.

"Doug would never have left if he'd known," she said softly.

"Cindy, you should write and tell him. Perry will give you his address. Regardless of his leaving like this, he's really a decent guy. He'd probably come back and marry you if he knew."

"Sure," I said bitterly, "but only because he'd feel obligated. I don't want to be anybody's second choice. Don't you tell him, either, Justine." I looked at her hard. "I'll manage somehow. I don't want him to know."

"I won't tell him," she promised. "But think about it. If you decide to keep the baby, Doug could help you out financially, at least. He'd want to. You know he would."

"I'll think about it," I told her, but I knew I would never ask Doug for anything. That would be asking for his pity, which I didn't want. The love I'd thought he had for me obviously wasn't strong enough to overcome his love for Annette—a love I had believed had died long ago. Pity was not only a poor substitute for love, but it was an insulting one. I would keep my pride, if nothing else.

Justine drove me home. Before I went inside, she had me wait while she wrote down her address and phone number. "If you need any help, call me," she said firmly. "Even if you just need someone to talk to, okay?"

I said okay and she drove away. I went down to my room, threw myself across the bed, and cried again.

After a while, I felt a headache coming on and forced myself to stop. Getting sick was the last thing I needed now. I had to pull myself together and decide what to do. How long would I be able to work, and what would I do for money from the time I had to quit until the baby was born? Justine's offer had been nice, but was probably no more than a gesture made in sympathy. At any rate, I couldn't go running to her and expect her to support me for several months. And what about the baby? The baby.

Suddenly I didn't feel quite so alone. It wasn't just me now. There were two of us. Nestled inside me was a tiny life, a child that would be mine to hold and love. This child and I were family—the family I'd never had. With this realization, I now felt fiercely protective of my unborn child. Maybe I couldn't give my baby a father, but it would have a mother—a mother who would make up for that lack by giving it more than enough love and devotion.

I felt a whole lot better. Getting up from the bed where I'd lain for nearly two hours, I showered and put on my nightgown. Then, realizing I hadn't eaten, I fixed myself some hot soup. While I ate, my thoughts turned more and more away from Doug and more and more toward my baby.

The next day, I made an appointment with a doctor I chose from the phone book and began to make tentative plans for the future. I concentrated on doing a good job at work. I couldn't afford to get fired now. The baby and I would need all the money I could possibly save while I was still able to work. During the months I'd been at Claude's, I had already banked a sizable amount of my weekly paychecks. Hopefully, by giving up all but the bare necessities from now on, I could add enough to it to keep me going during the last few months of my pregnancy and still be able to buy the things a baby would need.

I kept my pregnancy a secret from Vivian and Mr. Harrison, knowing that he would probably let me go if he knew. I lived only for the time I would hold my precious baby in my arms. After work and on my Saturdays off, I wandered through the infants' section of the department stores, gazing at all the tiny garments, toys, and furniture, dreaming of the days to come when my child and I would share life together.

Doug's letter of explanation never did come. I tried not to think of him, but sometimes his face would force its way into my thoughts, refusing to leave. And for a time, I would be surrounded by memories and feel miserable and depressed. But as time passed, Doug receded further and further into the past. I thought of him less and less.

The smock-style top and black slacks that made up my uniform at Claude's hid my pregnancy well, and it wasn't until summer rolled around that I realized my job would soon come to an end.

Vivian, who got off at the same time as I did and who always sat drinking coffee while she waited for her husband to pick her up, followed me out the door one day and fell into step beside me.

"Mr. Harrison's going to guess any day now, Cindy," she said. "Maybe this well help for a while." She held out the paper bag she was carrying in her hand. "It's a uniform top in a larger size. I snuck it out of the storeroom for you. The one you've got on is getting too tight."

I stared at her, wondering how long she'd known. As if she read my mind, Vivian told me, "I've known for a long time, but I would never mention it to Mr. Harrison. I know you're going to need all the money you can earn."

Her kindness and understanding brought tears to my eyes, which I quickly brushed away in embarrassment. Once again, I had refused to acknowledge the friendship she had always extended and I felt ashamed.

"Thanks, Vivian," I managed to choke out as I took the bag from her outstretched hand.

"That's okay." She smiled, turning to return to the restaurant. "See you tomorrow."

After the breakfast rush the next day, Vivian approached me again. "Are you going to keep the baby, Cindy?" she asked.

"Yes," I told her, then waited for her reaction.

She smiled knowingly. "I thought so," she said. "For a time after Doug left, I thought you'd never pull through. Then a little spark appeared and lately you've been positively glowing."

We laughed and then she grew serious again. "What are you going to do when you can't work and after the baby's born?"

"I've been saving money. I should have enough to make it until I can work again," I told her.

She studied me for a moment, then said, "How would you like to come and stay with us until the baby's born? We have an extra bedroom that usually gets used only when my brother or Russell's parents come for a visit. I'd be glad to have someone there to cook dinner and tidy up a little. I wouldn't charge you anything. You could save your rent money and be that much more ahead after the baby arrives.

"I've already discussed it with Russell," she went on, "and he says it's a great idea. But it's up to you. Think about it—there's no rush. Let me know when you decide."

She smiled again and went to wait on a customer who had come in a few minutes ago and who now sat glowering at the two of us from one of the booths. I went back to my own task of filling the napkin holders. Vivian's offer sounded too good to be true. I'd wait a few days and if it still looked as inviting then as it did to me now, I'd accept it.

At the end of June, I moved in with Vivian, her husband, and their son, Dean. The bedroom in Vivian's house was bright and airy. Up until then, I hadn't realized how depressing the room in Mrs. Ivers's basement really was. Russell drove Vivian and me to work in the mornings and home again in the afternoons. I planned to work until the day I got fired—which wasn't long in coming.

Two weeks into August, Mr. Harrison drew me aside and told me I no longer had a job. He was kind about it, but he said the customers were beginning to make comments and it wasn't good for business. I gathered from the way he spoke that he, too, had known for some time and had been putting off letting me go for as long as he could.

I loved living at Vivian's. Her place wasn't fancy, just homey and comfortable. Vivian had been firm about my chores not beginning until I was no longer working at Claude's, and even now that I wasn't, she didn't want me working too hard. But I did extra anyway, wanting to repay her in some way for her kindness. I had supper ready every night when she and Russell arrived home from work and Dean from school.

Besides the dusting, vacuuming, and tidying that Vivian insisted was all that needed to be done, I often spent an afternoon wiping out cupboards, defrosting the refrigerator, or waxing the kitchen floor. When Vivian noticed and commented, I would smile and say, "I got bored again." She would laugh, pleased anyway, and tell me I was spoiling her and that she'd never be able to survive again without me.

In the evenings, we played cards or watched television, and some nights I insisted that Vivian and Russell go out to dinner or to a movie they had mentioned they wanted to see. I would stay home with Dean, who was no trouble at all. At ten, he was a quiet boy who read a lot and spent hours painting the small parts of his model cars and trucks and gluing them together.

The money I was saving by living at Vivian's allowed me the luxury of a brand-new crib instead of the secondhand one I had planned on. And long before I was admitted to the hospital, three of my dresser drawers were crammed with blankets, bottles, baby clothes—everything I would need.

Amanda Lynn was born in October, and when the nurse placed her in my arms for the first time, I thought I would die of happiness. As I gazed in wonder at my daughter's small, red face, I vowed silently that I would never let anything separate us. My beautiful little girl would be my whole life from then on. When Mandy was a month old, I decided I'd imposed on Vivian and Russell long enough. It was time I found a job and got my own place. My daughter would need a loving, reliable baby-sitter, too. With this in mind, I searched for an apartment first, hoping to find one with a baby-sitter in the same building.

Russell and Vivian helped me here, too. Vivian looked after Mandy in the evenings while Russell drove me around to look at apartments.

I finally found what I was looking for just before Christmas. The one-bedroom apartment would be available on the first of January, and after hearing about my need for a baby-sitter, the woman who showed me the apartment told me she'd take on the job herself.

She was a pleasant, older lady, a grandmotherly type who told me she would just love to care for a young child again. I felt Mandy would get all the love and attention she could possibly need in Mrs. Webster's care.

The apartment was furnished, but I would have to buy dishes and bedding, which would take another chunk out of my savings but still leave me plenty until I could find a job, especially since only a small security deposit was needed. I gave Mrs. Webster a check for a month's rent and moved in.

Setting up housekeeping didn't turn out to be as expensive as I thought it would be, thanks again to Vivian. She and Russell gave me a set of sheets and pillowcases for Christmas, and Vivian dug out a few old dishes and pots and pans from the far reaches of her cupboards and told me I could have them.

"I was going to throw them out anyway," she said when I objected to her generosity. All I had to buy after that was a blanket for my bed, a few towels, some silverware, and a coffeepot. I would add whatever else I needed as it came up.

Although I appreciated everything Vivian and Russell had done for me, I was glad to be in my own place with the baby. The apartment seemed so cozy and private—a world where there was only the two of us. When I wasn't out job hunting, I was fussing over Mandy or cleaning when she was sleeping.

Mrs. Webster wouldn't let me pay her for baby-sitting while I was looking for a job. "I love having the baby," she told me. "You hold on to your money until you're working."

In less than two weeks, I landed a job in the dining room of a busy downtown hotel. Working there would mean taking the bus every day, but the Coach Lounge was a fancier place than Claude's had been, and the additional tips would more than cover the bus fare and extra hours of baby-sitting per week.

After my first week on the job, I was beat. I hadn't realized how hard working and caring for a baby full time would be.

I don't know what woke me up the following Monday morning. When I looked at the clock, it was twenty after six. In near panic, I jumped out of bed. I had less than half an hour to get Mandy and myself ready, deliver her to Mrs. Webster, and get to the bus stop in time to catch the bus.

I pulled a bottle of formula from the refrigerator and set it in a pan in the sink, turning the hot water on to warm it up. I enjoyed feeding Mandy in the mornings before I took her down to Mrs. Webster's, but today there wouldn't be time. But I knew Mrs. Webster wouldn't mind feeding her.

Mandy was still sleeping, so I decided to get myself ready first. I threw my uniform on and quickly brushed my teeth and then did my hair. I stuffed diapers, a clean sleeper, and bottles of formula into the diaper bag, then lifted Mandy gently from her crib, lay her on the bed, and changed her. It was now twenty-five minutes to seven. The bus came by in ten more minutes, but if I hurried I might still make it.

I picked Mandy up, grabbed my purse, the diaper bag, the warm bottle from the sink, and headed for the door. In my haste, I'd forgotten to dig my key out of my purse and was further delayed while I rummaged around furiously with one hand until I found it. After locking the door, I headed, downstairs to Mrs. Webster's. I practically shoved Mandy into her arms, explaining breathlessly that I'd overslept and that Mandy needed to be fed right away.

I set the bottle on the coffee table, the diaper bag on the sofa, then ran for the bus stop a block and a half away. Halfway there, I watched the bus cross the distant intersection and disappear behind the building on the corner. I'd missed it! Now I was going to be late for the breakfast shift.

When I got to the bus stop, I looked anxiously down the street. There wasn't another bus in sight. It was only my second week on the job. My new boss wasn't going to be too impressed. I paced back and forth in front of the bench, growing more frustrated as time passed, trying to will a bus to come.

Just then, a car pulled over and stopped beside me. I'd seen the car and the driver before. The man had driven by every morning while I waited for the bus. On Friday, he had smiled and waved, and I had waved back. Now he reached over to the passenger's side and rolled down the window. I bent down to see his face and found myself looking into a pair of friendly brown eyes.

"Are you late this morning, too?" he asked.

"Yes," I said sheepishly. "I overslept."

"Where do you work? If it's not too far out of my way, I can give you a lift," he offered.

I told him and he reached over again, this time opening the door. "No problem," he said. "I go right by there."

Without hesitation, I got in and shut the door. If the traffic wasn't too bad, I wouldn't be late after all. After we'd pulled away, the man explained that he had also overslept that morning. We laughed at the coincidence. His name was Glen and he worked for a printing company. I got to work with a full minute to spare.

The next morning, Glen stopped at the bus stop again. "Might as well ride with me and save your money," he said with a smile.

I rode to work with Glen every morning for the rest of the week, and by Friday I found myself enjoying his company and looking forward to seeing him. We shared similar unhappy love experiences. Glen had been through a marriage breakup and I'd known the heartbreak of a broken romance. I felt this created a bond of mutual understanding between us. It was comforting to know that I wasn't the only one in the world who had lost out on love. Glen's divorce had come through only four months before, he told me. His ex-wife had custody of their three-year-old son. He was twenty-eight years old and now lived with three other bachelors in a house they rented.

When I left work on Friday afternoon, Glen's car was parked outside. He motioned me over and said that he'd gotten off work early and thought he'd stop by and give me a ride home.

In front of my apartment building, he asked if I would like to go for a drive that evening.

"I wouldn't be able to get a baby-sitter," I told him. "I can't ask Mrs. Webster. She has Mandy all day. It would be too much for her, since she's not that young."

"Bring the baby along," Glen said matter of factly, then waited for my answer.

I thought for several moments. Just yesterday, I'd caught myself wishing Glen would ask me to go out with him, a wish I'd immediately chided myself over, remembering Doug's desertion and reminding myself that I wasn't going to get involved with another man.

But now that he was actually asking, the invitation was irresistible. It would be so nice to get out for a while. I hadn't been anywhere except apartment hunting, job hunting, and to work since Mandy's birth. A drive with Glen would be a welcome change from my boring routine. And with Mandy along, it wouldn't really be a date.

"Okay," I agreed. "What time will you come?"

"Is eight o'clock all right?" he asked.

"Fine," I said. "I live in 22B."

When Glen's knock came right at eight, I had Mandy wrapped up and lying on the sofa, ready to go. She was such a good baby. As long as she was fed and dry, she never cried. I proudly showed her to Glen, who grinned at my motherly adoration.

We drove out into the country, then stopped for hamburgers at a diner. When we got back, I asked Glen in for coffee. We'd talked during the entire evening and even now we hadn't run out of things to say. Glen told a lot of funny stories about his days in the Navy, and I told him about my life in the foster homes and about running away. By the time he left at midnight, it seemed natural and right when he took me into his arms to kiss me good night.

Now Glen not only drove me to work in the mornings, he often stopped by in the evenings as well. On weekends we sometimes went out. I had found another young mother in the building who was willing to look after Mandy occasionally.

Glen's kisses were becoming more and more insistent, but I was determined to continue resisting. I hadn't counted on the possibility that under constant temptation, the hunger that Doug had awakened in me might be stronger than I was. I gave in to Glen one night after we'd been dining and dancing at one of the local night spots. That night I also told him that there would be no more intimacy—not until I had seen a doctor and was safely on the Pill. He didn't object, agreeing that it was the only thing to do.

I got the prescription three days later and was to begin taking the pills five days after my next period started, which would be in a week. But my period didn't come.

I waited for another full week and still it didn't come. Was I pregnant again? So soon and after making love only once? It seemed incredible, but after another week passed, I had to face the fact that it was a very real possibility. The only other time I'd missed my period was when I was pregnant with Mandy.

The chance that I might be pregnant caused me to reevaluate my short relationship with Glen. I didn't love him, I knew that. I had loved Doug and this wasn't the same thing at all. And though I'd been trying to ignore it, I knew that Glen wasn't being completely honest with me, either.

In the two months I'd know him, I had never met any of his friends. And the one time I had asked to see where he lived, he'd refused to take me, saying, "It's no place to invite a woman. Four bachelors can be pretty messy." He'd smiled apologetically, but I'd had the distinct feeling that I'd been put off for some other reason. Though the idea that he could be married had entered my mind, I'd rejected it, thinking that no woman would allow her husband out alone as often as Glen was.

So the night a station wagon pulled up behind Glen's car just as I was getting into it, and the woman driver jumped out and yelled, "Just a minute, you little slut!" I was really stunned. At first, I thought she'd mistaken me for someone else, and I stood there frozen, watching as she slammed the car door and came angrily toward me. She looked bent on murder.

Just then, Glen stepped out from behind me and wrapped an arm around her, pinning her arms to her chest. I hadn't even known he'd gotten out of the car. "Settle down, Lisa," I heard him say.

The woman was struggling violently against Glen's grip. "Leave me alone, Glen!" she shouted. "I'll kill you, you cheap tramp. Nobody goes after my husband and gets away with it!" she screamed at me.

By this time, I'd gathered my wits a little and thought that the best thing for me to do was to get out of there and let Glen handle her, maybe calm her down. And I was angry now myself. Angry at Glen. Divorced, was he? I was glad I hadn't given in to him more than once, even though that once probably meant I was pregnant again. I was glad, too, that I hadn't told him that I suspected I was pregnant. A man like that didn't deserve to know.

But Glen did show up at my door—the very next night. When I saw him standing there, my anger came back full force and I had to grit my teeth to keep it under control. I couldn't contain the sarcasm, though.

"Did you bring your wife?" I asked. "Or did you manage to give her the slip this time?"

"Aw, Cindy," he pleaded. "I didn't tell you because I knew you wouldn't want anything to do with me if you knew. I don't love her, but I can't leave her right now. Every time I mention divorce, she threatens to kill herself. I need you, Cindy. The only time I'm happy is when I'm with you."

He sounded so pathetic, I softened a little, but not enough to relent. "I'm sorry, Glen," I said. "But I have enough problems without having to watch over my shoulder for a jealous wife."

He stood silently by the door, just watching me. Finally he asked, "Can I still give you a ride to work in the mornings?"

"No," I said simply, my eyes not leaving his.

He sighed in defeat. "Well, I guess that's it then."

He turned and walked away. I shut the door after him. Glen hadn't even said good-bye, and neither had I.

The pregnancy test I had taken the next week turned out to be positive, as I'd known it would be. Abortion didn't even cross my mind. Maybe because I was an orphan and had never had a real family of my own, motherhood was too precious to me to consider such an alternative.

I worked at the Coach Lounge until I was five months along. My boss was something of a tyrant and very few of the staff liked him. I knew he wasn't going to be as sympathetic as Mr. Harrison had been, and I didn't want to stick around and let him have the pleasure of firing me. I quit, and a week later I moved to another apartment on the far side of the city.

I hadn't told anyone that I was pregnant again, knowing that such a situation would be hard for others to accept. I left no forwarding address with Mrs. Webster, nor did I tell Vivian and Russell—who still stopped by occasionally to see how I was doing—that I was moving. Even though Vivian had always been such a good friend, the shame I felt over this second mistake was just too much, and telling her seemed unbearable. All I wanted to do was hide from my past and start out fresh.

When I had taken the new apartment, I'd told the landlord that I was expecting another child and that my husband had run out on me. As a deserted wife, I knew I would be treated with some respect. And now in my new home, I continued to tell the lie to everyone I met.

Having no means of support now, I had to turn to welfare for financial assistance. I was honest about my situation as an unmarried mother. Though the monthly checks were skimpy and didn't stretch nearly far enough, I was glad I could stay home with Mandy and be a full-time mother. Soon, I was looking forward to the birth of my second child.

I made friends with other young mothers in the building. We often got together for coffee, and we baby-sat for each other occasionally. I was grateful when Noreen, who lived directly across the hall from me, offered to keep Mandy for me when I went into the hospital. Although Social Services had made arrangements for her care during my hospital stay, I was afraid to leave her with strangers. It was comforting to know that Noreen would watch her.

My son was born three days before Christmas, and once again I experienced the joy of new motherhood. A brother for Mandy, I thought as I lay my cheek against the downy softness of my little boy's head. I named him Joshua, just because I liked the sound of the name.

After Josh's birth, I had no desire to go back to work. Caring for my two children was satisfying and fulfilling. Though I felt a little guilty staying on welfare, I devoted my time and energy to Josh and Mandy. Each new thing they learned filled me with happiness and pride. Loneliness rarely crept up on me and when it did, company was just down the hall. Having never had the comfort of sharing life and its problems with anyone, the lack of a husband in my life didn't really bother me. For nearly two years, I was content living as I was.

Having two young children didn't stop men from approaching me. In the apartment, there were several single men, and I was one of the only unattached women in the building. There were lots of requests for dates. Sometimes I accepted and sometimes I didn't. I never gave in to their advances though. I'd had it with men. I knew what they wanted from me all right, but this time they weren't going to get it under any conditions. If someone wanted to take me out once in a while, that was fine. But sex was out. I was through being used.

When Josh was nearly two years old, I began to think more and more about the future. I would never get married now—that was a certainty. No man would want a ready-made family of two illegitimate children with different fathers. But would Mandy and Josh be enough for me?

The idea of having another child crept in and slowly took hold. *Why not?* I asked myself. I had two already whom I loved dearly. A third child would bring me even more happiness. All I had to do was get pregnant again. I could easily maintain my pretense of being a deserted wife by moving to yet another area of the city where I wouldn't be known. Vance Whitney, who lived in 18C, would be more than willing to cooperate. Of course, I wouldn't be able to tell him that I wanted to get pregnant. But if he wanted to take me to bed—and I knew he did—then I could let him and become pregnant again.

It occurred to me that my plan was calculating and dishonest, but I immediately pushed all those thoughts from my mind. Holding another newborn baby in my arms, adding to my beautiful family, would be worth it. And the thought of turning the tables on the male sex was almost as satisfying.

My choice of Vance, who was the epitome of male chauvinism as far as I was concerned, reflected my opinion of men in general. He was tall, dark, and handsome—a real ladies' man. Both he and his roommate were electricians who worked for the city during the week, and they were both egotistical skirt chasers on the weekends. There was often a party in their apartment. I'd been to a few of them, but I'd never stayed very long, even though Vance always tried to talk me into it. He considered me a big challenge, I was sure, and he would have liked nothing better than to see me get drunk so he could drag me into bed.

Even though Vance's interest in me was beginning to cool after so many turn-downs, it wasn't hard to rekindle it. I dropped my cool reserve and flirted with him openly. He latched on to my bait with enthusiasm. Soon, he was in my apartment nearly every night. I went out with him, too, whenever he asked. He was puzzled over the change in my attitude, but I ignored the strange looks he often gave me.

I first let Vance make love to me after one of the parties in his apartment. After that, he walked around with his chest stuck out and a triumphant grin on his face. Secretly, I gloated. He thought I had fallen madly in love with him—that he had conquered where others had failed. He had no idea that I was just using him, and I felt a smug pleasure. Men thought they were so smart—that they could use a girl for their own satisfaction, then dump her when someone else came along. Well, here was one man who was going to be dumped himself, just as soon as I got pregnant.

But where it had been all too easy for me to get pregnant with Josh, two months passed and I still wasn't pregnant now. I was getting sick of Vance and his cocky self-assurance and lying. He was dating other girls and thought he was fooling me. He didn't know that I knew and didn't care. I told myself I would give it one more month and if I wasn't pregnant by that time, I'd find some way to get rid of him and try again later with someone else.

But luck was with me. My next period didn't come and I knew I had to be pregnant. I said nothing to Vance. I would just move away and not tell him where I was going.

I went to Social Services and told them I was pregnant again. My caseworker merely shook her head at my "stupidity" and then helped me search for a bigger place. I wanted a house this time, so it took us another two months to find one that was affordable on my welfare checks. The house itself was really run down, but that was probably the only reason I was able to afford the rent on it at all.

An ad in the paper provided me with a pickup truck at a cheap rate to move what few possessions I had accumulated over the last few years. I moved in the daytime while Vance was at work, even though I would have liked to have seen the look on his face when he found out I was ditching him!

The house was an older two-story place with three bedrooms. Mr. Murphy, the landlord, was a trim, nice-looking man who I judged to be in his mid-thirties. I told him my tale of desertion, adding that divorce proceedings were underway and I expected them to be final in a few months. He assured me that although the house wasn't much to look at, everything was in working order and that if I had any trouble, he would be around to fix things.

I didn't mind the shabbiness of the old house. After living in an apartment for the last three years, it was heaven to have so much space and privacy. There was a fenced-in yard in the back, and I spent a lot of time there with Mandy and Josh. It was the first yard they had ever played in and they were fascinated with it. I mowed the overgrown grass with an old push mower I'd found in the basement of the house, and I nailed the few loose boards back onto the fence so the kids wouldn't get out. Now they could yell and squeal all they wanted to. I no longer had to keep them quiet like I'd had to in the apartment.

Inside the house, some of the linoleum was torn in places and the wallpaper was stained and faded. But somehow it didn't matter. I scrubbed and scraped until I had the house as clean as I could make it. I bought curtains from the thrift store and soon had the house looking like a real home.

It was a family neighborhood, and soon I made new friends with other mothers. Lana, a pert little blonde who lived next door and who had a four-year-old daughter, a playmate for Mandy, was at my door nearly every morning for coffee. Though she tended to gossip, I was glad for her company. My kids were my life, but I still looked forward to conversation and activities with other adults. We often went for groceries together or took the children to the nearby park.

It was after returning from one of these trips to the park one afternoon that I found Mr. Murphy sitting on my doorstep. He stood up as we approached. "Hi," he said. "I dropped by to see how the house was holding up." He smiled pleasantly while he waited for my response.

"I haven't had any trouble with anything," I told him. "Do you want to come in and have a look?"

"I might as well as long as I'm here," he said.

I unlocked the door and shooed Mandy inside. Josh had fallen asleep in my arms, and as I laid him down on the sofa and covered him up, I turned to see Mr. Murphy watching me. "Just go ahead and look around if you want to, Mr. Murphy," I said. "I'll get my daughter washed up and down for her nap, then I'll have a minute."

"Okay," he said. "But please call me Derek. I hate formalities." He wandered into the kitchen while I took a protesting Mandy to the bathroom to wash her face and hands. It was past the time she usually took her nap and she had whined all the way home.

After I'd gotten her settled in her bed with her favorite doll, I returned to the kitchen to find Derek inspecting the plumbing under the sink. I was glad now that I'd taken the time to clean the house so thoroughly. Even the space under the sink smelled fresh and clean. I put a pot of coffee on while he went down in the basement to check the furnace. Lana would be coming over as soon as she got her daughter to sleep.

Derek came up from the basement a few minutes later. "I'd like to do some work around here," he said. "That is, if you don't mind having me underfoot on weekends."

He must have seen the look of dismay on my face and read my mind. "Oh, don't worry," he said, smiling. "I won't raise the rent when I'm done."

I breathed a sigh of relief. Welfare only allowed so much for rent, and I didn't want to move. In the two months we'd lived there, I'd come to love the old house. It was perfect for me and the kids.

Just then, Lana came through the back door. "Hi, Derek," she said brightly. "How was California? I didn't know you were back. How's Jeffrey? He goes to kindergarten this year, doesn't he?"

Lana had lived in the house next door for four years and it was apparent that she knew Derek Murphy quite well. As she stood there talking with him, I wondered why I hadn't gotten the rundown on him, like I already had about most of the other neighbors. I knew I soon would though. As soon as he left, I would get a detailed account of his history. I smiled at the thought. Lana wasn't a malicious person. She never told lies about anyone, but she sure did like to spread the truth around.

When Derek left, she started right in. "There's a man for you, Cindy," she said eagerly. "I never thought of it until now. His wife died about five months ago, so he's eligible. He has a five-year-old son, but I know you wouldn't object to that, the way you love children."

Lana had once said I was crazy when I told her that I was no longer interested in men—that my children were all I needed to make me happy. That was still true, but I couldn't help being a little bit curious about my landlord.

"What did his wife die from?" I asked.

"Some form of cancer," Lana told me. "I guess little Jeffrey was quite shook up about it, so Derek took him to California on his vacation. He'd be a good catch, Cindy. He's an accountant and makes good money. And he's cute!"

"You can forget any ideas you have about matching me up with him," I told her. "I'm already starting to show, and I'm sure Mr. Murphy doesn't want anything to do with a pregnant woman."

"Maybe not," she agreed. "But you're not going to be pregnant forever, you know."

"Lana," I said, leaning across the table, "I'm not interested, okay?"

"Okay, okay." She laughed. "It was just an idea. I won't mention it again." But I knew she would.

On Saturday, Derek came to the door with a ladder, pails, a huge steamer, and a small boy. "You don't mind if Jeffrey plays in the yard, do you? I usually leave him at home with my parents, but my dad isn't feeling well and needs to rest."

"Mandy will love it," I assured him. "Josh is still just a baby, so she loves it when she gets the chance to play with older children. You can bring him anytime you come."

"They'll be good for each other then," he said with a slight grin. "Jeffrey doesn't get much of a chance to play with other kids, either. There aren't many around our neighborhood. But he goes to kindergarten in the mornings now, so I guess that helps." He paused. "I'd like to start in the bedrooms if that's all right with you. I'll try not to make too much of a mess." He carried the ladder and his tools upstairs, then came back down for the steamer. "I have to strip the old wallpaper off first," he explained when he saw me looking curiously at the odd machine. "You steam it and it all peels off easily. I'll have you get your bedding out of the room, and I'll move the mattress and box spring. Otherwise, everything's going to get damp."

I followed him upstairs and into my bedroom and folded the sheets and blankets. I removed the pillows, too, piling everything on Mandy's bed. Then I went downstairs to check on the kids playing out in the yard. They were making tracks in the dirt with the toy cars Jeffrey had brought with him. Jeffrey and Mandy seemed to have become fast friends in the short time they had known each other. Josh watched them both, fascinated for the moment by what they were doing.

I turned to see Derek lounging against the door, smiling. "I got the steamer going," he said. "In about half an hour, I can start scraping."

"Would you like a cup of coffee while you're waiting?" I asked. "I have some ready." It seemed like the thing to do, and he accepted. I poured two cups of coffee, then I sat down at the table with Derek. The kitchen window looked out over the backyard, and Derek was now absorbed in watching the kids, a dreamy smile on his face.

Suddenly I felt nervous. What could we possibly talk about? Our worlds were so far apart. He was a good-looking widower who owned property and vacationed in California. I was an orphan on welfare with two, soon to be three, children and no wedding ring on my finger. Had I made a mistake in pursuing even this casual friendship? A lock of hair had fallen over Derek's forehead, giving him a boyish look, and he made no move to brush it away. He seemed perfectly at ease when he finally said, "Kids are great, aren't they? So straightforward and honest. I wish I was a kid again, don't you?"

"Not really," I disagreed. "I'm satisfied with the way my life is right now. My childhood wasn't that happy, so I don't regret leaving it behind."

Right after I'd spoken, I felt a flush creep into my cheeks. Why had I been so blunt about my childhood to this man who was a virtual stranger? I hoped he didn't think I was trying to get his sympathy. Apparently he didn't, judging from his next words.

"It seems we all get a portion of both sadness and happiness," he said. "It's a part of life, I guess."

I knew he was probably remembering his wife, so I changed the subject. "Lana told me you and your son were in California. Did you have a good time?" I asked, remembering too late the reason they had gone there and that this, too, would be a reminder of his wife's recent death.

But he brightened. "We stayed with my brother and his wife in Santa Monica," he said. "Jeffrey loved the beach. He brought home three boxes of shells. Now his bedroom smells like a fish cannery."

I laughed. "Well," I said, "if nostalgia ever grips you, a short time spent there with your eyes closed should bring the memories right back."

We were both laughing now and continued to do so as we dredged up funny stories about our kids. My nervousness left me. We shared a common concern—our children. Before we knew it, an hour had gone by and Derek went back upstairs to work on the walls.

Lunchtime came and I made sandwiches, mixed some juice, and carried everything outside where the kids and I had a picnic on a blanket I'd spread on the grass. Jeffrey became strangely quiet in my presence, and I felt sudden compassion for the small boy who had lost his mother so recently. I could understand his hurt, since I had lost my parents, too. I was glad he still had his father. At least he wasn't homeless like I had been. But his shyness left quickly, and soon he and Mandy were stealing glances at each other and giggling behind their glasses of orange juice.

After I'd taken the dishes back into the house, I stayed outside a while longer, enjoying the beautiful summer day, surrounded by the children. At one-thirty, I took Josh into the house to wash him and put him down for his nap. He didn't even protest he was so tired. Mandy and Jeffrey were having such fun, I decided to skip Mandy's nap that day and just let her play.

When Josh was tucked snugly in his bed, I put on a fresh pot of coffee. I guess the smell wafted upstairs, because soon after it started to perk, Derek came down looking worried. "I wasn't paying any attention to the time," he said. "Jeffrey must be starving. I'd better take him to lunch."

"He's had lunch," I told him. "I fed him with my kids." Derek seemed embarrassed.

"You didn't have to do that," he said.

"That's all right," I said. "It's the least I can do when his father is busy redecorating my home. You're the only one who hasn't eaten. Would you like a sandwich?"

"Only if you let me buy dinner." He was smiling now.

"It's a deal," I said, smiling back.

While Derek ate, I sat drinking coffee and we talked some more about the kids and then the plans he had for the house. He told me he would bring samples of wallpaper and flooring around and let me choose the kind I wanted for each room. Derek worked for two more hours that afternoon, then went out and bought a huge pizza and brought it back to the house. Shortly after we'd eaten, he collected Jeffrey, who had gone back outside with Mandy, and left, saying he would be back the next day to finish removing the old wallpaper from my bedroom. It was going to take him longer than he had figured, since there were three layers stuck firmly with age. I told him I didn't mind the inconvenience. I would just put my mattress on the floor in Josh's bedroom and sleep there until he was done.

That first day set a pattern for weekends that we followed almost faithfully. I would provide lunch and coffee, and Derek would bring supper in, sometimes pizza or chicken, and other times he would take us all out for hamburgers.

The work on the house went slowly, but after my bedroom was done, I knew it was all going to be worth it. Derek had done a beautiful, professional-looking job. Walking into the room, with its new wallpaper with the tiny rosebuds on it and the freshly varnished woodwork, was like entering another house altogether.

By mid-November, the upstairs had been completed and Derek was installing new cupboards in the kitchen. My pregnancy was coming to term now, and Lana was going to look after Mandy and Josh while I was in the hospital.

A week before my due date, I woke up in the middle of the night with a vague aching sensation in the small of my back. Having already been through this twice before, I knew that I was in the early stages of labor. There was no hurry, though. A glance at the clock told me it was nearly four in the morning. Maybe I could even get a few more hours of sleep.

I was just dozing off again when I felt an urgent need to go to the bathroom and was annoyed at being forced to leave my warm bed. When I stood up, I realized my water had broken. I would have to get to the hospital right away.

I considered waking up the kids, dressing them, and taking them over to Lana's, then decided that I'd better wake up Lana first. Already I was beginning to feel the increasing intensity of the contractions. I would need her help.

I got dressed and hurried over to Lana's, ringing the doorbell insistently. Bernie, her husband, came to the door. When he saw it was me, he ushered me inside and said, "I'll wake Lana up." He knew there was only one reason I'd be dropping in at such an early hour.

Both Lana and Bernie came down the stairs fully dressed a few minutes later. She headed to my house to get the children and Bernie drove me to the hospital.

At the hospital, I was put to bed, examined, and taken straight to the delivery room. Half an hour later, my new daughter was placed in my arms. I named her Elizabeth.

The next day, a Saturday, I was surprised to see Derek walk into my room, a pink teddy bear and a dozen long-stemmed roses in his arms. I almost cried. No one had ever brought me flowers before.

And when I returned home from the hospital, I found a beige desk phone sitting on the new kitchen counter with a note propped up on the dial. "Compliments of the management and included in the rent," it said.

Now why would Derek go and do a thing like that? I wondered. I'd once mentioned to him that I wanted to get a phone installed, but I'd told him that I would wait until the house was finished. His generosity embarrassed me, and when he came the next Saturday, I scolded him for it and tried to be insistent about paying the monthly service charge.

But he was even more stubborn than I was. "It's a small token of my appreciation for keeping my property so clean and tidy," he said. "The tenants before you were so messy, I'm surprised the Board of Health didn't get after them."

Life was hectic for a while after Elizabeth's birth. Lana was a great help. Every afternoon for the first two weeks I was home, she took Mandy and Josh to her house for several hours so I could rest.

Although I knew that the phone and the roses were given with no ulterior motive in mind, Derek's gifts still put a shadow of apprehension and guilt over my feelings for him. He didn't know that I didn't deserve his high esteem. I wasn't the poor little deserted wife he believed me to be. I felt like a thief, taking things under false pretenses. It made me feel self-conscious in his presence.

When Christmas time came, I got Derek a rib-knit pullover, the kind he often wore, in navy blue, and a matching one for Jeffrey. The weekend before Christmas, Derek arrived with presents for all of us as I'd suspected he might, and I was glad that this time I could give something in return. There were toys for Mandy, Josh, and Beth, and a tiny cross on a delicate gold chain for me. The exchange was a happy, boisterous affair, with Derek and me laughing at the children's impatience and excitement over the coming of Santa Claus in only two days.

Derek didn't work on the house that day, and he and Jeffrey didn't stay long. But the Christmas spirit we all felt reinforced our casual friendship and lessened my guilt. We were, after all, just a tenant and a landlord who had struck up a friendly bond. We would always be just that, and such a friendship didn't require the spilling of all secrets to make it right.

In the months that followed, Derek treated me as he always had before and I felt completely at ease with him. There were no more unexpected gifts or any signs that things would ever change. When the redecorating was finished in April, Derek still continued to come by on Saturdays with Jeffrey. We spent the day with the kids, playing games in the yard or going for a drive and stopping for ice-cream cones somewhere along the way. I was glad we could share our single parenthood in such an honest and comfortable way. The kids were certainly benefiting from it, and although Derek was a man, I didn't have to be afraid of him coming on to me and asking more of our relationship than I was willing to give. Things were perfect between us, I thought—and safe.

So the afternoon I went out to check on Mandy and Jeffrey and overheard their childish conversation, my sense of security was interrupted once more. Derek had gone to get tools from his garage so he could repair some of the toys that had gotten broken. Mandy and Jeffrey were playing in a "house" they had made from an old box and didn't hear me coming.

"Me and my dad are going to marry you," I heard Jeffrey say. "Daddy told me."

I stopped in my tracks several feet away.

"What's marry?" Mandy asked.

"That's when we all live together and I can play with you every day," Jeffrey replied.

At first I was thoroughly shaken. Had Derek really said such a thing, or had Jeffrey just made it up? Could a boy his age come up with something like that on his own? *He must have,* I thought. Why would Derek say it when we were only friends? Surely he didn't read marriage into a relationship like ours. He was too realistic.

I decided that Jeffrey was only trying to show Mandy how much more he knew than she did. He'd probably gotten the idea from some television show. I went back to the house without disturbing them, smiling in amusement. When Derek got back, I thought of sharing the incident with him, then decided against it. Telling him might make it look like I was hinting at marriage.

Two weeks later, Derek showed up, followed by a tow truck pulling an older blue car. He stood looking on as the tow-truck driver maneuvered it into the driveway beside the house. Jeffrey was already inside the house, calling for Mandy. I walked out with Beth in my arms, curious about why Derek had brought the car here. *Maybe there isn't room at his parents' house,* I thought. The car obviously wasn't running, and I guessed he couldn't park it on the street. But the body looked to be in good shape, so he was probably planning on fixing it. I knew he did most of the repairs on his car.

"I see you bought another car," I said.

"I didn't buy it," Derek told me. "A friend of mine was taking it to the wreckers and when I found out that all it needs is a water pump and some brake work, I asked him if I could have it. After it's fixed, it's yours."

I think my mouth fell open before I said, "Mine? I don't even know how to drive."

"You will," he said, grinning mischievously and taking Beth from my arms. "Lessons start next Saturday and continue every Saturday thereafter until you pass your driver's test. My niece will baby-sit while we're out endangering lives," he teased.

I had to laugh, although my insides were churning with indecision. Why was Derek rocking the boat again after we'd been sailing smoothly for so long? Favors like these created an imbalance in our friendship and made me feel uncomfortable. Didn't he realize that? But should I refuse him?

When I looked up at Derek again, he looked so pleased with himself that I just couldn't. Rejecting his offer would only disappoint him. I couldn't hurt him that way. And maybe someday I would be able to repay him by doing something equally nice in return.

The following Saturday, Derek arrived with Jeffrey and a friendly sixteen-year-old girl, his niece, Karen. The kids took to her right away, and after I'd given her a few instructions Derek and I climbed into his car to begin my driving lesson. On the third lesson, Derek sat back on the seat instead of on the edge like he'd done during the first two. He told me that I was going to make a good driver. But my initial apprehension about getting behind the wheel seemed to persist, and it was several more weeks before I could pin down the reason. It wasn't fear of driving that was making me nervous. It was Derek's closeness in the confining interior of the car.

Before the lessons had begun, I'd never really been alone with him. The kids had always been close at hand, no farther than the yard or the backseat of the car. Now it was just him and me, and even the daylight didn't seem to ease the nervousness I was feeling.

With this realization, I began really concentrating on my driving, trying to ignore Derek's presence. I was determined to learn as fast as I could. After I passed the driving test, the lesson would stop and life would return to normal. I would no long be forced to endure the turmoil and confusion I was feeling now. Soon I was driving confidently through traffic and busy intersections, and Derek decided it was time to teach me how to parallel park. We drove out to the suburbs and he found two cars parked along the curb that he thought were the right distance apart. I bungled my first two attempts. Once I almost hit one of the cars, and on the second try, I ran the back tire up on the curb. The third time I did it just right, and when I turned proudly toward Derek, I found myself in his arms, his lips on mine in a gentle yet passionate kiss.

It was so unexpected, I had no defense. I was totally swept away by emotions that I realized I had only been trying to hide. When at last I pulled away, Derek was looking at me with such love I thought I would melt. I looked away, confused. I couldn't handle this. I hadn't prepared myself for it, preferring to ignore the possibility that it would ever happen.

The second jolt was Derek's proposal—almost right on the heels of the kiss.

"Let's get married, Cindy," he said quietly. "I've loved you for so long. I wanted to give you plenty of time to get over your first marriage before I asked you. I think you love me, too. It's time to start living again, for your own sake as well as the sake of the kids."

I burst into uncontrollable sobs. Derek was right. I did love him, and I had for a long time. But admitting it only brought on the pain of its futility. I couldn't marry him. I wasn't the woman he thought I was. I had three children fathered by three different men. Derek was a decent, hardworking man. He deserved the best, certainly not a person like me.

"I can't marry you, Derek," I sobbed. "I just can't."

"Why, Cindy?" he asked, smoothing my hair with his hand. "It seems so right for both of us."

I pushed away from him and, taking a tissue from my purse, I wiped my eyes and blew my nose. "I just can't. That's all," I said icily, my tears now under control.

I put the car into drive and headed toward home. Derek didn't speak again as I drove, and I was filled with remorse for the pain I was causing him.

In front of the house, I reached for the door handle, but Derek took hold of my arm and held me back. I looked at him and was surprised to see that instead of the hurt look I'd expected, his eyes were still shining with love and full of self-confidence.

"I am going to marry you, Cindy," he said.

I didn't answer. If I had, the tears would have come again full force. He let go of my arm and I got out of the car and ran for the house, seeking the protection of the children's presence. Derek just strolled along behind me.

He didn't work on the car that day as he usually did after the driving lessons. After the kids had played with him for a while, he left with Karen and Jeffrey. "See you next weekend," he said casually as he walked out the door.

For the next few days I was absolutely miserable. It was time to reap the consequences of the way in which I'd chosen to live. I tried to remember when my feelings toward Derek had first started changing, but it had been such a gradual thing that I couldn't be sure. Always, it seemed, I had looked forward to the weekends, to opening the door and seeing Derek and Jeffrey standing there. But because I'd believed I would never love again—that the magic I had experienced with Doug for that short time would be all that would ever come my way—I'd chosen to ignore my feelings and label our relationship simple friendship.

I realized now that Doug had never truly loved me. Though he had been kind to me for a time, I had always been just a substitute for his old girlfriend, Annette. Now here was Derek, who loved me enough to offer me everything: love, marriage, security. But I had forfeited the right to those things long ago. All I would ever have now would be my children, and one day they would be grown and gone. Then I would have nothing but memories.

Sometimes anger at Derek would rise up and engulf me. Why couldn't he have left well enough alone? We'd been getting along fine as friends. Why had he made me face my love for him and spoiled it all?

I couldn't let him go on believing in me, hoping that in time I would marry him. I would have to tell him the truth and destroy his dream so he could be free. The love and respect he now had for me would die before my eyes, taking with it the friendship we had once shared. There wouldn't even be Saturday afternoons to look forward to anymore. He would want nothing more to do with me. I was sure of it.

By Thursday, I couldn't take it any longer. I needed relief and thought that the best thing to do would be to confess right away and get it over with. I phoned Derek at his office and asked him if he could come over that night so I could explain why I'd been so upset over his proposal.

He said he would come, and that evening I put the kids to bed early so we could talk without interruption. While I waited for Derek, I paced the floor, rehearsing what I would say.

By the time he arrived shortly after eight, I was a nervous wreck. He sat down on the sofa beside me, looking curious and concerned. Beginning my story was terribly painful. I knew it wasn't going to come out right, no matter how I put it. And I knew that once it was over, Derek would be gone from my life.

"I'm not the person you think I am," I began haltingly. I took a deep breath, searching for my next words.

"I'll be the judge of that," Derek said quietly.

I couldn't help it. I burst out crying again. His faith in me was too much to take. But the tears brought release, and the whole story poured out of me in a torrent of sorrow and misgivings. I made no excuses for myself, knowing there were none that would make up for my situation.

"And I got pregnant with Beth on purpose," I finished. "Just because I wanted more children. That's why I can't marry you." My crying had stopped now and I felt drained.

Derek hadn't interrupted again and he was still quiet. I was afraid to look at him, reluctant to face the revulsion I was sure I'd see in his face. I felt his hands on my shoulders, pulling me gently toward him, and I jerked away and stood up.

"No, Derek," I said, still not looking at him. "Don't make it any harder than it already is. You can go now. I'll be all right." I walked into the kitchen and stood by the window, looking out into the blackness of the night. I had thought that I'd cried myself out, but the sound of the door closing brought on a new wave of tears.

Sometime later, I dragged myself up to bed, but it was a long time before I fell asleep. I was wishing now that I'd never met Derek. Before he'd interrupted my quiet life, I'd been content and happy.

I was exhausted the next day, and even the kids didn't bring me the pleasure they usually did. I was glad when they were finally asleep again for the night. I ran water into the tub, hoping a nice hot bath would relax me and help me sleep.

I was just about to step into the tub when the doorbell rang. Thinking it was probably Lana coming to return the pie plates I'd lent her that day, I put my robe back on, went downstairs, and opened the door. But it wasn't Lana. It was Derek.

I just stood there, staring.

"Can I come in?" he asked.

Still, I stood looking at him blankly until finally he took me by the shoulders, moved me aside, and shut the door. Taking me by the hand, he led me to the sofa and sat me down. He sat beside me and from his jacket pocket he withdrew a small velvet box, opened it, and took out a sparkling diamond ring.

I couldn't move, couldn't believe this was really happening. Hadn't he understood what I'd told him last night? Derek picked up my limp hand and slipped the ring on my finger. "It fits!" he said, smiling at me tenderly.

I finally found my voice. "You mean you still want to marry me?" I asked, astonished.

"Of course I do!" he assured me. "I would have told you so last night, but judging from the mood you were in, you would have thought I was saying it out of pity. And I don't feel the least bit sorry for you. I'm a very selfish man. You're a wonderful, loving woman with three beautiful children, and I want to be a part of it—I want my son to be a part of it." He was grinning, his eyes twinkling happily.

I started to cry again, but this time they were tears of happiness. In Derek's strong arms, I said a silent prayer of thanks to God for sending me this miracle.

"We'll wait a few months to get married," Derek said. "I want you to meet all of the family, and I want to wine and dine you in style before we settle down."

"Oh, Derek," I said, "you don't have to do that."

"But I want to," he told me. "Then when we're old and gray, we'll have all those good memories to look back on."

On Saturday, we lined up all four of the kids on the sofa and made a big show of our announcement. Ten-month-old Beth didn't really care, and even Josh was too young to truly understand. But Jeffrey and Mandy sure did. Immediately after Derek had said the all-important words, Jeffrey turned to my daughter and said, "See, Mandy? I told you we were getting married!"

Derek and I just held each other tight and laughed, both of us knowing that now we would be sharing many more of these moments together as a close and loving family—the family I'd always dreamed of having. THE END

LOVE, HONOR, AND DECEIVE

The first time I ever saw Brian Meade, I had the strangest feeling that I should run away from him, that I should escape while I could, while there was still time.

I couldn't look away from his eyes. They were gray, disturbing and startling against the tan of his skin and the dark brown of his hair.

No man had ever made me feel so completely alive, the way he did. Those gray eyes took in everything about me at a glance, and even before I knew what his reaction was, I desperately wanted him to like what he saw. I wanted to be beautiful for him, smart and bright and important, and anything he wanted me to be.

The words of an old hymn we used to sing back home in the little church in Prewitt came into my mind: I'll go where You want me to go, dear Lord, I'll be what You want me to be.

Then, shame and panic and fear hit me, because I realized it was sacrilege to think of that simple, beautiful old song to describe the way I felt about a man I'd just met.

And it wasn't only the sacrilegious part that frightened me. I remembered so well how much in love my sister had been with Ed Connors, and what loving him had done to her. I didn't want to feel that way about any man. I wouldn't.

My cheeks burned with anger at myself for reacting as I had when this complete stranger walked into the office where I worked, but I used my most business-like tone when I asked what I could do for him.

He was obviously tense and upset. "I'm Brian Meade, from

Planning and Expediting," he said, mentioning another department in the company. "I'd like to see Miss Craig. Someone in this department made a big mistake, and if it isn't fixed, it's going to cost the company thousands of dollars."

Miss Craig, my supervisor, wasn't due back from lunch for another ten minutes. I tried to locate the necessary records and statistics, but I wasn't very sure of myself. I'd only worked at Sherman Electronics for two weeks, and it was my first job after secretarial school.

As Brian Meade followed me down the long row of files, I was so conscious of him that I was almost trembling. Later, after Miss Craig came back to the office and I transferred the problem to her, Brian said, "Thank you, Miss Scott. I hope I didn't terrify you. Actually, that magnolia-and-honey voice of yours calmed me down considerably."

His grin sent warmth all through me, and when I got back to my desk, I still felt shaken.

Later, Miss Craig, who was brisk and middle aged, said, "Sharon, you may as well know the facts right now. You aren't the first girl to be bowled over by Brian Meade, and you won't be the last."

I tried to tell her I'd just been upset because Brian seemed so tense, but she wouldn't listen. "He's attractive, that's for sure," she went on, "but he's also coldly ambitious. Just now, he's having a heavy romance with Regina Kelton, the daughter of the general manager. Incidentally, she works here in the publicity office. She took the job a few weeks ago, apparently because she was bored with being a debutante. And Brian is obviously out to marry her. You'll see them around. Everybody does, sooner or later."

I was embarrassed, but, at the same time, I was grateful that she'd warned me about the kind of person Brian was. I really had needed that warning, or I wouldn't have reacted to him as I had. I didn't want to love any man who could hurt me, as Leah had so blindly loved Ed Connors.

I was sixteen and Leah eighteen when our family moved up north to Chicago. We were full of dreams then about the glamorous life we'd have in the city, but it had been hard for us to leave Prewitt, our hometown. Our family had lived there for many generations.

As we'd grown up, Dad had often reminded Leah and me that our ancestors had come from Virginia in early pioneer days, and were close kin to Nancy Hanks, Abraham Lincoln's mother. We were always proud of that.

We left Prewitt because it was a dying town. The lumber yard where Dad worked closed, and there weren't any other jobs. We'd had our farm, but could hardly raise enough on it to pay the taxes.

Chicago was very thrilling to us at first, but it wasn't long until our whole family was homesick. My father found work as a warehouseman, but living costs were high, and we had to live in a tiny apartment in a rundown neighborhood.

We were happier after a church of our own denomination opened nearby in an old store off Wilson Avenue. We attended Sunday services and prayer meetings there, and there were church suppers like we used to have back home.

I wasn't allowed to date, even though I was in high school. My parents were very strict. Leah, of course, was out of school and over eighteen, so my parents couldn't forbid her to do what she wanted.

She found a job as a waitress in a restaurant in the neighborhood, and dated several men she met there. She earned a good salary, so she was able to buy pretty clothes and have her pale blond hair fixed in the latest style. When I saw her dressed in her cute new outfits, I prayed I'd be as attractive as she was when I was older. My hair was blond, too, but darker, and I wasn't quite so curvy.

"Don't worry, honey," Leah always told me. "You'll do just fine!"

Ed Connors wasn't from our part of the country. He'd lived in Chicago all his life, and he was a car salesman. The first time I saw Leah with him, I felt an aching, longing envy. He was so attractive, so tall and tanned, so attentive to my sister. She'd fallen very hard for him, and being so much in love made her more beautiful than ever.

Mother and Dad were dead set against Ed because he was over

thirty, didn't belong to our church, and because he drank. Members of our church weren't permitted to use liquor or tobacco.

Leah not only dated Ed, she admitted she'd let him buy cocktails for her. She said defiantly, "We're not living back in the sticks now. You're going to have to realize things are different here."

Finally, she went to live with three other girls. She came back to our apartment less and less often, but I went to visit her whenever I could.

She described her glamorous dates with Ed, told me the things he said and how wonderful he was to her. He was her whole life, and I knew that when I fell in love, I'd feel the same way.

But, suddenly, it was all over. Instead of wanting to marry Leah, Ed lost interest in her. I'd been so close to her that I felt as if I were going through her bewilderment and heartbreak. I longed to do something, anything, to make Ed come back to her.

The first time I found Leah in her bed on a Saturday morning, I didn't realize what was wrong with her. I was just frightened because she seemed so desperately sick. I wanted to rush out and get my mother.

One of Leah's roommates said, "Wait, honey. Don't you know a hangover when you see one? Leah was drunk last night. Again."

I didn't tell my parents about Leah's drinking. I just tried to get her to stop. Leah promised again and again that she would. Only she never kept the promise.

Of course, Mother and Dad found out about it finally. They were called down to the county jail when Leah was picked up as a common drunk.

All of us tried to reason with my sister after that. And more than once, Leah said, "I know—no man is worth it. But I love Ed. I just can't forget him. I guess that's why I drink. I don't care what happens to me if I can't have Ed's love."

Two or three times, we persuaded her to come back home and live with the family. But she always slipped away from us and started the whole heartbreaking pattern all over again. She'd get a job, and then begin drinking.

Worrying about Leah made Mother and Dad grow old long before they should have. It ruined my last year of high school, too, because I avoided dating or even being close friends with anyone. I was so mixed up and worried about Leah, ashamed, and yet heartsick because I loved her so much. I was afraid people would think I was like her. That was the one thing in life I was sure I didn't want to be—like Leah. I'd never let myself get hurt the way she had, and I'd never be as weak as she was.

After my graduation from high school, I took a one-year course at secretarial school, and on my nineteenth birthday, I began working at Sherman Electronics.

Miss Craig's remarks about Brian Meade, that day I met him, left me feeling terribly depressed, and I couldn't understand why. I just knew I felt a vague, senseless fear. . . .

A few days later, I went for a walk during my lunch hour. I was coming back, nearing the main entrance of the building, when a sleek convertible swept up to the parking area. Brian Meade was driving it, and with him was a strikingly attractive girl. She was very tall and dark, and dramatic in a suit the orangey color of bittersweet berries I used to find in the woods back near Prewitt.

Brian didn't notice me even though he passed very close to me. He was too attentive to the girl to see anyone else.

He certainly didn't mean anything to me, I reminded myself, and yet, watching him with that other girl, I felt stunned and sick.

A few days later, we met in the hall outside Miss Craig's office. Brian was hurrying, as usual, but when he saw me, he said, "Hey, there! You're the girl in the records department. How about having a quick cup of coffee with me?"

It was a fall day, and the cafeteria overlooked a park where the trees were turning red and gold. Looking at them, I felt a sudden wave of homesickness, not just for Prewitt, but for the old days when

Leah and I were small.

"Where's the place that makes you homesick?" Brian asked, and I was startled because I hadn't spoken my thoughts aloud. It was sort of weird, his reading my mind.

I felt suddenly as if I'd known him always, and to my surprise, I found myself telling him about Prewitt, and even about my being related to Nancy Hanks. All the time I talked, Brian never looked away from my face.

I came to myself with a start when I realized we'd been in the cafeteria twenty minutes. "Miss Craig will be furious!" I said.

"If she gives you a hard time, send her to me," Brian said. "I'll tell her it was all my fault."

He touched my hand, and I felt jolted, as if I'd come in contact with electric current. It seemed to startle and bewilder Brian, too.

I didn't see him again for a week. Then one night, there was a drenching rainstorm. I hadn't brought an umbrella, so I waited a while after work, hoping the storm would stop. Finally, I gave up and sloshed out to the bus stop.

Brian came out of the building after me. "Sharon," he called. "How about letting me rescue you?" He didn't wait for an answer, but took my arm and together, we ran to the parking lot, toward his car.

Neither of us said very much as he drove through the late-afternoon traffic, but I felt a deep sense of happiness, a crazy longing for the ride to last forever.

Brian said suddenly, "Tell me some more about Prewitt, Sharon. About what you'd be doing if you were there instead of here tonight." I thought at first he was making fun of me. But then he said, "I mean it. I need to hear you talk. You soothe me, and the day has been really rough."

I began to talk about what it would be like, back home, on a rainy night. It seemed as if Brian and I were the only two people in the world. We were shut in together, warm and safe.

He asked if I'd have dinner with him, so we stopped at a pay phone so I could call my mother. Then, we drove out to a restaurant where there was a big open fire flickering on a hearth.

There was only one awkward moment for me, and that was when Brian asked what I wanted to drink. As I told him I didn't drink, my own embarrassment shocked me. I didn't want to sound old fashioned.

But Brian didn't seem to care. He nodded casually and ordered a drink for himself.

He'd said he wanted to listen to me, but actually he did most of the talking. He described his job, and told me about some new ideas he was trying to get accepted by the management. I couldn't really understand the details, but the whole project obviously meant so much to Brian that after awhile, I found myself desperately wanting him to be successful.

He also told me about his family, which consisted of his mother and an older brother. "Mom had a pretty rough time, getting Bob and me through school," he said. "She always wanted everything for us, and worked hard to get it, as a real estate saleswoman. Bob was more help to her than I was, I'm afraid."

When he talked about his brother, his voice deepened with admiration. "There's no one like Bob. He won a scholarship to Northwestern University, and then went on to graduate at the top of his class in law school. When he passed the bar exams, several different big firms wanted to hire him. He's only twenty-seven now, but he earns over a hundred thousand a year. I wish I could believe I'd be doing that well two years from now."

"You'll be just as successful as he is," I insisted, and I believed it. But I didn't see that making that much money was as important as Brian seemed to think it was.

For a minute, thinking of his brother, Brian looked so unsure of himself he might have been a stranger, and not the ambitious, dynamic man I'd met at Sherman Electronics. And, I thought, he certainly couldn't be as conceited and selfish as Miss Craig had said.

When we left the restaurant, it wasn't raining, but the night had turned very cold. I shivered, and Brian got one of his old coats out of the back of the car and put it around me. His hand brushed my face, and I felt as if I'd been burned.

I'd never before wanted a man to kiss me, but I shamelessly wanted it then.

"Sharon—" Brian said, as if he could read my mind, and in a slow, deliberate way, pulled me to him. But there was nothing slow or deliberate about the kiss. It left both of us startled and shaken by dizzying, wild sweetness.

But almost immediately, the spell was broken, and Brian became distant and remote. When he took me home, he was almost impersonal. He didn't mention wanting to date me again.

I saw him at work the next day, but he was coldly polite, as if he'd never kissed me, as if we'd never been drawn together in a stormy, irresistible way.

It hadn't meant anything to him. I made myself face that fact again and again during the next week. But facing it didn't make it hurt any less, or make me feel any less angry with myself for falling in love with Brian.

The following Thursday, I saw him with Regina Kelton. They were in the downstairs main lobby of the building, standing apart from the crowd, talking in a low, intimate way. Suddenly, Brian looked up, straight into my eyes, and I realized I'd been staring.

I hoped desperately that my face didn't show the sick longing I felt, the stunning hurt, but I knew it probably did. I was so ashamed.

Brian picked me up at the bus stop that night after work, and we had dinner again at the same restaurant. I pushed the thought of Regina out of my mind and was happy in a crazy, half-hurting way.

Once again, Brian and I talked a great deal. I had thought I could never discuss Leah with anyone, but I found myself telling Brian all about her. He seemed very understanding and sympathetic.

"I wish I could give you advice on how to help her, but I can't," he said.

That evening, as he had before, he mentioned his admiration for his brother. "If I live to be a hundred; I'll never have a tenth of Bob's ability. I just never measured up to him."

Later, as he helped me into his car to take me home, it seemed as if we were both possessed by a sudden longing hunger. We clung to each other and kissed again and again. "Oh, Sharon, Sharon," Brian whispered. There was a kind of bewilderment in his tone, and it was almost as if he'd said aloud that the way he felt about me surprised him, that he hadn't meant for it to happen.

I suppose it gave me a thrill just to talk about Brian. The next day, when one of the girls at the office remarked that she'd seen him pick me up the evening before, I admitted we'd been dating, even though I knew the story would probably travel all over the office.

During the next few days, however, Brian was very impersonal to me again, and I couldn't fight the despair that haunted me. He and Regina were often together, and I was torn between hating him and remembering how we'd seemed to be so happy together.

One afternoon, Regina came into the records office and asked me to locate some statistics for her. Her eyes took in everything about me. She said suddenly, "You're Sharon Scott, aren't you? Brian has mentioned you to me. He worries a lot about other people's problems. He wishes he could help your sister."

I was really shocked to think that Brian had discussed Leah with Regina or anyone else. I'd taken it for granted that he'd hold our conversation in confidence.

While I was still stunned from her first words, Regina added, "You seem to be a nice girl, hun. If I were you, I wouldn't try to create the impression here at the office that you're dating Brian. People are laughing at you behind your back. Brian is only sorry for you because you seem rather—well, out of place, unsophisticated."

After Regina went back to her own office, I was numb at first, but then hurt and the humiliation made me so sick I could hardly go on working.

Late that evening, Brian called me at home. He'd had a rough day, he said. He was in the neighborhood and wondered if I'd have a quick drink with him.

I almost refused. Then I agreed. I was waiting for him outside the apartment entrance when he arrived. As soon as I was in his car, I told him what I thought of him for repeating my story about Leah.

"I told you about her in confidence!" I said. "Regina says you feel sorry for me. Well, I don't need your pity! And I don't want you talking to anyone else about me!"

To my horror, I began to cry.

Brian pulled out of traffic and parked. Then he said softly, "Sharon, I don't pity you! I did tell Regina about Leah. I have to admit that. I honestly don't know why. Or maybe I do. Please listen to me, and try to understand."

If Brian had tried to lie to me about himself and Regina, maybe I could have hated him. But he was honest with me, and he admitted he was confused about his emotions.

"I've been dating Regina for several months, and—until you came along, I thought I wanted to marry her," he said. "We aren't engaged, but we seemed to be moving toward an engagement. She heard I'd been out with you, and I suppose I told her about Leah because I was trying to convince myself as well as Regina that all I felt for you was sympathy."

I tried to get out of the car, but the instant Brian touched me, I just melted into his arms. The wild sweetness of our kisses left us more shaken than it ever had before. And finally Brian said, "It's you I love. I never felt this way about Regina. I think I've known that from the first time we were together. I just wouldn't admit it because you were such a surprise in my life. I want to marry you, Sharon, if you'll have me."

I couldn't answer. But Brian didn't need words. He had my lips, and my tears, and all my heart.

After we became engaged, I was secretly worried, and I think Brian was too, that Regina's father might do something to hurt him at work. After all, Mr. Kelton was the general manager at Sherman Electronics. He might have discharged Brian. But that didn't happen. Instead, Regina resigned from her own job.

My parents liked Brian, but I knew from the day I met his mother that she didn't think I was much of a prize as a bride. That disappointed me, of course, at first. But then, I didn't care what she thought of me, because I disliked her so much in return. She constantly taunted Brian in a sly way because he hadn't done as well yet as Bob. She would say things like, "My boys were always different. Bob was always the leader, always on the honor roll in school and college. He was the one who always made me proud."

Actually, when I finally met Bob, he didn't impress me as being so wonderful. He didn't have either Brian's personality or good looks. He was only twenty-seven, but he acted more like forty.

Around his mother and brother, Brian seemed very young and uncertain of himself. After we had dinner with his family, he was always quiet and discouraged, and starved for me to tell him I still had confidence in him.

Only one thing marred my happiness, and that was the sorrow I felt because Leah hadn't married the man she wanted, and because she seemed unable to overcome the terrible weakness that was destroying her.

Brian and I were married in the little store-front church my family had joined after we moved to Chicago. But as I walked down the aisle to the altar, between the rows of folding chairs, I had the feeling suddenly that I was back in our church in Prewitt. The old organ was playing my favorite hymns, and I carried my great-grandmother's Bible.

Then I looked up into Brian's face and saw tears in his eyes, and I knew that the solemnity of the moment touched him as deeply as it was touching me. Ours was going to be an old-fashioned marriage nothing could destroy.

On our honeymoon in Miami, Brian was so tender, so sweet, that he awakened passion and ardor in me that I hadn't even dreamed I would experience. The fulfillment of our love was so beautiful it made us both feel humble and reverent.

On the last night of our first week together, I tried to tell Brian in words how I felt about him, that I understood now that saying in the Bible about a married couple being one spirit, one flesh.

"And I didn't realize what marriage meant until you were my wife," Brian whispered.

Suddenly, I thought of Leah, and I was gripped by a new and deep understanding of my sister. With it, came terror. "Don't ever stop loving me," I burst out to Brian. "I'd be as lost as Leah if you did."

Brian took me in his arms, and the moment passed like a brief, bad dream. Then he kissed me, and our love flamed into the deep, exciting passion that was always just under the surface of everything we said or did.

Brian and I lived in a tiny new apartment not far from Sherman Electronics. The rent was outrageously high, and even though we were both working, it seemed as if we couldn't save any money.

As much as I loved Brian, his extravagance worried me. He never thought of being economical, and he loved for both of us to wear expensive clothes, to go out to dinner in expensive restaurants. It never bothered him if bills were overdue. Yet it seemed to gnaw at his self-respect because I was still working.

I insisted on it, though. I wanted to keep my job until we saved some money and started our family. But somehow, we never managed to live on the budgets I worked out. Occasionally, we even argued about money. We loved each other so much those arguments never lasted long, of course. They always ended in the sweet force of our love for each other.

One thing that irritated me, however, was that Brian tried hard to impress his mother with expensive presents. She barely noticed them, and went on bragging about Bob's achievements. For her birthday, Brian bought her some designer luggage. She thanked him casually, and then excitedly showed off the fur shawl Bob had given her.

Brian was upset. He was a grown man, and yet he reminded me of a hurt, worried little boy. It was all I could do not to tell his mother what I thought of her.

At Christmastime, Brian received a bonus from the company, and a surprise promotion. One of the other men had been transferred and Brian was given his job.

It was his idea that we buy a house. At first, we intended to buy in one of the inexpensive new developments, but Brian didn't like any of the places we could have easily afforded. I loved them, even though they were small. They were so bright and new, and I figured we could add on rooms when our family grew.

Brian wanted us to look at homes in the expensive Sheridan Acres development. Several Sherman employees, young executives, had bought houses there. "Nowadays, you have to look successful if you want to get ahead in life," he argued. "If you look and act like someone's poor relative, people treat you like one. They take you at your own evaluation. That's why I want us to have a decent home."

In the end, we did decide on a home in Sheridan Acres, and Brian borrowed most of the down payment from Bob. The Christmas bonus only covered the closing charges and some other unexpected expenses.

The day we signed the final papers, I was so nervous I felt sick, thinking of the payments we'd have to meet every month. But Brian was so thrilled and excited, I kept my worries to myself.

Yet soon after we had moved into Sheridan Acres, he started worrying about what people would think about my working. None of the other wives in the neighborhood needed to work to make ends meet.

I loved him so much I couldn't bear seeing him unsure of himself. I added up the amount of money I made at work, and I decided we could manage just as well if I resigned and then kept to a strict budget. Anyway, I left my job at Sherman.

The social leader of our neighborhood was Bette Harper. Her husband was an engineer at Sherman and had an important position, earning much more money than Brian.

Bette was the first to invite us to a party, several weeks after we'd moved to Sheridan Acres. Brian was really impressed by Bette's poised personality and the way she ran her home.

I didn't have such a good time at the party. For one thing, it bothered me that everyone drank so much.

Later, Brian said, "Maybe Bette could help you with the house, Sharon. You know. Give you some decorating ideas."

I felt like crying. I'd thought he loved our house. I'd spent weeks making curtains and draperies and slipcovers.

"Bette's husband earns more than you do, and they've been married for years. They've had time to accumulate things!" I protested.

"Honey, I didn't mean to hurt your feelings," Brian said. "I just mean—Bette might give you some ideas. And we'll have to buy some decent furniture—at least for the living room. I don't want people getting the idea that I'm not doing well."

Yet when Brian made love to me later that same night, I forgot my hurt in the sweet tide of longing and joy that overwhelmed me. I lay awake after he'd gone to sleep, and I made up my mind that I was going to make our home into what Brian wanted it to be. If it cost a lot of money, somehow I'd juggle our finances.

Actually, we didn't ask Bette Harper for tips on decorating our house. Brian decided it would be better not to. Instead, we got the services of a decorator in the store where we bought our furniture.

As soon as everything was in order, Brian began talking a lot about our giving parties. I'd always imagined that when we were really settled, we'd have cozy little dinners for other couples, really close friends, and have fun doing it. But that wasn't the kind of entertaining Brian was thinking about, and the more he talked, the more uneasy I felt.

"If a man wants to get ahead nowadays," he said, "he and his wife have to be active socially, and they have to do things right."

We knew quite a few people, but only casually. It worried me sometimes that we didn't have any really close friends. We were invited to cocktail parties given by other young executives in Brian's company, but I never felt relaxed or at home at those affairs. Most of the wives were college graduates, and I was afraid I might embarrass Brian with my lack of education.

During those early months in Sheridan Acres, I missed my family terribly. I'd hoped we'd still be close after my marriage, but it just didn't work out that way. For one thing, Mother and Dad were constantly worried about Leah because her drinking seemed to be getting worse. Then one day, Mother called me to say that my sister had eloped.

Brian and I invited all my family to our home for a celebration. But when I met Leah's new husband, I was secretly disappointed. Hank Phillips was years older than she was, and the two of them came to dinner already a little drunk.

Mother and Dad moved back to Prewitt that summer, hoping to make a living on the old farm, since it was just the two of them. I was sorry to see them go, but I knew they'd never been happy in Chicago.

After they left, I tried to keep in touch with Leah, but she avoided me. She and Hank were never at home when Brian and I went to see them. Finally, Leah moved without notifying me of her new address. Her landlord told us that she and Hank had separated.

It was weeks before I heard from Leah. Then, unexpectedly, she came to our house to have dinner one night. She wasn't drunk that night, but she looked shabby and unkempt, and she smelled of liquor. She insisted that she had a good job and was doing well, but I couldn't believe her.

Ironically, the debts Brian and I accumulated that first winter were a source of relief to me as well as worry. Because of owing so much money, we couldn't afford to give a party.

We borrowed money from a loan company to pay for two expensive wedding gifts. One was for Bob, who was getting married that spring. The other was for Regina Kelton, who suddenly married Bert Wheelock, an important executive at the office. Somehow, I felt a secret relief because Regina was settled.

I still couldn't seem to feel at home with any of the women in Sheridan Acres. I'd always pictured myself having close female friends after I married, sharing the fun of family talk and housekeeping with them. But I just didn't fit in with Bette Harper's crowd.

I'd never before been lonely, and at first I hardly realized that was what was wrong with me. Then I was ashamed of myself. But the days didn't really come alive for me until Brian came home from work. It seemed as if I hid in his love, in the sweetness and joy of being in his arms. The attraction between us was just as strong, just as intense, as it had been in the beginning.

At first, frankly, I was glad that I didn't get pregnant immediately after our marriage. I enjoyed having Brian all to myself. But after a while, I began to long desperately for a baby, and so did Brian. But I just couldn't seem to get pregnant.

We'd been married more than a year when we first heard that an important new position was going to be created in the office within a few months. Brian set his heart on getting it. At times, he would be confident that he had a chance, but just as often, his self-confidence would desert him and he'd be sunk in grim despair.

Mr. Kelton, the general manager, gave an annual cocktail party for the company executives. Brian had never been invited before, but this time we received an invitation. "We've got it made!" he exulted. "Honey, this means that they're considering me for the new job!"

I had a nice dress I hadn't worn since my honeymoon in Miami, but Brian insisted that I buy a new one. "Honey," he said awkwardly, "you always look sweet. But—well, maybe you should try to dress more like Bette Harper. I want to be proud of you at Mr. Kelton's party."

I knew my husband loved me, so I tried not to be hurt. But shopping for the dress became an ordeal.

Brian went with me, and nothing I liked pleased him. Before the afternoon ended, we were exhausted and arguing.

The dress we finally chose cost three times as much as we'd planned to pay. On the way home, Brian accused me of not caring what kind of an impression I made. "What do you want to look like at Mr. Kelton's?" he demanded. "As if you were all dressed up for prayer meeting in that store-front church you used to go to?" That really hurt. At times, I'd worried because we'd never joined a church. Brian liked to sleep late on Sundays, and I always felt guilty because I'd loved staying in bed with him, luxuriating in the sweetness of the attraction between us.

Later that evening, Brian apologized. "I'm sorry for what I said, honey. We were both tired. Surely you know I love you."

Our sudden rush of passion made me feel as if I were recovering from a kind of death.

But I worried more and more about making a good impression at Mr. Kelton's party. I didn't want to fail Brian. Still, I couldn't feel that the dress he'd chosen was right for me. It was black, a very sexy sheath, and it didn't seem to suit my type.

I couldn't sleep the night before the party, so even heavy makeup couldn't hide the dark circles under my eyes. I'd had my hair done in a new way Brian suggested, and it refused to stay in place.

A few minutes before we left the house, Brian came upstairs with drinks for us. Usually if he offered me a drink, I only took a sip or two. But I drank this one completely. I was desperate for anything that would give me strength to face all the important people Brian wanted me to impress.

The drink did help for a while, but the effect was wearing off by the time we reached the beautiful Kelton home on the lakeshore.

Brian whispered to me several times, "Can't you relax, sweetheart?

You're trying too hard."

He introduced me to several people, but then we were separated. Brian got into a conference with some of the men from the office. For a minute, looking at him across the room, I had the craziest feeling. It seemed incredible that I was married to him. He was so handsome and sophisticated and ambitious, and I didn't really belong in his world. For the rest of our lives, he'd be moving ahead, and I'd be fighting desperately to keep up with him. Suppose he stopped loving me?

The rest of the evening was a nightmare. I knew almost at once that my dress was all wrong. Maybe on someone else it would have been glamorous, but it just made me feel self-conscious.

A few of the older women talked to me, but most of the time I just moved around, a smile frozen on my lips, as I pretended to be enjoying myself.

I finally wandered into what must have been Mr. Kelton's study. It was so quiet and peaceful I just wanted to hide there until it was time to go home.

Suddenly someone called my name, and I turned to face Regina. Regina Wheelock, now. She'd followed me into the room.

"Hello, dear," she said. "Hiding? You should be out making friends with the company brass—for Brian's sake." She was smiling, but her eyes were like black ice. "Come on out," she insisted. "That's what you're here for—to be on exhibition like the rest of us."

During the rest of the evening, I really did try to be a credit to Brian, but I knew I wasn't really successful. I was too conscious of Regina. There was always a crowd of fascinated people around her. I just couldn't understand how Brian could have chosen me.

He was very quiet when we drove home. If he felt disappointed in me, he didn't say so, and I didn't ask him. I didn't mention Regina, either.

I almost cried with relief when, after we'd gone to bed, Brian's love and desire for me seemed more intense than ever. I gave myself up to the excitement of our love with a wildness that was almost desperate in its joy.

One evening about a week later, Brian came home for dinner looking haggard and beaten. I knew something terrible must have happened, but at first, he wouldn't tell me what it was. Finally he said, "They gave the new job to Clem Hardy. He's younger and slicker than I am."

He shuddered in my arms, and somehow, it was worse than if he'd actually cried. I hated the men who had decided against him. "They're fools, Brian, they're just fools!" I burst out, sobbing.

That night, when I couldn't sleep, I remembered the party. Was it my fault that Brian had failed to get what he wanted? Would he have gotten the promotion if I'd had a more sparkling personality and a college background?

Brian worked harder than ever during the next few months. In the spring, he was sent out of town for two weeks on company business. It was the first time he'd had that kind of assignment, and he was thrilled with the opportunity.

I was so glad for him. But after he had gone, loneliness hit me. By the end of the first day, I just didn't know how I'd manage for two weeks. I hadn't realized how completely he filled my life.

I watched television every night until very late, but I still couldn't sleep. That was why I started having a drink every night. It relaxed and warmed me, at least for a little while. I never drank enough to really feel it, but on the morning of the day I expected Brian home, I was startled to find that a whole bottle of whisky was gone. That shocked me, and I made up my mind I wouldn't drink alone again. The whole idea of it made me ashamed, even though I no longer considered drinking a sin. But drinking alone, using it as a crutch—that frightened me.

Brian's business trip was only the first of many. He was developing a knack for obtaining the raw materials the company needed at bargain prices, and now he was working officially for the procurement department.

I never did become accustomed to his being away. When he wasn't at home, I'd have an awful, lost feeling, as if he were never coming back to me. For the first few days he'd be gone, I'd fight my impulse to dull the edges of my loneliness with a drink. And then I'd give up fighting. One drink—two. . . Surely that wouldn't hurt me.

As the months passed, Brian spent less and less time at home even when he wasn't away on trips. He often worked late at the office, and his mind was always full of endless details and worries connected with his job. He was working very hard to get a raise.

That summer, my sister Leah was struck by a car and killed instantly. She was drunk at the time, and the newspaper story about her stated that she was a divorcee and had a long record of arrests for drunkenness.

I think all of us had known there was no real hope for Leah, but her death was still a terrible shock. Brian and I went to the room where she had been living to get her things, and found almost nothing there but empty bottles.

We made arrangements to have her body sent back to Prewitt, but we didn't go to the funeral. After almost three years of marriage, of hoping and losing hope, I was pregnant. My doctor felt I shouldn't take a long trip.

Only my lingering grief for Leah marred the months before the baby was born. I felt a secret joy and relief, during that time, when Regina's husband, Bert Wheelock, was transferred to the northern California branch of the company, and he and Regina moved west.

When our little girl, Kerry Ann, came into the world, and I held the sweet warmth of her in my arms, my heart swelled with joy. Beautiful, gray eyed, with a mist of blond hair, she was the physical symbol of the love Brian and I shared.

Even as a tiny baby, Kerry Ann seemed to have her own special personality. Within just a few weeks, she was smiling, watching me as I went about my work at home, and appearing to understand everything I said to her.

With Kerry Ann in the house, I wasn't nearly as lonely, even when Brian was away on his frequent out-of-town trips. I still missed him, but my loneliness wasn't the sick, frightening kind I'd known before the baby's birth. I hadn't realized what a companion a baby can be. I'd heard other women say that they got tired of being with their babies alone, during the day, but I never felt that way.

Brian received a salary raise a few months after Kerry Ann's birth, but not as large an increase as he'd hoped for. We had to use the extra money for payments on a new car. Our old one was five years old, still running well, but so shabby it embarrassed Brian to be seen in it.

We had our financial worries, but that first year of Kerry Ann's life was very happy for all of us. Brian didn't talk so much about the need for us to get on closer social terms with the families of the other young executives at Sherman. We couldn't eat out because we couldn't afford to pay the high prices charged by reliable sitters.

But then after a while, Brian began saying we had to give a big cocktail party soon. "We owe invitations to a lot of people," he kept reminding me. "We really should give dinners for some people, men who could really help me at Sherman."

If the idea of having a cocktail party panicked me, I just went sick when I thought of giving dinners for people I had to impress. I was sure I'd never be able to be the kind of hostess Brian deserved.

I kept trying to postpone the cocktail party, but I couldn't escape it forever.

Brian had taken up golf and was playing it with Dave Geery and Bob Harlan, men from the office. He didn't really like the game, but he felt that through it, he would meet influential people. He was hoping Dave and Bob would ask him to join their country club.

"But to get a bid," he said, "I'll have to show them that we're okay socially."

"I hate crawling to people, trying to please them!" I burst out.

It was one of the rare times Brian lost his temper with me. "It's not crawling!" he blazed. "These are the men I work with. I wish you'd realize you aren't living back in Prewitt any more. I want the best for you, and I want it for Kerry Ann. I should be able to count on you to help me!"

After that quarrel, Brian was out of town for several days. He didn't call me while he was away, as he usually did. Even though I had little Kerry Ann with me, all the old loneliness of the past seemed to come back to haunt me. I couldn't do anything to escape it. Even the drinks I had at night, after the baby was asleep, didn't help.

When Brian came home, he looked so haggard that I was frightened. But when he took me into his arms with hungry desperation, I knew he'd gone through much the same agony I'd had, because of our quarrel. I told him, "Oh, Brian, I'll make you proud of me. Somehow I'll do it!"

"I am proud of you," he insisted. "Most of all, I love you."

In the sweetness of our reconciliation, we started making plans for the cocktail party. Both of us felt that the more detailed those plans were, the more sure we would be that everything would go smoothly.

After the invitations had been sent, Kerry Ann came down with a cold. It wasn't serious, but she was fretful, and I got behind in my schedule of party preparations.

We had a lot of unexpected expenses just about then, so Brian had to borrow money from a loan company for the party. The liquor alone cost what seemed to me like a small fortune. He got the best brands, and much more than I thought we'd need. "We don't want to look like cheapskates," he insisted.

He worried as much over the food as I did. I'd made many of the canapés ahead of time and frozen them. After they were thawed, they seemed limp and soggy. Brian went out and bought cocktail shrimp and a lot of other fancy things, using up our week's grocery allowance.

Mother Meade was keeping the baby that night, and I knew she'd be very attentive to Kerry Ann. Still, I couldn't help worrying a little, and that added to my nervousness and tension.

Right up to the last minute before the guests began to arrive, I was so shaky I didn't see how I could ever get through the evening.

During the first hour, only a few people came, and we couldn't seem to get the conversation started. Then, at last, the house seemed to be crowded with people.

Maybe I'd forgotten to eat anything that day. I drank quite a bit, not just with the guests but because I had to get through the evening. Suddenly, the drinks hit me really hard. I drank black coffee, but I think the main thing that kept me from passing out was knowing that Brian needed me. So much depended on my being a good hostess.

I remember wondering once who the strange woman at the party was. She was laughing at me and waving her hands. Then it dawned on me that I was looking at my own reflection in a mirror as I talked to some of the guests. Only I didn't look like myself. My hair was a mess and my mascara was smudged.

I thought some of the guests would never leave. A lot of them did go away early—the important ones, Brian said later. But the others stayed on until after midnight. And when the last one had gone, Brian didn't have to tell me that I'd failed completely to be the smooth, sophisticated hostess I'd wanted to be.

Disappointment was stamped on his tired face. He went out for a walk, and I went upstairs to bed.

The next morning, I woke up with a terrible headache. Brian brought me coffee and tomato juice, or I don't know how I could have forced myself to get out of bed. He was very quiet, and wouldn't look into my eyes. I wished he'd tell me right out that the party had been a complete failure, but he didn't. He just said he had a date to play golf, but that he would be home in plenty of time for dinner. His mother was going to bring Kerry Ann home then.

After Brian left, I dressed and walked through the house. There were glasses everywhere, and stale food spilled on tables. The most awful thing about the rooms, however, was that they were so lonely. Crazily, I didn't feel as if Brian had simply gone to play golf. It was as if he'd walked out on me forever, because I'd failed him.

I had to have two drinks before I could face the rest of the day.

Brian and I never did discuss that party. But it was more than a week before he made love to me again, before his tenderness and passion brought me out of a state of cold, waiting despair. "Oh, Brian, Brian, I love you," I told him. "I'm not alive when you don't love me. I'm dead."

During the months after that, his business trips were more and more frequent, and even when he wasn't out of town, he brought home stacks of work to do. I knew at times that he was worried, but he never discussed business with me, or things that happened at work. I was so grateful when I could give him the comfort of my love. I'd think, after he'd fallen asleep beside me, "At least we have this." Then I'd be ashamed of myself. We had so much, so very much, not just physical passion.

Kerry Ann was the greatest miracle of all. I don't know what I'd have done without her. As she grew older, our companionship increased.

It was only at night, after I put her to bed, that loneliness completely overwhelmed me.

One of the houses in the next block was vacant for several weeks. When it was sold, and a new family moved in, I really wasn't very interested. I thought that the new neighbors would probably be like every other family already there, ambitious and wealthy. The wife would be a glamorous college graduate, and an expert at helping her husband get ahead in his career.

A few mornings later, on a really cold day, someone rang my kitchen doorbell. I opened the door just a crack and saw a bedraggled-looking girl carrying a baby in each arm. "Please, can I come in?" she asked. "I'm Sally Berringer. I've just moved in down the block, and something has gone wrong with the oven!"

She was so different from what I'd expected my new neighbor to be. Instead of smart slacks or stretch pants, she was wearing an old pink-checked cotton house dress that had been washed but not ironed. Her brown hair was in two braided pigtails. "Oh, gosh, I'm so worn out!" she burst out. "Do you have any coffee left from breakfast that you could heat up?"

I raced to make coffee. But before I plugged in the coffee machine, I looked up and my guest was crying, still clutching her two babies. "I feel like I want to run right back to Saint Louis," she said, only she called it "Saint Louie," in a soft southern voice.

I got Kerry Ann's old playpen from the utility room for the babies, who were just under a year old. Then I made Sally kick off her wet shoes and sit down in an old rocking chair I kept in the kitchen because it reminded me of home.

I insisted that she eat a complete breakfast. "I did forget to eat this morning, I guess," she said in surprise. I'd made biscuits. Brian didn't like them, but they always gave me a sort of homey feeling when I was blue. Sally was thrilled with them.

"Where are you from?" she asked after she bit into the first biscuit. "I thought you had that kind of accent. But now that I've tasted this, I'm sure!"

"Wait till you taste my cornbread," I said. I told her I was from Prewitt. She'd never been there, but some distant relatives had lived in a town nearby. Sally herself was originally from Tennessee.

"I haven't been back there in six years, though," she said. "Not since I married Ralph. We've lived in three different towns since then. Ralph is really getting ahead in business. This latest promotion is the best yet, and I know I should be thrilled at having a nice home like the one we just bought. But I'm just homesick, so far!"

Her husband worked for an electronics company, but not Sherman. In a way, I was glad of that. I felt I didn't want to have our friendship all mixed up with business and office affairs.

Sally and I spent the whole day getting acquainted. Even the children got along well. Kerry Ann was fascinated by the little boys, Bobby and Burl.

Sally's oven was working that evening, but not in time for her to prepare dinner for her husband. I insisted that she and Ralph eat with us.

I was disappointed when the dinner date didn't work out very well. Ralph and Brian were about the same age, and in the same business, but they were both tired and each of them had brought home work they had to do before they went to bed. Ralph kept insisting that they had to leave early.

After they'd gone, Brian said, "If I were you, Sharon, I wouldn't get too friendly with Sally. Oh, sure, she's a nice girl. But I doubt if she gets in with the right crowd here in Sheridan Acres."

"But I like her!" I protested. "I haven't felt so at home with anyone since I left Prewitt!"

"Now, look, honey, don't get angry," Brian said. "I've got a stack of estimates to get ready for presentation, and I can't afford to get all worked up over nothing. All I meant was, if you're with Sally too much, people might think you're just like her. She wouldn't fit in at the country club."

"What's wrong with being like Sally?" I demanded. It was one of the few times I'd been really angry with Brian. After all, we couldn't run our whole lives, even pick our personal friends, according to whether or not they could help him get ahead in business!

Brian went into his den and closed the door. It was an unwritten rule that when he did that, he wasn't to be interrupted. I was so nervous I was just trembling. To quiet myself, I had a drink. Then I had another one.

In some ways, Brian was right about Sally. She wasn't accepted by the social crowd in Sheridan Acres. I'd been invited to join the bridge club and the garden society when I first moved there, but Sally was completely left out.

She was a terrible housekeeper. Nothing about her home ever seemed to look right. She was always behind schedule with her work. While it was the style in the neighborhood to wear neat Bermuda shorts and polo shirts, or very plain dresses, Sally wore ruffles, big hats, and high-heeled, fancy sandals.

Bette Harper suggested once that I tell Sally in a nice way that she looked ridiculous. I wouldn't have dreamed of hurting her like that. I told Bette, "It's Sally's own business what she wears."

But Sally and I had a wonderful time together. Almost every morning we had coffee, either at her house or mine. We relaxed and talked. We did our shopping together, and took the kids on picnics in a nearby park. Our two husbands never did get to be close friends. And as much as I liked Sally, I never talked much about her to Brian. I knew he didn't approve of her, and I didn't want to antagonize him.

All that spring and summer, he was very moody. He'd had a deep disappointment. Dave Geery had nominated him for membership in the country club, but several of the members voted against Brian, and his application was refused.

He didn't know who the men were who voted against him, and that preyed on his mind. He couldn't stop wondering about it. Many of the club members worked for Sherman. "If any of them voted against me," he said, over and over, his face white, "it shows I'm sure not doing so well with the company."

It hurt even more when Mother Meade, on one of her visits to us, kept talking about the wonderful country club Bob and Helen had joined. It was much more important than the one Brian had hoped would accept him. "I couldn't even make it at a second-rate club," Brian said hoarsely. "Sharon, what's wrong with me? What's wrong with us? We never seem to click with the right people."

Nothing is wrong with you, I thought. *I'm the one who is all wrong.* But I didn't say it aloud. I didn't want to remind him that I'd never really been the kind of wife he deserved.

My friendship with Sally helped me get through the days when

Brian was out of town, but it didn't help at night. Instead of getting accustomed to loneliness, I seemed to be more afraid of it than ever. I still had to take a drink or two on the evenings I was alone. Otherwise, I couldn't face the long, dead hours. Sometimes it worried me that I was so dependent on alcohol. Then, of course, I'd reason that I never got drunk. No one knew about my secret drinking, so it was nothing to fret about. It was in no way like Leah's drinking problem.

A day or so after Christmas, when Kerry Ann was two, Brian was all set to make another trip East. The assignment was canceled. He came home in the afternoon with a strange, stunned expression in his eyes.

For a second I was really frightened. I had the crazy idea that he had lost his job.

Suddenly, he lifted me off my feet and whirled me around. "We're going to live in California, Sharon! I've been transferred to the northern California branch of the company. I'm getting a big raise. And this will be only the beginning, if I really click out there!"

I was so happy for him that I cried. He'd worked so hard for the promotion.

It wasn't until later that day that I realized that the idea of moving west frightened me. I didn't tell that to Brian, of course. I didn't understand my fear, and I was ashamed of it. But all the same, it existed.

I dreaded getting settled in a new place, meeting new people, trying to impress them.

And there was something else that disturbed and haunted me.

Bert Wheelock, the man Regina had married, was one of the executives in the office where Brian would be. Since the people who worked for Sherman always socialized a lot, we'd probably see Regina often, and I didn't feel any more like competing with her now than I ever had.

Even if I'd told Brian my fears, he wouldn't have had time to try to make me forget them. He was too busy with last-minute office details, selling our car so he could use the money to get a new one out west, and preparing to leave at once for California. I was to stay behind and sell the house.

The night Kerry Ann and I saw Brian off at the airport, I had the craziest feeling, at the last minute, that if I let him go I might never see him again.

"Honey, we'll be together again before you know it," Brian said.

Then he was gone.

I sat with Kerry Ann in the airport for nearly two hours simply because I dreaded going home to the empty house.

When we did reach there, Kerry Ann was whimpering with weariness. I was very busy for a while, fixing her dinner and putting her to bed. Then when she went to sleep, loneliness closed in around me.

Somehow, it wasn't just loneliness because Brian had gone to California. It was deeper than that, as if we'd never really be close to each other again.

My hands shook as I poured myself the first of the drinks that would help me get through the night. Did I think of Leah? I didn't dare think of her any more!

I was never more grateful for Sally's friendship than I was during the rest of the time before I left for California. She kept trying to get me to see the bright side of the situation.

"I've been to California," she said. "The weather is wonderful, and everything's brand new out there. People are relaxed. You'll love it. All that sun will be good for Kerry Ann, too."

No matter how many vitamins I gave her, or what the doctor prescribed, my little girl had a tendency to get colds.

"Well, if it helps her, it will all be worth while," I said. But I still wasn't very happy about it.

Brian had very little free time, but he called often. His voice seemed always to surge with excitement about his new job.

He loved California. The new plant was just south of San

Francisco, near Palo Alto. "Life here is great!" It took longer to sell our house than I'd hoped. The time dragged, and the empty nights were worse than the days. I knew I was drinking too much, but when I got to California, I promised myself, I wouldn't drink any more. I'd just stop it completely and finally. It wasn't as if I couldn't.

When the house did sell, we got the full price we asked. We planned to use our equity for a down payment on our new home in California. But as I told Brian, in our telephone conversations, I wanted us to be very careful this time about selecting a place to live. I hoped we wouldn't choose a place with payments too high for us, as we had in Sheridan Acres.

Three months from the day after Brian's transfer, I stepped off a plane at the San Francisco International Airport and carried Kerry Ann down a long ramp into Brian's arms.

I'd never seen him looking so well. He was tanned and energetic. "I'm a product of California living," he said, grinning. "Everybody swims and plays tennis out here. We're already members of the El Camino Country Club, I'll have you know!"

For a minute I felt as if he were a stranger. But then we were in the car, and Brian and I melted together in the aching longing of our love. That hadn't changed. It was still the same miracle.

Our sweet reunion and the shock that rocked me later didn't seem to belong to the same day.

Brian drove thirty miles south to Palo Alto, to the beautiful new hotel where he had rented a room for us. It was more luxurious and glamorous than the one where we'd honeymooned, nearly five years before.

"But this must cost a fortune!" I protested. "Brian, we can't afford to stay here while we find a house. That could take weeks! We'll have to get a cheaper place."

Suddenly, Brian was boyish in his excitement. "I was going to take you to see it later today and tell you then, but I can't wait. Honey, we already have our house!"

At first I thought he meant he'd rented a house, but then I realized he'd bought it. He'd put all the money from our equity in the old house on the new one. "I couldn't wait to talk to you, because there wasn't time," he said. "It was a fantastic buy, and I didn't dare wait."

Naturally, I was disappointed because I hadn't been consulted, and yet I couldn't blame Brian for taking advantage of what he said had been such a bargain.

"Tom Marshall, another Sherman man, was transferred," Brian continued, "so his house was available. I only had to borrow a little to add to our down payment cash."

Only a little. But the amount he said he'd borrowed made me feel actually sick. I sat there staring at him while he kept telling me that we couldn't possibly lose money and that the house and land would increase in value because California real estate was the safest investment in the world.

"This new development, Mission Hills, is really special, honey. It's only a little way from the country club. And most of the people who live there are big shots at Sherman. It was a real break for us that we got in. We may have to watch our pennies for a while, but it'll be worth it."

"You could have at least asked me before you agreed to buy!" I couldn't help saying.

"I've told you I just couldn't pass up this chance!" Brian shouted back at me.

Then he took Kerry Ann out for a ride. I refused to go with them. All I wanted to do was to shut myself in the motel and hide like a scared animal. But finally, I knew I had to face my disappointment and live with it. Brian was the man I loved, and I had to go along with his decisions.

I called room service and ordered a drink. As I swallowed it, I remembered I'd intended never to take another drink after I reached California. *But this really will be the last*, I thought.

Late that afternoon, I did go with Brian to see the new house. By that time, I'd made up my mind that I'd be a good sport about it. I'd be careful about the budget and pay off the new loan as soon as possible. And I'd make Brian proud of me.

Each of the homes in Mission Hills was different, but all were designed in sprawling ranch style and set on beautifully landscaped lawns.

Ours was a long, low redwood with brick trim. The living room, dining room, and hall were carpeted in thick wall-to-wall carpeting. "I just took over the payments on the rugs and draperies," Brian explained. "We didn't have to put a down payment on them. They were put in just two months ago, so they're new. Regina says they're okay."

Regina. Fear made me icy cold.

"Didn't I tell you? Regina and Bert live here in Mission Hills. You can see their house from that window."

Brian's voice seemed to fade for me, though he hadn't stopped talking. *Regina has been in this house,* I thought. I imagined I could see her walking through the rooms, laughing at me.

"She says she'll help you get started off right," Brian was saying. "Even in a place like this, you can get in with the wrong crowd if you're not careful."

At first I wanted to rage at Brian. I wanted to rebel against the fact that he had our lives all arranged, and had let another woman influence his choice of a home. But then suddenly, I was beyond anger, beyond hurt. I felt smothered, as if an invisible fog were enveloping me, choking me.

The next morning, Brian had to be at the office. He had borrowed a company car so I could use the new one he'd bought when he first came to California. I was going to go shopping and make arrangements to get a few pieces of furniture delivered at once, so we could live in the new house until our furniture arrived by van from Illinois. It would have been too expensive to stay at the motel and eat all our meals in restaurants. Besides, Kerry Ann needed the peace and quiet of her own home. Fortunately, the stove and refrigerator and other appliances were all built in, so I didn't have to worry about them.

At a nearby shopping center, I bought a bed, some folding chairs, and a crib for Kerry Ann. Then, I got groceries and we went on out to Mission Hills. I was giving Kerry Ann her lunch when Regina crossed the patio and came into the house through the sliding glass doors.

She was more beautiful than I remembered. Her skin was tanned to a dark gold, dramatic against the stark white of her blouse.

"How wonderful to see you, Sharon," she said, smiling. "I hope you weren't hurt because Brian had everything settled about the house before you arrived. I told him I was sure you wouldn't mind, since it was such a fantastic buy. He couldn't let it slip away." I tried to find my voice, but I couldn't. So Regina went on, still in that sweet, false way. "I told Brian I'd do everything I could to help you get settled. And then when you are settled, I'll give a party and introduce you to the right people. There's no point in wasting your time on the ones who don't count, is there? After all, Brian is going to go fast and far, and I know you want to help him."

My tongue felt stiff, but I said, "I've always liked to pick my friends for what they are, not for what they can do for me."

Regina's eyes glittered with malice. "I hope you don't think I'm a snob, darling. But after all, a wife who drags her feet and holds her husband back stands a chance of losing him. I'm sure you don't want that to happen." It was plain that, where Brian was concerned, Regina still hadn't given up. Her own marriage didn't matter. I felt like screaming at her, "I have Brian's love! Nothing can change that, even if I'm not the kind of wife you think he should have!"

But I didn't want to fight with her. Upset as I was, I remembered I shouldn't argue with the wife of an important official at Sherman Electronics.

After Regina left, I sat down in one of the folding chairs and cried. Kerry Ann kissed and kissed me until I stopped. But then she said, "Mommy, I want Aunt Sally and Bobby and Burl to come and see us." That just about broke my heart.

The routine of our lives in Mission Hills was much the same as it had been back in Sheridan Acres. Brian didn't make quite so many trips out of town, at first, but he worked late every evening and on weekends. We never seemed to see enough of each other. I worried because he was missing so much of Kerry Ann's development. She was almost three, an adorable little girl, no longer a baby.

Brian did take time off for social affairs. Regina gave a dinner party for us, and we went to all the country-club dances. Regina invited me to join the Assistance Auxiliary, a women's group that did all sorts of things to raise money for various good causes. I was glad of a chance to help in something like that, but Regina ruined even that for me when she kept harping to Brian about how no girl was invited to belong until the committee passed on her social desirability. It seemed so silly to me that you had to have the right friends before you could help raise money for sick people and crippled children!

Brian and I had a bitter fight about it. "You've made up your mind not to like Regina," he said. "Why? She's really a great person. Instead of being jealous of her, you should learn as much as you can from her."

I felt breathless, as if he'd slapped me. "She still hates me because I took you away from her," I insisted. "Her interest in me is all fake."

That was one of the few fights we'd had in our marriage that was difficult for us to make up after. It left us both cold and silent. Brian went on a trip to Los Angeles the next day, and I got through the endless week in the way I had so often before, by drinking almost constantly.

About that time, we joined the Village Community Church. "Most of the executives at Sherman belong," Brian explained to me. "It isn't denominational."

I had to bite back a bitter protest that I didn't think people should join churches for social prestige. Later, however, I was ashamed of myself for resisting something that could bring Brian and Kerry Ann and me closer together.

Actually, the church was a disappointment to me. It seemed so modern and impersonal, and I didn't get the feeling in it that I used to have back in the tiny church in Prewitt, or even in the store-front church in Chicago. The minister, Mr. Davidson, seemed so young.

We had to pledge a definite sum to support the church, and Brian signed up for much more than we could afford. "We have to," he said. "Bert Wheelock is on the finance committee."

"And he's the one we want to please," I said, before I thought. "God has nothing to do with it."

Suddenly, I was ashamed of myself. If I really wanted to worship God, I could do it in this new church as well as I had in a small, shabby one.

I apologized to Brian for my remark, and he forgave me. But I was frightened at how close I'd been to starting a quarrel with him again. I loved him so much that arguments between us actually made me sick.

By then, I wasn't drinking only when he was away. I often had to have several drinks to get through the days when he was at the office, or playing golf at the club. I would shut myself in the house and refuse to answer the door or the telephone. Of course, I never got drunk. I was always able to look after Kerry Ann. And before Brian came home, I always raced through the housework I let go of during the day.

But one day, he came back unexpectedly, in the middle of the morning, to get some papers. When he saw me, still in my housecoat and still with my hair uncombed, he looked puzzled.

"I've had a pounding headache all morning," I lied.

He accepted my story without question. "You'd better hop into bed, honey," he said. "I'll hunt up a sitter for Kerry Ann." He was so concerned, I felt guilty and ashamed, not just because of the drinking but because of the lie.

I resolved once more to stop drinking. I was still sure of one thing—I could stop. I wasn't like Leah.

Four days before her third birthday, Kerry Ann got one of her colds. She hadn't had as many since we'd lived in California, but she still seemed to have very little resistance to them. Dr. Stevenson prescribed an antibiotic for her and told me to keep her in bed.

Poor Kerry Ann. Her gray eyes were dark and shiny with fear that she wouldn't be well enough to have her party. We'd invited all the members of her Sunday-school class, and shopped for paper hats and favors.

She was miserable for about twenty-four hours, and then seemed to improve. Her temperature returned to almost normal.

Brian had to fly back to the main office in Chicago. "I'll call you tomorrow, a special telephone call all for you," he promised Kerry Ann. "And I'll be back before your birthday, I promise."

That night, around one o'clock, I woke up suddenly, not sure whether Kerry Ann had called out to me or if I'd simply dreamed she had. The house was very quiet as I hurried across the hall to her room.

At first I thought she was sleeping normally. Then her strange stillness terrified me. I tried to wake her and couldn't, and that was the beginning of a nightmare of panic.

Even as I called the doctor, I think I knew the nightmare was never going to end, that Kerry Ann was dead.

Later, Dr. Stevenson said she'd had a deadly, quick-acting form of pneumonia. There was nothing anyone could have done for her.

Before noon that day, Brian was home again. We were both stunned and dazed by the grief we still couldn't quite comprehend. We couldn't cry. And even though Mr. Davidson, our minister, prayed for us and said many things he meant to be comforting, it was as if we couldn't really hear him.

My mother and father were unable to come to California because of poor health, and Mother Meade was on a European vacation trip Brian's brother had given her. So Brian and I were alone in our grief, and Kerry Ann's funeral seemed that much more unbearable.

But somehow, Brian and I got through the first awful stunning shock of our loss, and settled down to learn how to live without Kerry Ann.

Brian went back to the office after a single week, because he was needed. He worked harder than ever, as if physical exhaustion could blot out heartbreak. I worked hard, too, cleaning the house over and over again when it didn't really need cleaning. But I could never get myself tired enough to make the hurt less. Before Kerry Ann's birth, I'd thought I knew all there was to know about loneliness, but I'd been wrong. Now, somehow, I felt cut off from every other living person in the world, sometimes even from Brian. I'd get to thinking of the years ahead, and I just couldn't face them. It wasn't going to be enough for me to be just on the edge of Brian's life. Even though he loved me, I realized that was really where I was.

And so, without really fighting it any more, I returned to my secret drinking. As soon as Brian left for the office in the morning, I started in. I had one drink—just strong enough to get me through a few hours until the next one. But the time between drinks got shorter and shorter, even though I still never got drunk. I clung to that fact almost desperately, promising myself that soon I'd be able to get along without liquor. after my grief was a little less sharp.

In the evenings, when he wasn't out of town, Brian and I went out a lot, to parties, nightclubs, and movies. It was better if you saw a lot of people, Brian said. And we had our love.

Sometimes, in Brian's arms, in the sweet oblivion of the passion that still could possess us, I'd think: *Tomorrow I'll be strong again. I won't drink.*

But when the day came, and Brian went to the office, or on one of his flights to Los Angeles or Chicago, there seemed to be only one way I could live through the hours.

Finally, because I was frightened, I confessed to Brian that I drank when I was alone. I guess I hoped he'd know how to help me.

Maybe he just didn't realize how much I was drinking, but he practically laughed at me. "Honey, you've never been drunk in your life," he said. "You're worrying too much—because of your sister. But you're not like Leah. Her trouble was that she never learned how to handle the stuff. Believe me, as long as you worry, you're safe."

I believed him. After all, he knew more about something like that than I did.

In one of her letters, Sally Berringer asked why I didn't get a job—for a while, at least. She said it would be good for me to get out of house.

I grabbed at the idea almost desperately. Not only would working get my mind off of Kerry Ann, we could really use the money, because we were still having a hard time financially. Our country-club and church dues were high, and we'd bought a second car.

"And if I'm working, I won't drink so much," I told Brian, though I felt ashamed and guilty because even my words seemed to embarrass him.

He didn't like anything about the idea of my working. "I don't want people thinking I can't support my wife," he said. "Anyway, your job is here in our home."

I was disappointed at his reaction, but I didn't go against his wishes. I loved him too much to hurt him. Every morning, right after he left, I poured myself a drink and turned on the television. Even though I didn't really follow the programs I saw, I liked the sound of voices in the house.

If Brian wasn't out of town, I managed to tidy up the house and get dressed in plenty of time before he came home for dinner. But if he was out of town, I didn't bother with dinner. I just had some soup or a sandwich.

One evening in late spring, he called at six o'clock to say he'd be late, that he'd have dinner in Palo Alto. But that evening, my own routine struck a snag. My last bottle of bourbon was almost empty. I got dressed and went out for more.

I had a rule that I never bought liquor in our local shopping center, or in any store twice in succession. So that night, I drove south toward San Jose, through the dozens of Santa Clara valley housing developments.

I chose a new shopping center I'd never visited before, and parked near the liquor store. It was after I'd made my purchase and put it in the car that I saw a woman come out of a cocktail lounge a few doors away.

The colored glow from the neon sign must have created an eerie illusion, because for a second I almost fainted. The woman looked like Leah! She had Leah's pale hair, but the weirdest thing of all was that she was walking as Leah often had when she was a little drunk—with exaggerated care, as if she feared the sidewalk might move.

I followed her, my heart pounding, around the corner and down a side street. Twice she leaned against a wall to keep from falling, and I felt nauseated because she was repulsive, sickening, all the ugly things a drunken woman is.

Sometime during those minutes, though, she stopped looking like Leah. In a crazy way, it was as if I were following myself!

The spell was shattered when a car drew up to the curb and the woman staggered into it.

I went back to my own car, several blocks away, still shaken. When I reached home, Brian's car was parked outside our house, and I almost broke down and cried with relief. Now I wouldn't be alone, I wouldn't drink. Brian was alarmed because I looked so sick. "Honey, you're getting so thin," he said. "You should take better care of yourself."

His love for me, his concern, was like a warm fire, and I wanted to reach out to it, get rid of the chill of terror that clung to me. In sudden desperate honesty, I burst out, "Brian, I'm afraid I'm going to be an alcoholic like Leah was if I don't stop drinking! I think I should get help! I could ask Mr. Davidson at the church—"

Brian grabbed my shoulders roughly. "Sharon, you're imagining things!" he told me. "You're making a big thing out of nothing. But Mr. Davidson might not understand that. Don't tell him—and don't tell anybody else! I'd know if you were in real trouble, honey, and you're not! All you need to do is use a little willpower. But if people ever got the idea you're a heavy drinker, I'd be finished! They don't hand out promotions to men with alcoholic wives. I haven't told you, but there's a chance I'll be put in charge of the whole procurement operation in a few more months."

When I saw how upset he was, how frightened that talk about drinking might get out, I wanted to comfort and love him. I was ashamed that I'd even considered going to an outsider for help. Brian was right. All I needed was willpower.

I suppose if we hadn't been struggling with our own private sorrow, we wouldn't have been so startled when we heard that Regina and Bert Wheelock were getting a divorce. We still went to all the country club affairs, so we were at the first big dance Regina attended after she came home from Reno. Brian obviously was very concerned about her. "She acts so darned lonely and lost," he said. "Bert wasn't right for her. He never was." I was afraid to look in his eyes, afraid to talk about Regina any more.

It had never been easy for me, even though I loved Brian so wildly, to be the one who initiated the times we made love. But that night I did, out of a bewildering need that was as much emotional as physical. I felt like crying with relief when he responded with the old tenderness and excitement.

Maybe no one is ever ready for a miracle. When I began feeling ill in the mornings, I didn't suspect that I might be pregnant. Actually, I was secretly ashamed, thinking I'd simply been drinking too much. But Brian insisted that I see the doctor. "Honey, I remember how you were before we knew Kerry Ann was on the way," he said.

So I had pregnancy tests, and it was true. I was going to have another child.

Grateful as Brian and I were, somehow at first, the old grief for Kerry Ann seemed refreshed and bitterly painful. But then, we began to accept the wonderful thing that was happening to us.

At first, I was sure I would stop drinking, now that I was pregnant. But Brian was still away from home much of the time, and I couldn't seem to get through the days without the only thing that helped my loneliness. I never told Dr. Bartell, my obstetrician, about the problem. He said that I was too thin, but otherwise, my physical condition was normal. Somehow I felt that if I told him about my drinking, it would mean that I couldn't stop whenever I wanted to. And I knew Brian wouldn't have wanted me to discuss it.

Even though I was happy about the new baby, I couldn't talk about it easily, even to Brian. Sometimes I thought: *Maybe I want it too much. Oh, God, don't let anything go wrong.*

I was just beginning my fifth month when Brian had to go on another trip to Chicago. He expected to be away a full week, but after three days, he was able to fly back to California.

About ten o'clock one evening, he telephoned me from San Francisco Airport. When the call came, I was watching an old movie on television, and having one last drink before I went to bed.

Brian had left his car at home, and he asked if I'd come and pick him up. He knew Dr. Bartell hadn't forbidden me to drive, and at that hour of the evening, the traffic on the freeway would be light.

I left the house within five minutes after I talked to Brian.

Sometimes I try to remember whether the night was bright or overcast, and when I can't, panic starts rising in me, choking me, terrifying me. There's so much about those hours I don't remember. What I do recall is a few pieces of it, like jagged fragments of a jigsaw puzzle.

One memory is of the dark outline of a car looming before me on the highway. It had no lights, and it was stopped in the fast lane. I remember that, and I remember the sickening impact that came an instant afterward, with the scream of crashing metal and glass.

Then I was driving in the dark again, racing along, with the car's horn blowing crazily even though I wasn't touching it.

I remember a highway patrol car forcing mine off the road.

"You're under arrest for drunken driving and for leaving the scene of an accident." Someone else said that to me later.

And I remember asking over and over again if anyone had been inside the car I'd hit, but no one would tell me. They just looked at me, while I cried and begged for information. I remember the flash bulbs popping. And then there was tearing, grinding pain. At first, in a garbled, confused way, I imagined I was losing Kerry Ann all over again. Then gradually I realized that it was the new baby I was losing. It would never have a chance to live.

Late the next afternoon, I opened my eyes to find Brian sitting beside my hospital bed. His eyes were swollen and puffy, as if he'd been crying. "Sharon," he said in a stunned, dazed way, "how did it happen?"

I expected him to blame me, to hate me, because I'd lost our baby. Instead, he insisted, still in that shocked voice, "You weren't drunk, Sharon! The newspapers are lying when they say that!"

Someone came and led him away. Then a nurse pushed a needle gently into my arm, and I slipped gratefully into oblivion.

I saw Brian again when, after another two days, I was no longer under sedation. He had recovered from his first shock, but he still insisted that I hadn't been drunk.

Somehow his love, his faith, made my own grief and shame deeper. Even before I was told that blood tests made at the hospital had positively proved it, I knew I must have been drunk. I'd been drinking all evening before Brian had called me from the airport.

I simply hadn't realized that I'd reached the point where I was in no fit condition to drive.

If there was any one thing that kept me from cracking up completely after the accident, it was the consolation that the people in the car I'd struck hadn't been seriously injured.

After a few more days, I was released from the hospital, and Brian took me home to Mission Hills.

The following morning, I had to go to court to answer the charges against me.

Brian kept insisting that I enter a plea of "not guilty" and ask for a jury trial. Our attorney, however, advised me to plead "guilty" and throw myself on the mercy of the court. I did this, because I just couldn't swear I was innocent when I knew I wasn't.

I received a stiff fine, but the judge suspended my jail sentence. "You've lost your baby," he said. "I think that is sufficient punishment." But he lectured me and said that drunken drivers are potential murderers.

As we left the courtroom, I was sure I saw Regina in one of the crowded back rows of seats. I couldn't read the expression on her beautiful face.

Just before noon, Brian and I reached home. I was afraid he would be furious with me because I'd refused to deny that I was drinking, but instead, he seemed very quiet and coolly determined.

"I'm going to see this thing through to the end, Sharon," he said. "I'm still going to find a way to prove in court that you weren't drunk. I'll have to raise money for the fight, but I'll manage that. They aren't going to ruin our lives."

"Brian, please listen to me!" I begged. "I was drunk. We have to face that!"

He didn't seem to hear me. A few minutes later, he left the house and drove away.

I was alone. Suddenly, I couldn't bear the awful emptiness of the house. It was emptier, somehow, than it had been even on the day after Kerry Ann's death. I had made up my mind in the hospital that I would never again take another drink, but as I sat there I knew I had to have one. I felt weak and sick, desperate for the only thing I felt could help me face not only loneliness, but the truth about myself.

My fingers were rubbery, but somehow I managed to get the bottle open.

I don't know how long the front doorbell had been ringing when I finally became really conscious of it. I sat and listened for a few minutes, but whoever was pushing the button just wouldn't go away.

Then I heard Regina's voice calling my name. She hammered on the door, insisting that I answer her. When she finally stopped, I was trembling uncontrollably. I didn't go to the door.

I had just filled my glass again when the double panels of the patio door slid open, and Regina came into the breakfast room.

"I had an idea you'd be doing exactly this," she said.

"Get out," I told her, and my voice sounded thin with panic. I was afraid of this woman because I knew she would have been a better wife for Brian than I.

Maybe I'd expected her to gloat, to warn me that she was going to try to take him away from me. I was amazed when she seemed more pleading than triumphant.

"Sharon, don't do this!" she begged. "Brian loves you. If you destroy yourself, you'll destroy him, too. I'm a fool, or I wouldn't try to stop you. I'd like to see you wreck your marriage. But I don't want Brian to be hurt any more than he has been in these last weeks."

Regina seemed to be fighting back tears. I realized that it wasn't an act. "Brian won't admit you were drunk at the time of the accident," she went on. "Ever since it happened, he has been telling anyone who will listen that the newspaper stories weren't true. It isn't simply because he loves you and is loyal to you. He's doing it because he can't admit to himself that you were drunk. He can't face the truth that his wife is an alcoholic."

Even then, Regina wasn't finished. "Find someone who can help you, Sharon," she said. "Do it before you smash Brian's life completely!"

I hardly knew when she left. I was sitting there transfixed, hearing again and again in my mind the things she'd said to me. And I knew that even though she hated me, she was right about many things.

Brian's love for me, coupled with his ambition, had made him blind to my need. I should have realized that and followed my impulse to talk to Mr. Davidson, even against Brian's wishes. If I'd done that, maybe I wouldn't have lost our baby. Maybe I wouldn't have brought scandal into Brian's life.

I was mixed up about so many things. But before me on the table was the bottle I'd just opened, and that was the biggest proof of all that I needed help.

I called Mr. Davidson at the church, and when I explained what I wanted, he came to see me within a very few minutes.

It wasn't difficult to pour out my fears to him. I wondered how I could ever have thought he was too young to be a good minister. There was a quiet strength about him. I also appreciated his being bluntly matter-of-fact about my problem, his insistence that I get help without delay.

"If you wait, you may lose your courage," he said.

He arranged for me to have an immediate appointment with a doctor in San Francisco who specialized in cases like mine. He even drove me into the city.

I didn't call Brian to tell him what I meant to do. In all our married life, I'd never gone against his wishes in anything important, and I didn't want to do so now. But I knew he'd object to my going to the doctor. I couldn't risk listening to him.

Dr. Bernard, the specialist, agreed that I needed help. He felt that I should enter a private rehab center for problem drinkers. There, my treatment would begin.

"If it's any comfort," he told me, "you aren't alone. There are many alcoholics and near alcoholics. Their tragedy is all the more poignant because they often quietly destroy themselves and their families in privacy. They can draw the curtains and lock the doors to hide their drinking. An even greater tragedy is that, many times, their families refuse to admit these women are alcoholics. So they never get the help they need. They die of alcoholism, or they commit suicide. And on their way to death, they hurt everyone whose life they touch."

Dr. Bernard went on to add that he was sure I had not reached the point of what he called complete personal disintegration. He felt I had an excellent chance of staying sober.

I entered rehab that same day, and Mr. Davidson went to tell Brian where I was and why I had made my decision to go there.

I braced myself to face Brian, but he didn't come to see me. Instead, he sent me a cold, shocked note in which he said, "I can't understand why you seem to want the whole world to know you consider yourself a common drunk. Apparently, you want that more than you want our marriage to continue."

Even as I read those bitter words, I pitied poor Brian. I'd hurt him so much, so very much. I couldn't go on making the tragedy worse for him.

I am sure now that I was able to make up my mind to continue with my treatment because Mr. Davidson was praying for me, and because God answered my own desperate prayer for strength.

I had memories to help me, too, the memory of Brian's love, even if I'd lost it now, and the memory of Kerry Ann. I had, too, the haunting remembrance of Leah, my sister, who hadn't had a chance at the kind of help I was receiving.

I was in rehab nearly seven weeks. During that time, my physical strength was built up. I had a great many psychiatric tests, and counseling from Dr. Bernard and other trained workers on his staff.

As much as I longed for Brian, I didn't try to contact him. I didn't blame him for wanting to forget me. I'd caused him such sorrow, such humiliation.

Part of my treatment was the conscious planning of a new life for myself. After I left rehab, Dr. Bernard helped me obtain work in a downtown office. I moved into a small, furnished apartment. At that time, I was still taking medication and seeing the doctor twice a week.

Little by little, I learned to face my problems without hiding in the oblivion of alcohol. I learned to search for spiritual strength, and to endure and face sorrow, self-condemnation, and loneliness. I was sure I would have to live with all of them for the rest of my life.

Loneliness was my oldest enemy. I'd first met it long ago, back in Sheridan Acres, before I met Sally Berringer. I saw now that it had haunted me for years.

Dr. Bernard also felt that the deepest mental conflict causing my drinking had been my feeling that I'd never really be the kind of wife Brian needed. I'd felt inferior and uneducated and ashamed, partly because of Leah, partly because I'd had such a different background than he had.

There's really only one way to get over feelings like that. You have to prove to yourself, if not to other people, that you aren't completely worthless. Each day I refused to drink made me respect myself a little more. Getting a job, supporting myself, helped too.

I'd been living in my apartment about three months when the bell rang one evening and I opened the door to face Brian. I couldn't speak for a moment. All I could do was just look at him.

He had changed. The change was a quietness about him, a maturity. He said humbly, "I know now why you drank, Sharon. The loneliness of these weeks, the emptiness of my life without you, has taught me that. You drank because you were lonely."

I wanted to cling to him, but I didn't move. Instead, I listened, because I sensed that Brian needed to talk to me.

"You were lonely since the beginning of our marriage," he went on, "because you never came first with me." His voice grated with bitterness. "Being a big success—that was all I could think about! I had to be more successful than my brother. I had to make my mother as proud of me as she was of him. I didn't have any confidence in myself—and yet I expected you to be perfect!" He grinned, but there was a terrible sadness in his eyes. "Being married to me was enough to drive you to drink!" he said.

I didn't know whether or not Brian was right to blame himself as he did. The important thing was that he'd come back to me, and that he believed now that I'd been right to get help for the drinking that had taken our baby and almost destroyed both of us. I knew, too, that he needed my love as much as I needed his—and that together we could save our marriage.

Brian still works for Sherman, but we no longer live in Mission Hills. We have a smaller, much less expensive house. We've paid our debts and are at last saving part of our income.

One of the things that I am happiest about these days is that Brian doesn't act so desperately anxious to advance in business. He isn't so tense. He tries to live more in the present than in some vague someday when he'll be a spectacular success. He still works hard and is ambitious, but he finds time to relax, too. Together, we've made friends we enjoy—people who like us for what we are rather than for what we have.

For a while after Brian and I got back together, I kept my job, commuting to the city. Dr. Bernard thought it would be good for me. I didn't resign until I knew that I was pregnant once more. Now I have only a few weeks to wait for the birth of this baby Brian and I want so very much.

I never saw Regina Wheelock again. She returned to Chicago soon after I went into rehab. But there is never a day when I don't think of her, never a day I don't realize I owe her a debt I can never repay. It was out of her love for Brian, her longing for him to be happy, that she made me see the truth about myself before it was too late. THE END

THE THREAT

I watched, engrossed, as Derek moved closer to Carrie.

"Don't look so frightened, Carrie," he murmured. "I promise nothing will happen that you don't want to happen. But if we are to stay warm—even alive—in this blizzard, we must sleep together."

"But, Derek," Carrie replied softly, "we've just met. I don't even know you—"

"Oh, but you will, my darling," Derek said as he reached for her…

"Mommy, me go wee-wee!" my daughter Tracy yelled, insistently tugging at my jeans.

With a jolt, I came back to real life and tore my eyes away from the TV screen.

"Oh, honey, why don't you ever tell Mommy before it happens?" I groaned.

"Me big girl?" She beamed at me hopefully, my sopping wet, seventeen-month-old angel.

"You're pretty sweet," I said. "But do you ever need a change!"

Suddenly, I remembered there weren't any clean training panties. Outside, a steady rain was dripping from the eaves, and I needed to go to the Laundromat in the worst way.

What burned me was that I had a perfectly good washing machine and dryer sitting unused in the back room, but we didn't have the right hookups yet. Jerry needed to put in new wiring and dig a bigger septic tank. The one we had was so small that soapy water backed up the pipes and flooded the linoleum when I used the washing machine.

Jerry was remodeling our old farmhouse slowly—very, very slowly.

Sometimes I felt so frustrated I could have screamed.

My little boy, Timmy, looked up from his coloring book.

"Tracy's pants stink," he announced with the smug disdain of a three-year-old who had finally mastered the bathroom bit.

"I know, I know!" I muttered.

Hurrying to the kitchen, I grabbed a clean dishtowel and used it to diaper Tracy.

"You're my angel-bug," I whispered against her blond curls. Tracy was beautiful to me even in her training pants, which were grubby indeed today. So what did it matter? Nobody would see my kids anyway. Nobody ever visited us except the door-to-door cosmetics sales lady.

Back home in Sweetriver, I had never been lonely on rainy days. Sometimes, I'd have a wonderful house full of company—my best friend Cindy, my two sisters, and all their kids. We'd try our hand at soft-sculpture dolls made out of dress scraps, or experiment with eye makeup and movie star hairdos. Sometimes, we'd bake gingerbread men for the kids, or just drink coffee and watch the soaps while our kids played.

Being alone was something I wasn't used to. I grew up in a big, warm-hearted country family, the youngest of six kids. Everyone in the county was related to us, it seemed. I had half cousins, step-cousins, and double cousins, besides the usual variety. There was always a wedding or family reunion, potluck suppers and birthday celebrations. Life was never dull.

And then the recession hit Sweetriver. Jerry lost his carpentry job and couldn't find another one, or any kind of work. There's no way you can raise two babies on unemployment checks, so we moved up here and I hated the place. Without Mom or Grandma to baby-sit, we couldn't afford to go out very often.

Worst of all, Jerry had turned into an absolute workaholic who spent all his spare time fixing up this awful old house we had bought outside the city limits. I hadn't wanted to buy it, but it was cheaper than paying rent.

Everything will be better when springtime finally gets here, I told myself firmly.

Somehow, it was hard to believe, looking out the rain-streaked windows at the sodden gloomy day. The huge maple tree on our front lawn seemed to shiver, standing naked under leaden skies. The kids' sandbox was half full of water, like wet cement.

Just beyond our country mailbox, I could see a huddle of yellow road machinery, looking abandoned in the rain. A highway crew had been building a new gravel road, but it was so muddy they'd had to stop work.

Half a mile farther on, the rooftops of a pretty little housing development, were barely visible through the trees. I could picture all those happy young couples living enchanted lives in homes with plumbing that worked and rooms that were actually warm. It seemed I was doomed to go shivering through life amid a tangle of extension cords and power tools, with the smell of paint thinner forever in my nose. . . .

Stop moping and get busy! I scolded myself. There was plenty of work to do. Two kids on a rainy day can really mess up a house.

Uncertainly, I glanced at the clock, which said three-thirty. I still wondered if Carrie would bed down with that handsome guy who'd found her lost in a blinding snowstorm. She'd been on her way to a ski lodge when the blizzard struck.

Well, why not go back to the TV and find out? Jerry wouldn't be home from his job until five-thirty.

I was still watching it later when Jerry walked into the room.

"Oh, my gosh!" I yelled guiltily, snapping off the set. "What are you doing home?"

"I usually come home after work," Jerry said wryly. "Look at the clock, Donna Sue. One of the kids pulled the plug."

I felt like an absolute idiot. "I haven't started dinner!" I moaned. "The chicken's frozen hard as a rock!"

"That's okay, just open some cans. No big deal." Jerry bent to pick up Tracy, who was tugging at his pant legs.

Jerry was only a few months older than I was, but somehow he seemed a grownup stranger in his dark blue coveralls with "Mike's Muffler Shop" embroidered on the chest pocket. It was like he'd become a settled, serious man while I was still a kid, and it bothered me. You read all this stuff about the man going out in the world and finding other interests, while the wife sits home growing dull and boring.

"We couldn't go out for hamburgers?" I suggested hopefully.

"In this rain?" Jerry looked aghast. "Donna Sue, I'm just not up to the hassle tonight. You remember the last time we took the kids to the drive-through—"

"Who could forget?" I said wearily. Tracy had spilled her drink all over the front seat of our pickup truck, and Timmy got catsup on my best blouse. I guessed because of that, Jerry expected us to live like hermits until the kids grew up.

"Okay, I'll fix something." I sighed. I went into our big gloomy kitchen and threw together an uninspired casserole of tuna and noodles that looked as drab as the room.

We were walking around on unpainted plywood flooring because Jerry had gotten sidetracked to another remodeling project before he finished the kitchen. Cartons of tile were stacked against the kitchen wall, which was plywood, too. I felt like a mouse trapped in a cracker box.

"Donna Sue, I can't find any clean underwear!" Jerry shouted from the bedroom.

"Nobody has any clean underwear!" I yelled back. "We need to go to the Laundromat tonight!"

"We?" He sounded horrified.

It's hard to argue with a disembodied voice. "You betcha," I said firmly, stalking into the bedroom. "The kids behave better when you're with us."

"I have a better idea. Why don't I keep them here while you go to the Laundromat? Maybe I can get a few squares of tile stuck down after the kids are in bed."

It made sense. Jerry was always very practical.

"Okay," I agreed.

Jerry loaded the baskets of dirty clothes into our pickup truck while I put on my best jeans and a pretty pink top. Maybe tonight, I'd meet someone my own age at the Wash-'n-Go, and we'd become real friends. What better place than a Laundromat to meet other young housewives with little kids?

"Mama's pretty," Timmy announced.

"Hear the boy! He knows how to spot the best-looking women already." My husband grinned.

Unexpectedly, Jerry kissed me good-bye, a warm, sweet kiss that set my spirits soaring. Maybe tonight we'd make love to the patter of rain on the roof. Jerry had been so tired lately, our love life was just about zero.

Driving into town, I started feeling a whole lot better about everything. I loved to drive in the rain. Everything seemed romantic, like a movie set—the wet, gleaming streets and the neon signs flashing in brilliant colors through a curtain of falling rain. On a night like that, you got the feeling that something wonderful could happen, which was dumb. All I'd get out of it was a bunch of clean clothes.

Some of my cheerfulness faded as I saw all the middle-aged faces in the Laundromat. *This place must give discounts to senior citizens,* I thought.

A big, dowdy woman was scowling as she hauled armloads of big, dowdy uniforms out of a dryer. At one of the long tables, a little old blue-haired lady was folding some of the cutest jogging outfits you ever saw.

It just didn't seem fair that young girls, like me for instance, couldn't afford nice things while old ladies went around in designer jogging suits.

"Excuse me," a man's voice said. "What kind of money does this coin machine take? Confederate?"

Startled, I whirled around to face a young guy who looked almost like Derek in my soap opera. He was younger, though, about my own age.

"I keep shoving in dollar bills and the machine keeps rejecting them," he said. "Are they the wrong color, or doesn't it like my looks?"

I couldn't help giggling at his bewilderment. "I don't think it's anything personal," I said. "Wait, I'll help you find Mabel—she's the manager."

Mabel was standing over an ironing board in the back room, carefully pressing a stack of dollar bills.

"This guy needs some fresh money," I told her.

"Sure." Mabel stubbed out her cigarette and handed over a couple of crisply ironed dollar bills in exchange for two rather crumpled ones.

"The machine won't take wrinkled money," she remarked.

"Oh, I see." The man's eyes were twinkling with amusement.

Somehow, we made it out of the room without cracking a smile, then we both just broke up.

"I've become so careless about myself, living alone!" my new friend said jokingly. "Just imagine, neglecting to press my dollar bills!"

"My money doesn't stay by me long enough for me to iron it!" I said.

He grinned at me. "Believe me, I really appreciate your help. My name is Brad Walker, and I work on the highway crew when it isn't raining."

"It's a mess right now, isn't it?" I said. "I'm Donna Sue Castlebury. Your road equipment is parked almost in front of my house. It's that old, unpainted farmhouse. . . ."

Suddenly my voice trailed off as I realized I'd just told Brad where

I lived. Boy, that was dumb of me! Would I ever stop acting like a naive country bumpkin?

Oh, well, I could sense that he was a nice, well-mannered guy who wouldn't try any funny stuff. He reminded me of my favorite cousin, Terry, except he was better looking.

"I'm a klutz when it comes to doing laundry," Brad admitted with a rueful grimace. "I guess Mom spoiled me. I'm an only child, and she always washed my clothes when I lived at home. She fusses over me like a mama hen with one chick. Here I am, a heavy-equipment operator, and my mom calls long distance every week to ask if I'm eating right!"

Well, that proved I was a good judge of character. Brad was a nice guy, with a mother who worried over him.

"Say, wait—can I ask something else?" Brad held up a plastic jug of bleach. "How do you use this stuff? They say it helps get clothes clean, but the one time I tried it, I got funny-looking spots all over my pants."

Men! I thought, trying not to giggle. Brad's mother sure raised a helpless child! I showed Brad how to dilute the bleach and how to sort things that should be washed together.

"I thought you just stuffed everything into a washer until it got full," he said.

"It's a wonder you haven't ruined your entire wardrobe!" I told him. Brad had some really nice Western shirts, besides the usual work clothes.

"I got lucky and met the prettiest girl in town, who also happens to be a housekeeping genius," Brad said softly.

"Thanks for the compliment. I'll tell my husband," I said. I figured I'd better mention Jerry pretty quick, the way Brad was looking at me with those smoldering dark eyes. He was attracted to me, I could tell.

"Donna Sue, are you serious? Where are your husband's clothes? I figured you were divorced," Brad said, looking startled.

"Jerry wears a uniform on the job. He works at Mike's Muffler Shop," I said. It seemed important to prove that Jerry was a real-life guy with a regular job, not someone I'd invented on the spur of the moment. "I haven't been wearing my wedding ring because the setting came out," I added.

Brad sighed. "Well, my heart will mend someday, and in the meantime, can't we be friends?"

"Crazy!" I laughed. "That sounds like a country music song title!"

"Well, you can't beat country music for telling it like it is."

I learned that Brad was a country music fan, like me. We talked about our favorite entertainers, and Brad bought me a soda because I had been such a help with his laundry. He was very good company, with a kooky sense of humor and a batch of funny stories about construction work. He'd learned to handle heavy equipment at a vo-tech school and now traveled all over the country, following construction jobs.

"It's an interesting life, but I get lonely sometimes," he admitted. "Maybe a small town guy will always feel lonesome for the settled life."

"I know what you mean!" I assured him.

Suddenly, I realized the last dryer had finished its cycle and clicked off, and Mabel was staring at us pointedly. Hurriedly, I jumped up and started folding clothes.

Brad insisted on lugging my clothes to the pickup truck. "It's been fun talking to you, Donna Sue. Maybe I'll see you again sometime," he said.

"Oh, I'll be back. It doesn't take my family long to get things dirty," I said lightly.

To be honest, I had enjoyed myself tremendously. I'd been feeling like last week's garbage, and now I was alive again. All it took was a little stimulating conversation. If I wasn't in love with my husband, I could sure go for this cute, sexy guy.

Jerry was snoring on the couch when I got home.

"I didn't get much work done," he mumbled, rousing groggily. "The kids kept calling for drinks of water and stuff." He got up and stumbled off to bed like a robot. Five minutes later, he was snoring again.

So much for nights of love with the patter of rain on the roof. All Jerry had on his mind was the kitchen tiles!

For quite a while, I lay awake trying to decide why Jerry and I seemed to be in opposite worlds lately. Back home, it hadn't mattered that we were different personality types.

Jerry was methodical. He kept his carpentry tools in perfect order and a neatly printed list of important telephone numbers taped to the wall by the phone. I was the impulsive kind. I stuffed things in drawers and forgot where I put them. Lately, my easygoing ways had started grating on Jerry's nerves, and sometimes he seemed to me like twenty-two going on sixty. That's scary when you live in a no-fault divorce state like this one. What if someday Jerry looked at me and remembered that incompatibility was reason enough to end our marriage?

It's all the fault of this terrible old house, I thought. My last waking thought was of Brad, who I was sure wouldn't let a house tie him down to a boring, everyday existence. . . .

We awoke to a gray, rain-lashed dawn and a screaming alarm clock. We'd overslept, and Jerry was grumpy.

"I met someone my own age at the laundry, for a change," I remarked, pouring Jerry's coffee.

"Huh? Tell me about her tonight, I'm running late."

Jerry grabbed the steaming mug and clattered down the back steps, slurping coffee as he ran. He didn't even kiss me good-bye.

Fine! I'll be darned if I tell you anything, I thought, annoyed. Yawning, I crawled back into my warm bed, and then Tracy started yelling. My long, dreary day had started.

By midmorning, I was so blue I thought about calling Mama long distance, but decided against it because Jerry had been fussing about the phone bills.

The telephone rang during the kids' afternoon nap.

Mama! I thought, racing to grab the receiver.

"Donna Sue, what do you do on rainy days when you can't work?" Brad's voice asked.

How did he get our number? I thought wildly. Then, I realized all he'd had to do was look in the phone book. We were the only Castleburys on Dawson Road.

"I can find lots to do, rain or shine. My kids keep me hopping!" I said.

"Want me to come over and lend a hand?" Brad asked softly.

"Sorry, my boss isn't hiring any extra help right now!" I said, laughing.

We talked for maybe an hour—just lighthearted, friendly conversation. We were laughing at a silly joke Brad told, when Timmy came padding in, sleepy eyed.

"Talk to Gwandma?" he begged.

"I have to hang up now!" I told Brad.

"Be a good child for Grandma, dear," Brad said in an old lady quaver. "Beware of tall, dark men who try to lure you into sin."

What a clown! I thought, smiling.

I felt prettier, livelier somehow, knowing someone thought I was special. It had been a long time since any guy had said anything about me. Was I glad Brad couldn't see me now, in my awful old sweat pants and a T-shirt spotted with taco sauce!

But that was how Jerry saw me ever day. Was that why the magic had gone out of our marriage?

The idea bothered me. I hurried around and shampooed my hair and prettied myself up before Jerry came home. I fixed fried chicken and mashed potatoes—Jerry's favorite meal.

"Tell me about your day," I said hopefully at dinner.

"What?" Jerry looked startled. "What's there to tell? One muffler job is just like another."

End of stimulating conversation. Tears stung my eyes as I watched Jerry gobbling down his fried chicken. I hated Jerry's job, I hated this town, and most of all, I hated the dumpy old house that took all my husband's time and attention.

The second time Brad called, I had just started out the door with the kids in tow.

"Look, I can't talk now," I said hastily. "I have to deposit Jerry's paycheck before the Metro Bank casts us into debtor's prison."

"That's okay, I understand." He hung up.

When I drove into the bank parking lot, the first person I saw was Brad. He'd parked just the other side of the drive-in window.

"You turkey!" I burst out.

Brad's dark eyes shone with mischief. "I decided to see the sights of the city. You're the best-looking one I've seen."

We talked for a while, and Brad told me the kids were cute. After all, it wasn't as if we'd met for a secret date. We were simply two lonely people reaching out for friendship.

For some reason, I didn't get around to telling Jerry about that friendship. I guess it was because he'd shut me out of his life recently, and I was getting even.

Brad usually phoned during the kids' afternoon naps. We'd listen to country music with our radios tuned to the same station, and kid around like teenagers. It was silly, but fun.

"Are you and your husband going out Friday night?" Brad asked once. "Maybe we'll run into each other."

"I doubt it. We're nearly broke. I wish I could think of something that would be lots of fun and didn't cost any money."

"I can think of something. Want me to show you?" Brad gave a lazy, sexy-sounding chuckle. "Of course your husband might not approve."

"This has to be recreation for both husband and wife," I answered primly, trying to keep the laughter out of my voice.

"Sorry, I'm not that kind of guy! Do I look kinky?"

After Jerry's deadly seriousness, it was fun to laugh and flirt like carefree high-school kids. Afterward, I flew around fixing a good dinner and whisked the kids through their baths. Nobody could say I was neglecting Jerry and the kids just because I had whiled away a rainy afternoon on the phone.

We were reading about Snow White when Jerry came home from work.

"What's in the paper bag?" I asked.

"Deadbolt locks."

Grinning proudly, Jerry dumped an assortment of gleaming brass knobs and hardware on the table. "You remember the old lady on TV who was beaten half dead for her pension check? That made me start worrying about our flimsy old locks," Jerry said. "I'm not going to leave my family unprotected. You never know what kind of weirdo could be prowling around while I'm at work."

"Don't worry. This place scares people off. They think it's a haunted house," I said grumpily.

I was so lonely, I'd have welcomed a visit from a pea-green space alien! Except for Brad, I hadn't talked to anyone except Jerry and the kids all week.

Jerry wasn't fooling me one bit with his blustering, protective-type speech about keeping his family safe. He just wanted an excuse to spend money on his home improvement hobby. We could've seen a movie or eaten in a nice restaurant for what those stupid locks cost!

My husband the compulsive carpenter, I thought. They should have a self-help organization, like they do for gamblers. Handymen Anonymous would be a good name.

Back in high school, I had felt proud that Jerry was the best student in carpentry class. Later, when his boss said Jerry was the hardest-working apprentice carpenter he'd ever hired, I had been real pleased. The trouble was, Jerry couldn't accept the fact that all those things were in the past. You heard on TV how the recession and tight mortgage money really zapped the home-building trade. Why didn't Jerry listen? Actually, he was darned lucky to have a job at the muffler shop, because his work wasn't affected by the weather. Poor Brad really had it rough—he'd been rained out for days.

Friday morning, I noticed a newspaper ad about a new supermarket that was holding a grand opening. They were going to give away a free microwave oven and other prizes, with balloons for the kiddies and a country western band to entertain the customers. We needed to buy groceries anyway, and the store advertised some fantastic specials.

Who says you can't find something to do that doesn't cost money? I thought, feeling a little smug. *Bring on the free ice cream and pizza samples!*

Jerry wasn't exactly thrilled when I brought it up Friday evening.

"Bet we could hear better music on TV without all the fuss," my husband grumbled. He was busy installing the new door locks and didn't want to stop.

So Jerry fiddled and twiddled until he decided everything was working right, and by the time we got to the supermarket, it was almost nine o'clock. The prizes had been given away and the musicians were packing their instruments.

I felt like bawling. Jerry didn't love me and the kids, or he'd want to take us places! That house was Jerry's mistress—an ugly, rawboned mistress who was probably seventy years old!

Saturday dragged by to the steady patter of rain and the thudding of Jerry's hammer from the bedroom, where he was building a closet. The Saturday cartoons roared full blast while Tracy and Timmy sprawled on the rug, enchanted. Two astronauts had landed in a different time warp and were being chased by bellowing prehistoric monsters.

Cartoons are noisier than they used to be, I decided wearily. My head was splitting.

With a sigh of relief, I tucked the kids into bed for afternoon naps and sat down to watch an old movie on TV. Jerry's power saw started with a screech and the picture dissolved into a million dancing splinters of light.

"It's on the same circuit as the saw," Jerry shouted. "It'll be okay when I get finished."

"Great! By then the show will be over!" I yelled back.

Disgustedly, I slammed into the kitchen and started washing dishes. It was almost time for the country music program Brad and I sometimes listened to, so I turned on the little kitchen radio.

There wasn't much static, so maybe the kitchen was wired on a different hookup or something. I didn't know, and I wasn't about to ask Jerry.

"Our next number is dedicated to a sweet little gal named Donna Sue, who's like sunlight on a rainy day," the deejay announced cheerily. "That's what her friend says who requested the song. We can use some sunshine, honey, keep up the good work."

"Oh, my gosh!" I gasped, almost dropping a dish. "That crazy Brad!"

My face felt as hot as fire. The song was about a rainy-night woman this guy met once and could never forget. I had the wildest feeling! Kind of giddy and tingling all over. What would Jerry think if he found out? A shivery, half-scared thrill of excitement raced over me.

Brad's only playing one of his silly jokes, I decided hopefully. Admittedly, I enjoyed a little harmless flirting, but I didn't want to get into anything heavy. I still loved my husband, in spite of his weird ways.

The closet looked nice when it was finished, I must admit. I had hoped Jerry would help me hang stuff inside, but instead, he dragged out the boxes of tile and returned to his first love, the kitchen floor.

No way was I going to attempt to cook dinner in the midst of Jerry's clutter! I zipped the kids into their jackets and told Jerry I was going to the store to buy something for a snack supper.

Tuna sandwiches tonight, my friend, and may you grow fins! I thought grimly.

Usually I loved to shop, but today, I pushed the cart around the supermarket aisles like a robot, picking up sandwich bread and chips mechanically.

I never knew you can feel so alone in the same house with someone you love, I thought. Something precious was drifting away from me a little bit more every day, and with a panicky feeling, I realized I didn't know how to stop it.

Someone called my name as I was loading my grocery bag into the pickup truck.

"Donna Sue!" Brad yelled. "Wait a second!"

He came running across from the discount store, grinning boyishly. "Guess what I found on sale?" He held up two of the latest country western CDs.

It will be nice to be young and free again and collect CDs instead of casserole recipes, I thought wistfully.

"Let's get in my car and we'll see how they sound. I've got a nice sound system—"

"Oh, Brad, I'd better not—" I began.

"Why not?" he interrupted. "I never attack women in shopping centers. It's considered very uncool." Brad's dark eyes danced with laughter. Unexpectedly, he tossed me his car keys in one quick motion. "Now you're in control of the situation," he said teasingly. "Nothing will happen to you that you don't want to happen."

Those were Derek's exact words to Carrie in the soap opera! Somehow, that made everything seem unreal and dreamlike, as if we were acting out a scene that fate had planned for us. All I had to do was relax and just go with the flow.

"Okay, but honestly, I can't stay long," I agreed.

When we got to the car, I told my kids, "Into the backseat, you two. We don't need your busy little fingers adjusting the stereo sound. And, Timmy, keep your feet off the upholstery."

Brad didn't offer to help me lift the kids inside. I wondered if he felt awkward around small children.

"Tracy loves to turn up the TV volume control," I added, smiling at my sweet baby girl. "Also the oven knobs, the furnace switch, and anything else she can."

"Sounds like my brother's kids," Brad said. He was looking intently at me, not at Tracy and Timmy.

The music was great, but I got distracted when Brad leaned against me to adjust the sound, which he did about every five seconds. Crazy skyrockets of excitement exploded inside me every time he touched me.

I should have put the kids between us, I thought weakly.

"Baby, this just doesn't do it, does it?" Brad said abruptly.

"What?" I felt confused. "I like the CDs a lot, Brad—"

He made an impatient gesture. "I mean, this is music to make love to, so what are we doing here making polite conversation?"

He really means it! I thought dazedly.

"You know I love you, don't you, baby? You can't tell me you don't feel it too." Brad was breathing funny, as if he'd been running. His voice was hoarse, not like Brad's usual voice at all. "Donna Sue, this morning I requested a love song for you—"

"I heard it."

"That's the way it is with me, baby. I can't sleep nights because I want you so bad. All I do is lie awake listening to the rain and wishing you were in bed with me. All I want is—"

"Brad, you don't even know me!" I protested. "We've only seen each other two or three times!"

"So? That doesn't matter when you love somebody. The first time I saw you in the Laundromat, I wanted you so much it nearly drove me up the wall."

It was all too fast for me. Brad came on so strong, it turned me off completely. The warm, sweet, sensuous feeling simply vanished, like water swooshing down a sink drain. I felt embarrassed.

"Let me show you what real love is like, baby," Brad said huskily. "How about us getting together when that wimpy husband of yours is at work?"

No way! I thought, shocked. Maybe Jerry and I hadn't been too happy lately, but that didn't mean I was going to crawl into the sack with some guy I barely knew!

"Something tells me you've never made it with a real man, right? Give me a chance, and you'll be ready to dump that kid husband of yours in a hurry," Brad went on.

Leave Jerry? Was he crazy?

"Brad, I like you a lot, but I'm a married woman." I had started edging away from him and now I was pressed against the door, wondering how to get away. "I'm sorry if I gave you the wrong impression, but I don't cheat."

"Some dumb kid marriage, what does that count? I was married myself at seventeen, no big deal." Brad shrugged. "This time is going to be the right time. The vibes are right."

My mind was spinning. Better not make this guy mad, a warning little voice whispered inside me. Brad's eyes had a funny, glazed look like one of those fanatics on the TV news.

"Come here, baby. You know I haven't even kissed you, yet," he said, and then he grabbed me so suddenly my head banged against the window glass and I saw stars. Brad's jacket zipper dug painfully into me, his lips ground hard against mine, and then he released me.

"That was really something," he said thickly.

"Mommy, me go wee-wee," Tracy's little voice piped up suddenly.

"Yuk. I think she did it already!" Timmy said disgustedly.

"Oh, man!" Brad burst out.

The tension between us shattered like breaking glass. I felt like giggling hysterically.

Saved by my daughter! I thought. Hastily, I grabbed Timmy's hand and hauled both kids out of the backseat. "Brad, I have to run now. We'll talk about this some other time." My words came too fast, tripping over each other in their haste. "I enjoyed the music, but really, I just want to be your friend."

"Sure, baby. Real good friends." Brad winked at me as I turned to go.

My face burned with embarrassment as I drove home. Boy, I'd goofed when I got so chummy with a perfect stranger! Brad wasn't just a friendly small town kid—he'd been around plenty. I remembered things he'd told me that suddenly didn't make sense. How could he have traveled all over the country and learned so little about things like help-yourself laundries? He'd also said he was an only child, so how could my kids remind him of his brother's children? I wondered how many of the things he'd told me had been outright lies.

One thing for sure, I didn't want to see him again! If he calls, I'll give him a polite but firm brush off, I decided.

A farm truck was parked in our driveway and Jerry was talking to a middle-aged couple on the front porch. Company at a time like this! I put on a bright hostess smile and willed my knees to stop shaking.

Our visitors were Mr. and Mrs. Gibson, who owned a chicken farm south of us. Mrs. Gibson gave us a bowl of big brown eggs and invited us to church. "I'd love to have those sweet kiddies in my Sunday school class," she said warmly.

Jerry showed off the house to a chorus of admiring comments. "It's going to be just beautiful, a regular showplace!" Mrs. Gibson beamed. "Earl and I were so glad to see a young couple move in and start fixing things up so nice. We'd figured some development company would buy the land and tear the house down."

"Folks don't appreciate an older home nowadays," Mr. Gibson said. "This was built around 1910. There's more good, solid wood in this house than there is in two of those cardboard boxes down the road." He nodded toward the development.

"I know. That's why I bought it," Jerry said.

The Gibsons were so friendly and nice, I got over the weak feeling I'd had since my parking-lot encounter with Brad. By the time they left, it had started seeming unreal, like a steamy seduction scene on TV.

"Those are nice folks," Jerry remarked later.

"They sure are." Tears stung my eyes unexpectedly as I watched Jerry carefully sticking down a square of tile. Jerry was so sweet in spite of his exasperating ways—so normal. How do you tell your husband you're sorry, when he doesn't even know you've done anything wrong?

Blinking back tears, I stared at the cardboard carton with its picture of a woman who was laying tile in a slinky dress and high heels.

"That doesn't look too hard. Can I try it?" I asked.

"It isn't. Just peel off the backing, and be careful to keep the pattern straight."

I got down on my knees and started helping Jerry lay tile. It was fun, once I got the hang of it.

"This is neat. Why didn't you show me how to do this before?" I asked.

Jerry gave me a funny look. "Donna Sue, you never asked if you could help before."

We turned on the radio, and the work went fast. At first, all we said were things like "Please hand me the linoleum knife," but before long, Jerry remembered a joke, and then we started kidding each other and telling funny stories. I had never dreamed that working with someone could be as much fun as going out on a date.

"This is how it used to be, remember?" Jerry blurted unexpectedly. "We always talked a lot. Somehow, all the good times ended when we came here." His voice was sad. "I know I haven't been any prize to live with, Donna Sue, but it's been rough adjusting to a new life. I never wanted to move here. I wanted to live in Sweetriver and build houses. It was what I loved to do. It was like somebody changed the rules of the game to where I was losing instead of winning. I couldn't handle it."

I could scarcely believe my ears when Jerry went on talking about how homesick he had been, and how he'd tried to bury his troubles in work.

"I wish you had told me," I said slowly. "Sometimes I thought you'd stopped caring."

Jerry shrugged helplessly. "Well, a man's supposed to be strong and keep quiet about his problems," he said finally.

I was just glad Jerry would never know how much trouble he'd almost caused by being so close-mouthed! I told him I thought he was more of a man if he could talk about his feelings.

It was after midnight when Jerry stuck down the last tile. "It's finished!" he whooped triumphantly, hugging me.

"Oh, Jerry, it's gorgeous!" I squealed. The radio was playing a slow, sweet waltz. Suddenly we were in each other's arms, swaying to the music as we danced across our shiny, beautiful floor.

"You're the prettiest girl at the prom, honey," Jerry whispered.

"That's because I'm the only girl at the prom." I giggled.

But you know something? I felt beautiful in my grubby jeans with glue streaks on my face. Beautiful is being loved, and I know Jerry loves me.

We went to bed and made tender love. *To think I could have blown all this over a silly flirtation with Brad,* I thought drowsily, cuddling in Jerry's arms. . . .

Sunlight woke me, streaming through the wide, old-fashioned windows. A bird was singing like crazy in the maple tree.

"Jerry! Wake up, it's stopped raining!" I yelled.

We went outside right after breakfast. All the world looked wet and sodden, kind of hung over, but the sky was brilliant blue and a warm wind was blowing. Spring was definitely on the way!

The kids yelled joyfully, splashing through puddles. Jerry and I found jonquils poking up in the flowerbeds and buds on the lilacs. We decided to start painting the house after we got our income-tax refund—pale yellow, with chocolate-brown shutters and trim.

"I'll help you paint," I said.

"Sure, if you want to. We're partners." Jerry grinned.

Partners. What a nice sound that had. Jerry and I were together again.

That Sunday was one of the best days of my life. We went to the zoo in the afternoon. Tracy was a little scared of the animals, but Timmy wanted to pet everything and asked where the dinosaurs were. We ate hot dogs and popcorn and had a great time.

The incident with Brad seemed far away, like a dream. Living with the guy you loved, making a home together—that was reality. I told myself that Brad would forget me as soon as he was working again and had something to occupy his mind.

Monday morning, some guys in a company truck were poking around the road machinery, but they drove away so I guessed it was still a bit too muddy to work.

During the morning, the phone rang several times, but I didn't bother answering. I was up on a high stool washing windows till they all looked real nice, all sparkling clean. I opened the windows to let in the sunlight and warm breezes, and thought how homey everything looked. Funny how I was beginning to love this old place.

Right after lunch, someone tapped on the kitchen door.

"Just a second!" I called, thinking maybe it was Mrs. Gibson.

Brad stood there, grinning possessively at me.

"Hello, sugar," he said softly. "I thought you'd have those kids stashed away in bed by now."

Oh, no! How can I get rid of him? I thought wildly.

"It's such a pretty day," I said distractedly. "I guess we kind of forgot about naptime."

Tracy was peeking around me, clinging to my jeans, while Timmy simply stared. "We can't have that, can we?" Brad leaned against the door frame confidently, Mr. Macho himself. "Grownups need time alone for fun and games, too."

Not this grownup! I thought quickly.

"I called you. How come you didn't answer the phone? You have some other guy in bed with you?" Brad asked suspiciously.

"I was washing windows!" I snapped, glaring at him. "I told you, Brad, I don't cheat!"

"Sure, sure, baby." Brad was grinning, but he had a strange look in his eyes. "Ready for a little fun?" he asked softly.

"No way!" I glared at him, wondering how I'd ever thought he was nice. "Furthermore, I don't want you coming around here anymore!"

"Oh, come on, baby. Drop the innocent act and let's get physical." Brad reached around the screen, trying to run his hand along my arm, but I moved faster. I slammed the screen door on his fingers.

"Hey!" Brad jumped back, shaking his wounded hand. "What kind of stunt are you trying to pull?"

"I'm not interested, Brad. I love my husband, and I'm not taking chances on breaking up my home!" I said.

I guess that was the first time Brad actually listened to what I was saying. His face turned blank for a second, then slowly hardened into a tense, mean-looking mask.

"Why, you lousy, no-good, little tease," he said thickly. "Lead a guy on and then say, 'I don't want to break up my home!'"

"You've got the general idea. So leave," I told him.

If I hadn't been so mad, I'd have been frightened by Brad's terrible expression. A muscle twitched in his jaw.

"So you don't want to break up your home, huh?" He was breathing hard and shaking all over. "That's just what I mean to do, baby. I'm going to break up your home!" With that he jumped into his car and gunned the motor, spraying sheets of mud as he roared away.

I ran around the house, locking the doors in case Brad came back. Believe me, now I was grateful for the strong locks Jerry had insisted on!

Trembling, I poured myself a cup of hot coffee and slumped into a chair, trying to think. I wondered if Brad really meant that threat about breaking up my home. He wouldn't try to find Jerry and tell him a bunch of lies, would he? Oh, how I wished I'd never met that creep!

Suddenly I heard some kind of motor running. The kids were perched on the couch, squabbling as usual.

"Twactor!" Tracy said.

"No, it's not." Timmy shook his head. "Mommy, Tracy's a dumb baby. That's not a tractor. It's a thing that digs holes."

"Well, whatever," I agreed wearily. "Quiet down, won't you?"

"What's it doing coming here?" Timmy persisted.

"What?" I jumped up and ran to the window. A yellow earthmoving machine of some kind was lumbering across the lawn. Brad was hunched over the wheel like an avenging demon, steering straight toward the house!

Frozen in shock, I stared numbly as the machine came up to the kids' sandbox and ran right over it. Like some outer-space creature, the monster lurched on, grinding the flattened sandbox into its muddy tracks. Brad was jerking levers that operated a long arm attached to a bucket—a boom, wasn't that what Jerry called those things?

Suddenly, the arm swung out like a striking snake and the bucket slammed viciously against the house. There was a grinding, crunching, horrible sound as a whole chunk of the front porch fell off!

"Take a good look, lady!" Brad howled above the roaring motor. "How do you like the way I'm breaking up your home?"

He backed away for another run at the house, swinging the boom for another terrible blow. Around it came, like a gaping jaw armed with hideous metal teeth. This time it struck one of the wooden posts that supported the porch roof, and it collapsed with a tearing, rending crash. The whole house shuddered as the porch roof sagged drunkenly.

Tracy and Timmy were screaming in terror. Somehow, the sound penetrated my dazed mind, and I ran for the telephone.

My fingers felt wooden as I dialed. The house shook under a

barrage of shattering blows. How long could it withstand such a brutal pounding?

"Police," a crisp voice said.

"Help—oh, please help me!" I screamed. Tracy and Timmy were wailing shrilly and it was hard to make myself heard. "There's a crazy man outside on some kind of big machine! He's tearing up the house!"

Terror choked my throat. "I live at 6089 Dawson Road—send someone quick!"

Just then, there was an explosion of sound as the boom struck the living room window and a shower of broken glass shattered all over the couch. The phone went dead.

Brad was backing the machine away for another attack, trailing a tangle of frazzled cables. Those were the wires to the phone! Nobody could help me now. The kids and I were going to die, and all because I'd been a silly, romantic fool.

Suddenly, I remembered the sturdy bedroom closet. My kids might have a chance, hidden there!

It was like running in some dreadful nightmare. Crunching on broken glass, I pushed the kids into the closet and pulled a blanket over them.

"You've got to stop crying!" I told them. "Don't make a sound until Daddy comes—even if it's a long, long time!"

Panting, I started to drag a heavy chest in front of the closet door, and then stopped. What if nobody thought to look in the closet—they'd be trapped.

Jerry will find them, I told myself.

Outside, Brad screamed something above the roaring motor. There was one last sickening wrenching sound as boards were torn away from the house, then the motor coughed and died.

That was when I heard the wailing of sirens, coming closer and closer. Weakly, I collapsed on the glass-strewn couch, trembling.

Someone pounded on the splintered, sagging door.

"Police officers. Open the door, lady," a man's voice called.

Shaking all over, I got up and turned the shiny new lock. "Please help. The door's stuck," I quavered.

Strong hands hauled the broken door aside and I climbed out over a fallen chunk of the porch ceiling. "Watch out for nails in those broken boards," the officer cautioned.

Later, they said I seemed very cool, but it was the eerie calm of shock. I told the police officer my kids were in the closet and he said he'd get them. I gave another patrolman the address of the muffler shop and he said he'd call through on his two-way radio and have someone contact Jerry. But it was all like something in a crazy dream.

Bright sunlight made everything unreal: The poor old house, like some bombed-out hulk from a war movie. Police cars parked on the lawn. Mr. Gibson's farm truck was there, too, beside the earth-moving machine.

Brad was slumped against the maple tree with his head in his hands. Two men in overalls were standing over him—Mr. Gibson and a younger man in overalls who turned out to be his son. They'd been driving past when they saw Brad attacking the house. They'd known we wouldn't deliberately wreck our home after all the work we'd put into it, and so they stopped to investigate.

"We didn't do much, just grabbed the guy when he tried to run away," Mr. Gibson said apologetically. "That backhoe ran out of fuel. It was running on the reserve tank, and there wasn't much left in it."

The police officer came up with both children. Timmy was protesting loudly that he was supposed to stay in the closet until his daddy came. Tracy's little face was wet with tears. I reached out my arms and she burrowed into them, trembling violently.

Brad just sat there, handcuffed. He acted almost bored.

It was all so crazy. Birds were singing in the maple tree, and the police radio was chattering away to itself through the open patrol car window. Then my heart sank like a stone because Jerry's pickup truck was turning up the driveway.

White as death, he stood there staring first at the shattered house, then at me and the kids.

"Jerry, I washed the windows, but he broke them all," I blurted. Tears made my voice thick. "I wanted to show you how pretty the house looked."

"Oh, honey, none of that matters." Jerry put his arms around me and held me close. "You and the kids are okay. That's what counts."

Brad looked up at me with sullen, hating eyes. "She was asking for it. The two-timing little tramp ran out on me."

Jerry gave me a startled look.

Here it comes, I thought, sick inside. The whole bit. The flirting and the phone calls, and maybe a lot of other stuff Brad had dreamed up in his twisted mind. Jerry would think I'd tried to come on to the guy, maybe even had an affair with him.

"That's enough, Whitson," the police officer said sharply. He gave us a sympathetic look. "Ignore the guy, he's a psycho. Lies as easy as he tells the truth."

The police knew quite a lot about Brad Walker—or Boyd Whitson, his real name. He was a heavy drinker with an uncontrollable temper, and he'd been in trouble most of his life. He'd received a dishonorable discharge from the Army, where he'd learned to operate heavy equipment, and he was wanted on a wife-battering charge in Tennessee. He'd been suspected of causing the unexplained death of an infant stepson, but his ex-wife was afraid of him and wouldn't testify.

"So that's why he didn't know how to use a coin machine," I said slowly. Brad had been in jail, or in the Army, most of his life. No wonder he didn't know about little, everyday things.

Well, I was lucky. Real, real lucky. All this happened months ago, and Jerry has never blamed me once. "You're just a friendly person, honey. You couldn't have known what that guy was like," he tells me.

Our insurance money enabled us to rent a house in the cute development down the road. I wonder now why I thought they were so great. The yard is the size of a postage stamp, and I feel crowded in the tiny kitchen when I'm in there alone. But none of it really matters, because we're not home all that much. Every afternoon and weekend, we drive over and work on the house. I've raked up shattered glass and helped Jerry replace broken windows and boards and rebuild the front porch. And you know something? I've really enjoyed the work. When Jerry goes into business for himself someday, I'll be a real help to him with all I've learned.

Another thing we had to learn the hard way was that you couldn't live just to work. Jerry and I have discovered flea markets, which we love. Sometimes we take the kids swimming and picnicking at the little creek that runs through the Gibsons' farm. We've started attending the Gibsons' church, too. Last night we went to a potluck church supper that reminded me of the ones back home. Several young couples seemed nice and I hope we'll become friends.

Sometimes I think of Brad, now in prison in Tennessee, and feel saddened by his twisted, abnormal life. I don't think of him often, though, because I'm too busy. Next week, we're moving back into our rebuilt huse! THE END

Printed in the USA
CPSIA information can be obtained
at www.ICGtesting.com
LVHW010408090824
787694LV00001B/54